About the author

Kate Jacobs left her native Canada to earn a graduate degree at New York University – and made her home in Manhattan for a decade, where she worked at *Redbook*, *Working Woman*, *Family Life* and *Lifetime TV.com*. Currently, she lives in Southern California with her husband. THE FRIDAY NIGHT KNITTING CLUB is her first novel. For more information, go to www.the fridaynightknittingclub.co.uk. To find out more about her novel, visit Kate's website at www.katejacobsbooks.com.

Praise for THE FRIDAY NIGHT KNITTING CLUB:

'The mother of them all: *The Friday Night Knitting Club* celebrates the power of women's independence' *New Statesman*

'Beautifully written with a fantastic cast of women . . . worth taking a duvet day for . . . you won't want to put this down' *Heat*

'Have a tissue box ready for this emotional rollercoaster of a book' *She*

'The fluffy escapism of this right-on read is bound to hook you in' *Eve*

'Funny, sad and effortlessly hip' *The London Paper*

'Thoroughly entertaining . . . with an unexpected twist' *Prima*

'A colourful yarn' *Woman & Home*

KATE JACOBS

The Friday Night
Knitting Club

HODDER

First published in Great Britain in 2007 by Hodder & Stoughton
An Hachette Livre UK company

This paperback edition published in 2007

2

A CIP catalogue record for this title is
available from the British Library

ISBN 978 0 340 92219 4

Typeset in Plantin Light by Palimpsest Book Production Limited,
Grangemouth, Stirlingshire
Printed and bound by
Mackays of Chatham Ltd, Chatham, Kent

Hodder & Stoughton policy is to use papers that are natural,
renewable and recyclable products and made from wood grown
in sustainable forests. The logging and manufacturing processes
are expected to conform to the environmental regulations
of the country of origin.

Hodder & Stoughton Ltd
338 Euston Road
London NW1 3BH

www.hodder.co.uk

The Gathering

Choosing your wool is dizzying with potential: the waves of colors and textures tempt with visions of a sweater or cap (and all the accompanying compliments you hope to receive) but don't reveal the hard work required to get there. Patience and attention to detail make all the difference. Also willingness. Challenge keeps it interesting, but don't select a pattern that is so far beyond you. Always select the best yarn you can afford. And use the type of needle that feels best in your hand; I always used bamboo. Even now, it still seems unbelievable to me that by pulling together a motley collection — the soft yarn, the sharp needles, the scripted pattern, the smoothing hook, the intangibles of creativity, humanity, and imagination — you can create something that will hold a piece of your soul. But you can.

I

OPEN TUESDAY TO SATURDAY, 10 A.M.–8 P.M. NO EXCEPTIONS!
The hours of WALKER AND DAUGHTER: KNITTERS were clearly displayed in multi-colored letters on a white sandwich board placed just so at the top of the stair landing, but Georgia Walker – usually preoccupied with closing out the till and picking up the stray ends of yarn on the floor – rarely made a move to turn the lock until at least 8.15 . . . and often later still.

Instead, she sat on her stool at the counter, tuning out the traffic noise from New York's busy Broadway below, reflecting on the day's sales or prepping for the beginners' knitting class she taught every afternoon to the stay-at-homes looking for some seeming stamp of authentic motherliness. She crunched the numbers with a pencil and paper and sighed (business was good, but it could always be better); she tugged at her long chestnut curls. It was a habit from years ago she'd never quite grown out of and by the end of each day her bangs often stood straight up. Once the bookkeeping was in order she'd smooth out her hair, brush off any bits of eraser from her jeans and soft jersey top, her face a bit pale from concentration and lack of sun, and stand up to her full 6 feet (thanks to the 3-inch heels on her well-worn brown leather cowboy boots that she kept as they cycled in and out of style).

Slowly she would walk round the shop, running her hands lightly over the piles of yarn that were meticulously sorted by color – from lime to Kelly green, rust to strawberry, cobalt to Wedgwood blue, sunburst to amber, and rows and rows of grays and creams and blacks and whites. The yarn went from exquisitely plush and smooth to itchy and nubbly and all of it was hers. And Dakota's too, of course. Dakota, who at twelve frequently ignored her mother's instructions, loved to cross her dark eyes and savor the fuzzed-out look of the colors all merging, a rainbow blending together.

Dakota was the store mascot, one of its chief color consultants ('more sparkles!') and, frankly, a pretty damn good knitter already. Georgia noticed how quickly her daughter was making her projects, how particular she was becoming about the tautness of her stitches. More than once Georgia had been surprised to see her not-so-little-any-more girl approach a waiting customer and say with confidence: 'Oh, I can help you with that. Here, we'll take this crochet hook and fix that mistake . . .' The shop was a work in progress; Dakota was the one thing she knew she'd done exactly right.

And yet when Georgia finally went to turn out the lights of her shop, she would often be met by a potential customer, all furrowed brow and breathless from dashing up the steep stairs to the second-floor shop, the seemingly innocuous 'Can I just pop in, for a quick minute?' out of her mouth before Georgia could even insist they were done for the night. She'd open the door a little wider, knowing all too well what it was like to juggle work and kids and still try to sneak in a little something for herself on the side: reading a book, coloring her hair in the bathroom sink, taking a nap. Come in, get what you need, she'd say, putting off the short climb to her sparsely decorated apartment on the floor above. And though she never let any straggler stay past nine on a school night because she needed to shoo Dakota from the corner desk where she did her homework, Georgia would never turn away a potential sale.

She'd never turn away anyone at all.

* * *

'You can go home, Anita,' Georgia would say over her shoulder to the trusted friend who worked in the shop alongside her. Anita always stayed until closing time, peeking in on Dakota's studies as Georgia wondered about keeping the older woman out too late. But even though she had the opportunity to leave, Anita, who still looked as fresh in her Chanel pantsuit as when she'd come in for her shift at 3 p.m., just smiled and shook her head, her silver bob falling neatly into place. Then Georgia would step out of the doorframe to let in the straggler, a resigned smile revealing the beginnings of tiny crinkles around her calm green eyes as she smoothed back a wayward curl. Here we go again, her face seemed to say. But she was grateful for every person who walked through the door and took the time to make sure they had what they needed.

'Every sale is also a future sale – if you please the customer.' Georgia often bored Dakota with her various theories on business. 'Word of mouth is the best advertising.'

And her biggest booster was Anita, who sensed when the day had been too long for Georgia and leaped in to assist. 'I'd be delighted to help you,' Anita often said, coming up to Georgia's side and reaching out to the last-minute shopper and ushering her inside. Anita knew and loved the nubbly textures and patterns as well as Georgia; both had been introduced to the craft by grandmothers eager to share their secrets. Talking about knitting with the customers at Walker and Daughter was Anita's passion – second only to working with the needles herself.

Anita was captivated with the craft from the moment her Bubbe asked her, as a chubby-cheeked youngster, to hold a skein of thick, warm yarn. She watched her grandmother work the needles quickly, fashioning the hunter-green string into a small smooth cardigan. With thick buttons for little fingers to grasp. And when that same grandmother presented the finished sweater to Anita . . . well, a knitter was born. Soon she was placing her hands over her grandmother's as she learned how it felt to work the wool, then mastered tying her first slip knot and relished the excitement of casting on for the first time. As a young woman, Anita kept up knitting to make herself the angora twin sets her parents couldn't afford, then to cuddle up her babies in thick blankets and booties while her husband worked on building his business. She just kept at it – long after she needed to make clothes for her family, long after her husband's hard work had built a life that was more than comfortable – and then, when she was well into middle-age, she threw out the pattern books and began experimenting with patterns and color to create unique designs. A mother of three grown sons and grand-mother to seven (handsome and genius) youngsters, Anita was surprised to add up the years and realize that she had been working with yarn for most of her 72 years.

'Anita is an artist, and knitting is her medium,' was what her husband Stan always told people who admired the colorful vests he insisted on wearing to the office. Stan. He had been so proud of her, encouraging her to work with Georgia all those years ago; she began going to the shop one day a week to test it out. Anita had had no need for the money and she worried that she seemed silly to work at her age.

'Does it make you happy?' Stan had asked her after her first day, and she admitted that Yes, yes, it did, as she rolled into his arms. Then keep at it, he murmured, keep at it.

Over time, young Dakota began to seem like another grand-child – especially precious because Anita could see her when-ever she wanted, unlike her own children and grandchildren, who had all moved away to Israel, Zurich, Atlanta. There were cards and phone calls, of course, but it wasn't the same; Anita had long harbored a fear of planes and all the psychol-ogists and Valium in the world couldn't fix it. Her grandchildren grew so much between each visit that it was like getting to know a new person all over again.

And then one day Stan was gone, too. A quick peck as she sat at the breakfast table with toast crumbs still on her lip, a sudden heart attack riding in the elevator to his top-floor office, a phone call telling her to take a cab to Beth Israel right now, then hearing there was nothing more anyone could do. And so it went.

Stan had taken care of the details as always, so she had no reason to worry about the bills. But financial security wasn't enough. Anita was alone. Really and truly on her own. She cried as she lay in bed, sleeping or with magazines piled all around her. And then, one month after the funeral, she got up, put on her lipstick and pearls, and made her way to see Georgia.

'There are more and more customers each day and you're going to run behind on your projects-for-hire, Georgia,' she had said. 'You need someone in here full-time and I need to keep busier than to just work one day a week.' It was the truth. Dakota was two then and Georgia had recently expanded from creating projects on commission to selling yarn and notions. She had worked hard to make her business float, had even worked the 6–12 shift for Marty in the deli below the apartment building, toasting bagels and pouring to-go cups of coffee. Branching out into sales meant she may soon be able to give up the second job and spend more time with Dakota.

They agreed that Anita would come in for the afternoon shift during the week and, while Georgia tried to insist on a dollar figure, Anita was adamant she would only work for yarn, never for wages.

'When the store is a booming success, then you can pay me,' she suggested that day ten years before.

Of course, the shop – with careful planning, slow growth,

and a lot of hope – had grown into something of a hit. Over the years, it had even popped up in mentions of local haunts in papers and such; recently an article in *New York* on mompreneurs had featured Walker and Daughter.

'Sure thing, it might bring your classmates and their moms into the shop,' Georgia had said when Dakota wanted to take the story to school. She planned to drop off her little girl at the front entrance as she did every morning, then go home to open up the shop. A quick hug and see you later; the usual. Instead, Dakota surprised her mother as she wheeled around, her winter coat already unzipped and revealing the bright turquoise sweater that accented her warm café-au-lait skin. It was one of Georgia's creations. Dakota spoke, pointing to the article in triumph, then dashed to the door before the buzzer sounded. Georgia barely remembered the walk home, fumbled with the keys to the shop before her face became wet with heavy tears as she let the years of fear and hard work wash out of her, Dakota's casual 'I'm proud of us, Mom' ringing in her ears.

Yet Anita continued to work only for yarn, and when she wanted to start a personal knitting project – she still made vest after vest even though Stan had been gone for a decade – she simply went to the shelf and chose something exquisite. When she wanted a hug, she wrapped her arms around Dakota. And that was enough.

So Anita always let out a deep breath upon seeing this last-minute customer skate into the store, felt the ball in her stomach begin to unwind. A few more minutes to be needed, a further delay to keep her from going home to the apartment at the San Remo that remained too big and too empty. 'Oh, come on in,' she'd say over Georgia's mild protests, walking right over to help the client. 'Tell me what you need . . .'

And so that's how it got to be that the door at Walker and

Daughter was open a little bit late and a little bit later than that, and soon enough, at the end of the long work week, a few regular customers took to popping in with their knitting – sweaters and scarves and cell-phone socks – and asking questions about all the mistakes they'd made while commuting on the subway.

'I just can't get the buttonhole right!'

'Why do I keep dropping stitches?'

'Do you think I can finish it by Christmas?'

Without Georgia ever putting up one sign or announcing the creation of a knitting club, these women began regularly appearing in the evenings and, well, loitering. Chatting with each other, talking to Anita, gathering about the large round table in the center of the room, picking up where they had left things the week before. And then, one Friday last fall, it became official. Well, sort of.

Lucie, a striking woman with short sandy-colored hair who favored tortoiseshell glasses over her big blue eyes and colorful funky outfits, was an occasional shopper at Walker and Daughter; she came in every few months and was always working on the same piece. A thick cable knit sweater; a man's garment. There were a lot of these types who came in to the store, folks whose knitting ambitions were out of line with either their ability or with whatever mysterious comings and goings kept them from sitting down and getting the job done.

But Lucie began appearing more and more often in the early evening, gazing wistfully at the fancier yarns but typically choosing a good quality wool that was just this side of inexpensive. Some days she sauntered in with a leather attaché case and suit jacket slung over her arm as if she'd come from a big meeting. At other times she looked relaxed in slim-fitting cigarette pants and a messenger bag draped across her body. But without fail she had a single bag of groceries in her hand, the makings of a simple supper, which she carefully placed on the counter as she paid for her yarn. After talking to Lucie on several visits, it became clear to Anita that she was pretty fair with a set of needles but simply couldn't find the time to get going.

'You could always knit here,' Anita suggested idly, not thinking much of it. And then, one Friday, Lucie simply pulled up a chair at the table and began to do her knitting right then and there. And Dakota, who had been idly milling about and rolling her eyes and making noises about being bored and wanting to go to the movies, sat right down beside her.

'That's pretty,' said Dakota, impulsively reaching out to stroke the top of the sparkling gemstone Lucie wore on her right hand.

'Yes, I bought it for myself,' said Lucie, with a smile that recalled happy times, but offered no more explanation. Dakota shrugged, then reached out to look at the big, thick sweater Lucie had on round needles.

'I'm pretty good, you know,' she said, nodding, putting out a hand to take a look at Lucie's stitches.

Lucie had laughed, kept clacking away. 'I'm sure you are,' she said, without looking up.

And then Anita sat down, ostensibly to keep Dakota in check. Other shoppers joined them at the table and suddenly, unexpectedly, it was a group. On a whim, Lucie pulled out the box of fresh bakery cookies she had just picked up at Fairway and had planned to savor over the weekend; instead, she offered them round. The polite 'No, thank-yous' echoed until Dakota declared that she most certainly would enjoy a treat, and then the laughter sliced through the awkwardness and they each took one, and then another. And somehow, between mouthfuls, they began to show one another what they had been working on. Anita talked button-holes and dropped stitches, and then she offered to put on a fresh pot of coffee in the back. More cookies, more conversation. It became late, too late to really stay on, and the women packed up their bags and made motions to move but lingered, reluctant to leave. It was Dakota who declared she'd bring muffins to the next meeting. Next meeting? I might be busy, the women said. I don't know if I can commit. Let me check my calendar. But the next week, Lucie did show up. Dakota brought her muffins. Georgia even sat down with them. And so the Friday Night Knitting Club emerged.

Six months later, the club was going strong even as the winter drew to a close. Lucie had finished her sweater and started another; Dakota was making a regular mess in the kitchen in their apartment above, experimenting with everything from pinwheel cookies to blondies to decorated cupcakes. 'Ever heard of June Cleaver?' Georgia would tease her. Big sigh from her sweet brown-eyed little girl who kept growing bigger.

'Yeah, I've seen TV Land, Mom.'

Then: 'It's for the club, Mom, the ladies are hungry!' A beat. 'What do you think about selling my creations?'

Ah, she'd raised another independent businesswoman with vision. It felt good.

Dakota's bake sale plans never came to pass – 'No, Dakota, this Walker still outranks the daughter!' – but the group continued to grow anyway. People told their friends, and women would stroll in after meeting up for drinks or a nosh. Coming to the Friday Night Knitting Club became a bit of a thing to do – different enough to be fun, refreshing in that it wasn't just another place to meet men.

One such drop-in – a woman who came once but never came back – mentioned the shop in a casual way to her cousin, Darwin Chiu, who arrived one evening and spoke in hushed tones with Georgia, then sat at the table with a serious expression and a note pad. She was no ordinary customer; in fact, Darwin wasn't a knitter at all. Instead, she was a struggling graduate student in search of a dissertation for her doctorate in women's studies. The knitting club became her primary resource for thesis research. A compact Asian-American woman in her late twenties, Darwin was all business. In the beginning, she rarely smiled; she just furiously scribbled and later moved on to interviewing the members of the club about their 'obsession with knitting'.

'How do you feel knitting connects with your conceptions of femininity?' Darwin asked of one quiet doctor who had popped by at the end of her shift and who never entered the shop again. No doubt, thought Georgia, due to Darwin.

'Does being an older knitter make you feel disconnected from the younger trendsetters?' she asked Anita.

'No, love, it makes me feel young,' Anita replied. 'Every time I cast on I feel the potential of making something beautiful.'

At first, Georgia tolerated Darwin because she was amused by her earnestness and because she admired the seriousness with which she approached her studies. Not to mention that she felt a certain sense of pride to have someone choose Walker and Daughter as a worthy place in which to do research. But in short order, Georgia put her foot down.

'You can't harass everyone who comes in here, Darwin,' she explained. 'You'll have to go if you can't stop interrogating everyone.'

'Aren't you disturbed that the renewed popularity of knitting is an alarming throwback? Can women who fritter away time on old-fashioned activities such as knitting realize their full professional potential?' responded Darwin, clearly missing the point.

'Disturbed? No, encouraged is more like it. As in, I'm

encouraged I can afford to send Dakota to Harvard.'
Georgia's mouth was a straight line. Knitting had done more
than provide her with a living; it had soothed her soul through
more struggles than she could count. 'Sweetheart, I'm
concerned you're preventing my shop from reaching its full
professional potential!'

The two women stood glaring at each other for a long
time. Darwin eventually turned on her heel and left.

And then she returned, two weeks later, watching Georgia
warily as she arrived for club. Their eyes met, the agreement
unspoken: You can stay, but don't upset the clients. Darwin
nodded imperceptibly. She selected one of Dakota's muffins
– Carrot Spice – and even gave it a try. It was a first. 'Hey,
this is awesome!' She was genuinely surprised. Dakota,
thrilled, told her she could request next week's flavor.

'I'm glad you're back,' said Anita. Darwin looked up, expecting
to see sarcasm but found only warmth and welcome in Anita's
eyes. A wide grin spread over her face. She was embarrassed
to admit it, even to herself, but Darwin was glad to be back.
She had missed them.

Officially, Georgia was nonplussed by the presence of the
club. 'You all sit here and no one buys anything!' she would
say to Anita during the day. Sometimes, when they had a lot
of drop-ins, she hung back at the counter. It felt overwhelming
to have this group here, laughing and chatting. Her adult life
had centered on work and her little girl for so long that Georgia
felt out of practice at just hanging out with women of her
own age. She'd felt awkward unless she was helping them to
calculate how many balls for this pattern or that. But she loved
that Anita had an activity for her mornings, getting revved up
about whatever knitting topic she would discuss that week,
and that Dakota was happy to stick around the store on a
Friday night and not retreat to watch the TV upstairs.

Keeping Dakota safe, making her happy: that was what mattered most to Georgia. The store was truly theirs together, because it was Dakota who began it all. And savoring the end of each day that they were still in business – and doing well, thank you very much! – was a triumph for Georgia. For she had been awash in panic when she discovered she was pregnant, barely out of college and working for poverty wages as some editor's assistant at an amorphous publishing conglomerate. Her boyfriend, James, had dumped her the month before, saying he 'just wasn't into exclusivity'. The truth of it was that he had already started dating a woman in his office. And not just any woman: he was fucking his boss, the lead architect in a major Manhattan firm.

Georgia had wanted James the first time she saw him at Le Bar Bat, had felt a connection to this tall, handsome black man. She tugged at her curls, walked over to him and popped the question: 'I like my eggs scrambled for breakfast. You?' It was a gambit. James looked at her with cool authority; he liked what he saw, charmed her with his lopsided grin. First waiting at the bar to get drinks, then standing off to the side shout-talking until the middle of the night. They went home together, something she'd always been too cautious to do, Georgia feeling that she had been chosen, believing everyone looked at her with envy. And without even having a big discussion about it, they became a couple, going to parties and to the movies and meeting for egg rolls after work. James was energetic and filled with big ideas; he loved to save up for more than a month so he could take them to luxurious restaurants like Le Cirque or wait in line to buy half-price tickets to Broadway shows. Other nights they stayed in, she reading manuscripts in bed, he working at the battered old drafting table taking up most of his living room. They were young, often broke, and infused with the energy and passion that fills the New York air. The relationship was easy, comfortable, exciting. It was meant to be. For eight months, they shuttled back and forth between apartments, had late-night chats in which they discussed whose furniture they'd keep when they moved in together, walked hand-in-hand through the city streets fantasizing about where they should live. The Upper West Side, they decided. Georgia recalled nights in bed with James, her pale hand tracing lines on his dark chest as she would ask in a sing-song voice, 'Will it reeealllly bother your family that I'm white?' and he'd laugh and say, 'Hell, yes!' They fell to giggles and tickles, empowered by the intensity of their recent lovemaking and not believing their relationship would fall to any challenge.

She never did meet his parents. She only realized that after he was gone.

And then James had moved on, having let himself into her apartment during the day and gathered up his clothes. He returned her things from his home, left them piled on the couch. Georgia's mind swirled. She called him, screamed, begged him to come back. She stopped eating, stopped sleeping, then began eating way too much. Snickers bars and Pringles and giant bagels with cream cheese, soda and ice cream and pizza and cookies. She ate anything she could get her hands on. Anything cheap and filling.

'If you keep eating like that, everyone will think you're preggers,' observed her wafer-thin, pain-in-the-ass cubicle mate.

A pause. Georgia did the math: her period was late. Way late. And then she knew.

Should she take it on the chin and go back home to small town Pennsylvania? Could she endure the humiliation of moving back home to her parents, of being a single mother

with a failed big-city career at 24? Or should she call her
doctor and then just pretend the pregnancy had never
happened? Georgia fretted over her lack of appealing options,
in between photocopying endless manuscripts and opening
looming piles of other people's mail and running out to buy
the oversized fat-free muffins her boss never ate.

Her indecision was her decision, and it became clear that
she and this baby were going to stick together. Then came
the day when Georgia, visibly pregnant, made her final
pilgrimage to Central Park. It was to be her last weekend in
the city before moving home to her parents; she'd dialled
them when there was no going back and choked on the news,
feeling brave and sorry for herself at the same time.

'We'd be happy to have you home with us,' said her father
with gusto, before being drowned out by his wife's sighs.

'You've made a stupid mistake by trusting this man,
Georgia,' said her mother. 'It's clear he only wanted one
thing. And you've set yourself up a hard road to hoe – not
everyone will be as welcoming to this child as we are.'

Georgia could see her mother's tight-lipped expression in
her mind; it was one she'd seen many times growing up. She
could barely hear them discuss the details of which train she
might take, too overwhelmed by emotional regreat and physical nausea.

The day was a scorcher. The air-conditioner in her Upper
West Side walk-up had konked out, leaving her sweat-soaked
and uncomfortable. Her dark curly hair had frizzed and stuck
to the back of her neck, her belly jutted out of her slender
frame, and her fingers, always so slim and nimble, were swollen.
Her eyes were red, puffy. Georgia had finally worked up the
nerve to call James and reveal the pregnancy in one of those
awkward late-night calls; he was shocked, angry, apologetic
. . . and bedded down with his newest girlfriend. And no, she
wasn't his boss. He had already found someone new.

'This isn't a really good time for me . . . perhaps we can meet tomorrow? At the park?'

And so she made her way that morning to an empty bench under the trees, sat down with the half-finished blanket she was knitting for her baby-to-be, and waited. James never showed.

'That's an impressive pattern you've worked out there.' Georgia was startled by the elegant older woman standing before her, her linen suit still crisp and a wide-brimmed sun hat framing her face. Georgia smiled weakly, embarrassed by her cheap clothes, her fat belly, her youth.

The woman sat down anyway, began talking about the blankets she had knitted for her own children and about how working the needles always helped her sort out her emotions. Georgia just wanted her to go away, but she had been raised to be a good girl, so she pretended to listen politely. Tears of rage and frustration stung her eyes. James!

'You don't find very many people who can knit with this type of precision,' she heard the woman say as she fingered the piece. 'It's a dying art, and one I imagine people would pay for.' She reached over and patted Georgia's left hand; there was no ring, but the woman knew that already.

'If I were you, I might start asking around, see if anyone needed sweaters or scarves for gifts. Perhaps see if you can put up a sign at the baby store over on Broadway and Seventy-sixth? Get the word out. Buy a classified ad in the *New Yorker* – it worked for Lillian Vernon.'

Georgia sat there, at a loss for words, doubt and confusion oozing from every pore. The woman stood up to leave, motioned to a man in the distance.

'You have a gift, my dear, and I have an eye for talent.' She handed Georgia a cream calling card on heavy stock. 'Just to prove it to you, I'll buy the first sweater you make. Make it cashmere, and make it quickly. I'll expect a call when

it's done.' Her heels made a soft clip-clop on the sidewalk as
she walked away.

Georgia turned over the card.

Anita Lowenstein. The San Remo. 212-555-9580

2

Marty Popper could set his clock by her: every afternoon at 2.52 p.m. Anita would struggle to open the heavy glass door of his first-floor deli.

He waited behind the counter, with the fresh-brewed pot of coffee, just as he had been doing every Monday through Friday for the past decade. The lunch rush had ended and his knife was down; only a few lonely sandwich rolls were left in the bins, the ham and smoked turkey breast lined up neatly alongside the Swiss in the refrigerated case. His broom leaned against a wall, resting after a recent push across the floor. Marty was a tall, solid sort of man who kept busy enough that his middle hadn't grown soft over the years. Now he savored the quiet, the chance to gaze at the potato-chip display he'd just rearranged, to survey the business that had once been his father's. It was a good operation and he liked getting people on their way to work, sending them off with a nosh and a joke, chatting with the same neighborhood faces day after day. The deli had provided well for him and for his younger brother Sam, paid for a fine home on the Upper West Side, season tickets to the Yankees, and a couple of weeks at the Jersey Shore each summer. Then came the day his brother was ready to make the long-awaited pilgrimage to Delray Beach, the permanent vacation for a generation of retirees. Marty bought him out, giving his brother his final payout the previous year. But Marty had no plans to shut down or sell out to a chain; he'd never

married and had never seen the need to come up with a
retirement plan. It was the family joke: Uncle Marty was
tied to his own apron strings.

Still, it wasn't exactly the life he had planned, years ago.
There had been the prospect of a high-profile business career,
his father making it clear that college was an option. But
things happen, in a way that most kids nowadays don't really
understand, he knew. Marty had snuck off to fight in the
Pacific, a few years underage, at a time when manpower was
so scarce that his recruiter made a point to not pay attention. It was colder and scarier than he'd ever expected, and
when he came home, he didn't really care so much about
going away to college. He just wanted to stay home and try
to shut out the images that haunted him. He had the blues,
they used to say. It'll pass, they said. And it did, eventually.
By then it was clear that Marty wasn't about to climb the
corporate ladder, even though he followed up on the GI Bill
and took a college course or two.

'I think I'll just stick with you, Pop,' he'd said over 50 years
ago. It was okay with his parents. They were thrilled he had
come home in one piece, and it eased his anxiety about coming
back to the world after the war. So he looked after his parents
at their home until the very end (no nursing homes for his
mom and pop), and let Sam take over the family apartment,
even suggested it. He was the kind of uncle who spent Sunday
afternoons with the kids at Coney Island so their harried
parents could get a little peace and quiet. That Marty's a good
guy, people said. And he was. But there was one thing he
couldn't do, not after everything he'd seen in the war. He
couldn't settle. Not that he couldn't make a commitment –
Marty had always wanted a wife, a family. You'd be a great
dad, his nieces and nephews used to say. No, it was more
than that. Family friends introduced him to daughters, nieces,
cousins – nice girls, then nice ladies, then sweet spinsters well

into middle age – but Marty wasn't willing to marry someone unless he absolutely, positively fell head over heels. He'd been in some serious like, even lust, but it was never the true love he was holding out for. I've seen the worst, he would tell his brother Sam, and I'm waiting for the best. And then came the day ten years ago that she walked into his deli and Marty had been overwhelmed by her citrusy perfume, her tailored clothes, her shimmering eyes, the soft hands he touched, ever so briefly, as he handed over her order.

Mr Marty Popper, war veteran, happy-go-lucky uncle, fell in love at first sight. The only problem was that he'd never said anything. All these years. Not one word.

Anita glided past the tables pushed up to the wall. Five or six school kids lolled on their plastic chairs, dazed from lugging their heavy homework-filled backpacks, fortifying themselves with black-and-white cookies for the assignments and television viewing that awaited in the evening ahead. The kids talked about who liked whom and said what when and why, occasionally glancing at the two old folks at the counter to see if they were listening.

'One medium coffee, white!' Marty chimed a little too loudly, the disposable blue cup looking small in his large hands. A dollar ready in hand, Anita smiled as she paid him. She took a sip; steam rose off the top.

'Thank you, sir, you remembered.' She said that every time even though Marty hadn't forgotten how she liked her coffee since the first day she walked into his deli and ordered a medium, to go. Please and thank you. Anita remained the most elegant woman he had ever seen.

'I always do, miss,' said Marty. Beaming. A pause. He handed her a white plastic lid, watched her take another sip, savoring. He had long ago stopped trying to convince her to take a donut or biscotti. Just coffee for me, she used to say, just coffee. As usual, he switched to their favorite topic.

'You know, Dakota stopped by not more than fifteen minutes ago, told me she needed to look around to do some research.'

'That might have just been an excuse to convince you to sell her muffins – she's writing a pitch letter to the Food Network about a show on kids who can cook.' Anita tilted her head, proud of Dakota's gumption, but also remembering the previous day when Dakota begged her mother to buy her a bike so she could sell her products to joggers in Central Park. Who will go with you? Georgia had asked, trying to lead Dakota to see the potential problems in her business development.

Anita knew just how much Georgia wanted her little girl to realize the world was hers for the taking. (She recalled Georgia telling her how she'd chosen the name Dakota, figuring they'd get a start by having the names of at least two states between them.) Yes, Anita knew the impulse, she remembered holding her own babies and promising to herself that they would be able to do anything. But she also knew that Georgia was flummoxed by the swiftly approaching teen years; many a night the two women would close up the shop together, Anita listening intently as Georgia fretted that she had confused setting limits with crushing the spirit. Sure, there had always been times when Dakota resisted not being the one in charge, when Georgia had to say no and suffer silently, secretly hating herself for seeming mean. But things had been increasingly tense. The push-pull had started in earnest last summer, when Dakota began going into her room and shutting her door with frequency.

'I need my space' she'd say to Georgia, acting more like a harried adult than a preteen. 'I have a lot to think about.' Georgia had always made it a point to allow Dakota her privacy, had always knocked before entering. So she was taken aback that her little girl felt she was being intrusive. Increasingly, her suggestions were met with resistance.

'How about we watch a DVD?' Georgia might ask, loudly, through the door.

'I'm not available right now,' her daughter might say.

Or the more curt, 'I'm busy.'

Other nights, Dakota would tumble out into the hallway, ready to pour out her heart to her mom, fascinating and confusing Georgia with the comings and goings of her classmates. Kids were in, kids were out; it was a never-ending merry-go-round of drama.

'You don't know what stress is,' Dakota told her one night, as they lay on Georgia's bed with a bowl of popcorn between them. 'You know how to handle things. But my life is seriously stressed out, Mom. Seventh grade is hard.'

And if the day-to-day business of growing up wasn't hard enough, there was now an added wrinkle. Shortly after the beginning of the current school year – after more than a decade of being completely absent (except for the sums, originally quite modest, that he wired into a custodial bank account for Dakota) – James had suddenly, inexplicably decided that he wanted to do more than send money. Now he demanded to be a part of things. And the man had returned to New York City to make it happen.

His preferred method, it seemed, was to buy his way into Dakota's heart. Not that she'd need much convincing, desperate as Dakota was for James's affection. Georgia had always assumed that if she could just be enough parent to Dakota, her little girl wouldn't miss James.

After all, it's not like she ever knew him, right?

It doesn't work that way with kids. She'd learned Dakota was ecstatic at James's appearance.

Georgia had first adopted her daughter's 'I'm busy' attitude when it came to James, trying to put him off seeing

Dakota. She took a gamble, figuring that if he'd given up easily the first time around, he was likely to do it again.

Wrong.

James had been an absolute pain in the ass, his assertiveness about his rights to see his daughter bordering on the aggressive. Calling, stopping by the shop, coming up to her outside Marty's deli after she dropped off Dakota at school. That was how she'd found out he was back in town. He just waltzed up to her, plain as anything, and said hello.

Her first impulse was to scratch and hiss. She considered it, briefly, then opted for the old maxim: kill with kindness. So she returned his hello as if seeing her former lover was no big deal, then walked up to her shop – back straight – without turning around.

Once safely inside the four walls of Walker and Daughter, she locked the door, ran into the office in the back and grabbed a pillow off the loveseat, holding it over her own face as she screamed with frustration and fear and shock.

Georgia didn't trust the man one bit and, as she confided to Anita, she feared that he would take some sort of legal action if she kept up with her stonewalling. She agreed to talk to her daughter. So she knocked on that damned closed door, waiting in the hallway between bedrooms in the apartment, admiring the carefully stencilled sign announcing 'Please request permission to enter.' Dakota cracked open the door.

'Yes, can I help you?' As if she didn't know who would be knocking in their own apartment.

'It's your mother,' said Georgia dryly. 'I was hoping to have a chat.'

They'd been talking about James, in a roundabout way, for years. That he worked overseas and that he and Georgia had come to an agreement before Dakota was born. Come to an agreement! Georgia always marvelled at how she said these things to her daughter with a straight face, how she had always been careful not to badmouth him – a decision she sorely regretted when she saw how eager Dakota was to meet the philanderer who was her father.

She'd gritted her teeth through a soda at Marty's and watched with increasing anxiety as Dakota fell for James's hearty laugh and his praising compliments. And especially in the first few weeks of the father-daughter reunion, for Dakota there was only the joy of knowing that he'd come for her.

Her father had finally arrived. Oh, Dakota had a lot of emotion about James's return, but she saved most of her questions and hostility for Georgia.

'Did you do something to make him leave?' Dakota stared down her mother over cereal one morning. (It was these times that Georgia repeated Anita's advice like a mantra: The truth about her father will only hurt Dakota – and she'll hate you for telling her.) Georgia danced around the subject, talked vaguely about relationships not working out, repeated that Dakota was loved and had nothing to do with their break-up. The recriminations continued, more a drizzle than a downpour, as fall turned to winter.

'You may not have loved him but I'm the one who has been punished,' said Dakota, leading Georgia to muse that she was hiding self-help books between the covers of *Cook's Illustrated*.

Around this same time, Dakota stepped up her challenges to Georgia, demanding to wear flashier, more grown-up clothes and eyeshadow and mascara to school. She wanted to go to PG-13 movies by herself with her friends. (She tried to sneak in the occasional R-rated horror flick too.) There was the night when Georgia overheard Dakota and a friend talking animatedly about some teacher at school, sentences sprinkled liberally with the 'F' word.

'I don't approve of that language I heard last night,' Georgia said while doing dishes the next night, in what she thought was a casual reprimand. Dakota pulled a face, burst into tears.

'So now you're policing what I say in private?' she screamed. 'What are you, the CIA?'

She stomped out of the room and slammed her door shut with such force that her sign fluttered down to the floor.

Who could match it up to the times when she was all soft little girl, wanting cuddles and foot fights on the couch? Was it seventh grade? Was it the crazy hormones of puberty? Was it James's sudden drop into their lives? It was as though Dakota was caught in a tug-of-war, not just the one simmering between her parents, but within herself.

'I just want her to like me,' Georgia had sniffled to Anita after saying no to the bike that Dakota desperately wanted. The very expensive bike that cost almost $1500 – and that Georgia strongly suspected would be a passing fad, like the keyboard and the music lessons her daughter simply had to have when she was a wee thing of nine. Back when she still thought Georgia was cool.

'In the teen years, it's better she hates you now and loves you later,' Anita had said, patting down Georgia's wild curls.

Now Anita looked at Marty, admired his thick salt-and-pepper hair, the neatly trimmed nails on his large, strong hands, the almost-dimple on the left side of his mouth.

'You won't believe it, but our little miss has found out that I don't know how to ride a bike – and she's decided to teach me once the weather gets warm!' Anita shook her head at Marty and sighed. 'She doesn't know that you can't teach an old dog new tricks.'

'Not so old.' Marty's eyes were warm. 'With more than a few tricks up her sleeve, I'd bet.'

And so, as they did every afternoon, Marty and Anita would speak Dakota, the language of mutual love. She was the granddaughter that Marty always wanted but would never have and the proxy for the grandchildren that Anita hardly ever saw. And she was always a safe topic.

They had talked all through diapers and the first days of school and summer camp. For years, whenever Anita would mention taking Dakota to see the latest tween movie or treating her to ice cream at Serendipity on the East Side, Marty would make a sincere suggestion of how he and Anita should go down to Film Forum and catch something with more appeal to the older generation, or try a more sophisticated dessert at Café Lalo. Maybe a little slice of German chocolate cake. Anita would agree with enthusiasm, laughing at how Dakota kept her young but adult company was in short supply, though neither of them ever went so far as to actually pick a date. Or to exchange phone numbers.

Then the moment would fade away, or a new customer would pop in for a bottle of water, or one of the afterschool kids would shuffle over and buy a pack of gum. Better be off so I can start my shift, Anita would say.

Marty would follow up with a round of 'say hi to . . .' all the mutuals at the knitting shop and she would be out the door, feeling lighthearted and desirable, coffee in hand, her low heels making a muted click-clack on the concrete as she walked speedily up the flight of stairs to Walker and Daughter.

And then Marty broke the pattern: he cleared his throat, uttered several ums and ahems, and asked Anita if she would be so gracious as to accompany him to dinner. On a date. Anita felt as though all the oxygen had been sucked out of the room.

'It's Friday,' she squeaked, nearly spilling her coffee as she grabbed her purse and coat in a swoop and made a beeline for the door, overwhelmed by a potent mix of white-hot anger in her face – how dare Marty upset their regular routine –

and bubbles in her tummy. 'I have the knitting club. The girls need me there. I have to go.'

And she was gone.

Upstairs, the redhead rushed into the shop for the seventh time that day, a manila envelope peeking out of her messenger bag and a newsboy cap on her head; Georgia had stopped asking if she could help her by the third visit. They'd had a lot of looky-loos since that magazine article and she wasn't sure if that was good or bad, to be honest. Now she just raised her eyebrows at Peri, her paid morning-shift employee, who was walking into the store from the back and flipping through a new knitting book. Georgia knew just how lucky she was to have Anita – she'd never have been able to pay for two employees – but she was also grateful that the twentysomething Peri was comfortable doing much of the physical work that would have been too taxing on Anita. She'd just spent the morning in the back opening boxes and cataloging the latest inventory of yarns. Not to mention she was fun company in the front of the store, always up on the latest fashion trends and eager to try them out.

'Watch this,' Georgia murmured to her employee, giving a slight nod in the redhead's direction. 'She's bought and returned the same tape measure I don't know how many times today.' The flame-haired stranger did a quick scan around the room, then sidled alongside a brunette with long hair and looked her up and down. Suddenly the young woman walked over to the register.

'I'd like to return this tape measure, please,' she said, while continuing to scan the room.

'Were the measurements off?' Georgia kept a straight face. The girl looked at her blankly, then went and sat at the table, drumming her fingers on the top. Some of the customers seemed mildly perturbed; still others didn't seem to notice, engrossed in difficult stitches or daydreaming about cashmere.

'What is that all about?' said Peri under her breath.

'She's been in and out every hour since I unlocked the door – and I'm pretty sure I saw her in the deli on Tuesday,' Georgia answered in a whisper. 'I can't tell if she's nuts or just creating some sort of performance art, waiting for everyone to react.'

After ten minutes of sitting, the girl stood up and slowly, slowly dawdled her way out of the shop, peering intently at any new customers as she headed towards the door. A moment later, Anita ran through the doorway, her cheeks flushed pink, a little out of breath.

'I think we should offer extra classes in manners,' Anita huffed. 'I was nearly plowed down as I came up the stairs by a girl with a giant handbag!'

'So you've met our mystery shopper – or nonshopper, as the case may be.' Georgia shrugged. 'She was loitering here this morning so I thought she might be a shoplifter. I pointed her to the remnant bin and told her she could pick whatever she liked free of charge. But she just looked right through me and then she bought a tape measure.' Her face was impassive but her eyes revealed worry. The store attracted all types, it was true, but typically they weren't certifiably nuts, just mildly annoying. 'Then she returned it and bought it over and over again. I wonder if she just needs a place to get out of the cold?'

'Drugs. She's high out of her mind.' Peri was definite. 'Ladies, I advise you to watch your purses and arm yourself with some knitting needles if she comes back. Ta ta for now, I've got to catch the train in time to get to class.' She buttoned up her red cardigan, pulled on an overstuffed navy parka to protect her from the icy March air, and smoothed a knitted cap over her dark cornrows. A glance in the mirror by the door as she checked for smudges of eyeliner, smoothed her fingers over her rich mocha skin and reapplied a dramatic red stain to her lips, a quick smooch to leave a big red mark on Dakota's cheek as she strolled in with the friend she walked home with every day. Then Peri waved behind her as she walked out the door. If Anita was Dakota's fairy grandmother, Peri was her fashion idol Barbie doll come to life.

'So it's going well for her?' Anita was hopeful. Georgia nodded. She knew that employees came and went – for most years of running the store, she hired students who were happy enough with minimum wage and part-time hours. She accepted that her shop was just a way-station until they journeyed to better things, however sweet or hard-working they may have been. But Peri Gayle was different. She had graduated from college three years ago and had been well on her way to NYU law school; working at Walker and Daughter was supposed to be a summer gig while she learned her way around the city. And then, just as Georgia was on the verge of making a new hire to replace her, Peri asked if she could stay on.

Peri's family was outraged; her mother flew in from Chicago and came to the shop to make a personal appeal to Georgia: fire her and she'll have to go to law school. But Peri insisted she wanted to keep her job. Georgia gave her a tiny bump in wages, and waited for Peri's case of cold feet to subside, for the potential of making $325 an hour to beckon her downtown. But Peri stayed put, working the first shift every day, making sweaters on commission after hours, and reading issue after issue of VOGUE – the British, French, Italian *and* American versions – during her down time. She was smart, creative, boisterous and her boss loved having her there. Georgia spent the majority of her waking hours either in the shop, thinking about the shop, or stocking the shop. Running

Walker and Daughter had become her entire life: she was a mom and a business owner and she didn't make much room for anything else. Of course, she had Anita – she adored Anita – but Peri was hip and young and energetic. And she was around the same age as Georgia had been when she'd discovered her pregnancy; perhaps, she thought with more than a hint of guilt, she was so willing to keep Peri on for the chance to relive her own twenties, sans baby. She thought it unprofessional to seem interested in all the gossipy tidbits of Peri's life and often seemed preoccupied as she shared the latest with Anita or one of the many regular twentysomethings who loved to come in and chitchat with her young employee. Peri had a great ability to turn customers into friends, Georgia had noticed.

And, secretly, she loved to hear about Peri's crew of friends and their forays to champagne bars and speed dating and winter skating at Wollman Rink. Georgia remembered times like that, too, when she'd skip breakfast, allot $1.35 for lunch (a nutrient-lacking pack of red Twizzlers and a can of root beer) and eat just a slice of pizza for dinner; pocketing her so-called food money until she and the other assistants went off to Webster Hall or some other club at the weekend. Yeah, she'd had many a night when she walked all the way uptown in the cold because she couldn't afford the buck for the subway, not sorry to be going home with empty pockets and hazy, beer-soaked memories of fun. Then she'd met James and settled into a cozy sort of domesticity that seemed so natural at the time. It had to be love, right? Now she recognized it for the playing house that it was. Had they ever sat down to pay the bills? Argued about cleaning the toilet? No, they ordered in pizza and had great sex and laughed and watched movies. That's what monogamy meant to her when she was 24: watching movies on the VCR instead of going out to the Cineplex. When she was with James, she splurged on taxis she couldn't afford and pricey designer shoes (but quality lasts – she still had those cowboy boots and wore them damn often, thank you very much) and gobbled up smoked salmon when she would have been smarter to buy a case of tuna fish. Sure, she had her worries then (the demanding boss and uncertain prospects for promotion, natch) but all was overshadowed by her confidence in a bright personal future and a partnership that would sustain her.

Ha! She gave up on love after James. No, that slimeball didn't just break her heart; she held him responsible for stealing her ability to trust. Georgia hadn't been in a serious romantic relationship since James had returned the sweaters and toothbrush she had left at his place. Hell, she wasn't even good at making friends – just friends – with either sex, especially with people her own age. 'I'm stunted,' she once told her long-time friend K.C., who was bemoaning her own latest sexual misadventure. She met Anita when she was pregnant, she found her current apartment above Marty's deli around the same time. And when Dakota arrived on the scene a few months later . . . well, that was it for new people. In the shop, Georgia was knowledgeable, professional, friendly, definitely welcoming. In that running-a-business kind of way. She could talk your ear off about stitches. But chitchat? Georgia always hung back, letting Anita – and then Peri – get to know the names of pets, spouses, in-laws. Ms Walker was a listener, not a sharer. Which made her, by her very nature, just that little bit lonely.

There it was. Georgia Walker was lonely.

And so having Peri around, day in and day out, was like drinking a cool glass of water on a steamy New York-style summer day. More than refreshing. Life sustaining.

Still, after a year had passed since Peri arrived at Walker and Daughter, Georgia's maternal instinct kicked into high gear and she decided it was time to sit Peri down for a big talk. She had a place at the shop, to be sure, but was that what she wanted? And then Peri came out with it: she had designs on becoming the next Kate Spade, and had been secretly taking fashion marketing classes at FIT all along. She worked during the day and went to school at night. She had even registered a URL – PeriPocketbook.com – that was idling while she figured out how to build a damned website. (She was taking a class on that, too, and had offered to create a separate one for the shop – WalkerandDaughter.com.) Oh, she had plans, all right, Georgia needn't worry about that – but Peri knew her parents would want her to take a more certain career path so she kept her design ambitions to herself. As for the knitting shop, well, it was a good job. A toe in the fashion world. And she planned to make a specialty line of knitted bags, so if Georgia didn't mind displaying a few . . .

Georgia didn't mind at all.

'I don't want to hear "I told you so" from my mother for the next fifty years,' Peri had confessed. 'If it doesn't work out, I'll just claim I've been finding myself and reapply to law school. Let's be real: I had straight As at Smith, my LSAT kicked ass, I'm West Indian and I'm a woman. It's a double win for the quota freaks and a bonus for the profs who actually care about ability.'

Georgia admired Peri's chutzpah, her daring to take chances because she could, not because she had to. Now, two years later, Peri still took classes and the website remained under construction, but she had started selling her knitted and felted bags in the shop and hit the flea-market scene with her fabric purses as often as she could. And, when she wasn't planning to be a playwright, pastry chef, or archaeologist, Dakota had informed Georgia that she very much intended to become Peri's vice-president. Or the model for her ad campaign. She wasn't sure which.

'So it's been a strange day up here too.' Anita watched the door close after Peri; her voice was mild but it was shaking ever so slightly. Georgia assumed she had been startled by her run-in on the stairs.

'I'll say – mystery girl has been making frequent appearances. But don't worry, I don't think she's dangerous, just a bit mixed up.' Georgia wanted to sound reassuring. 'She's not our only new visitor for the day: Peri said some wafer-thin fancypants – Mrs Investment Banker So-and-So – came in with that magazine clipping from *New York* and said she wants to hire me to make a very important gown. She arrived when I was at the bank.' Georgia was secretly thrilled at the prospect. 'Here's the thing: she wouldn't leave any details with Peri, just a name and number and said I was to call her immediately. With a big stress on the "immediately".'

'So naturally you haven't called yet?' Anita knew Georgia too well, knew her automatic distrust of people with money to burn. 'Being wealthy doesn't make someone a bad person, sweetheart.'

'I love to knit, I love to work, I loathe being treated like the hired help,' said Georgia evenly. There was a certain kind of New Yorker whom Georgia had always had trouble accepting. The entitled. The demandingly entitled. The trust-fund babies she once worked with at the publishing house who hadn't fretted over supporting themselves. Who had treated everyone as just a little less than they were. As for how she felt about the stereotype of the pushy New Yorker? That was almost redundant. And Georgia had never had a problem with a person who knew her own mind. But she simply couldn't abide anyone who believed a moneyed background made them better.

And maybe she was a little envious, too. Not that she'd admit it – to herself or anyone else, for that matter. Anita after all was well off. Rich, even. But Georgia's problem wasn't really people with money. It was people who thought money was what mattered. People like James.

Anita was smiling benignly, waiting for Georgia to come back from her thoughts. 'That's the nature of business, my dear, making your client feel that somehow she's got something over you. It makes her want to come back again and again. And that's what you want: for your customers to spend loads of money.'

'I promise I'll call this woman tonight, before everyone gets here for your regular extravaganza.' Georgia raked her curls with her hand. 'I think I'll sit in. Dakota is planning to make cookies tonight – something about extending her product line. She's given up on the bike sales and is working on a plan to convince Marty to invest in her little enterprise; I've got to warn him. She's been asking me how to write a business plan.'

'He's on to her already; she popped in after school to snoop around the Little Debbie cakes.' Anita took a sip of her coffee.

'If I know Marty, he probably put in an order with my kid! No wonder she's upstairs making a double batch!' Georgia laughed. 'That man is the best – I don't worry so much knowing he's just down the stairs.'

Anita nodded, seemingly preoccupied with her gloves.

'You missed your cue!' Georgia chided, hanging up Anita's coat for her. 'That's the part where you tell me something funny Marty said today, or tell me how he donates his leftover bagels to City Harvest, or how he's really a very good-looking man . . . Anita? Don't worry so much about that kid on the stairs – I don't think she'll be back. Do you want to sit down for a bit?'

Anita turned to Georgia. 'I don't need to sit,' she said. 'But Marty asked me out to dinner. On a date. I think. A dinner date. I don't know how it happened. He just said it and there it was.'

'Did I just hear you? Oh my God, Anita, that's fantastic!'
Georgia gave her a quick squeeze. 'What did you say?'

'Oh, Georgia, of course I said no! We have club tonight,
and I'm talking about Continental style.' Anita turned so
Georgia couldn't see her face, wouldn't notice the look of
excitement mingled with fear, wouldn't sense the flip-flops
in her lower abdomen.

'People eat dinner every night of the week, you know,'
Georgia teased gently; she wasn't about to be put off. 'And
you've never really dated since Stan passed.'

'That's not true, I shared a subscription to the Met with
Saul Ruben back in ninety-six and we had a lovely time.'
Anita turned to face Georgia, her expression stern, her eyes
troubled. It was clear to Georgia that time to discuss Anita's
private life was running out fast.

'It's one thing to share an evening with another heartbroken
widower – and quite another to be asked out by the man
who's so perfect for you!' Georgia spoke quickly. 'Marty's a
great guy – and seriously, the two of you have been flirting
with each other like two teenagers for years now!' Georgia
held her breath, worried she had crossed the line. Even though
they were close, she felt uncomfortable, as though she had
just asked Mom if she wanted to get it on with Dad.

Anita looked her full in the face, her eyes moist. 'Stan was
a great guy, too.' Her voice was higher than usual. 'And if it
didn't work out with Marty, where would I get my afternoon
coffee?' She flashed a small, tight smile and turned to the
table in the center of the room, where a few customers sat
around, trying to decide between yarns. 'Becky, are you still
working on that scarf?' She spoke loudly. 'Just wait until
tonight, I am going to show you a much faster way to get
going on those stitches. Let me come over and take a look
. . . Georgia, don't you have a call to make?'

*   *   *

Georgia headed to the back of the shop as though being sent to the principal's office. 'Aaaaagh!' She screamed as loudly as she could. Well, inside her head, anyway. On the outside, she was just as competent and disheveled as ever. Georgia stuck her tongue out at her desk, then plopped down in her seat. There, on top of the month's bills, lay a large, too-brown cookie, a yellow Post-it stuck to the top. 'My first batch!!!!!' The 'i' was dotted with a smiley face. Georgia felt the ball of tension in her heart begin to ease; she peeled away the sticky note, and broke off a piece of cookie to nibble. Not bad. Then she moved the cookie off the bills, rolled her eyes at the big greasy patch left on the papers, and sighed. She touched the phone but hesitated. Then she swirled her chair around to face her PC. She'd need to check her email anyway, she told herself. Why not now? Then I'll call that woman. She popped open a window on her screen and got ready to do her daily airfare watch, plugging information into a flight search on the Internet. Then she opened another window, scanning her messages. 'Can this really be my life?' read one subject line, sent from one of her closer friends in the city. Tell me about it, she thought. She clicked open the message.

> *What a waste of time. Got yet another pep talk: we love you but the economy sucks, we had to lay off so many people last fall, yadda yadda yadda. When does it get easier, kiddo? You were the smart one, to get out when you did. I'll see you tonight; tell Dakota to make a double batch of anything. Absolutely ANYTHING.*
>
> *K.C.*
>
> *p.s. Did you hire a publicist? I saw another bit about the store! Something in the Daily News about celebs frequenting an unnamed Upper West Side craft shop. Sweetheart: are you holding out on me???*

Nine years older and half a foot shorter, K.C. Silverman had been the newly minted Senior Editor when Georgia was hardly more than a kid. Far from being aloof, or adding yet another coffee to her list of daily duties, the always energetic K.C. had shown Georgia the ropes when she started in book publishing, even taking her to lunch when her pregnancy had started to show. Gradually their professional roles had morphed into a kind of easy friendship that made few demands of the other; certainly working in entirely different worlds made it simpler. K.C. could talk about jobs she wanted, co-workers she hated, and have both the satisfaction of knowing Georgia understood where she was coming from and the relief that she wasn't going to tell on her. Not to mention the value of having a friend who'd been around during the early days of James; K.C. knew about Georgia's pain, having survived two short-lived marriages that sputtered more than they failed. ('I did starter marriages before the world knew about starter marriages,' she insisted.)

In return for their friendship, K.C. had been buying wool and starting a new sweater with regularity. That she never seemed to quite finish her projects, well, Georgia sometimes offered to put it all together for her. What she did with the rest of her half-knitted creations was anyone's guess. It was a comfortable arrangement: they saw each other at the shop, talked easily, emailed, but never really got together. They'd never been in each other's homes even though they had known each other for fourteen years. Still, to be fair, Georgia reminded herself, that wasn't really all that unusual in the city. They had hardly even chatted on the phone. It was what it was – a very New York kind of friendship – and yet each felt, in the city of strangers, that they had a good friend in the other. But it wasn't like having a very best friend whom she could call at all hours. With K.C. it was more a . . . relationship than a friendship. K.C. was no kindred spirit. Just a nice enough person whose life choices had meant her path intersected with Georgia's. And that was okay, right? It had been a long, long time since Georgia had had the type of friend who knew what you wanted to say even before you said it. Who was always in your corner. Who actually enjoyed talking to you every day. And Georgia noticed the difference.

The Web results blipped onto the screen: 2 tickets to Edinburgh by way of Heathrow. $1,473. Maybe we'll see you next year, Granny, she thought. I'll bring Dakota when I win the lottery.

It had been years since she'd seen her grandmother Walker and Georgia longed to go, wanted to step back into an old ritual and sit under soft blankets before a coal fire, knitting and talking. Georgia's father was a cheery man, a hardworking Scottish emigrant in love with the size and possibility of his Pennsylvania farm, but taciturn; his wife was the talker and the taskmaster. From her earliest days, Georgia remembered disagreeing with her mother, a trend that continued even now. Hers was the type of mother who was all empathy and caring to just about everyone – the other members at her church thought Bess Walker was simply precious – but to her own family, it was all about bucking up and being ready for life's disasters. Not bad training for life, Georgia thought privately sometimes, but not exactly the warm cuddles and apple pie an All-American (and one-half Scottish) kid hopes for, either. Without a doubt, it was the dread of the 'I told you so' natter that really spurred her to take up Anita's offer that day in the park. What amazed her most about her mother – always distant, often preoccupied – was just how much she could yabber. Georgia took after her father in that regard, ever so slightly suspicious of idle chatter. But her mother seemed to possess endless energy to make her irrefutable – within the family, at least – pronouncements. Such as 'People who tell their children they love them every day are just phoneys.' (Georgia made it a point to tuck in her daughter, even now that she was twelve, with words of love and cheeks covered with kisses.) Or 'Boys who give you expensive presents are just hoping to get you into bed.' (Well, James had always been a big one for flowers; maybe Bess was onto something with that one.) Still, there was a reason why Georgia hardly ever saw the woman. The trouble was, she didn't see her dad too often because of it.

Her parents' marriage was one of those strange matches that left friends and neighbors curious about the connection, whispering on the way home. 'What do you think he sees in her?' the farm friends might ask; 'What do you think she sees in him?' the prim church ladies would say to their husbands after coming by for a Sunday tea. Georgia suspected her mother fell for a lilting accent before she realized the man and his deep voice came with a newly acquired farm. With chickens and cows and crops. Or maybe she thought it would be easy to convince her stocky dark-haired boy to give up on the land and head to a big city, not realizing the earth was Tom Walker's first love. As for her father, maybe he had fallen for Bess's attractive figure or perhaps, ever practical, suspected the brisk efficiency hiding within.

Tom had been Georgia's touchstone growing up, a quiet man sitting in the corner after supper, sneaking her a gentle smile over the corner of his newspaper even as her mother went on about her little girl's misdeeds and all the lessons she needed to be taught. Still, he never interfered. Just about the only thing her father had insisted on when she was a girl was that the family go over to Scotland every three years or so. The trip to his mother's farm near Thornhill, not far from the small city of Dumfries, was a great expense for them at the time. (Her mother would harp, all the while, on the new washing machine or sofa she couldn't afford to get as they squirreled away the funds for the journey.) Then, more often than not, he was unable to accompany them, asked by a neighbor to help with a late harvest or struggling with equipment in need of serious repair. For Georgia, those fall days, after the crops were done, were glorious – pulled out of school for two (or sometimes three) weeks to tramp about in the fields with her granny, her feet toasty in her rubber boots and her hand held tightly by the older woman. In the afternoon, they'd rake up the coals and get the heat going in the small stove, sitting in just their socks on the two-seater sofa. Those were the times when her gran would take out her big bag of knitting – a hold-all she'd sewn herself of sturdy canvas and that closed by means of several snaps – and pull out the small needles that were Georgia's and Georgia's alone. Their first lesson was all about the garter stitch, sliding the right needle behind the left, Georgia's six-year-old fingers fumbling, her eyes rolling as she forgot which hand was which. And then when Gran tried to switch it up with purling, putting the right needle in front of the left! One way, then another way – ridiculous. She clearly remembered throwing the needles across the room in frustration, stitches falling off and the yarn unraveling, the cats – Gran always had several kitties around the house – chasing in delight. And Georgia hadn't forgotten her quick hand on her bottom – just enough to get the young girl's attention – and the long talk about taking things as they come and the virtue of keeping at a lesson without giving up. They agreed, over hugs and tears, to leave that crazy knit-a-row-purl-a-row stockinette stitch until the next time they saw each other. Which came earlier than predicted, as her grandmother made a rare visit to see the unexpected (and much hoped-for) arrival of Georgia's only sibling, her little brother Donny. She brought presents, certainly, and an assignment for little Georgia: do ten scarves between now and the next trip to Scotland and the two of them would make a sweater.

Her mother hated those trips. Hated the rain and the

lingering damp and the long, boring days playing cards until a rare sunny break meant a chance to tend the garden or sit outside. Bess didn't knit, didn't want to learn from her mother-in-law, and wasn't so keen on Georgia spending all her free time learning an old-fashioned skill. But Georgia loved her Scottish adventures, loved how her gran could be so delighted about everything she did, how a simple 'very good' from her lips could mean more than a paragraph of praise. And that left her with an intense attachment to her memories of child-hood vacations and the skilled master knitter who had intro-duced her to the craft that had saved her life.

Dakota had never met Gran, a fact that rested heavily on Georgia as the years went on and her grandmother strug-gled with bouts of flu that lasted longer than normal, or slipped and, while not breaking a bone, managed to bang herself up. It was always there, the fear of death that hovered.

If only she didn't have so much going on. If only life wasn't so complicated.

Georgia closed her eyes and leaned forward, resting her head on her hands. Her mind swirled.

She wanted to keep crazy kids out of her store, wanted Anita to fall in love again so she wasn't so lonely, wanted Peri to land a big account at Barney's and have her bags featured on *Oprah*, wanted to hire people to make her a wardrobe instead of the other way round, wanted her heart not to hurt with so much pride and love for her beautiful, ambitious almost-teen who spent more time plotting a takeover of Martha Stewart's empire or Rachael Ray's show than she did anything else, wanted some cute forty-some-thing version of Marty – a phantom Marty, Jr – to take her out for oysters and whisper sweet nothings over the table, wanted him to make love to her for hours and bring her cups of soup in the middle of the night while they snuggled and laughed.

'Knock knock.' She heard the deep voice as though it was far away. 'Hey, you okay over there?'

Her stomach fell to her knees. Georgia looked up, her forehead streaked with red marks from where she'd been pressing, and saw James, impeccable in his navy pea coat and camel leather gloves. It figured. She didn't smile.

'Every other Sunday, that's the deal, James.' She was calm. Calm. Breathe in, she told herself, breathe out.

'I know, I was just meeting with a client and thought I'd stop by, see if I could maybe take Dakota out for a quick bite.'

'What day is it again? Did I get mixed up on the calendar?' Her voice was icy. Where was that calm? It just slipped out the door when she wasn't looking, leaving its familiar neighbor, rage, in its place.

'It's Friday, Georgia, I know. But I didn't figure it was a big deal.' He leaned on the edge of the desk, grinned, ignoring her obvious anger. He was as handsome as ever. More handsome. Could dropping by unannounced qualify as trespassing, she wondered? Just what type of violence was allowable when throwing out your baby's father? She scanned the desk, clutched the computer mouse.

'What's the problem? You always said I was welcome to drop by anytime.'

'Well, I didn't mean it!' Georgia jumped up, slamming her hands on the desk. It stung. 'That's just something people say – especially to someone who hasn't been around for the previous decade!'

'It's a little hard to find the time to pop over for tea when you're living in France,' said James dryly. 'That job made my career and you didn't return the money I sent, did you? Well, now I'm back in the city and I'd like the chance to get to know my daughter. I don't see how that should be such an inconvenience.'

'Every other Sunday, goddammit.' Georgia's face was pinched. 'It's not Sunday. It's not Sunday. It's not Sunday!' She began rearranging her desk, picking up the stapler, setting it down, the tape, the paper clips, the pens. Inhale, she told herself, exhale. 'It's not Sunday and you know it.' The smell of warm peanut butter drifted into the room. No, God, no, Georgia pleaded.

'Daddy!' Dakota stood in the doorway, holding a plate of cookies. She ran over to James, spilling cookies on the floor, and launched herself into his arms. 'I baked these cookies just for you!' Georgia shot her a sharp look. Don't tell lies, it said.

'And for the women in the knitting club, too.' Dakota was all giggles. 'Want one?'

'I sure do, darling! I smelled those cookies all the way out on the street!'

Georgia watched James charm his daughter, sent him a telepathic message. Don't tell lies, it said. Don't tell lies.

'This Mrs Phillips said she would come tomorrow morning at eleven, on her way home from a Pilates class, to go over the details of her evening gown. She seemed very eager to get started so I told her that was fine. I think it's going to be pretty lucrative.' Georgia sat at the register, talking to Anita who was greeting the club members at the doorway. Their earlier tension was tucked away and she was more than happy to let it go. She felt drained, had watched Dakota run upstairs to grab her coat and scarf and head off to dinner with James. Wait, she wanted to call out, you're taking my heart with you. 'She has to be home at nine-thirty and not a minute later,' she said instead, as she watched them bound out of the shop, arm in arm. 'You're going to miss club tonight,' she told Dakota, feebly.

'That's okay, Mom, you can just set out the cookies.' Dakota was positively glowing.

God, she hated that bastard.

'Let me guess which bastard.' Georgia looked up; she had been muttering aloud.

'K.C., I am losing my mind,' she admitted.

'Happens to the best of us, babe.' K.C. removed her long camel coat, dusted off the flakes of snow on the shoulders, hung it up on the rack by the door. She was still in her interview suit and pumps; Georgia could see the goosebumps on her legs through her nylons.

'I'm starting a new piece today: I'm going to put together a sweater with the words "Hire me" over my tits. Then I'll wear it around town until some schlub hires me.'

'To do what?' Georgia chided, confident that K.C. would land on her feet; still, she knew that a lot of the reason the shop was having such a boom was because the economy was hurting and these women had no place else to go. And K.C., she could guess, certainly didn't want to spend her afternoons staring at the walls of her apartment. She was a born-and-bred New Yorker, all tough cookie outside with a surprisingly soft center. She respected a person who could match her brash personality – the cabbie who talked back, for example, or the woman elbowing her on the way to the sale bin – but at the same time, K.C. knew just when to reach out, as she did when Georgia was new to the city and being buffeted around.

K.C. had managed to survive the recession of the early nineties, waited out the ebbs and flows, and stayed intact at Churchill Publishing until her recent lay-off.

'It hurts, let me tell you,' she said to Georgia. 'I worked my ass off for them in that dark, dingy little office. And now they've given me the boot.' It wasn't her, she knew; the entire city was still reeling. But now she was stuck, having reached that dangerous point where she was too expensive for her old position, yet too mature for potential employers to risk hiring her, sure that she'd bail at the first opportunity of a better gig elsewhere.

She wouldn't, of course. K.C. couldn't imagine a life anywhere but in New York. She loved a good summer street fair, scoping out sample sales for the latest in cheap(er) designer duds, waiting on line for tix to Shakespeare in the Park, and getting exasperated with all the tourists clogging up the sidewalks in midtown. It was her city, her home, and she couldn't fathom being in a different place. She wasn't the type of person to get stuck in a rut – K.C. changed her hair color with regularity – currently sporting a dark auburn pixie cut that highlighted her lively hazel-colored eyes – but she could never understand anyone who would voluntarily leave the most vibrant city in the world. It was a constant: her one true love was New York and she was never going to cheat. Or change. She hadn't even moved apartments in years. Sure, K.C. had ventured around the globe (the requisite post-Barnard backpacking around Europe circa 1978), but she barely paid attention to the rest of America. Tough, feisty Manhattan was the only world that mattered. That Georgia had stuck it out and made a go of things earned her K.C.'s eternal respect.

Just then Lucie strode through the door clutching a plastic grocery bag stuffed with a selection of medium-weight alpaca yarns in olive and heather gray, a pair of needles sticking out the bag, ready for another session of the knitting club. K.C. pounced, eager to have a new listener to her week's tale of woe. Georgia could see that the sandy-haired woman was rather startled to be the recipient of K.C.'s unique brand of something akin to charm.

'Hi, Georgia.' Lucie spoke softly and nodded in her direction, then let herself be led to the table by a chattering K.C., murmuring hellos with Anita and Darwin, scooping up a couple of cookies along the way. Georgia ambled along behind them. She missed Dakota, was storing up all the raves about her peanut-butter-crumble cookies so she could share them when she tucked in her little muffingirl later. She grabbed a chair and sat down at the table. Darwin, she noticed, still seemed painfully conscious of her presence, and went out of her way to sit at the opposite end, next to a recent newcomer to the store. The kind of woman her mother would have called a trouper, who kept trudging along in life but would never quite get to the front of the line. In fact, this customer had been sitting in the shop all afternoon, bound and determined to be farther ahead than she was last week. She had asked Anita to teach her several different ways of casting on, which she performed methodically. So far she'd made a long practice piece but hadn't yet started on a pattern. Maybe, Georgia thought to herself, she should offer a special class: Is casting on all you want to do? Over and over and never getting started? Come to Georgia's shop because she can teach you everything you need to know about getting stuck in a rut!

And then it came to her. That was it! A lot of the women were coming to the meetings to work on their personal knitting projects, but they weren't getting too far ahead. They were stuck. Something was missing.

'I think I have to tear the whole thing out again!' The woman with the practice piece moaned to Darwin, who frowned and backed away almost imperceptibly. She was still reluctant to touch a stitch lest it sully the nature of her research.

'Maybe you could get tutoring,' Darwin offered. 'I make a lot of money helping out undergrads with their women's history courses – I edit essays and, you know, just spend a lot of time explaining how we're all bound by patriarchy.' She was pleasantly matter of fact, nibbling on a cookie. She spoke to the group. 'Because we are. Just so you know.'

'Uh-huh. Well, maybe in the meantime someone could teach me how to transfer stitches.' She was glum. Anita went over to look at what she was tearing out. And so, Georgia thought, a typical gathering of the Friday Night Knitting Club. There was no official proceeding: at some point, Anita might begin whatever chat she had prepared, though there were many nights when she didn't even get to it, so busy was she sorting out everyone's individual mistakes or lending a sympathetic ear as someone (more often than not it was K.C.) related the bad dates and work mishaps of a busy week.

What they needed was a plan. A pattern. An organization.

'Everyone?' said Georgia. 'I was thinking it might be nice to all work on one project together.'

'Like the archaic model of the quilting bee?' asked Darwin.

'Um, that's actually quite effective – and fun, if you're a quilter,' Georgia told the academic. Then she turned to face the group. 'I know a lot of you pop in to work on your own projects – which is great, you're more than welcome – and I know we have knitters of all different levels. But for those of you willing to try it, I thought it would be neat if we all took up the same pattern. That way, the beginners could really watch the more experienced knitters. And it might be easier on Anita!'

Her silver-haired mentor came over to stand beside her. 'I think it's a great idea,' she said to the group, then whispered to Georgia: 'I'm glad to see you're really getting involved!'

'And I'll offer a ten percent discount on all the wool you need,' concluded Georgia. 'Are you in?'

A few steps over to some of her beginners' pattern books, and Georgia had selected a stockinette-stitch sweater with a garter hem and a slashed-neck opening – eliminating any need for round needles or extra finishing on the neckline. It was basic, looked good, and would be more than challenging for the beginners, while easy and relaxing for the experienced knitters like Lucie.

She was unusually quiet tonight. Georgia watched Lucie sit with her hands in her lap for a full fifteen minutes, staring out the window, before she picked up her needles. And the grocery bag? Lucie was always so put together but tonight she looked as though she'd got dressed in stuff from her father's closet. Her top seemed to be several sizes too big and her usually manicured nails were chipped. She looked . . . tired. Still, Georgia didn't disturb her reverie, understood when life could feel so overwhelming. Was Dakota laughing her way through a plate of fries and ketchup, a little dash of vinegar on the top? 'Ha, ha, Daddy, you're so funny,' she might be saying. 'Mom's always cranky and she works all the time. Will you buy me a bike?' Georgia felt hot, stood up, mumbled something about needing to check something in the office, and took a few steps across the room to the door, absentmindedly thinking about locking it early. She figured everyone who was going to show up for club was already there.

Just then the door flew open and Georgia was knocked to her knees as a figure barreled past her into the shop. 'Robberrrr . . . !' warbled the intruder, as though announcing her intentions. She seemed to be pushing forward, pointing to the back of Darwin's long dark hair; something glinted in her hands.

'What the—?' screamed Georgia. As if in slow motion, she felt herself twist, then dive at the person's legs to knock her down. 'Help me!' she screamed, as chairs tipped over and the women ran to her aid. Papers seemed to fly around the room. Everyone was yelling; the intruder was kicking near her face.

'Help!'

'Call the police!'

'Keep her down!'

'Georgia, oh my God!'

'Robberrrr!'

'Call nine-one-one!'

Suddenly K.C. was sitting on the struggling figure. The body was noisy, snuffling and screaming. Georgia felt herself being pulled up, was surprised to be upright, to feel Anita's familiar hand rubbing her back. The faces of her friends and customers stared at her and then at the floor. She looked down.

And there, in a lump, lay the mystery shopper from the afternoon. The crazy redhead. Though now her newsboy cap was halfway across the room, no doubt kicked about in the commotion. The group kept her down easily; the girl was slight. Mascara and tears ran down her cheeks, her coat was torn. A tiny camcorder lay smashed nearby. She had a cut above her eye. Did I do that? Georgia wondered. Wow. She felt both impressed and horrified. The shouting in the room began to subside as the adrenaline slowed down. Everyone quieted down . . . except for the girl. A horrible moaning sound was coming out of her. 'Robber,' she seemed to sob. 'Robbbberrrr.'

And then Anita, always Anita, took charge. Lucie was dispatched for water, Darwin was sent for tissues, K.C. was convinced to get off the girl, and Anita settled the stranger on a chair and wriggled off her coat. The unexpected visitor looked more like Opie's cousin visiting from Mayberry than a crackhead or a burglar. Georgia rubbed at her knees, felt the beginning of a bump. The girl continued to cry, taking noisy, ragged breaths. 'There, there,' Anita said. 'There, there.' Still whimpering, the redhead looked up, her freckles streaked with globs of black, shrinking back ever so slightly from the crowd that stared at her. And then she spoke, in such a whisper that everyone

leaned forward as if to hear a long-awaited pronouncement. Georgia held her breath. The redhead cleared her
throat and tried again, haltingly, her voice scratchy and fat
droplets still running down her cheeks:

'Has . . . has anyone . . . has anyone here seen Julia
Roberts?'

3

Early morning sun streamed in the windows; Dakota stretched out on the faded peach and yellow sofa in her pajamas and let the warm light fall on her face, her head cradled in her mom's lap.

'It was quite a ruckus last night, kiddo. Yarn and needles everywhere! Everywhere! Everywhere!' Georgia reached over to tickle Dakota, who squirmed and jumped off the couch, jog-shuffling to the kitchen in her oversized lime-green slippers. Georgia followed her, grabbing a couple of bananas out of the fruit bowl on the sturdy IKEA table as she walked by. She went over to the counter to slice up the fruit, her back to her daughter; still, she watched out of the corner of her eye as Dakota moved stealthily to refill her bowl of Fruit Loops. The two Walkers shared breakfast every morning but Saturday meant sweet rolls and sugared cereals and lots of cuddles.

'Did anyone get hurt?' Dakota was sorry she'd missed the action and yet elated to have gone out with her dad the night before. He'd bought her a bike! She couldn't wait to tell her mom. But she wasn't totally sure how it was going to go over. Well, no, that wasn't true. She knew exactly how her mom was going to react. Badly.

'Darwin was yelping about Peeping Tom psychos and K.C. could hardly be persuaded to get up off this girl. Poor Lucie – she looked like she was going to throw up. I think she was really scared. And I have a bump on my knee the size of a bowling ball. It wasn't one of the shop's better moments.' Georgia popped a slice of banana in her mouth, then offered a piece to her little girl, who shook her head, a drop of milk running down her chin. Nope, Dakota was confident her mother hadn't noticed that she'd doubled up on cereal. Excellent. 'The next thing you know, Anita's got this girl sitting up and she's blathering on and on. And then she starts crying all over again.' She leaned over with a napkin to wipe off Dakota's face. 'And that's enough cereal, sweetie. No third-sies.'

Georgia reached for the coffee pot, filled her mug, and took a gulp. 'The meeting broke up early thanks to the arrival of this nuthut but you'll be happy to know that Lucie and Darwin took home several cookies each.'

'Did they fill out the comment cards?' Dakota looked up, her eyes filled with excitement and perhaps a little trepidation. Baking and this kid! Still, better she obsessed about flour and sugar than midriff-baring tops and boy bands. Though Georgia suspected she was starting to think about that stuff, too. She shook her head.

'Oh, darling, with all the commotion, I completely forgot to hand out your comment cards.' She leaned over and whispered, conspiratorially, 'But they all loved the treats. Why don't you just ask them their feelings about the cookies and muffins next week?'

'Because people never tell what they don't like when you ask them face-to-face. They only give you lots of compliments and that doesn't always help.' Dakota was silent for a moment, her brow furrowed. 'What about that crazy girl? Did she eat any cookies?' Georgia was always cheered by Dakota's single-minded ambition.

'Yes, my little Martha Stewart, she ate about fifteen cookies, I'd say.' Georgia grinned back as Dakota's eyes lit up. Score! 'That girl may be rather obsessive about Miss Julia Roberts but she had more than enough time to eat everything in sight.' Georgia looked out the window and spoke softly. 'The end of the evening was a bit of a bang-up but she doesn't seem like a dangerous type. We all sat down with her for a long time and got quite a story.'

Georgia smiled to herself as she remembered. So far that magazine article had brought both good and bad. The redhead wasn't actually crazy. Or even a druggie or a psycho. No, she was something worse: an NYU student who was hell-bent on making a film. Only there were around a million issues with getting it done, starting with the fact that she and her group had next to no money. And somewhere along the way they had realized they really needed a Big Name to make a go of the project. A few too many drinks while reading a *People* article about celebs who love knitting crossed with a mention on *Page Six* that Miss Julia was in town and then that *New York* mompreneur piece; it just seemed so perfect. Julia would probably need wool while she was in town and they would catch her off-guard, convince her to do a cameo in their searing crime drama! And so the young woman used the entire $12.75 she had in her pocket to buy odds and ends while she scouted out Walker and Daughter. Which, by the way, she had said to no one in particular, is really cute. You've done a lot with this place. Ever thought about making a commercial for cable? Because I could help you with that.

And then she slowly took a cookie off the plate on the table and ate it. And when no one said anything, she ate another. Cookie after cookie after cookie while the members of the club stared. And stared.

Of course, Georgia couldn't deny that she'd had many a young actress come in to learn how to knit, desperate to while away the waiting time during auditions. And she had several local celebs pop into the store now and then. In fact, two of her regulars included the 6 o'clock anchor on Channel Four – who was a first-rate knitter to boot – and that sweet girl from the soaps who won the Emmy for Outstanding Younger Actress last year. But Julia Roberts? It may have been a long time since Georgia had seen a movie that wasn't rated PG but even Georgia would have recognized a mega-watt movie star like Julia Roberts. And no matter what the *Post* was reporting, there'd been no A-listers in Walker and Daughter for some time now. Well, ever, to be honest.

'So then she liked the cookies? She didn't find them too rich? Too . . . peanutty?' Dakota was nothing if not focused. She pulled out a notebook from the backpack that she'd slung over the chair back instead of putting it away after school on Friday, opened it up to the middle, and began to write in glitter ink. Georgia leaned over to see the title, Peanut-Butter Cookies with Crumbles, Recipe #2, and a line drawn down the middle of the sheet of paper. On one side of the sheet was the word Comments; Dakota hesitated, then wrote 'Took cookies home – positive sign'. On the other side was the word Name. Darwin Chiu and Lucie. Dakota looked up at her mom.

'Mom, what's Lucie's last name?'

'Brennan. She was more than a little exasperated with that film student crashing club last night. Said she came to the store to get away from her type.' She tugged on one of Dakota's braids. 'Turns out she's a freelance TV producer. She's so quiet I'd never really talked about what she did outside of knitting. It's like Peri with her handbags – women do amazing, creative, wonderful things.'

'Like us, Mommy.' Dakota was nodding. Georgia winked.

'Yup. Now I've got to hurry and get dressed for work. Finish up and rinse out your bowl in the sink, muffingirl.'

'Hey, Mom, would you ever do it?'

'Do what?'

'A commercial, like that girl said!' Dakota had turned to a new page in her notebook. 'I could write a script for you, even go on-camera.'

'I'll tell you a funny thing,' answered Georgia. 'The last thing that Lucie said before packing up was that the meeting-crasher may have given the store a jolt in the right direction. A commercial probably doesn't make sense, she said, but Lucie's asked me to think about creating a series of how-to videos, said she'd help with making it happen if we were interested. I mean, I don't know, those things could take a lot of time and money.' She shrugged. 'But we've started on everyone doing one sweater pattern. So we could track everyone's progress with that and make a how-to sweater video.'

'We could do a cell-phone sock,' Dakota pointed out. 'It's easy, a little decreasing, a buttonhole. And then maybe I could get a cell for my birthday.'

'Aha, now the reason comes out.' Georgia pretended to swat Dakota's butt. 'Your birthday isn't until the summer. So we'll see. Got to run, hon, I've got an appointment down-stairs.'

Georgia went to her small bedroom and changed, pulling out underwear from the chipped white dresser that she used as a nightstand, her full-sized bed right up against the walls that she had recently painted sky blue. She'd been lucky to afford a two-bedroom all those years ago, had put Dakota into the bigger bedroom from the beginning, figuring she'd need room for baby things, then toys, then sleepovers. (At least one of them got to have sleepovers, right?)

Now Dakota had a large desk in one corner for homework or art projects: in the early years it had been the home of a Barbie McMansion and her fleet of tiny pink convertibles. All provided by Anita who, as the mother of three grown sons, was simply thrilled by everything girl. She'd showered Dakota with Barbies of every hue, and Dakota, in turn, had named her favorite doll in her honor. Watching Dakota play with the white and blond 'Mommy' doll and the dark-skinned African-American Barbie named 'Anita' had prompted a line of gentle questioning from Georgia. 'Why did you name that one after Anita?' she'd asked her daughter, then four years old.

'Because it looks like her,' Dakota had answered, not looking up from the engrossing task of sliding plastic Barbie shoes on those tiny curved feet.

'How does the doll look like Anita?' Georgia prodded.

'It's pretty,' said Dakota, then handed Georgia a Skipper. 'You can drive the convertible or the Barbies are all going to be late for a news conference. They're opening a knitting shop.'

Who could argue with that?

Though, of course, they'd had talks, especially as Dakota grew older. About how she and her mom looked different from each other. Each beautiful in their own way. About being prepared for people whose prejudices might lend them to say stupid things. And about how Georgia loved Dakota more than anything in the world. That was the constant. Though it helped too, that at her Upper West Side public school there were other kids whose parents didn't look the same. Some were foreign adoptees, others whose parents were from different backgrounds, like Dakota.

Sometimes they talked about it a lot. And then long stretches would go by and it didn't come up. Dakota would be preoccupied with a new recipe or arranging a massive sleepover party ('Can I just add two more people?') or getting her mom to lend her a favorite sweater from her prized collection of handknits.

None of which she planned to wear today.

Georgia's closet was cramped, her main storage space for more than just clothes and it took some effort to begin to sort through her dressier outfits. First, she stepped into gray crepe pants and a silk blouse, then into a black skirt. Finally, she settled on a simple navy shift with a camel-colored cashmere cardigan, one she'd knitted over the winter and had yet to wear. She liked to look as elegant as possible when meeting a new client, with just a piece here or there that she had knitted herself. Though she had grumbled to Anita about meeting this Mrs Phillips, designing and creating clothes was the part that Georgia secretly loved most of all. She kept a small red leather journal in her office in which she jotted down pattern ideas for all sorts of pieces she planned to make someday. Sure, she loved the shop and she was thrilled to be her own boss and she enjoyed teaching classes but there was something so significant about being able to make a gorgeous item of clothing from almost raw materials. It gave her a feeling of her own power, to make something practical and beautiful just by using her own skill and creativity. It inspired her.

Many nights, before drifting off to sleep, Georgia imagined an alternative life in which she would be a reverse immigrant and head to Scotland, back to the house where her father had been born and her grandmother still lived. She and Dakota would buy the farm next door and raise their own sheep. Walker Sweaters they would make, using only their own wool and never anyone else's. Their creations would be unique and they'd be coveted by Madonna and Sean Connery and Gwyneth Paltrow and she and Dakota and Granny would live together, happily and never getting any older, for ever. And even her parents would come to visit and Bess would say that she'd never have thought that Georgia could make a go of it, but boy had she proved them wrong. And then they'd all laugh and eat shortbread that Dakota had doctored up with bits of fruit and drink cup after cup of sweet tea. Anita would come to visit, of course; James would disappear from the scene. She didn't exactly wish him dead, mind you, just missing in action.

Because that's what he'd been – absent. So what was he doing back in the city?

Perplexed. That's how she felt. Oh, there was always that core of anger, the little nub that she polished with resentment when she felt overtired and exhausted but still had to dash to yet another PTA meeting or run down for milk even though she was already in her pajamas, there being no one else to go but her. But the acuteness of her pain had cooled over the years, more simmering than seething. Now, all those dormant emotions were stirring again, even as she remained utterly confused as to why James had popped up again. With some vague mumblings about how he regretted he hadn't been around more often. (More often? Try at all, buddy!) Georgia prided herself on learning how to be a shrewd judge of character, thanks to the smarting betrayals she'd received in the past, James being the most notable. The problem was that she just couldn't seem to figure out his angle this time.

Obviously, in the early days, it had been about sex for him, right? (Georgia could barely remember sex with a partner. There had never been anyone significant at all after James, just a string of blind dates during an optimistic '97.) Maybe because the memory of James loomed large. It had been impossible, immediately after he dumped her, to reconcile the man she had loved – her smart, funny, gorgeous best friend who loved to do crossword puzzles and go rollerblading in the park – with the same person who had bailed on their relationship. There was James . . . and then there was *James*. The real James. It wasn't a question of if he was coming back, it was when. That's what she had expected, back when her body was growing too large for her clothes. Georgia remembered long-ago lunch breaks from the office with K.C. during which she insisted, with confidence, that the two were just on a short-term break. It's a misunderstanding, she'd told her colleague. K.C., for all her brashness, was too kind to insist on the opposite. Because Georgia sincerely believed all would work out, had sold herself some bullshit theory about James needing to sow his wild oats. He'd definitely return to the woman having his baby.

Or not.

Then she went into labor – twenty painful hours on her own – and a new little face stole her heart. And energy. Twelve years of being a single mom can make anyone tired. Or cash-strapped. That was the thing about being a success in New York: you could still feel the pinch. There were always too many bills to pay. Even though she'd done the impossible for Manhattan and lucked out into a great space for her home and her business, even though her lease had held steady for years. Everything – utilities, equipment, inventory, Peri's wages, the cost of personal items such as food and clothes and extracurricular fun for Dakota – was just too damned expensive. Twelve-and-a-half years old and nearly 5'5, Dakota seemed poised to grow her way through several pairs of shoes and pants this year alone. There was never any time to slow down if you wanted to do more than merely survive. If you wanted to save for your kid's college, get life insurance, squirrel away for your own retirement. Pay for your own healthcare, dammit. That was the beauty of being self-employed and being a solo parent: It was all on you. Sure, James had often wired money into that custodial account he had set up for Dakota and Georgia had access to it at any time, but it wasn't a huge amount in the preschool years. A couple of hundred bucks every month or so. Later on, he began sending more substantial sums with regularity, especially in the last few years. (Georgia figured he'd either had a big promotion or he'd finally developed a guilty conscience.) Her pride kept her from dipping into the funds unless it was really necessary and besides, she liked to think of Dakota using the money for school. Either way, the fact of the matter was that the two of them had never really settled on a dollar figure. That was another reason his return made her nervous – they'd never discussed, let alone worked out, a legal arrangement when it came to Dakota. Oh, Anita had told her she should, even offered to pay for a lawyer, but Georgia just wanted to have nothing to do with that damn man.

And now he was back.

Georgia smoothed down her dress, chose a pair of open-toed shoes that wouldn't work on a March day in New York except that she only had to exit her squeezed little apartment and take the stairs down to her similarly cozy second-floor shop. It had to be the shortest commute in town.

She opened a tube of lipstick. Too red. Chose an almost nude sheer, put on a light coat of brown mascara, a dusting of powder. Done. Goodbye, tired momma. Hello, savvy businesswoman.

The opposite of love, she'd always heard, is hate. Certainly that was what she felt for James. Well, more like hatred lite, seeing as it wasn't quite so intense as it used to be. But James? He'd moved from love straight to disinterest. Not exactly evil – he'd always made a contribution financially – but he'd never actually wanted to pursue any sort of role in Dakota's life. Until now. Georgia gave her cheeks a pinch to bring up a bit of color and turned to pick up the cardigan.

'Mom! I've been calling you! For, like, ever.' Dakota hung in the doorway of her bedroom.

'Uh-huh. Well, what do you need?' Georgia knew Dakota was excited that later in the afternoon, Anita was taking her to see a matinee on Broadway. The two of them always went out for a special outing on the second Saturday of every month. And she even enjoyed hearing Dakota warble the songs all day Sunday. She waited, expecting to hear the pros and cons of possible outfits.

'I just wanted to show you my new helmet.'

'Helmet? For what?'

'Daddy took me to look at bikes.' Georgia felt her whole body grow hot, then cold, then hot again. 'I just remembered that I forgot to tell you about it.' And Dakota was a terrible liar, she noticed.

'And did your father make any other grand gestures?'

'Just that he'd teach me how to ride once the weather warmed up. I said you wouldn't mind.'

Georgia felt exhausted even though it wasn't yet 10 a.m. She left the apartment with some vague mention of discussing the bike when she was finished with work, then walked slowly down the stairs. She unlocked the door to the shop, still able to hear, ever so faintly, the sound of cartoons from her apartment above. She waited a moment, then tilted her head slightly as the din grew quieter. Yes, she could just make out the change in tempo. It was MTV, definitely. Dakota was watching music videos. But why did she feel she had to sneak? It wasn't as though Georgia censored her music – though she'd made it a habit to secretly read lyrics – or even that Dakota had been that interested in all those midriff-baring teen queens singing about love (and sex!) before a few months ago. Was Georgia that secretive when she'd been in middle school? She couldn't remember, and it wasn't as though she could just call up her mom in Pennsylvania and ask. Theirs wasn't that kind of relationship, hadn't been since she'd announced she was single and pregnant and then, when her parents finally felt ready to welcome her home, told them she was staying put to support herself by knitting. Even though she and Dakota took the train home to Harrisburg every Christmas, her mother and father had never really quite got over the hurt.

'My goodness, the baby appears to look very much like her father,' her mother had said curtly that first holiday. 'She's beautiful enough but I imagine we'll get stares at church.'

Dakota was four months old then and Georgia, working in Marty's deli and taking knitting commissions on the side, had to dig deep to afford the train fare to Pennsylvania. But blood can trump all, it would seem. Georgia caught her mother singing late-night lullabies to the gurgling baby girl. And she was buoyed when her parents surprised her with a handmade crib that her father had built out in the barn, painting the wood white and dotting it with soft pink flowers. He'd always had a bit of an ability that way. But as her parents went out of their way to make an effort, Georgia suspected they were overcompensating for their apprehension over meeting their new biracial grandchild. (All these years later, she could honestly say she'd been wrong on that front.) Not to mention that she was frustrated by her mother's criticisms that first Christmas, from how she bathed Dakota to choosing disposable diapers over cloth to the endless repetition that she had made a poor choice by sleeping with James.

'First comes marriage,' said Bess. 'Then the baby carriage, Georgia.'

So when her parents made the great reveal at the end of her short stay – the attic done over into a nursery/playroom – they were shocked and hurt that Georgia met them with resistance. She couldn't give up on herself. Not yet. But they saw only rejection when Georgia had felt mostly the potential for independence. For setting an example for her daughter.

And to show James that she didn't need him anyway. There was that, too.

⋆   ⋆   ⋆

Saturday mornings at the store were always slow; most of New York was sitting on their respective sofas downing fresh-squeezed juice and bagels and lox while they tried to make a dent in the early edition of the Sunday *New York Times*. Peri was probably doing the same – she wouldn't be in until noon. Anita supposedly took the weekends off, but she was frequently in and out, what with coming by to spend time with Dakota or making up reasons to stop by the deli to see Marty. But even though the shop was closed on Mondays and Peri often took Tuesdays off, Georgia never really felt she worked too much. Sure, the hours were long and often busy (though there were days when the store was far too quiet and she fretted about the lease, held by the institutional-sounding Masam Management Co). But most of the time Georgia felt a tremendous excitement each and every morning she opened the door. And she felt most excited when she was going to meet a new client for the first time. Dakota and the bike situation were pushed into some back corner of her mind.

So she felt fairly giddy when Mrs Phillips walked through the door, just as thin and glamorous as Peri had said. Hey, if someone could impress Peri, she had to be well put together. And this woman was like a perfect piece of art. The hair was blond and sleek and fell in a crisp blunt cut; she was dressed casually in a pair of wool slacks and a creamy wide-necked blouse that probably cost more than the sum of Georgia's entire wardrobe. Her ears were adorned with simple diamond studs that Georgia suspected were very much the real thing and her leather boots looked as though they never really braved the elements. If she looked outside the window, Georgia was pretty sure she'd see a car waiting.

'Oh, Georgia, it's you!' The woman stretched out both of her hands, ready to grab hold and air kiss a cheek.

'Mrs Phillips, so nice to meet you. I'm very much looking forward to designing this gown for you.' Georgia came out from behind the counter, went to shake the woman's hand. As she came closer, she could see the smooth skin; the timbre of the woman's voice said 35 but her face and figure said 25 and holding. She was in her own shop yet somehow Georgia immediately felt as though she was the new kid on the first day of school.

'Sweetie, what's with all the formality? It's so great to see you! Oh, this is too much, isn't it?' Georgia was smiling and nodding, but inside she felt tingly and confused. Did she know this woman? College? Churchill Publishing? That summer she'd had a share with some friends in Southampton? She heard a strange sound coming out of her, something like 'Yeah hah hah' that conveyed, she hoped, some sort of recognition. Not that it mattered much. The blonde kept talking and talking.

'I just wondered if it was you when I saw that article in *New York* – and you have a daughter now! Is your little precious here now?'

'No, no, she's at home.'

'Oh, so you have a nanny then? That's smart, got to keep up with your work. You are the little mompreneur, now, aren't you? Georgia the mompreneur. And I hear you do fabulous designs. Fab-u-lous.' She smiled but no warmth reached her eyes. Her pearl teeth glinted white and shiny.

'I want my husband's eyes to pop when he sees his friends eyeing me up and down in this dress. Know what I mean, sweetie?' She snapped open her tiny purse and handed Georgia a piece of paper neatly cut out from a magazine, folded once. It was a photo of some young model in a pair of cut-offs.

'See how the girl looks in that snap? Her attitude is all "try and stop me" and that's what I want to say with this dress. Know what I mean?'

'But this is a woman in a pair of jeans.' Georgia had the

feeling she was treading water in a fast river. 'I thought you wanted me to design a knitted outfit for a Very Important Fundraising Dinner.'

'Exactly. Now you're getting it. I want to look like that model. Only in a gown. A tight gown.' The blonde leaned over to whisper in Georgia's ear. 'And we won't hesitate to play up my décolletage, will we? Show it off a bit.'

She walked around the store, arms outstretched. 'Oh, it's so precious, Georgia. I love how you stay small to keep that homey feel.'

Who *was* this woman? Georgia felt inadequate and stupid and couldn't make sense of anything, as though she had a mysterious hangover but couldn't remember drinking.

'Think you can have a design by next week? I do like things to get done quickly. Then I'll fix up what you've worked on and we can get started, can't we?' The woman walked over to Georgia and put a hand on her shoulder. 'It's so special, reconnecting like this. I can't wait to see what you come up with.' And the moment, if one could call it that, was broken by the shrill ring of Mrs Phillips's cell phone. 'Oh, dear, it's my chef, checking on tonight's dinner menu. I'm having a small gathering. You know how it is. Hello? Yes, yes . . .' The blond woman walked away from Georgia, into the center of the room, talking loudly.

And then James nudged open the door, pushing a shiny green mountain bike. For the first time in oh, about twelve and a half years, Georgia was very happy to see the man who stole her heart and then smashed it all to hell, if only because it gave her an excuse to wrap things up with her new client. Her new obnoxious client. She was less pleased, however, to see the bicycle. It was clearly an expensive model. Too expensive.

'What do you think? Pretty spiffy, right?' James was positively strutting with his purchase. 'Dakota told me about how she wanted a bike and how it was maybe a little pricey and I thought, hey, here's something I can do.'

'It wasn't too expensive for me. I just thought it wasn't worth it for the amount of use she'd get out of it.' Georgia was speaking softly and calmly but her voice was firm. 'How much do I owe you? I can write a check in just a moment . . .'

In her mind she was calculating the cost of the bike and the fee she could charge Mrs Phillips for the dress. She waved in the blond woman's direction, didn't want her to think she'd forgotten about her. The woman, still on the phone, gave a curt nod and turned her back to address the clearly more important details of fish forks and butter balls. Georgia returned to James.

'I don't need money,' he said.

'I can pay, I will pay, and no, you can't just go around buying things for Dakota without asking me, mister,' she hissed. 'Do you know she thinks that you are going to take her for rides?'

'I am – and so are you.' Why couldn't James talk in a whisper, like she was doing? The regular stream of Saturday customers was starting to come in and she didn't want to be the entertainment.

'I don't have a bike, James!' Why couldn't he understand that when she had disposable income, she stuck that extra money into Dakota's college fund along with what she put in there every month. Georgia wasn't poor, but she watched her funds carefully and she had no damn money for bikes, that was for sure.

'That's why I bought you one, too. It's on the landing – Marty brought it up with me.' And with an elaborate bow to her, he opened the door of the store to reveal a woman's mountain bike. For a half-second, Georgia had that feeling of joy everyone feels when they get a new bike. The expectation of rolling down a hill as the wind ruffled her hair, of being able to do and see anything, anywhere. Then she remembered to be mad.

'I can't take a bike from you! What are you thinking?' Damn Mrs Phillips and that expensive dress order, Georgia had had just about enough of people making her feel small. And it was time that James understood just how this getting-to-know-Dakota situation was going to work. Because she was going to call the shots.

'And who is this now?' Georgia was ready to let it rip when the blond Mrs Phillips glided smoothly across the room, her voice deep and honeyed.

'This is my . . . someone I know.' Georgia was curt. She was so done with people.

'James Foster. How do you do?' James reached over to shake the woman's hand; the blond woman's eyes flashed.

'Not the same James Foster who designed the "V" hotel in Orsay? Oh, that place is so darling.'

'One and the same. I'm back in the US creating a series of boutique hotels for Charles Vickerson.' James was obviously enjoying the recognition and was going into great detail about his latest project in Brooklyn. Georgia felt conflicted and mentally dizzy. Aha! See, Mrs Phillips, she thought, I do know a person or two. Then again, it's not like James was really any friend of hers. Just a guy who had shared her bed and left her with a baby. She watched the two of them gush and coo over buildings she hadn't seen and people she didn't know, watched the two of them lean over the two gleaming and beautifully seductive bikes, felt herself smiling awkwardly and making little noises of agreement. Oh, yes, it was fantastic. Fan-tas-tic.

'It's a scream, isn't it, Georgia?' The woman lightly touched James on the hand. 'I mean, meeting up after all these years and getting Georgia to design a little something for me? It's just really special.' The woman tucked her arm into Georgia's but smiled only at James. 'I don't think I've properly introduced myself to you, Mr James Foster. I'm Cat Phillips. And it . . . is . . . such . . . a . . . pleasure . . . to . . . meet . . . you.' She spoke with exquisite slowness, then brushed back a hair that wasn't out of place. She didn't break her gaze from James while she continued to speak.

'And can you believe that Georgia and I went to high school together?' She gave Georgia's arm a squeeze as Georgia took a frank look at this blond woman she'd never laid eyes on in her life. And then she saw it. The eyes. The hair, the nose, the lips – those were all unfamiliar and probably cost a pretty penny. But the eyes. Georgia knew those dark brown eyes. And yes, she knew this woman. Oh, God, did she know her.

'We were the best of friends, weren't we, sweetie? Until Georgia dumped me, that is.'

Casting On

The only way to get going is to just grasp that yarn between your fingers and twist. Just start. It's the same with life. Of course, every beginning won't be the same: there are dozens of ways to cast on and they vary based on skill or design or even just relying on the tried-and-true. My point? Sometimes what works for one piece isn't the right way next time. You have to experiment to see what works. But there's a similarity no matter the method: you either try or you don't. So form a slipknot; make a series of twisted loops on one needle and then use its partner to reach through and make a stitch. Casting on is as much leap of faith as technique.

4

Georgia felt a hard knot in her stomach. She looked straight through Mrs Phillips's carefully applied mascara – were those fake eyelashes? – and saw into the eyes of Cathy Anderson, saw reflected long-ago evenings of sleepovers and munching on untoasted Pop Tarts and dancing all night to the music from *Flashdance*. *Thriller*. The Thompson Twins. Madonna in her *Like a Virgin* era. Could this be the same girl who'd bleached her light brown hair with Sun-In until it turned orange, who once tried to cut Georgia's hair short in an attempt at high style (say hello to Orphan Annie!), and who had spent long evenings chatting about boys and periods and the meaning of life while locked in the bathroom with Georgia, desperate as they were to get away from her little brother Donny?

She hadn't seen the woman in nearly twenty years. And there she was: a sophisticated, sleeker, slimmer version of Cathy Anderson. The girl who had once been her right hand at the Harrisburg High *Gazette*. Her comrade-in-arms. Her best friend forever. Now Mrs la-di-da Phillips. With more than enough disposable cash to commission an expensive, hand-knit dress.

Georgia felt her cheeks turn red, embarrassed by her inexpensive shift and inappropriate shoes; was her hair sticking up again? Still, she squared her shoulders and prepared to do battle. Don't lose focus, she whispered to herself, caught off-guard to see someone she had never expected to see again. Someone who had hurt her, too. And yet some secret part of her wanted to wrap her arms around Cathy and fly back to the past so they could sit around dreaming about a future that involved buddy trips to Europe, endless closets of shoes, and a great big corner office for a Big Fat Career. Raising a child by herself while running a yarn shop? Knitting outfits for well-heeled customers? Or even just knitting at all. Her 17-year-old self would have rolled her eyes given a glimpse of this life, muttered a curt 'I don't think so' before turning back to her fashion magazine to pick out a red power suit with Dynasty-style shoulder pads. No doubt Mrs Phillips could buy all the shoes and shoulder pads she had ever desired.

'Cathy?' Georgia was pleased to hear how neutral her voice seemed. Good girl, she told herself. Cucumber cool. Keep at it. 'This is such a surprise.'

'It's Cat, now, darling, I don't think anyone's called me Cathy in nearly twenty years!' The woman unhooked her arm from Georgia's as she spoke, looking over to James as though she and he were sharing a joke: ha ha, our life is so much different since high school, her look seemed to convey. Better. While Georgia's life . . . well! And there was James, clearly taking it all in. He'd always had a thing for beautiful women. In fact, he'd cheated on her with a blonde. Though Georgia knew well enough that Cathy had a stylist to thank for her shimmering golden locks.

'I can't believe you two went to school together!' He was right in on the action, of course. Georgia flashed him a secret telepathic message: Shut. Up. Now. And. Go. Away. Oh. And. Take. The. Bike. With. You.

'Have you really not seen each other since then?' Clearly James was on another frequency. Just as he had been for the past twelve years.

'Not a word. Right, Georgia?' Cathy's – make that Cat's – voice was light but Georgia was wary. She'd been surprised by this girl before.

'No, I haven't heard from you in a very long time, Cathy.' She tilted her head. 'Cat.'

There was a long pause as the two women regarded each other, half-smiles on their lips, eyes cool. Then James, clearly uncomfortable, broke the deadlock.

'Well, you know, I have several buddies I haven't seen since those days. We all do get busy. Speaking of . . .' He smiled at Georgia, made a motion to the door.

'Don't tell me you're leaving already?' Cat's focus was right back on James; Georgia bristled. 'I don't normally do this so last-minute, but I'm having a wee soiree tonight and I'm expecting the architect who designed the latest Trump building.' Cat leaned in to James. 'Have you ever met her?'

'No, but I've always wanted to,' he said, impressed.

'Why don't you come then? To the dinner?' Cat turned to Georgia. 'It's not really your kind of thing, Georgia, but you're welcome to come along. James, if you'll walk me to my car, I can give you all the particulars.'

'Can you give me a sec? I'd just like to finish up here.' He gestured towards the bike. As if on cue, Dakota – all dolled up in a plaid jumper and a glittery black scarf she'd made herself – floated through the doorway.

'Daddy! You brought the bike! Awesome!'

'Is this your little girl? Oh, James, she's absolutely darling,' cooed Cat, reaching out towards Dakota. 'Do you like to knit, sweetie? Are you having a big shopping day? Here to pick out something fun with your daddy? Georgia over here can help you choose some yarn. She's a knitting expert.' Cat spoke very slowly, a bit too loudly, her voice lingering on the word 'expert'.

'Hiya,' Dakota looked past Cat to her mom, raising her eyebrows in the universal sign for 'What's going on around here?' Georgia was too mad to speak.

Cat beamed at James. 'What a cutie-pie! Why don't you

two do your shopping while I just finish up with Georgia? Then we'll all walk out together?'

Dakota had had enough of listening to the loony lady. Whatever. She had serious business at hand. 'Mommy?' She walked over to Georgia for a big hug. 'Can I keep the bike? Pretty please?'

'Of course, babycakes,' said Georgia with warmth, enjoying the pleased look of surprise on James's face – she suspected he'd just been planning to seem generous by offering the overpriced bike and then make her the fall guy when Dakota couldn't keep it – and really savoring the shock on dear old Cat's. Yes, honey, this handsome man (bastard!) is the father of my gorgeous daughter. She wasn't about to air her private issues with James in front of this bitch. Holding her little girl in her arms gave her all the strength she needed. Even the strength to take a gift from the man who broke her heart and a job from her former best friend-turned-obnoxious-lady-who-lunches.

'I didn't realize the two of you were . . . that she was . . .' Cat started and stopped, started and stopped, as she looked from James to Georgia to Dakota, who was giving her dad the thumbs-up sign: we won her over! Suddenly, the feeling in the room had shifted, and Cat, who was used to holding sway, felt that awkward sensation of being just an extra in a scene that didn't need her. She gathered her things and made to go.

'Georgia, let's talk later in the week to discuss the designs.'

'Oh, Cat, I'll still take you to your car – and I don't have your address.' James seemed oblivious. Or just eager to make connections. Georgia couldn't get a full read on his enthusiasm. Cat quickly proffered her card, told him to arrive at 8 o'clock. 'And it will be the two of you, of course,' she said hollowly.

James hesitated.

'Of course,' Georgia assured her. 'We'll be there.'

*   *   *

Anita pushed the door open with her back, her arms filled with garment bags. Georgia rushed over to help her.

'I've brought you a few simple choices, nothing too fussy. Good thing I always wore my skirts long or you'd be in a miniskirt!' Anita laughed. 'Did you call and make that hair appointment like I told you?'

Georgia nodded as she carried the outfits to the office and hung them on the door; Peri had come in for her regular shift and waved to Anita as they scurried to the back, where Dakota was playing computer games. Her face lit up at the sight of Anita, ready to head to the musical. And to tell her the latest Big News.

'My mom and dad are going out tonight,' she blurted out. 'Together! I think it's a date.'

'It's not a date, muffin. We're just going to the same event,' Georgia corrected her. It wasn't a date, was it? True, they'd agreed that James would pick her up and bring her home. But that was just about logistics. Too much had gone on for them ever to pick up that thread from long ago. In fact, she dreaded the party more than anything else. Felt quite wary of it all. It had been years since she'd been 'out' for something other than a movie with Anita or Peri and longer still since she and James had spent any amount of time together. If they weren't careful, they'd have to move on from discussing Dakota and no-you-can't-yes-I-can and have an actual conversation with each other. (So, James, been screwing around on anyone lately?) And talking to James was pretty far down on her to-do list. Cat had been right – this wee soiree really wasn't going to be her kind of party. But, dammit, she wasn't about to have anyone – let alone Cathy Anderson – suggest that she wasn't quite up to standard. And thanks to Anita, she was going to look the part. Let James see what he threw away, let Cat see that she wasn't the only thing going.

Georgia zipped open a garment cover and pulled a beautiful dress off its hanger, admiring the light beading at the hem and neckline. Anita had brought quite a selection from her own closet, all sumptuous fabrics and designs.

'Everything old is new again – and besides, most of these outfits were worn twenty pounds ago,' chuckled Anita, who still looked trim. Georgia had called her as soon as James and Cat had left, knew that Anita would understand, would be on her side. How did she get herself into these messes?

'Pride,' Anita said. That was good old Mrs Lowenstein. Just out with it.

'I just didn't want to seem to think they were better than I am.'

'There's money, and then there's class,' Anita told her. 'The two are often separated. You, my dear, have a ton of class. Money, not so much. So whatever you do, don't blow off this client. You need to build on your exposure from that article. Besides, it's high time you got out of the house.'

While she knew she could count on a sympathetic ear, she hadn't expected Anita to come over and dress her. Georgia had just planned to wear the one suit she kept for important events, a classic Chanel style that had been waiting, covered in plastic from the drycleaners, since the last time she'd needed it several years before. 'Are you planning on wearing the red blouse or the gray?' was all Anita had asked. And now she was here, with several choices of outfits.

'I brought you something else.' Anita was pushing a box towards her. 'Just a loan but it will look so nice when you're dressed up.' Georgia opened the lid, saw the long strand of pearls, and pulled Anita into a tight squeeze.

'What would I do without you? You're the kind of mom I always wanted.'

Anita gave a modest shrug though Dakota, unable to miss

out on the action, jumped out of her chair and threw her arms around Georgia. 'And you're the mom I always wanted, too, Mom.'

The three set to work, watching Georgia jump in and out of clothes, holding up earrings and trying on lipsticks before dashing out to get the once-over from fashionable Peri. Yes to the pearls, no to the orangey lipstick. Too many sequins. Not enough skirt. And lose those old pumps! Finally they narrowed the choice to the black sheath dress and silver silk wrap – knitted, of course, by Walker. And about time: Dakota was zipping up her coat and following Anita out the door as the two headed off to make the curtain of their matinee. Anita turned and whispered in Georgia's ear: 'Stick with the black and the long pearls and wear a push-up bra. Hike it up to your eyeballs!' And with that, Anita patted her cheek, took Dakota by the hand and strolled out the door.

The bikes. Ack, they were still on the landing. Georgia had been so flustered over the change in plans – er, make that the actual having of any social plan for an evening – that she'd completely forgotten about them. James! It was his fault for bringing them up and he didn't even ask. He was just such a bulldozer. When he wasn't charming everyone. A charming bulldozer. Georgia caught sight of her squinty face in the little mirror on the office wall. Did she always frown like that? She took her hands and smoothed them over her cheeks, practiced smiling at her reflection.

'Hello, I'm Georgia Walker. Perhaps you read about me in *New York*?'

'How do you do, I'm Georgia Walker. Oh, Cat and I are old friends. Recently reconnected.'

'Oh, pleasure. I do love what they've done with the place – very mod. What, you're her decorator? Well, I'm her designer.

Knitwear.' She lowered her voice to a stage whisper. 'Isn't she a crank to work with?'

Georgia sighed. Hello, you, she said to the mirror. We'll get through it all and we'll look damn smashing. She hefted up the clothes and walked out of the office through the shop, told Peri she'd come back to deal with the bikes later, and marched up the stairs to her apartment. Did she even own a push-up bra?

As Georgia carefully hung the dress in her closet, a tattered cardboard box on the upper shelf caught her eye. Her memory box. Some crazy idea she'd seen on a talk show, to sift out all the little odds and ends and keep only the most precious items. Well, it had saved on storage space, a precious commodity in a New York apartment. But the truth was that she hadn't looked at the items inside in a long time. Even though she knew exactly what was in there. She quickly dragged a chair into the room, stood up, reaching, reaching, to the top shelf until she was able to tap tap tap the box forward. She let a corner fall off the shelf onto her body, then eased the container onto the chair as gravity worked its magic. Georgia coughed; the top was covered with dust. A deep breath. And then she took off the lid.

Dakota's baby blanket. Her first pair of shoes. Lots of photos – loose and in envelopes. Random holiday cards from her granny in Scotland: 'When are you coming to visit?' written in Gran's scratchy hand every year. A family photo taken in front of the fireplace circa 1970, her hair in pigtails, her brother making a V behind her head. Her parents. Young and looking happy. Then, clipped together, the two thin letters that James had sent her, with the Paris postmarks. She'd never opened either. The original business card Anita had given her. And there it was. The high school year book. Georgia opened it, knew that she'd find the entire inside cover taken up with just one person's inscription:

Crazypants!

I'll always remember: our heart-to-hearts sitting on the bench at Smithie's, getting chewing gum stuck in my hair at the game (thank you, peanut butter!) and sneaking in from Homecoming at 4 a.m.!!!!!! (No, Mom, I just got up to go to the bathroom!) Seriously, G., you're the funniest, smartest girl I know – and the best friend I'll ever have. Where would I be without you?!!! Who else will listen to me cry about Barry F. all night long and then double date with us the night after???? You're the best. It wasn't easy coming into this town and being new. (Insert a certain gesture to you-know-who and her minions here.) Okay, okay, being serious. Georgia, the day you invited me to join the paper changed my life! One day I'm going to write a Pulitzer-Prize-winning story and you'll be my editor. We're always a team, right? The two of us together! So even if things change or don't come out exactly as planned, we'll always stick together and be there for each other. Because it's where our hearts are that matters.

You're my sister in spirit forever.

C.

Funny how she could read so much into Cathy's note that she'd missed the first time. So clearly Cathy knew in June? Too bad she didn't find out about Cathy's treachery until September. Theirs had been a stupid plan – foolish, she realized now. Their pledge to only go to a college if they both got in. So Georgia ignored her parents' and teachers' pleas and turned down a partial scholarship to Dartmouth because Cathy didn't get in. Instead, they agreed to go to the University of Michigan. A fine school, indeed, but it wasn't an Ivy. But who cared? They'd be together, meeting guys and taking

classes, signing on with the college paper. And eventually in
their junior year they'd move off-campus so they could get
a taste of apartment living before they moved to New York
after college. To begin those great careers they were going to
have. And they'd be together for ever! Why did teenage girls
use so many damn exclamation marks? There ought to be a
tax on unnecessary punctuation, thought Georgia. Especially
when the writer is lying to you.

Because Cathy had been waitlisted at Dartmouth all along.
And when a spot opened up – the placement that had been
Georgia's, maybe – she leaped at it. Never breathing a word
of it to Georgia all summer. The moment when she went
over to Cathy's house to coordinate whose parents would
drive them to the University of Michigan, Cathy wasn't home.
Oh, dear, her mother had said. Didn't she tell you? Her father
drove her to New Hampshire this morning. Oh, Georgia, she
said. I thought you knew.

Georgia could still recall standing stock-still in the doorway
of Cathy's house, the rush of hot-cold shivers going up and
down her spine, the twist in her stomach, the gasping realization that she'd picked staying true to her best friend over
leaping at her big chance to go to an Ivy. And then Cathy
had simply ditched her. Gone off to Dartmouth without a
word.

That was the last time – before this morning – that Georgia
had ever been in contact with her best friend. She had waited
for the guilty phone call, hovering in her Michigan dorm
room, debating how long she'd make Cathy grovel. But the
call never came. And the long-awaited, much-dreaded run-
in over the December holidays – how much time had she
wasted that first semester imagining what she would say to
Cathy? – never took place. Mr Anderson was promoted at
the bank and she heard from some classmates that the family
had moved to a big old house just outside of Pittsburgh. And

that's where Cathy must have gone for holidays and summers until she eventually landed in New York. Because Georgia never heard from her again, moping around the Ann Arbor campus and not making much of an effort to get to know anybody. It took her until her junior year to even darken the door of the newspaper. It wasn't until she got a summer internship at a publishing house that she began to perk up, wasn't until she fell in love with James Foster that she really felt complete again. To have a friend who really cared, who really got her. And we know how that story goes, she thought. A walk-up on the Upper West Side and single motherhood. Or a gorgeous daughter and work she loved. It all depended how you looked at it, Georgia told herself. Were there things she'd change? Yes. Did she truly believe her life would have been better if she'd gone to Dartmouth? That she'd missed out on some secret world of connections and money? Only every other day. But would she change her life if it meant there wouldn't be Dakota? Never. Never ever.

The dress she could handle. The doorman, no sweat. But the dinner? Now that was another question. Georgia secretly tried to rub her clammy hands on the wrap she held in her arms, still wearing her good cloth coat.

'Don't be nervous,' James said, sotto voice, as they stepped into the elevator.

'I'm not!' Her voice had a squeaky edge.

It had been one hell of a cab ride, sitting next to him, discussing the weather. Sort of.

'How long do you think things are going to stay chilly?' he'd asked, his tone ever so slightly challenging.

She'd been quite prepared to ignore him when his cell phone rang, and she sat there, pretending to be disinterested.

'Lisette! Lisette, il est après minuit,' he was saying. 'Avez-vous l'insomnie encore?'

Lisette? Poor *Lisette* can't sleep? Georgia rolled her eyes as the car sped down Broadway. Some things never change.

'Oui, oui,' said James. 'Ma fille est belle. Et aussi intelligent.'

They pulled up to Cat's building as James made his goodbyes.

'I'll come around and help you out,' he said to Georgia, who ignored him and made her own way out of the taxi, marching through the front door.

Now they stood side by side inside the elevator.

'Don't be fidgety,' he repeated.

She coughed. 'I'm not – I'm just not used to leaving Dakota . . . on a Saturday.' Oh, that was lame. She knew Anita and Dakota had made it back from the show and were busy eating popcorn and gossiping on her sofa. Probably talking about her going out with James! No, not going out. Not like that. Attending the same party together. Still, she was glad Dakota had someone to share secrets with, was glad that Anita often spilled the beans later, revealing her baby's crushes and feuds and worries. Especially since the closed-door policy meant she and Dakota weren't talking quite as easily as they once did.

'She's fine with Anita, I'm sure,' said James. 'She's a pretty amazing woman.'

Georgia gave him a sidelong glance. It was not as though he knew Anita; he'd met her only a few times in the store. 'Yes, Anita is the kind of person you feel special to know . . .' Georgia stopped short as the elevator opened. Directly into the apartment. A beautiful, huge loft apartment. She could easily fit her shop – and her own apartment – into this space several times over.

'May I take your coat?' A thin young woman in a white blouse extended her hands.

'Hello, it's nice to meet you. Do you know Cat? I'm Georgia Walker, I'm . . .' Georgia, juggling her handbag and wrap from hand to hand, faltered as the girl eased off her long coat.

'Thank you,' said James, then turned towards Georgia, briefly touching her back to steer her into the room. Of course, that was the coat check. Who threw parties that required a special coat-check girl? Who had elevators that opened up into their apartment? Cat, apparently. Georgia quickly slipped her wrap around her shoulders as she scanned the room and the backs of several well-dressed individuals, huddled in conversations.

A long exposed brick wall faced the elevator; across the room and to her right was an entire wall of windows and the ceiling was twice the normal height. She'd read about the conversion of Soho warehouses and factories to prized – and pricey – lofts but Georgia had never been in one of these apartments. It was simply stunning. From the gleaming stainless-steel appliances in the open kitchen to open pipes along the walls and ceiling to the modern *objets d'art* on smooth white pedestals to the fireplace surrounded by a matching set of sleek leather chairs to the long marble dining table in the middle of the room set with silver and crystal . . . the loft was huge. And richly decorated with sumptuous upholstery, gigantic vases filled with fresh calla lilies and paintings large and small on the wall. The look was modern, sophisticated, intimidating. The loft was a showpiece.

'This architecture is fantastic,' said James, reaching out to take a mushroom tartlet from another white-bloused server. 'I have been away for a long time but clearly, the gentrification of Soho is complete.' He smiled at Georgia. She glared back.

'And here is our hostess,' said James as Cat walked over to greet them, in a slinky, shimmery off-the-shoulder crimson dress. She motioned to a tall man by the fireplace, talking intently with another man, made a small wave as if to get his attention.

'That's my husband Adam. Doing a little business. We'll

meet him later,' said Cat, looking ever so slightly over Georgia's head to James.

'This is a fantastic loft. You have celebrated its warehouse past while making it elegant. It's a true tour de force,' said James, his focus still on the building. Georgia noticed that he didn't look over to Cat at all.

'I'll have to give you the tour after dinner – I think you'll like how we've managed to keep the loft feeling while setting off some private bedrooms at the back. We had a wonderful architect – I should connect the two of you sometime. And now, come, let me make introductions.' Cat's face lit up as she smiled warmly at James before bringing her gaze to her old friend.

'Welcome, Georgia,' she said evenly, her eyes scanning Georgia up and down. Her hands motioned in the direction of the knit wrap as she made a soft murmur of approval and then she looked at James. 'Come in, you two.'

They followed her as she made introductions; James got the big build-up, filled with his illustrious career details (had Cat Googled James? She certainly knew more about him than she had this morning) and then it was finished off with 'and this is Georgia'. A pause. Cat smiled and mentioned checking on the other guests, then walked away, leaving James and Georgia to mingle. Everyone looked the same, men and women alike: well coiffed, well dressed, well manicured, well mannered.

'That's quite an impressive résumé, James.'

'Clearly you've done well.'

'It must have been difficult for you, facing all the challenges out there for someone like you.'

'You must be quite exceptional.' James acknowledged the comments without actually saying anything.

'And Georgia, what do you do?'

'Ms Georgia Walker is an independent businesswoman. She

runs a knitting boutique on the Upper West Side.' James spoke before she even opened her mouth. This was good because her mouth felt a little dry. Georgia took a sip of wine. Okay, more of a gulp.

'And I design knitwear for independent clients,' she added. Her voice was soft but at least it didn't squeak this time. 'The Upper West Side store is where I display new creations.' Her voice grew stronger. 'There's a place in fashion for unique knitwear – everyone wants to own a garment of beauty without worrying that it's also owned by a jillion other people who went to the same store.' No one laughed. In fact, they seemed to be listening to her every word. Maybe she wasn't so out of her league after all.

Or maybe she was. The evening had gone downhill after the canapés. She pressed a five-dollar bill in the coat-check girl's hand, made awkward small talk in the elevator, hit the street with James hot on her heels. C'mon, James had said, let's have one quick stop at a coffee shop before going home. It'll be a chance to discuss the bike and visits with Dakota – and all the other guests. Remember how we always loved to gossip about people? Believe me, there were some real caricatures there. Georgia had put up a token resistance – got to get home so Anita can get some sleep – but the wine made her feel tired. And she didn't really want to argue. And, well, she was enjoying being with James just enough to spend a little more time together. Okay, she said, one coffee. And then a cab to home.

Two coffees later – even though she'd switched to decaf – Georgia felt energized, sitting there with James, talking architecture. Doing a breakdown of the evening's conversations. Just . . . chitchatting. It was satisfying to feel that they were on the same side for once.

'Cat's an all right sort – she's better than many of them,' ventured James.

'What do you mean?'

'The bored housewife. Or, in the case of those with money, the bored trophy wife.' James laughed. 'She's not stupid, Georgia. Girls may grow up dreaming about marrying a rich man but when their whole life becomes about being an appendage, the appeal tends to diminish. Look, you knew her when she was a kid. Was she intelligent?'

'As brainy as they come.'

'Then you tell me: is she satisfied throwing parties and being afraid to eat the food she serves lest it go to her hips? You wouldn't be.' James took a sip of coffee. 'I've seen her kind many times before – worked with more than a few too.' And bedded them, no doubt, thought Georgia, with the full-on charm-and-roses treatment. She doubted that wedding bands ever stood in the way of James's conquests.

'She seems perfectly content to me,' Georgia insisted. 'And more than happy to be chilly towards me.'

'Oh, that. She's jealous – you're independent, you live by your own rules, you have a great life and a handsome man who hangs around your shop vying for your attention.' James winked; Georgia shot him a dirty look. 'Her comments?' he said. 'She's just getting a little Botox for the ego.'

Georgia rolled her eyes, thinking back to the party. She had held her own at first, emboldened that some of the guests had read the article about the shop. Still, she felt jittery – and the feeling began to take over. It was as though she had stepped into an alternate world. The party was one thing – how often did she eat risotto drizzled with truffle oil – but that was just set decoration. No, it was as if by some miracle she was given the chance to see a future that might have been. With James. If he hadn't slept with his boss all those years ago. If they had stayed together, even married. He was so attentive in the early evening that it hurt, and she shooed him off. Mingle, make connections, she'd said after finishing her great chat about knitwear. I want to check in with Anita on the cell.

Instead, she walked to the bathroom and splashed a little cold water on her face. The truth was that acting as James's 'date' at Cat's loft had left her with a racing pulse and a gripe in her stomach – and not in the cute butterfly way. She felt there and not there. As the night progressed she could sense the pressure building behind her eyes, wanting to cry as she watched James work the room. A few times she even heard the word 'Dakota' and saw him making gestures to her and smiling. She smiled back and raised her glass. She was too practiced at stuffing it down to actually worry that she'd blubber in public; she'd shed years of tears already. What surprised her was how she felt devastated all over again. Sure, she could always remember, intellectually, how difficult it had been to get over him, but it had been a long, long time since she'd actually physically experienced those feelings. The anxiety, the nausea, the hope. But that wasn't the problem. What sent her reeling is that she remembered just how much she had liked James. Just how much she did like his wit and intelligence and handsome looks. Even if she hated him, too.

Georgia had returned from the bathroom, nursed a glass of white wine at the party until it got so warm from her grip that it wasn't even enjoyable any more, and then got another. Just so she'd have something to do with her hands. She was grateful, too; one of the quieter guests, a woman who was a plastic surgeon, seemed content to stand off to the side and didn't seem to mind that Georgia stood next to her. The two wallflowered the loft, occasionally commenting to each other on the decor or some oddball human interest story that had just been in the Sunday *Times*. Dinner hadn't been much better, across the table from James and sandwiched between two guys more interested in arguing about the Harvard–Yale game the previous fall.

And Cat did not speak to her at all.

Now, in the coffee shop, Georgia took a sip of her drink. It was bitter. 'So, James, you were a real hit with that old guy, Edgar Edward What's-his-name. He couldn't stop talking about everything you've done.' Georgia stirred more sugar into her decaf.

'You must be quite exceptional? Oh, Walker, you spend too much time in the shop – and to think you're raising a black daughter.' James made a wry face and leaned forward, dropping his usual light manner. 'Exceptional is the modern version of "You must be a credit to your race." It's code. Doubletalk.' James looked deeply into Georgia's eyes. 'I know people. I know they say things to you.'

Georgia looked away, embarrassed, even feeling slightly guilty. It was true. Too often she'd seen the look of surprise flash in a stranger's eyes before being replaced by a PC neutrality when she introduced Dakota as her daughter. And how many times had new customers looked at Peri and assumed she must be Dakota's mother? She'd lost count. Georgia faltered, looked at James. 'I do the best I can,' she said softly. 'It's not my fault people act the way they do.'

He sighed. 'It's not about fault, Georgia. It's about teaching her how to deal with that crap,' said James. 'Can you honestly do that?'

'Don't be angry with me! You're the one who wasn't around.' Georgia didn't know where the conversation was going but she knew they were back on opposing sides. Again.

'I'm not mad – I'm just saying that I'm here now and I need more time with my little girl. I have things to teach her that you'll never be able to –' James's voice was rising but he caught himself. 'Do you think tonight was the first time I was the only black person in the room? And how do you think that feels?'

'So what do you want? Do you think I've just wandered about in a vacuum? I've read books about being black, about being half-black, about mothers whose daughters look different than they do. Just so I could understand.' Georgia was riled. 'She's smart, healthy, happy. A beautiful little girl. You know, I didn't grow up learning how to style black hair. But I learned, Mr Foster. I learned. I learned because I was here, at home, working hard and doing my best. Being Dakota's mom isn't about being black or white. It's about being here. Which I was. Am. Not like you, slinking your way through Paris and fucking every woman you met!' So this is what he'd wanted to talk about all along? The reason he'd come back? To save the daughter he abandoned from her inept white mother? The familiar comfortableness of sharing a coffee the moment before might not have been real, she thought. James was just manipulating her. Again. Why was she always so stupid? She stood up quickly, both hands flat on the table.

'If your daughter needed a black mother then maybe you should have screwed a black woman!' Georgia was out the door and in a cab, her purse in one hand and her cloth coat over her arm, getting goosebumps from the chilly March air, before she realized she'd left her silver wrap on the coffee shop chair.

'Broadway and Seventy-seventh,' she blurted to the taxi driver. Georgia felt blindsided. Was he going to make some sort of power play? She wanted to get home to Dakota and hold her. There is never such a thing as being too ready for the bad, she thought. But why does it never work? Georgia knew how impossible it was to recognize the moment that everything changes; it's only with hindsight that the hidden clues are sussed out: that a night of intense lovemaking is revealed to be the last night of being together, that a casual conversation about how many towels to pack can be the last words shared for over twenty years. And suddenly her carefully created world was invaded, her little shop hosting her two greatest enemies on the same morning. James was back and he was everywhere – in the shop, out with Dakota, in her thoughts. And now there was Cathy, Cat, too.

The bright yellow car screeched away from the curb, picking up speed, as her tears finally started to fall in ugly hulking sobs.

5

The hall light was on as James turned his key in the lock with his left hand, Georgia's wrap folded neatly in his right. Forty-year-old men don't leave a light on when they go out at night.

Except, of course, that he did. Always had. James could never stand to come home alone. To an empty house. An empty bed.

He walked into the kitchen, opened the fridge door to survey the contents. Several bottles of water stared back at him. Grabbing one, he twisted off the cap and sat down, in the half-dark, on his black leather sofa, surprised to discover just how uncomfortable his minimalist furniture really was. James didn't lounge around his place too often. Well, ever, really. He got up, pacing. The wrap was still in his hand; he brought it up to his nose and took a deep sniff, felt the softness of the yarn, ran his finger over the perfect stitches. She had talent, all right.

He breathed into the wrap again. It was weird, being this close to something of Georgia's. It felt illicit, exciting, unbelievable. Arousing. Even after more than a decade, he marveled at how she still smelled the same. Floral and fresh. His pillows would carry her scent for hours, days even, after an evening (or morning or afternoon) of nibbling and tasting and touching. James knew it: he'd shared a good thing with Georgia.

But new sex is hard to turn down.

Back then he hadn't realized the challenge of clicking with a woman. Of actually liking her. That a beautiful woman can turn out to be boring and a quirky-looking chick can keep you guessing a lot longer than you anticipated. Like Sabrina, with the gap between her teeth, who had settled into his pricey Paris digs shortly after he first arrived, who behaved in the French way and turned a blind eye to his indiscretions.

They had been happy together. Happy enough. Only it wasn't, he hated to admit to himself, as good as when he was with Georgia.

James tossed the wrap onto the couch. A man can't turn the clock back, he said aloud, get it through your head. Still. He'd expected Georgia's anger, prepared reasons and justifications for why she should let him back in his daughter's life, anticipated Dakota's confusion (which, thankfully, there hadn't been too much of – he was beginning to suspect that Georgia hadn't spoken ill of him over the years judging from his daughter's willingness to get to know him). But then to meet Georgia again, see the girl he knew grown up into a woman. The sarcasm given way to a wry humor, the cleverness deepened into a savvy business mind. And the way she held herself at the party last night! It was a revelation: he hadn't expected to find Georgia so capable. So confident. So . . . alluring.

So much his equal.

If it was morning, it had to be coffee. And lots of it. With just a few sprinkles of Lo-Cal sweetener. And maybe a piece of fruit. A tiny piece. To celebrate. The party had gone quite well; James Foster was a real find. The guests had loved him. Even Adam was smiling today. 'That was an interesting evening, Cat, I think Stephen and I worked out the details of our latest deal.' Adam Phillips was tucking in to a plate of eggs and bacon. He gave her a satisfied grin, a tiny bit of yolk slopped on his chin.

'And I think you were the third-prettiest woman in the room.'

Cat looked out a window as Adam continued to eat. 'Don't you agree? I mean, Madison Fleischman always had just that edge on you. And that curly-haired woman just looked ripe. Where did you find her?'

'She's an old friend from high school. I just ran into her again.'

'Well, she's certainly come a long way from Bumpkinland, I'll give her that much. Nice ass, too.' Cat was used to Adam's behavior after fifteen years of marriage, accustomed to the way he assessed women's bodies in the same reasonable tones as he talked about the stock market. As if they were on view precisely for his evaluation. There was no leering with Adam, just a calm expectation that he could choose to have whatever appeared before him. He didn't care that much how Cat felt, having long ago stopped thinking about her as something separate from him.

'I'm going in to the office to finalize this thing with good old Steve-o.'

'It's Sunday,' answered Cat, still staring out the window, not that she wasn't secretly hoping he would go.

'Right,' he said, picking up the front page and the business section of the *New York Times* and walking to the elevator, grabbing his coat along the way. He left without saying goodbye.

Cat slowly let out her breath, easing back into her chair. She took in the room, all put back together by the catering and cleaning crew, no sign of the event the previous evening. Nothing to tidy. Not that she was eager to clean. Far from it. But it's just that there was nothing to do. There never was.

Oh, she could fit in an exercise class. Review her social

diary. The fundraisers. The dinners. The lunches. Go shopping. Plan yet another party.

But what she wanted to do was go into her own office.
Have a business card – not a calling card – to hand to friends
and colleagues. To sit in on meetings and make decisions that
mattered.

When she was 17, she'd wanted to be a journalist. When
she was 19, she'd wanted to be an artist. And by the time
she was 21, art history degree in hand, she had a vague notion
about curating at a museum. But she'd been sidetracked, in
lust and love with Adam and the life he offered.

'Be a docent,' he had said when she revealed her desire to
go back to school, to get a Ph.D. in art history. 'We'll have
kids soon enough and they'll keep you busy.' But there weren't
any children – Adam shot blanks thanks to a childhood acci-
dent, though he adamantly refused to accept it, instead
sending Cat for every manner of invasive procedure.

She flipped on the TV, caught the last moment of a PSA.
'Don't be a fool – stay in school!' bellowed some sitcom actor.

No kidding, thought Cat, no kidding.

The graduate students' lounge hadn't been redecorated in
far too long, the tiny kitchen area still awash in avocado green
and harvest gold. It was Friday, the end of a long, long week
for Darwin. Her research wasn't much farther forward than
it had been at last week's knitting club meeting. Darwin lifted
the mug to her mouth and took a tiny sip of hot tea.

'Ouch, that's toasty!' she commented, a bit too loudly, to
a woman sitting nearby. Women and beer-making in the 12th
century. Darwin knew about her thesis; they shared the same
advisor.

'I always do that. Drink too soon. I should just wait a bit.
Do you do that?' she asked.

The woman made an uh-huh sound, didn't look up. Darwin

moved closer to her, sat in a chair opposite. The woman was reading the newspaper. Darwin scrunched up her nose, read the headlines upside down. More bad news about the economy. She cleared her throat.

'So how's your research coming along?'

The woman looked up. She did not look happy. 'Can't you see I'm trying to take a break here? Let it be, Darwin!' The woman folded the paper, glared at Darwin, and exited.

'I thought that's what we were doing?' said Darwin to no one in particular. There was no one else in the lounge. She sat, drinking her tea, waiting. A cookie would go well with this, she thought. Darwin zipped open her backpack, rooted around for a treat, but all she came up with was an apple from yesterday's lunch. Nah. She saw her notes from the last meeting, hesitated, then zipped up the bag. She held the cooling mug in both hands, savoring all the warmth, blowing on the hot drink. Soon enough another student sauntered in.

'Hey, Jeff! How's your research coming along?'

The student stopped, looked quickly at Darwin, hesitated. Then he turned on his heel and walked back just the way he'd come.

She sighed. Darwin had been at Rutgers for five years, and if she could name five friends, she would have been rounding up.

'They're jealous of you because you're so smart,' her mother used to tell her as they sat at the kitchen table, watching the dreary Seattle rain out the window. Darwin became suspicious of her mother's advice somewhere around sixth grade though she didn't let on; she didn't want her mom to feel bad. But she knew the drill: the other kids loved her to help with their homework, but few of them ever wanted to hang out with her. There was the girl from across the street; she played with her often until the family moved away. And Darwin tried to be funny, checking out joke books from the library. But all she learned was that staying up all weekend memorizing knock-knock jokes did not guarantee popularity by Monday. 'Be good and people will come to you,' her mother insisted. Be quiet. Work hard. Listen to your mommy and daddy. Don't make waves. Never make waves.

It wasn't Darwin's natural inclination to be a goody two-shoes. She didn't want to sit silently while adults were in the room, and she didn't want to help her little sister, Maya, clean up her room, and she didn't want to wipe the table after dinner. (When her mother's back was turned she swept the crumbs right onto the floor.) No, she didn't want to burn money for her ancestors on Chinese New Year and she didn't want to go to Sunday school and she didn't want to wear knee socks and a camisole when everyone else had training bras and nylons. But she did. There was some secret part of her that didn't want to jinx the chance that her mom was right and that if she just did as she was told, a best friend forever would appear. Poof! Like magic.

'Someday my best friend and I will share all our secrets,' she told herself every night before she went to sleep, repeating it over and over until the loneliness of the day began to subside. Who would her friend be? Maybe someone like Princess Leia, ready to stand up for her, or more like Patty from *Square Pegs*, or even like Mary from *The Secret Garden*. Someone good and true and who always picked you first in gym class.

And so Darwin Chiu was good, the best good girl there ever was. She didn't spill lunch on her dresses and she always did her homework as soon as she came home and she made sure she was the first one to put her hand up in class. 'I know, I know,' she'd burst, reaching high, glancing to the side and grinning, certain to impress her classmates with her quick answers. The wait for a friend dragged on. But few invitations ever came for a birthday party, only rare phone calls on a Saturday morning to ask if she could come over and play. And no, it didn't count when cousins came over; it's not as though they had a choice.

High school was more of the same. No date for the prom. Check. No Saturday night parties. Check. No boyfriend. Check. No first kiss. Check. Too smart, no friends, a seething layer of resentment: it was the foundation for turning into a serial killer, Darwin told herself. So by the time she hit her sophomore year of college, she officially quit playing the role of Hello Kitty. The new Darwin had a criticism for every wrong answer from a less gifted student, a comment for every fashion disaster, a smart retort for every request from her sister. And what did she care? She was going to go on to grad school, move out of her parents' home, and get the hell out of there.

And then came Dan. He sauntered into the History of Midwifery in Colonial America when she was a junior in college and, unlike the lazyasses sitting in the back row, actually participated in the lecture. Dan tilted his head and paid attention when Darwin made a point. And then, after that first class, he caught up with her as she headed to the doorway and touched – reached out and touched – her shoulder: 'Hi, I'm Dan,' he said, his voice low and rich. 'Love what you said in there. Hey, I bet you've already planned your final paper but I was wondering if you'd like to study together sometime . . .'

Handsome, quick with a joke, easygoing – Dan Leung was a natural leader, the kind of guy who held court in the dining hall and nailed impressive internships during his summers. Ambitious, he had stacked up AP credits in high school and was set to graduate in only three years. Even Darwin hadn't done that! But most of all he was cute, impatiently brushing his too-long hair out of his eyes, laughing. Darwin met him for study time once, twice, and soon enough they were talking movies and music instead of midwives. She loved how he listened, really heard every word she was saying.

She loved how he didn't seem to think she was a geek.

Not to mention that he'd never been in chess club.

'Why me?' she asked him once.

'You look like every girl I'm supposed to date – and you act like none of them,' he'd answered, crushing her lips in a too-hard kiss, slightly sloppy. It was her first. (Check!) And it was delicious, made her insides all gooshy and twisty and jingly-jangly.

If never having had a real friend in all of her 19 years was because the She-spirit of the Universe had been waiting to bring her Dan, then it had all been worth it, she told herself after that kiss. He never asked her to tone it down. Darwin, he said, was the sharpest girl he had ever met.

And when Dan was on your side, no one ignored you. Suddenly girls were talking to her on the way to seminars, in class ('Shhhh, I'm listening,' Darwin would tell them, annoyed), in the campus café, at the mall. 'Oh, you have so many new friends, Darwin,' said her mother. 'You should have them over.' But just Dan was enough for her. He said he found Darwin beautiful. From her early protests – you're just saying that – to her slow acceptance that maybe, just maybe, there *was* something in the way she carried herself, to letting him gaze into her deep brown eyes as he brushed her long, dark hair before he began to lick her neck and work his way down: Darwin began to feel differently about herself. She was proud of her intelligence, sure, but there had always been something else. Dan's attentions were as if her deepest, most shameful hope had been discovered, examined, and found to be true. She was *pretty*.

Of course, how the two of them looked was the catch. He was also Chinese-American – the one thing that would make Darwin's mother so delighted, so ultra-satisfied that she had raised her daughter right, it might even repair the years of screams and slammed doors. Her family, in her opinion, was far too sheltering and Old World. She'd begged and pleaded to go to a school out of state – 'It will test my character!' was argument No. 9; 'I hate you' was reason No. 31 – but ended up just where she had always been, sleeping under her flowered duvet in her single bed and sharing a bathroom with her little sister. The road to a graduate program studying women's history was paved with clichés about earning As and respecting her elders and, oh yes, finding a nice Chinese boy. The thought of living up to traditional expectations made her want to scream herself hoarse.

'So you're going away to study the history of famous women?' asked her father, a literal-minded biologist who seemed confused why she wasn't going into law or medicine as he and his wife had advised.

'No, Dad, I'm going to research women's history. Regular women. Everyday women. You know, the part all the male historians ignored.'

He frowned but her mother jumped in, always ready to smooth things out: 'Well, at least we can call her a doctor!'

Although she never let on to Dan, Darwin toyed with the possibility of dumping him – her one friend, her dearest friend – simply because she had been adamant about not loving a Chinese boy. But she wanted him more than she wanted to be defiant. Dan saw all the good that was inside her, and imagined even more that she suspected really wasn't there.

And then the Universe tipped its hand again: he got into med school at NYU and Darwin got into a top women's history program at Rutgers. A night of celebration with just enough red wine and, um, conversation, and Darwin had talked Dan into moving in with her. We'll be able to spend so much time together and save money, she had said. As expected, her mother was horrified (Check!); as an added bonus, Dan's mother refused to speak to her for years (Check check!). And when, in a rare argument, Dan accused her of being anti-tradition for its own sake, Darwin followed up with a spur-of-the-moment proposal, offering no ring and no change of surnames. Let's elope, she whispered. Affable as ever, Dan thought that sounded just fine to him. They settled for swapping vows at City Hall. He wanted a partner and the woman he wanted was Darwin. And so it was: no red dress for Darwin, no shark fin soup, no Double Happiness for her mother. Perfect.

But now their life together wasn't exactly going according to schedule. For one thing, Dan finished up med school in the city but ended up with a residency in Los Angeles; Darwin was still fighting her way through her dissertation.

'I can't just toss aside everything I've been working on because you need to go to LA,' she had cried the previous summer. 'My dreams are important too!' She needn't have worried, of course. Dan was as understanding as he had always been. No, no, he said, stroking her hair, you'll stay and study and I'll fly back when I can. It'll all work out. And soon enough we'll be together again. You'll see, Darwin, you'll see.

She wanted to believe Dan. She really did.

But his unwavering support just made it harder to see him go.

Now she woke up every morning alone, knowing that the best she could hope for would be a stolen moment from his shift when he could call from his cell phone.

'Hey, Darwin, how are you?'

'I'm okay, Dan, but I miss you . . .'

'Me, too, babe. Holy cow, gotta go already, I'm being paged—'

And that would be it. Click. Call you again in another 36 hours.

There was another obstacle, thought Darwin. One that was

pushing them farther apart than the physical distance between them.

She'd lost the baby.

The one Dan had really wanted.

Oh, it had been a stupid idea to begin with: she was still in school and he had years of residency ahead of him and neither one of them had ever changed a diaper in their lives. They were too busy. Too unprepared. It was too soon. Then again, is there ever a right time? That's what Dan had said. And imagine how cute the baby would be if it looked like its mother, he would tease. They'd debated the pros and cons of getting pregnant and looked at calendars – will it fit into our schedule? – and worked out a budget and even read a book on positive parenting. They made a deal about how they would split the childcare 50/50 and then they tried the craziest of all marital ideas: Dan and Darwin had unprotected sex. On purpose. And it worked. Just like the science books say.

But that baby was never born. And she'd never told her husband what she'd done.

And then her original research just fell apart. Darwin couldn't sit still and write about childbirth customs in the Victorian era. Not any more. So that left her with no brilliant dissertation almost finished, no impressive graduation ceremony for her parents to fly across the country to watch. All she had was a stack of student loans and an uncertain future, anxiety attacks that awakened her in the middle of the night, a distant voice on a phone line for a life partner, ('Won't you please tell me what's wrong, Darwin, I've been up all night with patients . . .') and an empty apartment to go home to after a frustrating week.

But it was Friday, and that meant it was time for that knitting group. She could watch them all tackle that sweater pattern, click-clacking away.

'I think I'm changing my thesis,' she had told her mom on the phone a few weeks ago. 'I'm curious about why women cling to outmoded craft activities in the modern era.'

The owner of the store, Georgia, didn't like her very much, but that was same story, different day. Since never had she been popular. So what? What Darwin cherished was eating that little girl's cookies. (Should she warn her about the perils of domesticity?) And seeing Anita's big smile every time she walked into the shop. She even practiced clever little small talks – the weather, the traffic, the man selling purses on the sidewalk – so she could draw out her weekly hellos, grab a little bit more of Anita's attention.

Darwin sighed. Even though Georgia had tried to kick her out that one time and even though Lucie was always giving her these weird looks and even though she absolutely disapproved of knitting in the first place . . . that club was really the only place she had to go.

A guy poked his head into the lounge. No doubt he was checking to see if it was Darwin-free. She scowled at the sight of him.

'Bye,' Darwin said, pushing past him in the doorway. 'I'm off to meet people. My friends.'

It was past 6.30 and Lucie should have been packing up her messenger bag by now. Her boss had come by at the last minute, saying he wanted to get back to her about her request. But so far he'd just been talking in circles.

'. . . and just the way you pitch in, Lucie, and help everyone around here is fantastic. Your work ethic is so impressive . . .' Get to the permanent offer, thought Lucie, get to the money. She'd already worked it out – going full-time would mean she could just barely cover the latest round of bills but at least she'd stop going further and further into debt. And if she could bank her vacation time . . .

'Lucie?'

'Yes, Anthony, you were saying?'

'Just seemed like you drifted there . . .'

'Oh, just a little tired lately. Sorry.'

'As I was saying, Lucie, you're our best producer here, and boy, are we lucky to have you. We'd love to hire you. But if there's one thing we don't have too much of at a public access station, it's money, and with this year being the way it has been . . .'

Back at her desk, Lucie crumpled up the slip of paper on which her boss had written his calculations. The salary was half of what she was making as a freelancer. And even if you factored in health care, she just didn't know if she could make a go of it.

Shit. She sucked in a fast breath. Yeah, well, maybe next year she'd win the lottery. Thank God it was time to head uptown to Walker and Daughter. Knitting was the one thing that took her mind off everything, that distracted her from the impulsive – no, not impulsive, naïve – decision she had recently made. The one that meant she would need to take this full-time job. Unless something better came along. It was just a seed of an idea that planted itself when she became an insomniac. Lucie hadn't had a really good night since her fortieth birthday party, two years ago. She sat at the kitchen table in her parents' Long Island rancher, picking at the left-over birthday cake her mother Rosie had baked. Every year it was her favorite: iced lemon. She savored each moist bite, the lemon frosting tangy on her tongue, waiting for her mother's annual year-in-review.

'Always you have the boyfriends, never the husband,' her mother was saying. The usual. 'You don't want to miss out on your chance to have a baby.'

'It's fine, Mom.'

'No, there's something special about a baby from your only

daughter,' Rosie admitted, patting Lucie's cheek. 'Don't you want to make me happy?'

'Yes, Mom.'

'I knew it. So, okay, I have just the boy for you. But don't get all carried away. Don't fall into lust. Wait for love.'

'Mom, I'm a grown woman.'

'I know, I know. Time to get married,' insisted Rosie. 'But you'll lose your head if you have sex. That happens when it's new.'

Omigod. Did her mother actually think she was still a virgin?

That's how it started. She'd returned to her one-bedroom apartment on Amsterdam and 101st that night, making the requisite 'Can you believe my mother thinks I've never had sex?' phone calls to her friends. 'I'm forty years old, for God's sake, forty years old.' Forty. Four-O.

And still single.

She stopped sleeping.

Night after night, it was as late as 3 or 4 in the morning before she could rest. She'd tried Ambien, St John's Wort, camomile tea and acupuncture. The only thing that lulled her to sleep was the click-clack of the two needles as the stereo softly played the strains of Chopin. Lucie had been a good knitter when she was a young woman and she'd been rusty trying it out again, knitting up a few bookmarks to remind her fingers of how to work the needles. Then she had made an olive and light gray alpaca V-neck for herself, blocks of color dividing the front, then stepped it up to four needles and made a cable-knit cardigan for her dad, a cream fisherman's knit. Her knitting saved her sanity; she knew it. Lucie favored traditional projects that took time and focus – an afghan, a Fair Isle sweater – that would give her something to think about during the day, not make her dread the night ahead. At night, she would work the stitches until her fingers would hurt, her eyes were weepy, and the exhaustion let her know that, finally, the sleep would come. Then she'd tuck the rosewood needles and the attached ball of yarn into the empty half of the bed beside her, drifting off with her hand resting on her knitted stitches – a sweater front, a sleeve – and dreaming, as she did every night, of a time when her apartment wouldn't be empty.

When she'd have a family of her own.

Lucie's Aunt Doris had taught her how knit during a long-ago summer vacation; Doris had just got divorced again – from the rebound guy between uncles Les and Paul – and had driven Lucie's mother nuts with her constant crying.

'I need help with Lucie,' Rosie Brennan had whispered to Doris late one night, hoping to quell the dramatics and refocus her sister-in-law. 'She's fourteen and won't give me a moment. She won't tell me what goes on at school, all she does is come home and play Bay City Rollers in her room, painting her toenails bright red and writing in her diary. I'm worried she's going to try pot. Smoke her brains right out. That's what all the kids are doing nowadays. Please, try to get her to open up, Doris, I need you.' It was classic Rosie. Molding the truth . . . for a good cause, of course.

In fact, Lucie wouldn't have recognized pot if you'd handed it to her and at fourteen, she was still sharing all her secrets with her momma. The two were close: Lucie was the late-in-life surprise for the Brennans, a precious daughter after a houseful of boys.

What details Lucie didn't cough up willingly, Rosie read every morning after her daughter left for school, carefully using a bobby pin to pick open the locking journal she'd given to her little girl on the day of her first period. 'So you'll have your privacy,' Rosie had said. 'Keep it somewhere safe.'

Rosie's plan worked; Doris took to her new project – becoming Lucie's confidante – with vigor. She took her niece swimming, taught her how to apply lip liner, asked her about boys, and, after a glass of Coca-Cola every day at 3 p.m., showed her how to knit and purl. It became their special afternoon ritual. 'My finger gets sore when I try to slide the stitches off the needle, Aunt Doris,' Lucie had complained.

'Honey, being a woman is all about being sore. Get used to it.' Failed romances had left Doris with an edge. But then she softened. 'The stitches are too tight, sweetie. So you'll do better next row. But remember, you might just have to toughen up your skin to get the job done. Okay?'

As high school picked up in earnest and Lucie joined the volleyball team, knitting became just another pastime she tucked away, along with Shrinky-Dinks and Monopoly. Armed with twelve lip-smacking shades of Bonne Bell gloss, an enviable collection of wide-legged slacks, and the attention of a relatively acne-free boy in his senior year, teen Lucie had been good to go.

And now, all these years later, she was back at the craft, the memory of Doris's voice soothing her heart. It was like reconnecting with an old friend. 'Be careful not to use the short end of the yarn,' her aunt had advised her when she was a girl. 'Make a knot, or put a smidge of tape on it, or even just put a paperclip on the end – that way, you won't end up wrapping it around the needle.' This only after Lucie had used her short end to knit five stitches. But Doris had waited quietly to see if she'd noticed, then simply pulled the yarn off the needle to pull out the mistakes. 'Try again.'

Try again, try again. Isn't that what everyone says? When your heart is broken they tell you that love will bloom again, thought Lucie, but they never ask if you're the one who is causing the problems.

'Why aren't you married yet? You were always such a popular girl, always going to beach parties – you remember those parties? Out on the shore?' Riing, riing, riing went the phone, every Friday night for twenty years. Rosie. Calling to see if Lucie had met anyone yet, even though she'd just talked to her mother a few days earlier. What about a blind date? Rosie knew just the boy for her . . . it was the same phone call every week; only the names and professions of Mr Potential changed. The conversations were worse after the holidays, of course, when her mother had to confront the year gone past and her brothers all married, Lucie still alone.

But who wanted to be married when it meant you'd be living with someone who wanted to know everything about you? All your thoughts and habits? Weighing in on every decision, large and small? It would be like having two Rosies. Love, Lucie had learned over the years, can smother you.

Her friends – from college, from work – had mostly settled down, to marriage, to live-in arrangements, to kids and dogs and houses in Long Island or Jersey. Come out for the weekend, they'd say. And she did go. At first. But then it became clear to Lucie that their lives were hurtling in a direction she couldn't follow. There she was, smiling stupidly at christenings, housewarmings, cook-outs. And any single male guests shied away – bald and annoying though they might be – convinced that she was desperate to bed them and wed them. And it's not as though Lucie hadn't dated over the years: she canoodled with her college sweetheart well into her twenties ('Where's the ring?' Rosie would ask every Thanksgiving) and then, once that relationship had tired itself out and they'd mutually come up with the guts to move on, kept up with a series of steady 'significant others'. Bill, Todd, Angus. And a Howard lasted briefly in there too. She would tell everyone – Rosie, her brothers, her friends – that each guy was 'The One'. At first it really seemed that way. But then, little by little, her boyfriends became annoying. Wanting more of her time. More of her soul.

What Lucie didn't reveal to anyone was that it was she who bailed on each relationship. Every time the dum-dum-da-dum seemed inevitable.

Oh, she could stay faithful, all right. She was a serial monogamist, more than happy to settle in and stop looking around. Just as long as no one exchanged keys – let alone vows – it was a-okay with her.

Because she was independent, see? Except that she wasn't. Not really. Lucie's entire life had been defined by her relationships to other people. Daughter, little sister, girlfriend. She had simply bounced around.

'Why buy the cow when she's offering the milk for free?' It was one of her best lines, trotted out when a fellow seemed promising boyfriend material. Who wouldn't want a girl that only wanted to see you on Wednesdays and Saturdays?

A lot of men, apparently.

So there was a reason why Lucie Brennan couldn't sleep at night. She was too busy trying to figure out how she'd gone from pretty young thing with an up-and-coming TV career to a struggling, still-single freelance producer. Still living in the same one-bedroom apartment after 20 years in the city. Still living paycheck to paycheck. Still waiting for someone, somewhere, to give her the answer.

'You need to shake things up a little,' Lucie's friends told her, suggesting treats at the spa or splurging on some Jimmy Choos.

'I can't wear heels,' she said. 'And my skin breaks out if I use anything harsh.'

But she did need something different. So when one of the other producers at the station suggested on-line dating, Lucie laughed it off. Then logged on at home to give it a whirl.

She felt a little embarrassed, a little shy about her online forays. So she kept it to herself. But there was something so liberating about having a private life that Rosie knew nothing about. That no one knew about. It made Lucie feel like a real adult. Finally.

And without even trying, she fell in love. Not with some guy who sent her an email or posted a profile.

No, she'd found someone else.

Someone who'd always been around but to whom she'd never really given a second thought.

Herself.

It was great. She went to museums and plays alone, and ate in restaurants at tables for one. Without even a book as a cover. She took a pottery class. She turned up the music and danced by herself in the apartment. There was the experimental solo vacation – a quick weekend getaway to Boston – and its follow-up: a week-long Caribbean cruise, a steal of a deal with a last-minute rate. (Then she turned around and used the difference in price to rationalize the purchase of a shiny ruby ring for herself.) Lucie hadn't shut her heart to the idea of love. She'd embraced it.

And she'd done something else, too. She had written down a list of everything she wanted to do – make a film, have a baby, fall in love. Which of these things can I make happen, she asked herself? What is my top priority?

The baby, she realized. The baby before the opportunity had passed and her body was too old. She couldn't afford a clinic – she wasn't on a health plan – but even a good Catholic girl whose mother thinks she's still a virgin knows how to make a baby. The old-fashioned way.

So she began using her online dating for sperm donor selection – unbeknownst to the nice enough fellows she invited home after three or four dates. She settled on Will, a good-looking researcher at Sloan-Kettering, a shy kind of guy who had been in school so long he'd kind of missed out on dating. He was a good eight years younger than Lucie, which didn't hurt, either.

He probably would have made good boyfriend material. But Lucie wasn't looking for that. She convinced him to do the modern thing, to get tested and get into bed.

She told Will she used birth control. She didn't.

Hey, Lucie wasn't a saint. She was a woman on a mission.

And she began spending more and more time at the knitting shop at the end of every work week, eager to avoid the Friday-night phone calls from her mother. (So, okay, maybe she felt a little guilty over her baby-making antics.)

But it worked. It all worked. She was sleeping better, her knitting was going gangbusters, and, oh, yeah, there was that other little situation, too. Will had hit the target. Her boobs were puffy and sore and her butt was growing exponentially; it wouldn't be too long before it was impossible to hide the fact that, at 42, Lucie was really, truly going to have a child.

'Order! Order!' Dakota was banging the end of her needles on the table in the center of the shop. Darwin was scribbling furiously in a notebook as K.C. was chatting animatedly to anyone who would listen about the fab skirt – black, very chic – that she'd picked up at a DKNY sample sale the previous day.

'I said "Order!" I now call this meeting of The Friday Night Knitting Club in session,' shouted Dakota.

Georgia looked up from canceling the register. Clearly her daughter had mixed up what she'd learned from her classroom's mock trial of James Booth and Georgia's speech about time management the night she didn't leave enough time to finish her math homework. It looked as though she just might have to go over there . . .

'Our first motion of the day will be for everyone to show what they've worked on since last week,' said Dakota. 'Okay, I'll go first.'

So that was what it was all about; Dakota wanted to show off the green felted purse that Peri had helped her to make, complete with handle and buttonholes, last Sunday afternoon. And, of course, a few sequins were sewn on to the finished product – Dakota showed no signs of moving out of her sparkle phase. It had been nice to have a little project to help her with – lately Georgia was so tired from working on Cat's ever-changing dress design and struggling with James's increasing requests (why could he never call more than a few hours ahead?) to take her girl out on shopping trips and to movies and dinners at Ellen's Stardust Diner in midtown. Dakota just loved those annoying singing waiters; Georgia got indigestion every time she tried to eat a bite, conscious that her server might suddenly burst into an Elvis number. It drove her absolutely nuts that James was willing to go there week after week in his bid to win gold at the Good Dad Olympics; she knew he hated shtick. Who knows? Maybe he kept busy talking to French women on the cell phone while Dakota sat there, entranced by yet another condition of 'Rock Around the clock'. Still it had been gratifying to know that, even without a stop at Marsha D.D. for Paul Frank monkey face tees or the big ticket bike that still sat in the stair landing, her baby muffingirl had been just happy enough to chill out on the couch and have foot fights and cuddles and then work on their own stuff, side by side. That's 'cause we're Walker *and* Daughter, mused Georgia.

Though at the moment the Daughter needed a little reining in. Pronto. She must be getting this bad attitude from spending all that time with her father.

'So why are you here if you didn't make anything?' Dakota was confronting Darwin who, while plenty bitchy when she did her so-called interviews of the women in the group, seemed completely flustered to be the recipient of investigative questioning by a twelve year old. 'Don't you think it's a little weird to come to a knitting group if you don't knit? Hmmm?'

'Hold on there, little friend.' It was Anita to the rescue, her arm on Dakota's shoulders. 'Our group isn't about having to show or not show. It's about helping each other, sweetie, sharing a love of craft. We look after each other's knitting – or not knitting, as the case may be.' Anita flashed a grin at Darwin and winked; Georgia was surprised the way Darwin's face broke into a rare smile. Even Ms Chiu, it seemed, was not immune to the Anita Effect.

'All right, feel free to use this time to work on your own projects. But a word to our new drop-ins that several of us are sharing a sweater pattern. Though, as always, we're here to help you with anything that's particularly challenging,' said Anita, catching the eye of some recent customers who'd come by the shop and decided to stay for the meeting. They waved her off and smiled.

'Yeah, I have a problem – everything takes too long!' K.C. had been making a big effort lately; she'd purchased some merino wool for the sweater but hadn't even started the front. So far that month she had quit on a cotton scarf and declared it was going to be a dishtowel and then downgraded that project to the much smaller dishrag. And now, after four weeks, she still wasn't finished. 'I don't know that I'll ever get to this sweater.'

Georgia could accept that K.C. had a unique knitting style: her rows were filled with dropped stitches and she was often asking Anita to 'show her some shortcuts' so she didn't have to go back.

'I don't do backwards, Anita, it's not on my path to enlightenment,' she would insist, half joking. She only knitted on

Fridays during club and then maybe only for fifteen minutes total – she was too busy talking or adding to-dos into her PDA. If K.C. had been six years old (instead of 46) she would have been labeled ADD; by virtue of maturity, she had lucked into the opportunity to describe herself as a multi-tasker. Now people just put up with her energy and mile-a-minute mouth. By the same token, her liveliness had rescued Georgia from a one-person pity party many times over the years. So if K.C. wanted to come and just be with the group, her old friend let her know she was always welcome.

Reassured that Dakota wasn't getting out of hand, Georgia went back to closing out the till and then planned to do more paperwork in the back; some new customers were demanding some very high end yarns and she was thinking of trying a new supplier. She was just getting ready to do some Internet research when a bedraggled Lucie made her way in the door, struggling heavily with several plastic bags and her winter coat over her arm. Georgia was really taken aback: Lucie's roots were showing in her sandy hair and her clothes looked rumpled and, frankly, too damn tight. Her overcoat looked as though it had a streak of grease or mud on the hem. Lucie had a funky style, sure, but Georgia had never seen her look anything but professional.

'Hey, hey, you missed my description . . .' Dakota's voice petered out; even she could see that Lucie was not her usual self, '. . . of felting a purse.'

Georgia looked to Anita, expecting her to walk across the room and do her comforting thing. Instead, Anita raised one eyebrow and tilted her head ever so slightly to Georgia, communicating the silent message: go to her. Hesitating, Georgia stepped out from behind the counter and walked over to the door.

'Hey, Lucie, how are you?'

'Oh, I'm good. Good.' Lucie was nodding, her head bobbing

as she spoke. 'Just, you know, good. I worked up the entire front of the sweater in that purple angora. Looks good. I'm good.' She tried to follow up with a smile but her lips began to tremble. 'Or maybe just okay. I'm okay, Georgia. Tough week. Trying to decide if I should take a job that doesn't pay so much. You know.'

'Yeah, we've all been there.' Georgia didn't think she was doing very well at this comforting thing; she looked to Anita for guidance but Anita was pointedly staring out the window. Georgia inhaled quickly.

'Hey, why don't we all slurp back some coffee and try out Dakota's latest concoctions? Tonight is a departure from muffins and cookies – we're trying a loaf cake.'

'Sure, I loved those peanutty cookies. But no coffee for me,' said Lucie. 'Just water.'

'Water it is then – Dakota, grab the Tupperware and napkins. Darwin, could you hand those out, thanks.' Georgia busied herself with the details. She was surprised at how much she enjoyed seeing everyone gathered around the table. These women like to come to my shop, she thought, and they like to visit with my daughter and savor her culinary experiments. This is our place, and it's a good place to be. And kudos for us that we all come together every week, no matter how difficult the days have been . . .

'Hear hear!' It was Anita. Oh, God, Georgia had been talking aloud. Why did she always do that? Her face flushed.

'And here's to us, the best damn group of girls I've ever had the pleasure to hang with in an after-hours knitting shop!' said K.C. 'Well, actually you're the only knitting group I've ever been invited to join and that's 'cause I've known Georgia since forever.'

Even Darwin had stopped writing long enough to join in the talk; Dakota was comparing her purse to a hobo bag Anita had knitted and put on display long ago; Lucie seemed to be relaxing ever so slightly and helped Dakota slice up the cake. 'I christen this dessert to be calorie-free,' K.C. told anyone who asked for a smaller piece.

It was all just a bit too loud as the cream and sugar and cake were passed around and everyone laughed when Dakota realized she'd forgotten to bring forks.

'It's fingers, girls, fingers,' K.C. piped up.

Her shop was crazy busy messy, Georgia realized, and it was wonderful. She felt Anita's hand rubbing her back lightly. The store was more alive than it had ever been.

'Oh!' All eyes turned as Lucie let out a cry of surprise. 'It's iced lemon cake. Iced lemon cake.' Her expression was impenetrable as she stared at the dessert on her napkin. And then she looked up and smiled at Dakota. 'It's my favorite,' she told her. 'It just hasn't tasted right in a very long time.'

Dakota, so pleased to be the bearer of such delight, impulsively ran over to Lucie and kissed her cheek. Georgia was surprised, but fine with it.

'This is my favorite,' repeated Lucie, looking around at the women. 'And one of my very favorite places in the city.'

6

Lucie arrived at the shop shortly after noon. It was a few weeks since her cake outburst and, instead of feeling embarrassed every time she walked into the shop, she actually felt more comfortable. As though she didn't have to wear the armor of her professional Lucie persona all the time.

'Hey, guys,' she called out, and Anita waved back excitedly. Peri sat at the counter, ringing up a customer with one hand while trying to hold one of her fashion merchandising textbooks with the other.

'Hey, handbag lady,' Georgia said, her tone both joking and warning. Peri dropped the book, mouthed 'Sorry' in her direction, and refocused on the customer.

Motioning to Anita to join her at the table, Lucie pulled out a large binder.

'We're going to go over our game plan,' Anita announced to Georgia. 'Come on over. I want you to look at these scripts Lucie has prepared.'

So far Anita had been completely gung-ho on the idea of knitting videos – even though Georgia wasn't sure if the costs made sense. She suspected Lucie had only been half serious when she'd mentioned the idea.

But then Anita continued to bring it up and insisted she wanted figures and projections and Lucie, who was really growing desperate, decided she needed this video project to supplement her public television gig or she was going to be short on the rent again. Every time she went to the ATM, she said a little prayer that the machine would spit out any money, having long ago stopped looking at her ever-declining balance.

'I don't know about being on-camera,' Anita was saying, 'I don't want to project an old-lady type of image of knitting. Even though I'm not. Old, that is.'

'Don't worry – have you seen my hair?' Georgia said. 'And I've never even been on a home camcorder before.'

Lucie was feeling anxious – if she saved this project, she saved herself.

'Okay, let's tape the knitting club,' she blurted, launching into her director's spiel, thinking back to her days at SUNY Purchase when her dream had been to make avant-garde films.

'Real women, real questions, real-life knitting,' she continued. 'Are you in? 'Cause I think this could be a block-buster.'

Just as she did on the first of every month (even when it was April Fool's Day), Georgia reviewed the books with Anita; the previous weeks had been great for business. They were even this close to giving Lucie the cash to get going on her knitting-club videos. And a large part of the business boom was because Cat was willing to pay for fast delivery.

On Anita's advice, Georgia had delivered her first set of drawings and tossed out an amount for the gown – from fitting to final – that she thought was just this side of astro-nomical. She had never asked so much. But she gave her quote while looking Cat straight in the eye and without blushing. Believe you're worth it and you'll get it, Anita had advised her, passing along a lesson learned from her late husband. Hesitate and you'll have a hard time getting even a low price.

People may love a bargain, Anita said, but even more they

love to feel they're getting the very best. Anita was right, as usual. Cat hadn't blanched at the high price.

'Complete the gown in half the time and I'll pay you double,' she countered, without smiling.

They set up regular appointments at the loft. Working with Cat had been awkward for the first hour or so, and then, as they were busy taking measurements and going over Georgia's initial vision of a figure-skimming full-length A-line with a shrug, the work took center stage and the tension became more of a hum in the background, less of a jackhammer. Cat took her to a back bedroom to look at expensive accessories, entered a massive walk-in closet and opened the doors of an intricately carved Chippendale-style armoire within. She pulled open a drawer and removed several velvet jewelry cases, Georgia inwardly wondering about the price tags of the chunky ruby earrings, the jeweled dragonfly brooch, the solid diamond tennis bracelet that demanded its own wrist workout.

'That's just in your closet?' she asked.

'Yes, Adam won't have it out. He has no use for old furniture,' said Cat.

'I meant the jewelry. Shouldn't you lock it up?'

'Oh, that.' Cat shrugged. 'Whatever. Let's see what I could wear with the dress.'

And they went back to the dining-room table to return to work. Sketching, laughing, disagreeing, ripping out pages from magazines, over time the two women began to experience a feeling of *déjà vu*: they liked working together. Even if Cat kept changing her mind about what she wanted! Georgia went home many times wanting to pull the curls out of her head. Cat was still a perfectionist, annoyingly so.

'In some ways, you haven't changed a bit,' Georgia told her. 'How so?'

'I remember you and I going out for sales calls for the school newspaper – and I was out the door while you were still adjusting your shoulder pads in the bathroom!'

Cat laughed, more at the thought of her 1980s attire than anything else.

'Well, a woman always has to look her best if she wants someone to invest in her,' she said. 'But you were always the one to close the deal. I'll give you that. Even if you did insist on wearing a Members Only jacket.'

'Touché.' Georgia crumpled up a sheet from her design pad, made as if to throw it at Cat, before remembering. They were all grown up now. And she was working for Cat.

And yet the frustrations of dealing with the fussy socialite were outweighed by the sense of excitement Georgia felt at designing her own gown. She had long been fascinated by fashion and watched Peri's handbag business grow while feeling a combination of pride and envy. If she hadn't had to look after Dakota, she might take a chance that she couldn't risk right now, might plunge all her savings and the college fund into a line of gowns and wraps. For too long, people had looked at knits as something casual – chunky ski sweaters and spinster cardigans. Georgia wanted to shake off the cobwebs and reinvent knitting style, wanted it to say something other than warmth and comfort. She wanted to see delicate stitches and silk threads. And Cat's project – she was going to wear the gown to a private gala being held at the Guggenheim – was the first, she hoped, of many commissions in this new direction. Sure, she enjoyed all the baby blankets and cozy sweaters she knitted for customers too busy to do it themselves – and Georgia guessed that more than a few of them had passed off her handiwork as their own. (One client, in particular, paid her to make several baby booties and caps every year, and Georgia envisioned the oohing and aahing at shower after shower, the recipients none the wiser that the guest in question had never picked up a knitting needle, let alone a ball of yarn.) But those were the types of items she could make in her sleep, and her desire was to experiment with textures and colors and push people to view knitwear as so much more. When she wasn't planning her country life in Scotland, she fantasized about buying Marty's deli and turning it into a boutique selling her knitwear creations, the yarn store still above. Maybe she'd buy the entire building, and create a duplex apartment – or maybe she'd rent out the apartments and build a penthouse with an entire wall of glass overlooking the brownstones on the side street and all the way to the Park.

First, though, she had to make Cat sparkle. This hadn't seemed all that difficult when she'd been hired. The truth was that Cat was absolutely striking – the sleek bob, the smooth skin, the just-so arches of her eyebrows – and her body was toned and taut in places that Georgia didn't even think you could exercise. But though her shoulders were straight, somehow she seemed increasingly brittle; being a mother had turned Georgia into a quiet observer and she frequently noticed Cat biting her lip or rubbing her fingers together so that it would not be obvious.

Georgia really needed Cat to sell this gown and to walk with the same type of sexy, obnoxious swagger as when she'd entered the shop that first day and she fretted as Cat kept changing her ideas. One day she was bold – 'I'm not even going to wear a bra!' – and the next session she thought the dress should sway more over the hips and bust.

Throughout the last week of March, Cat had started to seem preoccupied and less certain.

'Georgia, please tell me what you think about me in this dress,' Cat said very quietly one afternoon, remarkable because she had spent the previous meeting telling Georgia exactly what to change and nixing any suggestions. 'I just don't know any more. I just don't know anything any more.'

And then she'd walked to her bedroom and shut the door; Georgia waited a good twenty minutes before quietly letting herself out.

But then they'd get together again and the energy would be back, Cat would be witty and bitchy and ready to hold up a front piece and sashay in front of the mirror.

'Why did we pick gold yarn? I'm going to look like a life-size Oscar!' she said, before cackling, 'Or like an expensive piece of quality ass – am I right?'

When each afternoon planning session was over, Georgia invariably headed back to work while Cat consulted her ever-ready PDA and went to Pilates or an acupuncture appointment, a quick workout or an even quicker stop at the dermatologist for her regular collagen. There wasn't any sort of gabbing on the phone in between their meetings – and the two always conducted themselves professionally – but slowly a quiet feeling began to build. A sense of reunion. Georgia looked forward to seeing 'C @ 2p.m.' scribbled on the calendar taped up over her computer, and Cat found herself clearing the decks on Wednesday afternoons in case the meeting went long; she'd rather skip spinning than her design meeting with Georgia.

'I think I'm having fun,' she told the couple's counselor who had transitioned to becoming her personal confessor after her husband Adam declared he wouldn't waste time dithering about their relationship. 'This woman – Georgia – is a complete stranger. And then she's not and we both talk at once about an idea. When she's around I feel different. Better.'

Better had been something Cat had wanted to feel for a long time.

Only 22 when she married Adam, she had never been fully embraced by his family. Oh, Adam's mother and father had always been welcoming when she was still a student at

Dartmouth and asked questions about her studies and her plans, often including her in dinners out when they came to school to visit Adam. She joined them on ski trips and summer weekends to Nantucket and even spent one Thanksgiving with the family. But she hadn't realized there was an implicit understanding between Adam and his parents: small-town Cathy may have been a looker but she certainly wasn't in the same league as the Phillipses, all Mayflower and DAR. Date her but don't marry her.

She knew they suspected a pregnancy or else they would have kyboshed the whole plan for the garden party wedding. Under that assumption, they put on brave smiles and raised their champagne flutes and set up Adam and his new wife in a large Tudor-style home in Westchester while he started at an investment firm on Wall Street.

'Cathy sounds like the name of a truck-stop waitress,' she overheard her father-in-law tell Adam after they returned from their honeymoon. 'Tell her to call herself Cat and, for Christ's sake, get her to stop biting her lip all the time.'

Her in-laws' unexpected visit a few months after the wedding – and the apparent shock upon seeing no sign of a swelling belly – led to a series of closed-door conversations to which Cathy had not been invited. She sat silently at the table during meals, pecking nervously at her food, as the family stared, assessing her potential; she went out in the yard, conscious of her mother-in-law watching from the window.

'My father says we can get this thing annulled,' Adam panted as he moved inside her that night. 'But I told him "Hell, no!"'

'Because you love me,' Cat prompted him.

'Sure thing,' he said. 'Let me focus, babe.'

It was only at that moment – after two years of dating and five months of marriage – that it occurred to her that Adam had never actually told her he loved her. He'd always responded to her pleading little questions – 'Do you love me?' – with a 'Sure thing' or a 'Yup' or an 'Of course.'

She was rigid that night as Adam finished, feeling numb. 'When I knew how much my father disapproved, I just had to have you,' he whispered in her ear as she lay there, unable to move. 'Besides, Pudge, you'll never find anyone better than me. And I just couldn't deprive you of that pleasure.'

Cathy turned to face the wall as Adam sauntered out of bed to go have a shower, flooded with a moment of total clarity: there was no special love between them. Adam treated her with the same disdain as he treated everyone else. She was just another one of his pretty playthings. Not for the first time did Cathy feel an intense wave of regret, and once more she felt powerless to do anything about the situation. She couldn't stand up to Adam, as she lay, naked and vulnerable, just like she couldn't stand up to her father when he insisted she take that place at Dartmouth and leave Georgia behind. 'Chances like this make or break your life, Cathy,' he'd yelled. 'Why would you want to disappoint us?' Her mother insisted that high-school friends grow apart anyway, so no point wasting a precious opportunity because you made a silly promise to a girl you won't remember in five years. The daily harangue wore her down and she accepted the offer, struggled with a college world that was a lifetime away from good old Harrisburg. She met Adam at a party, invited as the date of his best friend, Chip. Adam was intrigued when she didn't respond to his come-ons.

'We expect great things of you, Cathy,' her father had said to her when she received her college acceptance. 'Don't let us down.'

So she let herself down instead.

Her marriage had pleased them – Adam Phillips was quite a catch. 'You've done well,' said her mother, admiring the mega-watt ring as Cathy grinned, flushed with pride to make her mother so happy. If she left then, she'd have had nothing. No marriage, no approval, no something akin to love.

And that's when it started: the obsessive dieting. ('If I eat only three bites, Adam will learn to love my self-control and tight ass.') The intense exercising. The experimental sex – all her new moves captivated Adam for a while but it didn't stop him from sampling other women when he felt the desire. ('It's what men do, Pudge. Get over it.') The name change. ('Call me Cat,' she'd purr, her face never betraying the sick feeling inside. 'It's an absolute pleasure to meet you.')

Fifteen years later, the reinvention was complete. Cathy had been replaced by a smooth tiger Cat, the kind of hard woman whose physical attractiveness and veneer of bitchiness made her fascinatingly attractive to men who wanted to tame her.

Adam, however, wasn't interested. He only saw her when she was reflected in another man's gaze, he only wanted her when it was time to prove she belonged to him.

That's why she couldn't wait to wear Georgia's knockout knitted dress, to walk into the foyer at the Guggenheim and feel the eyes of all of Adam's friends and family and colleagues watch her slink into the room.

And then, in front of everyone, she was going to dump the bastard.

Still, after the design was finalized and the work underway, there was really no need to see each other until the first fitting. But it hadn't seemed so out of the ordinary when Cat suggested they meet in midtown to look at shoes, said she appreciated Georgia's eye and would love her help picking out this and that from Bergdorf's and Henri Bendel.

'I could use the store's personal shopper, but can you really trust them?' she offered by way of explanation. And, after all, the dress had led to Cat's decision to have Georgia make her a twin set for everyday and then a luxurious cardigan that Cat gave as a gift to one of her siblings. Keeping Cat happy was good business and Georgia had already received a commission from a guest she'd met at her *petite soirée*.

So Georgia asked Peri to come in a little earlier on Tuesdays and Fridays and she took the train to midtown and walked over to meet Cat in front of whatever shop she wanted to check out. Cat would wait in her car until Georgia arrived (though Georgia refused to rap on the glass and would wait outside the vehicle until Cat exited) and then the two of them strolled block after block. Meeting in midtown – not so far uptown as the store, not as far south as Cat's loft in Soho – was neutral territory and it was there they did some of their best work. And so it made perfect sense, as they shopped and talked, for Georgia to answer Cat's questions about the store, even to tell her about the club.

'So everyone comes in and just knits? Like some pioneer lady thing?' Georgia suspected Cat was mocking her. As usual, she was hard to read, her face impassive, her eyes flat. Cat had been more exuberant in the old days.

'I'll admit I wasn't so keen on the idea at first, but it's really grown on me,' said Georgia. 'And Dakota loves it.'

They were strolling up Madison, looking for luggage. I just need to pick up a few things for a trip I'm taking; you don't mind if we go off the list today, she'd asked. Georgia shrugged even though she was feeling tired, just reminded Cat that she needed to be back in time for the night's club meeting.

'What do they say when people show up who can't knit?'

'You mean do they boo and jeer? Cat, you've got to hang out with some knitting women.' Georgia laughed. 'It's so awesome – everyone just pitches in and shows each other little tips. We have one member who was just too afraid to try a pattern – any pattern. She did thirty-two practice pieces in different yarns! And then Anita told her she needed to look at all those practice pieces and secretly sewed them together and said there, now you have a crazy baby blanket. So she'd already made something. And then Anita gave her the easiest beginning – just cast on thirty and knit every row for two hundred rows. *Voilà* – a scarf! And everyone applauded when she'd finished.'

'But surely you have some really good knitters?'

'Well, we have our die-hard regulars, but they're not like me – knitting isn't their career.' Georgia turned to Cat, began ticking off names on her fingers.

'There's Lucie, who's working so quickly on the sweater pattern we're all doing, kind of a group thing, and K.C., an old friend of mine from publishing, but I wouldn't qualify her as anything close to an expert. More like a lunatic enthusiast. Peri from the shop comes to the club if she's in the mood – she usually just pops in if she's meeting friends uptown for dinner. And then there's Darwin. I don't think you could say she actually belongs to the knitting part of the club – she doesn't even knit – but she does come faithfully every week. Of course, there are drop-ins, or folks who come for a bit and then beg off, depending on schedule. You know the city – it's hard to keep up.'

'I know! I wanted to join a book club but I balked at someone else telling me what to read!' Cat laughed. 'Everyone wanted to read Sartre. And I just wanted to read something fun!'

'Sounds more like school than fun,' Georgia said.

'Oh, you know, everyone's overeager because it's a Dartmouth club—' Cat realized too late what she'd said. In all the weeks they'd been working together, shopping together, drinking tea and splitting a quick sandwich when they were hungry, they had, without ever saying a word, made a tacit agreement to not bring up The Past. They made it all the more 'normal' by politely inquiring about each other's parents and siblings while still not talking about high school. In fact, Georgia realized for the first time, she didn't even know what Cat had majored in.

'Ah, Dartmouth.' Georgia looked past Cat's shoulder, then breathed deeply and looked her old friend in the eye. 'So how was that for you?' She wasn't surprised by the twist of frustration in her tummy; what shocked Georgia was that she was actually interested in hearing about Cat's experiences.

'I'd really like to know,' Georgia repeated.

Cat let out a little snorty bark-laugh: 'Of course you would.'

'No, really, I . . .'

'It was just . . . college.' The laughing Cat of a few minutes ago had vanished. 'You know. Skipping classes. Taking exams. Meeting nice boys. Sleeping with bad ones.'

Cat looked hard at Georgia. 'Stupid choices you regret but can't undo.' She bit her lip. 'I have to go, Georgia, I forgot I have a masseuse coming over this afternoon. I'll see you next Tuesday.'

She began to walk away and then turned on her heel sharply, strode back with a fierceness that made Georgia take a step back.

'It wasn't like you think,' Cat said. Then she walked straight across the middle of the street to her car waiting on the opposite side.

7

James lay in bed, staring at the ceiling, deep in contemplation. Life doesn't always turn out like you think.

Sometimes, it's even better.

He had finally figured it out. Or, more correctly, Georgia had pointed it out. If he wanted to spend more time with Dakota – and he did – then he simply called in advance and made an appointment. Georgia had relented on her Sundays-only policy, had made it clear that she would let him get to know his daughter – and she'd also been adamant that the little unannounced drop-ins weren't cool. He took the hint, er, the dressing-down fairly well. His ears had forgotten how much volume Georgia could produce.

Now, at the office, he found himself thinking about what Dakota might like to do on the weekend, or rushing in to a store if he saw something in the window she might need or want. She was his insta-family. And it was fantastic.

He took Dakota to the butterfly exhibit at the Museum of Natural History and watched with a weird sense of pride as dozens of butterflies landed on her shirt and another time they went to a movie about some kid named Lizzie McGuire. More than once they'd eaten at this crazy diner with singing waiters and he even took her out on that overpriced bike he'd purchased, discovering too late that his legs weren't in quite the shape he'd assumed.

'Daddy, why are you breathing so hard? Like, I wasn't even going full-out fast,' Dakota hollered when he caught up to her, then rubbed his shoulder. 'Don't worry about it. You're pretty old.'

James was almost 40 but his step was becoming lighter by the day. Being with Dakota was more exhilarating than any party or club – and God knew James had been to more than a few good-time places. He'd met a lot of good-looking women in Europe, dated many, and even had a handful of seemingly serious girlfriends who had waited around for a proposal that James had no intention of making. His last live-in left after she snooped upon the photo he kept behind the expired New York driver's license in his wallet. It was a photo of Georgia with baby Dakota; her friend K.C. from the publishing house had sent it to him in Paris with one line scrawled on the back of the snapshot: 'See what you're missing?'

He intended to contact Georgia when she was pregnant. But he didn't pursue her. Not the way he pursued everything else. It had been less complicated to push it aside, bounce from bed to bed, to leap at the great job offer he knew would make his career. He partied hard when he first arrived in France, out of some combination of guilt and desire to put his new baby out of his mind. Then he made an attempt to touch base with Georgia by sending a letter or two; when he didn't get a reply, he let it go, sending money but never offering his affection.

It was easier that way.

And harder, too.

And now here he was, getting ready to paint pottery with his little girl. He soaped up in the shower, feeling the warm suds wash him clean. The first of April marked eight months since he'd come back to the city with a vague idea in the back of his mind about meeting his daughter. Before letting anyone know he was back in the city, James took a cab over from the East Side and stood across the street from

Georgia's shop until he began to see children walking to
school. When he was growing up, September had always
seemed like a time for new beginnings – new classrooms,
new friends. Why not a new father? (He had been so unsure
of when school started that he showed up at 6 a.m., running
in for a coffee from Marty's deli and then crossing the
street. He waited for an hour and a half, fretting that he'd
somehow missed seeing his daughter, then worrying that
he looked like a crazy stalker as he paced up and down the
block. But hey, it was New York. No one paid a damn bit
of attention.)

And then came the first fall day he saw that amazing café-
au-lait girl stroll down the street in sparkly jeans and a newsboy
cap, talking animatedly with a serenely beautiful woman with
a thick mane of curly hair, her smile lighting up as her little
girl gestured wildly to tell her story. James had felt so sick
with fear and regret and excitement that he had to turn away,
had to walk fast to West End Avenue and bite his cheek to
hold back the stinging wetness behind his eyes. How could
he have stayed away so long?

Sometimes the good moments hurt much more than the bad.

For two weeks after his first glimpse of Dakota, he filled
up his work schedule with punishing assignments that hardly
left time for sleep – let alone the idea of going to see Georgia.
But then he found himself standing across the street from
the store on weekday mornings again, until the late September
day when he finally crossed Broadway and waited until
Georgia returned from dropping off her daughter. His
daughter. Their daughter.

'Hello, Georgia,' he said, wishing there was some more formal
greeting that implied 'I'm sorry' and 'Please forgive me' and
'How the heck are you?' all at once. He cleared his throat,
spoke more loudly. 'Hello.'

Georgia didn't miss a step. 'Hello, James,' she said without looking at him, unlocking the glass door to her building and then locking it firmly behind her. Standing on the sidewalk, he could see her walk up the stairs to the store.

He stood there, flabbergasted, until he realized she wasn't coming back down.

The older guy who had sold him his coffee all those mornings walked out from the deli. 'Can I help you, buddy?' he asked.

'No, thank you,' said James, then caught the man's eye and the look of warning within. 'Just trying to reconnect with an old friend.'

'You might want to keep your distance. It looks like the feeling is far from mutual,' said Marty as he walked back into his business.

The day after that he had gone to the store during lunchtime and tried to speak with her. Again, Georgia wasn't interested. He didn't bother with flowers or candy or showy displays of his success; James wasn't trying to buy Georgia's affection. He'd done that once and then frittered it all away, created a debt of the heart. No, he would settle for the chance to see his daughter. It had taken weeks of negotiation before he finally met Dakota. And it was more than worth it.

Meeting his daughter was like finding out he had a fan club that he never knew about. They'd been in touch for what? Just over six months. And it was a never-ending discovery. Of Dakota's hobbies – she was all about baking, that one, giving him little care packages of strawberry cupcakes or blueberry muffins – or trying to learn her taste in music – she stared at him blankly when he offered to loan her a Lionel Ritchie CD: 'Do you mean a DVD of Nicole's show, Dad?' she'd asked, genuinely perplexed. Not to mention their get-togethers were a nonstop rollercoaster of emotion for him. 'I missed you, Daddy, but I'm glad you're here now,' she had said one day, all casual, as they walked to Marty's to get a snack. It was their third week of knowing each other, their first outing without Georgia (only to the deli for half an hour and then back, he promised her). James thought then that it was the best afternoon of his life and he found himself wishing he could get back the twelve years he'd pissed away. Nothing on the Champs-Elysée or in the Louvre could compare to his brilliant, captivating little girl.

First came the joy, for both father and daughter. Then Dakota followed up with the questions and the anger.

'Didn't they have planes in Paris?' she said to him one night as they sat, yet again, listening to the poodle-skirted actresses singing at the Stardust Diner. Dakota had been sullen all evening, not even impressed that he'd scored Broadway tickets and convinced her mom to let her stay out late. ('I go to shows with Anita all the time,' she'd told him when he'd picked her up. 'It's no big deal.')

That evening she had gazed at him with cool authority.

'Why didn't you come visit me?' asked Dakota. 'Or send me an email? Do you know that I've lived at the same address my entire life? And I'm twelve and a half. That's a long time, you know.'

'I, uh, um, yeah,' James said. Oh, that was so lame. He'd practiced answers to these questions so many times but he was struck dumb when he looked into Dakota's wide, sad eyes, the look of defiance within. 'I'm sorry I wasn't around. But I am here now.'

Dakota gazed at her newfound father thoughtfully.

'I want dessert,' she had said finally. 'Something big.'

'Okay,' he said, glancing at her as he motioned for a singing waitress and knowing she had his number. 1-800-GIL-T-DAD.

But even that phase had evened itself out. Well, okay, he was still overcompensating with the gifts. Still, the two of them had developed a sort of easy rhythm, walking around the West Side as James pointed out historical buildings and shared his love of architecture, going to movies, watching the Liberty basketball team at Madison Square Garden.

The bigger surprise over the past few months was that he was finding himself lingering around the knitting shop when it was time to pick up Dakota. He was showing up earlier and earlier and popping into the office for a quick chat. Georgia always seemed vaguely annoyed but some days the mood might pass and they'd spend a few minutes making small talk. James felt supercharged when that happened, though careful not to seem that way. (A decade with the French had taught him the fine art of seeming uninterested.) Other times Georgia completely ignored him and he left with Dakota, still happy but less so.

And then came that party. Seeing Georgia outside her shop made her seem more vulnerable and more impressive. She was smart and funny and he could see where his daughter got her enthusiasm and optimism.

James Foster was not a stupid man. He recognized that some way, somehow – maybe that time he helped an old lady who'd fallen down the stairs in the Metro? – the universe had given him an opportunity to make things right. He also knew, with growing conviction, that he wanted more. He had a great career, a long list of sexual conquests (some of them even memorable), journeys from Mount Fuji all the way to Mumbai, and a finely honed lust for luxury goods from his Rolex to that uncomfortable black leather sofa. None of it mattered as much to him any more.

'Something crazy weird has happened,' he found himself confessing the night before to Clarke, his best friend from Princeton days, as the two met for a beer. Clarke had never approved of James's decision to go overseas.

'I think I've fallen in love with my family.'

Clarke laughed, then clinked his bottle with James's beer. 'Congrats, old friend – today you've finally become a man.'

Georgia folded up her laundry while Dakota practiced baton twirling in the living/dining/everything room. It was just the way she liked to spend her Saturday nights, hanging with Dakota. Though more and more often, her daughter was being invited to sleepovers and movie outings and Georgia was home alone. Tonight, thankfully, it was just the two of them and a million loads of laundry to lug up and down the stairs.

'I wish we lived in a big house with its own washer and dryer,' said Georgia, starting the 'I wish' game that she and Dakota loved to play. There were also the 'Someday' and 'When I'm Grown-Up' variations, depending on her mood.

'I wish we had our own gymnasium,' countered Dakota.

'I wish we were spending Easter with Gran in Scotland,' said Georgia. She had looked at the savings account and decided that this was going to be the summer she finally took Dakota to the UK. She needed her baby to see the country that she loved, and the grandmother who, while not exactly effusive with the hugs, held her tightly when she did so. She wanted to show her gran just how well she was doing with her little girl and what an accomplished knitter Dakota was becoming. And hey, let's be honest, thought Georgia. She wanted to get one of those tight hugs for herself.

'I wish we were spending Easter with Dad,' said Dakota, interrupting her reverie.

Georgia stopped folding mid-sheet and tossed it back into the basket; it was a fitted one and she could never do those right anyway.

'What do you mean? Do you really want to have your father over for Easter? We typically just have us and Anita, baby,' reminded Georgia. Thank goodness for Anita, who always included Dakota in her Passover Seder and then didn't hesitate to come over a few days later to eat lamb and choco-late bunnies, always bringing some leftover matzoh ball soup.

'It's not like I have to believe in Jesus to eat the celebra-tion dinner,' Anita had pointed out with a wink over Dakota's head at their first Easter. So far, for a little girl whose mother was Presbyterian and whose up-until-now absentee father was nominally Baptist, Dakota had been receiving quite an interfaith training.

'I'm sure Daddy has plans for Easter, sweetheart,' said Georgia gently, wondering if her daughter could pick up on her reluctance. If so, Dakota didn't let on.

'Oh, no, I asked him when we went to the pottery studio this afternoon. He's cool with coming by – said he likes lamb.'

'We'll see, honey, we'll see,' said Georgia. The last thing she wanted to do was to let down her guard with James. She still suspected he was up to something.

And Georgia was done with making stupid mistakes.

Darwin rolled over in bed and looked at the clock. 1 p.m. Could that be? She never slept past noon, even on a Sunday. It was leftover training from when she was a kid – she still woke up at 9 and felt guilty about not going to church.

Damn, the blood in her brain was aching and her mouth felt fuzzy and dry at the same time. And did she ever have to pee! She swung her legs over the side of the bed and went to stand, discovered the floor was rolling – were they having an earthquake? – and so she fell, awkwardly, back on to the covers. She looked at the ceiling, which was spinning in circles. She closed her eyes. The spinning got faster. She opened them and groaned.

'I think I have a hangover,' she whispered, then paused a moment to consider what she was saying. A hangover! She squinted her eyes as if trying to see a long distance but really just tried to think back to the night before. She remembered waiting to hear from Dan and when he missed their call time for the third day in a row she decided to go to the West Side and see if Peri wanted to move up their interview. They were scheduled to talk today for the thesis research but Peri seemed comfortable with switching it up, even if it had been a Saturday night.

'Come on down,' she had said. 'It'll be fun.'

Darwin was simply exhausted with being home and waiting by the phone, hoping it would ring and that Dan would have more than three minutes to talk; their conversations were becoming ever briefer and more strained. So she pulled on a pair of mules and her spring coat and headed for the train-station to travel in from Jersey.

What she'd hoped to be a diversion turned into an awesome evening: even Georgia had been pretty friendly, heading upstairs early to do laundry with Dakota, leaving Peri to lock up, Darwin following behind with her notebook. Peri had shown Darwin the handbags she sold in the store and then even revealed a few designs still in the works, telling Darwin all about her ambitions. It had been fascinating. And then Peri showed her the most expensive yarns in the shop – $89 for that little ball!

It was like being let into some strange inner world of knit-ting. Kinda, she'd had to admit, cool. She'd gone to the shop to interview Peri, yes, for the thesis, but Darwin gave in easily to Peri's insistence that she join her at a Greek restaurant and meet her friends from FIT. They were all friendly – Henry, Elon, Bridget, and Anjali – even if they did talk nonstop about all these people Darwin had never heard of. Who cared whether or not Anna Wintour wore fur? But the evening was truly fun, especially because Elon genuinely wanted to hear Darwin's thoughts about mid-century styles as a form of repression. She may not care that much about design, but Darwin loved to talk corsets and all the ties that bind.

Last night was the first time she had tried hummus, startled by the texture of the chickpea mixture and yet savoring it as well. Souvlaki she could gladly skip forever, baklava left her salivating for more. Oh, and then there was the Ouzo. Yes, they had had a few glasses of the liquor. Darwin had loved licorice candy since she was little – who knew they made it into a drink? Delicious. She made a smacking sound with her mouth, then felt slightly sick at the remembrance of the alcohol. She gently rubbed at her lips.

Lips.

A memory flashed, so briefly, that Darwin shook her head as if to dislodge it.

Lips.

Warm, soft, nibbling at her mouth.

Lips.

She put her hand to her face and then looked down, realized she was still in her blouse from the night before, although it was adjusted awkwardly, the first button through the third loop and so on. Her legs were bare: jeans lay crumpled on the floor, along with her shoes and one of her socks and a pair of pink-striped panties. Darwin reached out to take her underpants and put them on for the trip to the bathroom when she heard a low moan from the bed.

'Dan?' she said softly, afraid to turn around. 'Did you fly in last night? Dan?'

'Hey,' came the croaked reply. 'Darlene, baby, come back here.'

Darwin felt a shiver of revulsion run down her back. She turned round, one hand clutching the headboard to steady herself.

There, his head on her husband's pillow, his arm lazily reaching out to her, lay Peri's friend from the restaurant.

It was Elon.

Doing the Gauge

Just as you have to take baby steps before you walk, you can't get going with your garment until you make a practice piece. So try out a few stitches and measure your handiwork against the pattern. Take the measure of yourself against the expectation. (Otherwise what you make just won't fit!) And then you make adjustments. Too tight? Try bigger needles. You might have to adjust again or make another gauge before you're done – your stitching may change as you become more experienced. The mystery is that two people using the needles of the same size and type can make stitches of varying size and tension. The magic is that, even though they have differences, they can both create something equally wondrous.

8

Pacing up and down Mott Street, Darwin could barely keep herself from crying. Or vomiting. Or hyperventilating.

'Oh my God, oh my God,' she repeated under her breath, startled every so often by the bleating horns just blocks away on Houston Street. It was Monday and the cars and cabs were ferrying the expense-account bohemians from their Soho lofts up to their midtown advertising offices and the young Masters of the Universe from the Upper East Side south to their finance jobs on Wall Street. It was the way of the city that no one lived near where they worked. And it was a typical bustling, energy-filled day – except for Darwin. She'd left her house early to get to Planned Parenthood before it opened, then realized she hadn't emailed her advisor that she wouldn't be making her teaching assistant gig for the undergrad class on women in Victorian times. Fishing in her backpack for her cell phone, she realized she'd left it at home as well. Which meant that at least she wouldn't have to lie about not answering when Dan called. 'Sorry I couldn't pick up, honey,' she imagined herself saying. 'I left the cell at home and had to go in to the city.'

'Didn't you have class?'

'Oh, I had to go . . . into the knitting shop. Do some interviews.' Darwin was deep in her fantasy.

'That's so great,' he would say. 'You're going to get this dissertation completed and everything is going to fall into place. We'll get settled together again and then we can get back to making that baby.'

Darwin's lips began to tremble. She didn't deserve to have a baby with Dan any more.

God, she missed him so much. It was funny: the last person she wanted to know about what had happened last night was Dan. For obvious reasons. But he was her best friend! She told him everything. He always had the smartest advice. And even though the past several months had been excruciatingly lonely – for both of them, right? – Dan still took the time to scribble little notes and mail them from the hospital. Darwin had a hefty stack of Hollywood post-cards, all with a similar theme: Miss You! Love You! The occasional smiley face on his prescription pad, too, ordering up long-distance hugs from the office of Dr Dan Leung. She tried to reciprocate with emails and phone calls. Long emails. Pages and pages. Pouring out her heart to him. The breezy little messages she got in return irked her. They did. She could admit it. Initially she was thrilled to hear from him, then she was mad that he was fitting their relationship in between morning rounds, cups of coffee and catnaps.

Why did he have to go so far away? They had excellent hospitals a hell of a lot closer. Lots of cranky, sick people in New York. Who needed good doctors.

Was she going to be one of them?

Elon had tried to reassure her that they'd used a condom – 'You seemed totally into hooking up, Darlene,' he told her as she sobbed hysterically, demanded he leave the apartment. 'You made the first move, not me.'

'I was drunk! Drunk!' she'd screamed.

'Not that drunk,' he'd answered. 'I asked you if you were sure and you said yes, come home with me.'

Elon stood there, his shirt on and his leg in one side of his pants, his wire-rimmed glasses on the top of his ruffled hair. A little too scrawny, this sort-of stranger looked just this side of nerdy. Not threatening. Not particularly suave. Not concerned enough to actually get her name right, but not a complete jerk, either. He'd just, as they say, got lucky.

Darwin remembered enough from the night before to know there was truth in what he was saying. Shit.

'Get out, get out, get out.' She flew at him, hands flying, pushing, throwing him out the door. Then she crumpled onto the floor and sat there, too long, too shell-shocked to cry or even move.

There had been short-lived relief at learning they'd used protection. A blip. A second of thinking, 'Thank God I won't have to get an HIV test.' Now she just felt dirty. Darwin had never wanted to be just a good girl but she didn't really want to be bad, either. Breaking her vows and for what? If only Dan really knew her. He'd leave her.

And then she'd be alone.

The 'why?' in her head became a constant echo through Sunday afternoon as she eventually heaved herself up off the floor, took a long, hot shower, and then fell into bed at 7 p.m. She lay there, awake, for hours, plugging her ears when the phone rang and Dan's voice boomed out over the answering machine. Sure, she knew how to turn down the ringer, turn off the volume. But she wanted to hear his voice, wanted to think about what she'd done. She wanted to suffer.

Darwin knew, in that moment, just how much she loved Dan. Because the thought of losing him made it impossible to think of going on.

What was she going to do now?

Even though she'd been tracking her cycle for ages and had a pretty good idea that she couldn't have got pregnant the night before, somehow, someway, she needed to remove all traces of Elon. She needed to get the morning-after pill.

★   ★   ★

The security guard was bored.

'Bag to me here and then walk through,' he said, giving her a quick glance up and down.

Lucie walked swiftly through the metal detector, grabbed her purse on the other side, and waited to be buzzed in. She'd given up on her pricey uptown gyno when she went freelance (goodbye, affordable healthcare!); it would be three more months before the health plan from the public station job kicked in. And even then, her pregnancy might be considered one of the 'pre-existing' conditions that they wouldn't cover her for. So Planned Parenthood it was – and thank God for them. Of course, her original motivation for showing up at the door of PP was something else altogether. She'd been surprised by her late period, assumed it was – what do all the magazines call it? – perimenopause. Even though she wanted a baby. She'd been afraid to hope. And then the stick turned blue.

'Let's talk,' the counselor had said after her physical exam. It had been a long morning, that initial visit. First the wait in one room, then finally being buzzed in, again, to a smaller waiting area. God, the security in this place! It was a far cry from her sedate doctor's office. Yet she felt protected, safe. And certain she wasn't going to run into anyone she knew. 'You're among friends here,' the counselor prodded upon meeting Lucie. 'I want to help you do what's right for you. Is this pregnancy a positive experience for you?'

That's all it took – a few kind words – for Lucie to crack. Well, in truth she'd had no one to talk with about her situation. It had seemed easy when it was theoretical. Now she was freaked out by the prospect of having a baby and, for all intents and purposes, raising it alone. On very little money.

She wasn't sure she could do it. That's why she hadn't told anyone. Not a friend, no one at work.

'Do you want to have this baby, Lucie?' The counselor waited for her answer.

'More than anything.'

'Then we're here to help you. We typically encourage women to see their regular doctor but because you're in limbo in terms of insurance, we can deal with your prenatal care here for the time being.'

The counselor looked at her until Lucie met her eye. 'Eventually everyone *will* know, Lucie. There's almost no way to hide your stomach in the later months. So you may want to consider talking with your family, especially if you want them involved in the baby's life. But, until then, let's get you on some vitamins and get you some literature.'

Lucie had been so relieved that February morning, just to have someone treat her so . . . matter of factly. To not react when she told her story.

Now it was April and she sat, 13 weeks pregnant, waiting for her name to be called. Easter was coming up and she was going to be spending the holiday all alone; she hadn't told Rosie and she wasn't about to show up at home in the family way. It hurt, her self-imposed exile, to know the entire family was together and she was alone in her apartment. Coming up with plans to make extra money, like with those knitting videos.

She squeezed her eyelids shut as she fought back a stress headache. She'd had a lot of those lately.

'Lucie?'

Her eyes opened rapidly, blinking. There, standing just in front of her, was that annoying woman from the knitting club. The blah-blah, I'm-too-good-to-knit-and-I-can't-believe-you're-all-here-but-let-me-eat-a-muffin-anyway academic. Darwin Chiu.

'Hey, Lucie, I had no idea. You always wear such big sweaters at the store. I just thought you were, you know . . .' Darwin made a vague motion with her hands. 'Fat.'

Fat! I barely look pregnant, thought Lucie, indignantly.

And then she was called to the back for her weigh-in, leaving Darwin standing there, clutching an old copy of *Reader's Digest*.

So much for not meeting anyone here.

Lucie walked all the way to Astor Place and got a chai tea at Starbucks. She took two sips and then threw it in the garbage. Damn that Darwin Chiu! If she told anyone, well, they would have a problem. Marching back down Lafayette Street, Lucie made a plan to tell that woman to keep her mouth shut. She crossed the street at Bleecker and returned to the entrance of the clinic, then stood there, realizing she had no way of knowing if Darwin was still inside. Or if there was a more serious reason why she might have been there.

Mad at Darwin for ruining her plan of secrecy and mad at herself for not considering what Darwin might be dealing with, Lucie began to slowly walk up and down Mott Street. Aaagh, she thought. What now? Do I know her well enough to reach out? No. Is she so much a stranger I can just walk away? No. I'm stuck, concluded the TV producer, I'm stuck. I'll just wait five minutes and then go.

Fifteen minutes later, Darwin emerged, her face in a frown. She was clearly startled to see Lucie just outside the doorway.

'Goodness,' she said, then repeated it. 'Goodness. I didn't expect you to wait for me. I didn't think you would.'

'I forgot something and had to come back,' Lucie lied, all too familiar with the desire to be by herself and out of judgement's way.

'Oh.'

'But here I am anyway. And it's nearly lunchtime, you know,' said Lucie. 'Have you eaten?' Of course Darwin hadn't eaten, she thought to herself; she's just been in the clinic all morning. Stupidhead.

'No.' Darwin seemed subdued; she hadn't asked an inappropriate question or commented on Lucie's condition in several minutes.

'Let's get a bite, come on, over here at Noho Star.' Gently touching her forearm, Lucie motioned for Darwin to follow. 'We'll eat something healthy like spinach salad and then spoil ourselves with chocolate cake. And not even to share – we'll each get our own. Come on, it's my treat.'

Darwin followed, about a pace behind, until they came to cross Lafayette again. God, I'm getting my exercise today, thought Lucie; at this rate, she'd be able to keep off the pounds for a long time.

'Please don't tell anyone you saw me at Planned Parenthood,' blurted Darwin.

Lucie threw her a sidelong glance, slowly nodding her head.

'Right back at you, kiddo. Now let's go get a nosh and I'll be like Anita, patiently letting you ask me crazy questions about knitting.'

9

Anita spread a thin layer of seedless strawberry jam onto her toast, then put her knife down and took a tiny bite. She looked up and was surprised – but only for a moment – to see her husband Stan drinking his coffee, sitting at the far end of the table. He met her gaze and smiled, the lines around the corners of his brown eyes crinkling.

'Hello, my dear,' he said. 'It's a lovely day today.'

Glancing to her side, Anita could see the sun's rays glinting off the shiny hardwood floors. She could feel the warmth on her skin.

'Yes, it looks lovely,' she answered. 'We should go to the park.' Anita had the strongest feeling that something important was going to happen in Central Park today.

'You know, Stan, I had the most terrible nightmare. I dreamed you weren't with me any more.'

Stan frowned with concern, then his face relaxed.

'Don't worry, sweetheart, I'm right here across the breakfast table, just like I am every morning.'

Anita was flooded with relief, then felt foolish, a bit embarrassed. She took a sip of coffee, then another. Coffee. Suddenly a man's face flashed in her mind. Marty. Anita felt a rush of guilt and confusion. If she knew Marty, then how . . .

She took a breath.

'I don't know why I had such an awful dream because you're right here,' she murmured, then peeked across the dishes and coffee cups to get a better look at her husband.

His appearance always made her feel so proud; he was a very handsome man, the kind of distinguished older gentleman whom passers-by nodded at almost imperceptibly, pleased by the very look of him.

But the sun hit her eye and it was difficult to make out Stan's shape clearly – Anita could see his charcoal cardigan, the one she'd knitted on the Panama cruise, but it was hard to find the features of his face. She felt a tingling in her limbs and a mounting sense of worry. He had to know it was him, he was the one she wanted, that there never would be anyone else. Certainly nothing had happened with that Marty fellow. 'I love you, Stan,' she said, her words a rush.

'I know you do, sweetheart,' he replied, his voice deep and strong. 'And I love you. Always and forever.'

Anita's eyes flew open, her upper lip beaded with perspiration, a feeling of dread and heaviness coming over her.

She moaned softly to herself as her mind raced through the last fifteen years of her life, always leaving her with the same conclusion: Stan was dead. Really gone. And she was still here, alone.

Groggy, Anita remained motionless in her bed, staring at the ceiling. How many times had she had that dream? The grief seemed to cycle in endless phases; sometimes she dreamed about Stan night after night, and other times months would pass between seeing him in her sleeping hours. And then the dream would return. Always it was the same – Stan was alive! – and always the waking reality was the same: Anita was a widow.

She would see him in the living room, on the street, at a party. The sequence never altered – the shock at the sight of him, the embarrassment over her mistake – what sort of wife would believe her husband was dead when he was right there in front of her? – then the intense relief that left her wanting to fall to her knees and thank God that he was still alive.

It seemed so real. Each and every time. She felt stupid when she woke up but everything seemed so logical in the dream. So matter of fact. Anita would tell Stan how she had worried and he would laugh and call her his sweetheart and she would feel so goddamn overwhelmed that his supposed death had all been a misunderstanding. Of course it was! Everything was okay! And that meeting, the moment of talking with Stan, would be so raw and exciting and truly perfect that she would be enveloped by a happiness beyond any she had ever imagined.

The feeling was pure joy.

Just at that instant she would awaken, right when she had sorted through all the possibilities and come to the conclusion that yes, Stan was alive, and all was right again.

And so the waking up meant everything was all wrong. The regret was much worse than during the day, when she gazed at his photo on the mantel or thought wistfully of the good life they had shared. At those times, she was in her warrior mode, her shields and defenses at the ready. In her sleep, she was vulnerable to her hopes and to her sorrows. 'The grief will pass,' she had heard from mourner after mourner at Stan's funeral. That's what everyone had said to her, in quiet tones, briefly touching a shoulder or offering a gentle kiss on the cheek. 'Give it time,' her loved ones told her in the days after Stan's heart attack. She knew the words; she had certainly said them often enough herself to friends and relatives.

So Anita gave it time. She waited for the day that she felt better. And yet the feeling of loss just didn't fade away. Certainly, the pain was not as acute as when she sat shivah and her sons held her hands and their capable wives asked if couldn't they please just get her to eat a little bite, just something to keep up her strength? (Which they couldn't; Anita lost far too much weight after Stan had died.) No, the cold shock of it had long ago settled into acceptance.

For Anita, what lingered all these years later was something just as uncomfortable. It was heartbreak that remained. She lived with a constant, nagging sense that something was missing, that Stan was just out of reach, and the loneliness was often overpowering. There were days when she felt he was so close that she only had to talk aloud and other moments when he felt so far away that it left her feeling lost and newly abandoned. On a see-saw that never stopped.

Of course, who could she tell? Anita knew that no one really wanted to listen to the tales of woe from an old woman: her friends were all dealing with sick or deceased spouses themselves and her family wouldn't know what to do if she told them. It would only be a burden. She hadn't wanted to talk with her own mother about the loss of her father, she'd been too busy raising her sons and being Stan's charming better half at the dozens of functions that filled up their social calendar. It was enough, wasn't it, that she had invited her mother over every Saturday after shul and taken her out to the hair salon on Wednesdays? That she called several times a week? Anita had made a fuss over her mother at every holiday and made sure she had a place of honor at every recital and graduation. It was enough.

Now she knew it hadn't been enough.

This generation was different, but not so much. Her friends were all atwitter now that their adult daughters were on a kick of getting to know them as equals. 'I want us to be friends,' she heard that these grown children kept insisting to their mothers. Of course, what these daughters really wanted was to be able to bare their souls to the one person in the world who would love them without restraint, whose approval was priceless, who would find them and their myriad life issues endlessly fascinating. It is a beautiful gift, thought Anita, to have your mother be your very dearest and best friend. It is quite another to try to be hers. Then you'd have to actually get to know her. As a real person.

Being the mother of three sons, well, it wasn't as though they were going to call and have great heart-to-hearts. Maybe some boys did? Not hers. Too busy with providing for their own families, they left the chatting up to their wives. All good girls, too, but too busy with the day-to-day business of running a family, just as she once had been. It was no wonder then that she loved Georgia as much as she did, their friendship precious and free of the mother-daughter acrimony that would linger after a decade of teenage rebellion. But even her relationship with her beloved Walker girls was unbalanced. It wasn't as though she would pick up the phone to tell Georgia her secrets; that wasn't the role she'd signed on for.

Young people – whom Anita counted as anyone under 50 – never really thought about the generations ahead being the same as they were, she knew. Every pair of lovers thinks they invented sex. No one wants to consider that at 72, she'd like to be kissed quite thoroughly by a man who loved her, that she still felt desire and that not having anyone to whisper to under the covers was louder than silence.

And so there is the trouble, thought Mrs Stan Lowenstein as she turned on the water for her morning bath. She remained a vibrant, sexual, smart creature, nursing a broken heart for a man who was never coming back. And a guilty conscience for hankering after a certain man who *was* around.

If she'd been wiser, Anita told herself often, she'd have just shriveled up, instead of hanging on and duking it out with the universe. She watched the tub fill. 'If one more person tells me I'm feisty I'm going to scream,' she told the soap. 'I'm not a spitfire. I'm just me, the same me I've always been. Only now I look wrinkled.' She marveled at her body, its lines and soft skin. How did she get so old so quickly? She couldn't believe she was a grandmother, so many times over. And most of those little faces would be at her table for Passover in just a few days, flying in from Atlanta. And Israel. She would hug and inspect and admire and then they would all be on their way again, back to their own lives and leave her alone with hers. Of course she would have loved to see all of them more often, but Anita had always been afraid to fly. And her sons found wives and careers that took them all around the globe, doing good things, raising good families. It was okay. It was enough.

'I am not alone,' she said aloud as she stepped into the water. They were the same words she said to herself every morning. 'I am not alone.'

She rested her head against the tub, closed her eyes as she lay back into the steamy water. Thank God for her family, far-flung though they were. She loved them more than they could know. And thank God for the steady diet of opera and Broadway matinees with Dakota and knitting club and working at the shop. It was what sustained her.

And yet, Anita thought, and yet. She was still hungry.

At precisely 11.27 a.m., James picked his sports coat off the back of his Aeron chair and headed out of the office. He had to catch the C train up to the West Side for his noon appointment with Anita. 'Try not to be tardy,' she had warned the first time. 'I have to be at the shop in the afternoon.'

It was true that he'd pushed for some time to talk with Anita, knowing that she was Georgia's most trusted confidante, but he had expected to meet her for a quick coffee, on neutral ground. James was used to driving every situation.

But then he hadn't met Anita before.

'Hello, Anita,' he said upon initially meeting her in the shop many months ago. She smiled pleasantly, though not exactly warmly.

'Oh, please,' she said. 'Do call me Mrs Lowenstein.'

The next few times he had dropped by the shop – sometimes scheduled, more often not – he'd received a similar formal treatment. When he got into his new program (the calling ahead, double-checking major purchases thing), Anita had been much friendlier. Georgia too, of course. But anyone could see that you had to go through Anita to get to Walker and Daughter.

'Yes, James, you're right,' she responded to his suggestion that they get to know each other better. 'It looks like you're staying put on this go-round.' Anita looked him straight in the eye, daring him to leave.

'Yes, ma'am,' he answered lamely, feeling more than a decade's worth of guilt and shame in one moment.

'Very good then. I'll see you for lunch on Monday at my apartment.'

And that had been that. Once a week during the previous month, James had been making his way to the San Remo to sit at Anita's dining table and discuss everything from the latest headlines to his work projects to the time he was spending with Dakota to his shock over the booming New York real estate market. The one thing they did not discuss – ever – was Georgia.

James had tried, feebly, to press Anita on the matter at the first lunch.

'So I think Georgia is a bit surprised by my relocating to the city,' he said casually while spearing a potato in his Salade Niçoise. He pretended to be more interested in his food than in Anita's response.

'You'd have to ask Georgia how she feels about that, James,' Anita had said reasonably, her fork at the side of her plate and her hands in her lap. She was a vision of repose, her expression impenetrable. 'But I, for one, am not surprised. It is never too late to make a different choice and it is never too late to make the right one. Do you agree?'

'I don't know,' he'd replied, losing his appetite although half of his salad was still untouched. When he was with Anita, he had a sensation of being Dakota's age and being found with his hand in the cookie jar. She was a wise old bird, he could see that. She enjoyed laughing at his jokes, was quick to join in his banter, could hold up her end of a conversation on the state of the global economy or talk just as comfortably about a current movie. She was equally elegant and intelligent. Anita would have been a great CEO, he thought. Especially because she never fell for his practiced charm. He wanted – he needed – her to be on his side. And he was learning, quickly, that the only time he had her full attention was when he was being sincere. It was new to James, dropping the act of the suave man-about-town, and just being himself. More than that, it was liberating. 'I know it, Mrs Lowenstein, I know what I did,' he told her that first lunch. 'And I'm sorry.'

'Very good, then,' she said, then looked past him and smiled. 'We both know Dakota is a delight and she gets half her genes from you. Keep that in mind, James. There's hope for you yet.'

James nodded to himself as he remembered her words, stepping out of the subway on 72nd street and walking up Central Park West. The weather was getting so warm he didn't really need his jacket; it was a late Easter this year and April was already winding down. Georgia having graciously agreed to invite him over for lamb, he was looking forward to telling

Anita that he would see her for dinner the following Sunday, eager to get Anita's input on what sort of gifts he should bring. He was wary of going overboard yet again. A lily bouquet, for sure, but should he bring two chocolate rabbits or just one? And what about a new Easter outfit? Growing up, he had always received a crisp new shirt and pair of pants on Easter morning, his sisters getting new frilly pastel dresses, the entire Foster clan gussying up until they were the most handsome bunch ever to appear at the First Baptist Church in Baltimore. Come to think of it, should he ask to take Dakota to a service? Not like he had been to church in years, but still. Maybe he should.

James waited as the doorman called up to Anita, then received the nod to proceed. Anita stood in the open doorway as he approached.

'Hello, James,' she said. Her voice was strained. 'Come in.' James stepped through the threshold, getting a better look at Anita as he came closer. Her lipstick was feathering at the corners and her shoulders drooped ever so slightly.

'Come in,' she repeated. 'I'm glad you're here but I'm just a little tired.'

'No worries, Anita, let's go have a sit down.'

James took her hand and led her gently to the sofa, for once being in charge instead of the other way around. His mind flashed quickly on his parents, worrying for a moment about his father getting up on a ladder to empty the eaves troughs as part of spring cleaning. They were all getting older.

'Hold on,' he said, then walked back towards the bedrooms. He hesitated, only briefly, then stepped into the master. It was scrupulously neat, the king-sized bed made up with dozens of silk pillows. His eyes caught what he was looking for, a soft sage-green afghan resting on the footboard. James picked it up and carried it out to Anita, who was almost dozing on the sofa.

'Oh, excuse me.' She perked up at the sight of him, but only for a moment. 'I didn't sleep very well last night.'

James lifted her feet up on the sofa as she made clucking sounds of protest, then just gave up as he covered her with the afghan she had knitted years ago.

'I'm so sorry about this, James, I should have called,' she said, her eyes barely open. 'It's all rather embarrassing.'

'I'll see you Sunday, Anita,' he said. 'I'm coming to Georgia's for Easter dinner.'

'I'm so glad, James, so very glad that you'll be there.' And then she was out, asleep and peaceful. James pulled up the afghan gently so it was resting under her chin. He didn't want her to be too cool. For a moment, he stood still, watching the older woman who had looked after his family all these years, then quietly made his exit. In the elevator, he pulled out his cell phone and scrolled through his contact list, hitting the dial button as he stepped out on the sidewalk.

'Hello, Mom?' he said as he strolled to the subway, his sports coat over his arm. 'I was just wondering how you are . . .'

Georgia slowly put down the phone in her office, then walked over to look at the knitted gown on her dressmaker's model. Damn, did her body hurt! It had taken six weeks from that first meeting but it was finally finished, every stray end sewn in, the final product blocked and steamed. Gorgeous. Cat hadn't even seen it yet – Georgia had been expecting her to drop by in a few hours, after her Tuesday afternoon Pilates class. So she was surprised that Cat had just called, even more taken aback with what she had to say.

'I positively adore the direction we're going,' Cat told her, 'but on second thought, the gown might look better in a light pink instead of gold. Metallic but not so shimmery. Something softer, more feminine. Don't you think so?'

No, thought Georgia, I don't think so. Exasperated, she blurted out a sum to remake the dress that was beyond astronomical, mainly to deter Cat from wanting them to start over. Couldn't that spoiled socialite see how difficult it would be to complete in time for the museum gala?

'That's fine – we're going to need it quickly,' Cat answered, unfazed, as always, at amounts of money that Georgia felt embarrassed just saying aloud. 'And we'll need all new accessories, too. I think we ought to step up our meetings. Are you free tomorrow?'

'I have to check my calendar,' Georgia retorted, frustrated that Cat seemed to think she was always on call and always available. There *are* no knitting emergencies, she had told her former best friend during one late-night phone conversation. Though they had ended up talking for such a long time that it had actually been quite fun, chatting as they once used to do daily in their teens. But not now. No, at the moment, Cat was in full-on lady-who-lunches mode, filled with ideas and details and all manner of demands.

Georgia was dazed by the prospect of making another gown over the next few weeks – Cat had changed her mind so many times during the creation of the first one and she couldn't bear to remake the pattern again. But good money was hard to refuse.

'Anita,' she called out wearily, standing in the doorway of her office. 'I think I'm going to need some help here.'

'I just don't think I can do it,' Georgia found herself telling Anita when the day was done and she was tallying up the register. 'It's like she's punishing me. Trying to prove how rich she is or something.'

Anita tilted her head as though considering what her friend was saying, but didn't speak a word.

'It's not right,' Georgia whined. 'I'm tired. And I have to roast a lamb for Sunday.'

'Well, surely you won't be putting it in the oven yet, love,' Anita replied. 'It's only Tuesday.'

'I told her it would cost fifteen thousand dollars – and that I might have to do some machine knitting to get it done.' Georgia spoke in a low voice even though no one else was in the store. 'And she agreed to pay it. Just like that.'

'Fifteen thousand dollars?' Anita repeated calmly as Georgia nodded. 'Tell me again about what happened in high school,' she prodded, then listened intently to the tale of how Georgia passed on Dartmouth to go to the same school as Cathy and her shock at learning that Cathy's name had come up on the waitlist and that she'd taken Georgia's place at the Ivy, without breathing a word of it.

'And we never spoke again until she showed up here and whipped out her checkbook,' Georgia finished, her voice trembling ever so slightly.

The older woman reached out and led the way to the back of the office. The twosome settled on the worn loveseat wedged into the corner opposite Georgia's desk, which was covered in invoices and yarn samples.

'The thing is,' Anita began quietly, 'that when you're young, you always think you'll meet all sorts of wonderful people, that drifting apart and losing friends is natural. You don't worry, at first, about the friends you leave behind. But as you get older, it gets harder to build friendships. Too many defenses, too little opportunity. You get busy. And by the time you realize that you've lost the dearest best friend you've ever had, years have gone by and you're mature enough to be embarrassed by your attitude and frankly, by your arrogance.'

Smiling at Georgia, Anita spoke softly. 'Why do you think Cat Phillips would want a second dress made? With all the accessory shopping afternoons and all that?'

'Because she's a bitch!'

'Okay. She's a bitch with too much time on her hands,'

said Anita. 'Or maybe because she has something to say but she doesn't know how to start.' Her arms wrapped around her dear protégé, Anita continued. 'I don't claim to know the woman and her motivations, Georgia, but it seems to me that she's just looking for an excuse to spend time together and you – yes, you! – are so damn valuable to her that she's willing to pay any amount just to have your attention.'

'Ha! I don't think so!'

'I do. I think if I'd lost a friend like you I'd go on missing you for a long, long time.'

Anita gave a gentle tug on a curl.

'Why is this all happening?' Georgia moaned. 'Why are they all coming back now? First James, now Cathy. And suddenly the business is booming. And you're making videos with Lucie! It's all too much going on – it's not the right time. I'm not ready!'

'We're making videos, dearest, you and me.' Anita held Georgia close as she sniffled. 'And there's always a better time than right now and there always will be. But right now is what we've got.'

'I don't want them around!' Georgia insisted.

'I know, sweetie, I know. It would be so much easier if you really didn't care.' Anita hated to see Georgia upset but, at the same time, her heart expanded with the satisfaction of being needed. Her daughter of the heart. 'Sometimes God answers a prayer you didn't know you had,' she continued, thinking to herself of the day when she met Georgia in the park.

Georgia's response was inaudible.

'I missed her,' Georgia's voice was less than a whisper. 'All this time, I missed Cathy. I wanted to get in touch with her so many times over the past twenty years – but fear of seeming pathetic always stopped me,' she said. 'Hey, still mad about the Dartmouth thing. But boy-o-boy, I sure do miss you. Won't you be my friend again?' She shrugged her shoulders.

'See what I mean? Stupid. Sillier as you get older. Even if it's the truth.' Georgia threw back her head of curls and exhaled loudly. She stood up, giving Anita a 'thank you' squeeze on the arm as she did so, and squared her shoulders. The tough cookie, Georgia Walker, was back.

'Now she's rich and I'm Cinderella, dressing her for the ball. And if I don't get started right away, I'm going to turn into a pumpkin, too.'

10

'Help! Someone take this from me,' puffed K.C. as she nearly dropped her veggie lasagna through the door of the shop at 8.55 p.m., the last member of the Friday Night Knitting Club to show up.

'You went home and cooked? I don't believe it.' Georgia took the warm Tupperware dish from her friend.

K.C. looked Georgia squarely in the eye. 'I turned on the stove and heated up this sucker. Which, if you want to know, has its own particular challenges.'

Georgia laughed as she walked K.C. over to the big table in the shop. It wasn't that surprising, in a tiny NYC kitchen, to never actually turn on the stove. Before Dakota was born, Georgia had never cooked anything other than pasta in her apartment share. After Dakota, well, it had just been too pricey to do take-out. And it's not like babies can be raised on pizza by the slice. Toddlers, perhaps. Of course, by the time Dakota was a toddler, Georgia had learned how to cook. And do the books. And run a store while keeping an eye on her little one playing in the yarns. Now her baby girl stood before her, backpack over her shoulder, waiting for her sleep-over date to pick her up. Georgia had fallen short of the good mom award tonight, having earlier fed Dakota a tuna sand-wich instead of a home-cooked meal. It was really going to be a grown-up evening.

'Wow,' said Georgia, surveying the food on the table. Lucie had carried in a cake that didn't have that distinctive scent of cake mix. (Maybe it really was homemade?) Darwin had brought bags of pre-washed salad and plastic bowls and forks (but no dressing, Georgia noticed; she would have to run upstairs and get something out of her own fridge). And Georgia – although worried about the idea of having a dinner party in her shop – had even made some chicken and red pepper kebabs for the shindig.

Georgia marveled at how Dakota's idea of sharing snacks had been the seed for this potluck dinner concept. Secretly, Georgia was glad she'd gone along with the idea, feeling rather pleased and proud to have assembled such a great group of women, cooks and non-cooks alike. Though the timing could have been better, wedged between the week's Seders and Easter coming up on Sunday. Georgia noticed that only the true diehard regulars had shown up: Darwin, Lucie, K.C., and Anita, who had quietly excused herself after Shabbat dinner with her sons and their families and walked over. Hers had never been a particularly religious home; her oldest, Nathan, had married into a far more observant family and Anita often found her daughter-in-law's presence in the kitchen stressful. ('I just wanted to see how it's going,' she whispered to Georgia when she arrived a short time ago. 'Also, I got a little tired of you-know-who and her insistence on eating off paper plates because I'm not kosher enough.')

Georgia heard the zip of a bag being opened and saw K.C. pull out a bottle – no, make that three bottles – of Chianti.

'I didn't make this either, sport,' she said with a wink at Georgia. 'Ladies, let's start our engines.'

'Just a drop for me, it's Passover,' started Anita, though she still took the full glass offered by the evening's sommelier. Darwin began passing the wine around, discreetly skipping Lucie, who was dressed, as usual, in a very baggy sweater.

'Attention, attention. I have an announcement. I'm quitting publishing,' said K.C.

'But you don't actually have a job, do you?' Trust Darwin to say the wrong thing, thought Georgia.

'No, honeybuns, I don't. I've been unemployed for months. That's just the point.' K.C. made a show of taking a seat. 'I thought I'd take it easy for a while. Get off my duff. But now it's time for my second act.'

'As what?' asked Lucie, more intrigued by the idea of re-invention than she wanted to let on.

'That's just it,' heaved K.C. 'I haven't a fucking clue. I always wanted to be a lawyer but I'm worried it's too late for school. So if you have any suggestions, don't hold back. Okay, who wants some of my not-quite-homemade lasagna? It was very expensive at Zabar's, I'll have you know.'

The women sat down and filled their plates, undressed lettuce and all. The kebabs were a hit, Georgia was pleased to see. So was the wine. 'K.C., you brought so much,' she told her friend, sotto voice. 'You didn't have to spend like this.'

'It's part of my last hurrah,' explained K.C. 'If I don't figure out things soon, I'm going to be so broke I'll have to go from couch to couch.'

Their attention shifted as Anita returned from upstairs with the salad dressing, an extra wine bottle in tow.

'This really warms you up,' she told Lucie. 'Don't you want any?'

'She's allergic . . . to grapes,' interjected Darwin with light-ning speed, then turned on her official professorial drone. 'Grapes are a very interesting fruit, in fact, coming in many different varieties and shapes . . .'

As if on cue, K.C. rolled her eyes to Anita and changed the subject. Which was good because Darwin didn't really know a damn thing about grapes.

There was nothing left of the cake but a few crumbs on a plate. The club had mainly been about snacking and chatting tonight. Though Lucie had actually taken out her knitting, Anita noticed. The TV producer, she knew, had several projects on the go – but was trying to pace herself on the sweater to keep time with everyone else. But she was already on to the sleeves while the rest of the group was still plowing their way through the back. Well, good for her.

They couldn't just party like Judy Garland all night. And she'd have to get back to Nathan and Rhea soon enough. Anita felt giddy, both from the wine and from spending the evening how she wanted to instead of how her sons expected she should. It felt good. Liberating. Maybe even a little bit naughty.

'How's everyone's knitting coming along?' she asked, slurring just slightly on the letter S. It was really a question for K.C.; Lucie was an accomplished knitter and Darwin, well, was Darwin.

K.C. picked up on the comment.

'I know who you're talking to, Miss Anita, and I have a second announcement to make,' said K.C., who stood up somewhat unsteadily. How many glasses of wine had she drunk? 'From now on, I'm only going to make things that are E-A-S-Y. If it has more than fifty rows, it's out. So forget what I said about scarves last week – now, it's only Barbie scarves. And only in garter stitch. I am *so* done with purling.'

The women's laughter was interrupted by a sharp knock on the door. Anita walked over and turned the lock.

'Ah, Anita,' breathed Cat, a vision in a very Easter-egg pink swing coat and matching clutch bag. Her sharp, flowery perfume wafted in though her body was still in the doorway. 'I hope I'm not too late for the knitting club.'

'Um, do you knit?' asked Anita, displeased to see Georgia's troublesome old friend. It had been gratifying to see Georgia finally relax tonight; Anita wanted to protect her from anyone who could tramp all over that good feeling.

'I didn't know that was an actual requirement,' Cat responded curtly as she blew past Anita into the shop. 'Hello, Georgia! Hello, everyone!' She spoke as if addressing a convention. Too loudly. 'It's delightful to meet you all. I'm Cat Phillips. Georgia is making me a dress.'

'Cat! This is unexpected.' Georgia was somewhat embarrassed by the wine bottles on the table. She looked down automatically, as if her eyes could prevent Cat from seeing them. Of course, Cat followed her gaze.

'Thank God. I'd love a glass,' she said, settling herself at the table and raising a plastic cup to the light to make sure it was clean. 'I was wondering if all you did was play with yarn. This will do fine.'

'Fill it to the rim for our friend Mrs Phillips,' said K.C. dryly.

Darwin picked up the bottle and brought it over. Cat downed her first glass.

'Hit me again, wine lady,' she said, surveying the room. 'Georgia, nice club you've got here. Festive.'

And with that, she raised her cup, as Georgia simply shrugged her shoulders at Anita. What can you do? She refilled her own glass and took another to her friend and mentor, who was relieved to see that Georgia was calm about Cat's presence.

'If you can't beat 'em, join 'em,' she said.

'Time for "Truth or Dare",' announced K.C. soon afterward, the small talk having dissolved into an awkwardness with the presence of Cat.

Georgia hated games. Always had.

'I don't think so . . .' she started.

Darwin perked up. 'I love games,' she said. In truth, she'd never been anywhere, like a sleepover, where she would have played a game like Truth or Dare. But she liked the idea of being part of the gang.

'I do, too – my whole life is a joke,' muttered Cat. 'I'm in.'

'I'm out,' said Lucie. 'It's time I went home.'

'Can't,' responded K.C. 'It's against the rules in the knitting club handbook.' She consulted her empty palm. 'Yes, yes, rule #577-B. No one, not even Lucie, may opt out of mandatory games that have more than two players.' K.C. looked up. 'Guess that means you're in. Anita, you first.'

'First? First what? I don't think they even had this game when I was a girl, K.C. We just played potsie on the sidewalk. I can't help you.'

'Just ask Truth or Dare, Anita.'

'Here's truth: you've had too much to drink.'

'No, you *ask* "Truth or Dare", you don't make a pronouncement.'

'I'm ready! Truth or Dare, Georgia?' Darwin was earnest.

'Neither,' responded Georgia definitely.

'Okay, truth!' Darwin was undeterred, at 27, from playing her first-ever game. 'Why are you so grouchy all the time?'

'Yes, that's it. You're so aloof!' interrupted Cat. 'Brilliant analysis, whoever you are. Georgia the Grouch.'

The knitter fumed as she regarded her bitchy old friend and the irritating grad student. If there was one thing Georgia was never good at, it was handling criticism. ('You're oversensitive,' her mother Bess used to tell her. 'You'll never be able to handle the real world if you don't get a thicker skin.')

A nasty retort jumped out of her mouth before she could stop herself. Before she could remember to be professional.

'Stress. Ever heard of it? Oh, no, you're too busy spending your husband's money, Cat. Or you, Darwin, avoiding the real world by staying in school.' Aack. Was she drunk too? She looked up at Anita, who winced.

'I think the gloves are coming off, people,' said Cat sharply. 'So don't hold back, Georgia Walker. Tell us what you really think.'

Georgia paused for a moment, facing down her old friend.

Her first impulse was to gloss over her mini-outburst. Return the club meeting to its festive spirit. Instead, other, different words came out of her mouth. Honest ones.

'Maybe I am grouchy. Maybe what I really think is that I am just a little bit envious of some things,' she admitted with a sigh. 'It's just really hard being a single mom – there's always a new bill or a new worry and no one to share it with.' Georgia looked at Anita and reassessed. 'No husband to share it with, I mean. Because I wouldn't survive without Anita. I think you all know that.'

A cheering round of agreement went through the group. Even Cat's expression had momentarily lost its hard edge. Georgia continued.

'I'll tell you the truth, Ms Truth or Dare Darwin. I'm really tired. The shop takes a lot of juggling and as Dakota gets older, she seems to need me more rather than less. My whole body aches and I just want to sleep for a thousand years.'

'And now that handsome James is back on the scene,' crowed Cat, looking around the room, nodding.

'He is not,' insisted Georgia.

'Oh, believe me, I saw how he watched you at my party. Maybe you need your camera checked, Georgia, but that man is completely back in the picture.'

Georgia folded her arms and made a face.

'What about you, Cat? What's your big truth?'

'My truth – and I'm completely comfortable telling all of you – is that my husband is a snaky little tightfisted two-timer who thinks I'm on the road to getting fat.' Cat turned in her seat to look at Darwin, the youngest woman in the room. 'Are you married?' she asked. Darwin hesitated.

'Keep it that way if you want to be happy,' said Cat with a shake of her head followed by a gulp from her plastic cup. 'I spend my life poking and prodding my muscles, my fat cells, my old bones. You name a treatment, I've had it. But it's never enough.'

'That behavior is a type of control—' Darwin began a lecture but Cat stopped her with a snotty laugh.

'I took psychology 101. I know it,' she said matter of factly. 'What I don't know is how I became a victim to it. I don't know how I went from being me to becoming Mrs Needs-to-Fix-Herself.'

Cat addressed Georgia directly in an icy voice. 'I bet you have an answer, Ms Walker. Maybe something to do with selling out?'

Looking at her hands, Georgia chose her words carefully.

'We all find ourselves in places we don't expect, Cat. Situations that seem out of our control,' she said. 'The challenge is making our way out of them.'

'And so it is, old friend,' replied Cat, sounding satisfied yet still needling Georgia, ever so slightly, with her attitude. 'So who's with me?'

'Who's with you to what?' asked K.C., fading fast from too much wine.

'Ah, yes, the loud one,' said Cat, appraising K.C. 'Let's all make a pledge to do something that scares us. Something that will challenge us. Make our way out of our situations, to quote the always successful Ms Walker.'

Cat drew out the 'always successful' part a few beats too long. Just enough to raise Georgia's hackles.

'I don't know about this—'

'I do. I'll do something,' Darwin spoke quickly. 'I'm going to learn how to knit.'

'Brava, but not exactly the earth-shattering thing I'd expect to hear at a knitting club. However, there you go.' Georgia marveled at Cat's command of a room. 'Any other takers?'

'I'll call my mother,' said Lucie.

'When's the last time you spoke?' Cat inquired.

'Over a year.'

'Now we're cooking with gas, folks! Excellent. And I pledge to . . . lay off Botox and stop thinking so much about what I look like. And maybe to mend some fences along the way.' Cat smiled at Georgia. A beautiful, defiant, happy smile. 'It's your turn.'

'I don't know. What scares me? Having James snake his way back into our lives.'

'And I am going to take the LSAT,' yelled K.C. 'Screw it all, I'm going to go for it.'

'Yes,' said Anita. 'Let's all go for it.' And if Marty asks me out again, she thought to herself, I'll say yes.

'Let me carry the dishes into the kitchen – please, it's my pleasure,' said James. 'You must have worked for hours on that fantastic Easter meal. The lamb was really tender.' It was a perfect Sunday evening. James had been great company all night, sharing stories about Easter in Paris – Georgia noticed he never mentioned if he shared those holidays with a special someone – and tall tales about growing up with his sisters back in Baltimore. Dakota had been entranced.

'So I have how many cousins?' she asked, marveling at the idea of her family expanding. Georgia's younger brother didn't yet have children and besides, they only saw the Walker clan once a year, around Christmas. Her brother Donny drove in to take Dakota to Pennsylvania as soon as school let out and Georgia went up on Christmas Eve, closing the shop at noon and coming back with her muffingirl on the 27th. The way Dakota was reacting, though, was as though she'd never seen an actual blood relation. It left Georgia feeling a little ticked, to be in James's shadow whenever he was around Dakota.

'Three aunties and seven cousins, plus a whole other set of grandparents.'

Dakota was thinking hard, she could see that. 'Do they know when my birthday is? It's in July. I'll be thirteen, you know.'

Georgia had explained, awkwardly, over the years about James and his family not being very involved in their lives. But she always told Dakota that she was loved. And she'd never revealed the details of why James wasn't around – simply that he had a job in Paris that kept him busy. Her daughter had rarely complained to her directly, choosing instead to funnel her questions and frustrations through Anita. A good thing, because Georgia was quite sure – definite, in fact – that the charming Mr Foster had never actually told his parents about her, let alone about their baby. And she had a few choice words to say about that. But now was not the time.

'That's enough, Little Miss I-Made-Dessert-All-By-Myself,' she said, hoping to distract her daughter. She didn't want to see her get hurt when she realized the Fosters wouldn't care about her birthday. Anita, as always, picked up the cue.

'So what delight are you going to tempt us with tonight? A baked Alaska?'

'No! It's something for our guest of honor. And I'm having it delivered.'

'Delivered? There's a carrot cake in the kitchen, honey,' Georgia whispered. 'The one we made this morning . . .'

'That's just for our second dessert, Mom,' Dakota whispered back. 'I'm having the special one delivered.'

James, Georgia, and Anita all exchanged confused glances over the table.

'Ummm, how did you order this dessert, sweetheart? When? Where?' Georgia wasn't sure how to handle the situation; Dakota looked so pleased with herself and she didn't want to have to launch into being all strict mommy. Not when they were having such a nice evening.

'Oh, I just put the order in on Friday. It's a little something I read about in your Julia Child cookbook but I had trouble getting some of the ingredients,' explained Dakota, patting Georgia's hand the way she'd seen Anita do so many times. 'I ordered it for right about now . . .'

Just then the doorbell rang. Not the buzzer for a deliveryman, Georgia noticed, but the doorbell. She went up to the peephole while Anita and James also got up from the table.

'Special delivery!' rang out the deep, loud, familiar voice. It was Marty – dressed in a suit and tie, no less. Georgia opened the door to her good friend.

'Special delivery,' he said again, handing over a large covered metal dish to Georgia. She motioned him inside with a flick of her head and walked the dish over to the table. Anita smiled, ill at ease, as Marty joined the party. She hadn't expected to see him tonight. Quickly, she turned her head, ran her tongue rapidly over her teeth. Just in case. One never knew what could get stuck when you had broccoli.

'Ta-dah!' yelled Dakota. 'Hurry, Anita! It's Bananas Foster! Get it? Bananas Foster! For our guest of honor.' Dakota grinned and put her arm around her father, pumped her fist in the air a few times, jubilant over successfully planning a secret dessert. And at having her mom and dad in the same room with her. 'And it's for me, too. I'm half-Foster, you know.'

Georgia's face froze in horror; James caught her eye and shook his head slightly. He hadn't put her up to the idea.

'That may be true, Dakota, but all the best parts are pure Walker, I assure you,' said James smoothly. 'The good looks *and* the good manners.'

Dakota shrugged, busy explaining to Marty that they still had a chance to light things up if they struck a match to the heavily liquored dish. 'Stand back, everybody,' she yelled. 'It's Bananas Foster! Go go go!'

The match struck but the flame only lasted a moment on the top of the liquid, then petered out. Dakota looked glum. 'Let's try it again! Get me another match, quick!'

'I have a better idea,' said Anita. 'Why don't we get out the ice cream and serve this up? It looks delicious, dear, and what a brilliant idea. I see a great future for you as either a party planner or the President.' She smiled, blushing ever so slightly. 'And Marty, you'll stay, of course.'

Marty straightened his tie as his face relaxed into a toothy grin.

'I was hoping you'd say that, Anita,' he said. 'Because I'd love to.'

Knit and Purl

These stitches are the fundamentals of knitting and are the basis of every garment. The knit stitch is a series of flat, vertical loops that produces a knitted fabric face and the purl stitch is its reverse. One side is smooth, the other bumpy. Knit is what you show the world; purl is the soft, nubbly underside you keep close to the skin.

11

Two popcorns, a soda, and a bottle of water. Should he ask for butter? What if it was that awful greasy golden topping? Surely Anita wouldn't enjoy that. No, he'd skip the topping, but add a pack of M 'n' Ms in case she liked chocolate.

Goodness, he'd known her for ten years and he didn't even know what she liked to eat.

Marty entered the theatre, arms full, blinded by the darkness for a moment before seeing Anita's head, looking back towards him. He walked over to their row.

'There was a big line,' he told her, handing her a large popcorn and a large soda.

'Oh, Marty, I don't think I can eat all this, let alone hold it in my hands.'

He knew what he'd been thinking – sharing one popcorn would be too presumptuous for a first date. But he should have chosen a smaller size. He just didn't want her to think he was being chintzy. He felt his face redden – he couldn't even get their food order right! – and pivoted ever so slightly, trying to hide the bag of candy in the pocket of his sports coat. He stood there, the second large popcorn in his hands, looking sheepish.

'But, I'm glad you did!' Anita was beaming. 'I haven't eaten popcorn in years. I love it.' She put a fluffy piece in her mouth, enjoying the squeak and crunch.

Marty got himself straightened out (he always hated those fold-up seats) and sat down to enjoy the show. If it had been

1953, he would have spent the entire time worrying about when to put his arm around Anita. Age brings wisdom, he told himself, and women like you to take things slowly. So he settled in to enjoy the show, planning to offer his arm as the lights went up.

'Let's stroll off that popcorn,' he suggested.

'Yes, let's do that,' she answered, easing into her cardigan and letting him help her up, hold out her spring coat. She slid her hand into the crook of his arm quite naturally – it felt good to hold onto a strong male arm, one that belonged to a man who saw her as a woman and not as a frail senior. He guided her through the hordes of moviegoers talking about this performance and that. Anita didn't have a clue what all those kids were talking about; she hadn't watched a minute of the show. No, she'd spent the entire evening watching Marty out of the corner of her eye, admiring his profile, the clean lines of his jaw, privately wishing, just a little, that he might reach out and take her hand.

The phone began to ring as she was changing into her nightgown; her hand caught in her blouse because she'd tried to be clever and pull it through the sleeve without unbuttoning the cuff. She gave a quick tug, then grabbed her robe to cover herself, in case it was Marty calling. 'Hello?' She kept her voice low, a little bit of flirtation on the edges.

'Mother? Do you have a cold? You sound funny.' It was Nathan, calling from Atlanta. He'd been phoning often since he brought his family down for Passover, always trying to convince her that she was looking strained. His words.

'No, Nathan, I'm fine.'

'Well, I've been trying to call you all night and I kept getting the machine. Is your phone not ringing?'

'I wouldn't know, Nathan, I was out this evening.'

'Mother, you really need to take some time for yourself.

You can't always be running out to solve all of Georgia's problems.'

'I wasn't—'

'I know, I know, you love that Georgia and Dakota.' Nathan was working himself up into a rant, just like he used to do when he was a kid and her middle son, David, always the cool operator, would hide one of his baseball cards and then try to ransom it back to him for his share of the allowance. Oh, how Stan would give it to those two, knowing full well that David took the card not for the money but for the pure fun of making Nathan squirm by disturbing his exquisitely organized collection. Now they were all grown up, David working for the World Health Organization in Zurich and Nathan married to a Southern girl and practicing law in Atlanta. It was surprising, really, how they'd all grown up before she was ready for them to be men.

'It was obvious just how much she has her hooks into you when you ran over there during our visit,' Nathan continued. 'You know, you really hurt Rhea's feelings, Mother, by leaving dinner.'

Anita grimaced inwardly at the mention of the daughter-in-law who tried her patience above all others.

'Nathan, I would never want to hurt you. But I chose to attend my regular knitting club meeting that night; it had nothing to do with Georgia and certainly was no criticism of Rhea.' Anita caught sight of herself in the mirror, wagged her finger at her reflection. Okay, it had been a little criticism of Rhea. A tiny one.

'Well, at any rate, I've discussed this situation with David and Benjamin' – Anita smiled at the mention of Ben, the most easygoing of all her sons; she couldn't imagine him actually listening to Nathan's 'concerns' at all, he was too busy with his various businesses in Israel – 'and we've all agreed that you're working too hard. It was one thing right after Dad died, keeping busy and all that, but now you're completely mixed up with this single mother and her daughter to the exclusion of your own grandchildren, Mother.'

'I hardly ever see them, Nathan, except when I travel to see any of you.'

'That's just it. That's the problem. So Rhea and I have decided you should move in here with us.'

'I beg your pardon? You've just decided this, have you?'

'Not just me, Mother. David and Benjamin, too. There's no point in you staying in New York any more.'

'No point for whom? I'm just supposed to up and move to Atlanta? Become the old lady in the basement?'

'Mother. Mother, Mother, Mother.' His tone had turned placating, as though he was talking to a two year old. 'No one is trying to warehouse you. Besides, we don't even have a basement – you'll be happily ensconced in the guest house by the pool. Or you can stay in the main house, with us. We'd love to have you.'

Ensconced. Patted down and powdered and hustled out only for weddings and bar mitzvahs. She'd finally be the gray-haired old lady, just like her mother had been. Of course, whose example was Nathan following but her own? It was karma.

'I don't think so, Nathan—'

'No, Mother, I've already purchased you a train ticket for the Memorial Day weekend later this month. You'll come down, check it out, spend some time. There's even a few New Yorkers, you'll be right at home.'

Anita had had enough of her son's presumptions about her empty life and her supposed exhaustion. In truth, tonight's evening at the movies had made her feel more alive than she had felt in years. She recalled the end of their evening, when she said it was time to go home and Marty flagged a cab for her. He'd opened the door to help her inside and, as she turned towards him to say her goodbyes, Marty had hesitated. He leaned in then made a last-minute switch to cheek from lip. She'd found herself reddening at the memory.

'So, what, you've decided not to ship me off to Florida but to let me come live with you. I see. Well, I'm not ready to pack it in!' Her tone softened. 'Let's get one thing straight here, Nathan. You may be forty-nine years old but I am still your mother. And that means that I am still in charge of me. End of discussion.'

'So you won't even consider it?' She could hear the hurt in his voice, the slight whine.

Anita loved all of her sons, still marveled at how three boys raised with the same rules and the same parents could turn out to be so different in their personalities. Nathan the worrier, David the risk taker, and Benjamin, who just wanted to go his own way in the world. But there it was.

'Of course I'll come down to visit you, Nathan. I'm touched that you would buy me a ticket and I'd love to see the kids.' Anita paused. 'But next time, check in with me before you make a plan. I have more going on than you seem to realize.'

She heard the beep of call waiting, the feature her sons had insisted she install but that she'd never had cause to use.

'Nathan? I have a call coming in.'

'Just let it go to voicemail, Mother.'

'I can't use voicemail! Oh, hold on.' Beep. Beep. Beep. Which dratted button was it? She pressed this one and that until, finally, she heard a familiar voice on the end of the line.

'Anita? Are you there? It's Georgia. What's that beeping?' Anita explained her little technical problem and got some help toggling between phone lines from her good friend.

'Go back to Nathan but then call me back right away. I have to talk to you – something crazy has happened.' Georgia's voice was breathless. 'I kissed James.'

*　　*　　*

Wow. James was walking so quickly back to his apartment, he was practically running. The night air was cool but he didn't notice. His heart was racing. He'd kissed her, just reached out and pulled Georgia to him and planted one on her. And then another. It had just been so intense, like some animal pull between them. And so fantastic. God, she tasted so good. Better than he remembered. It had all happened so naturally, returning Dakota from their afternoon of bike riding. (He was finally getting the hang of all those hills in the park.) And there was Georgia, casually dressed in a pair of shorts, her legs toned and smooth, sitting on the couch – that same peach-colored 1980s sofa he'd helped her find at the Salvation Army the year Dakota was conceived – and he sat down, wanting to talk about his idea to bring the little girl out to Baltimore, but instead being distracted by those legs.

She'd noticed.

'Earth to womanizer,' Georgia said, Dakota having wandered off to change out of her sweaty clothes. 'Those legs belong to me. You know, the one you left behind.' Georgia made a face at him. 'So, James, some reason you're sitting on my couch?'

'Uh, yeah, I'd, uh, well, work is going well – we scouted out a location for a V hotel in Park Slope.'

'I wouldn't expect Brooklyn to be the logical choice.'

'It's booming out there – you should leave the island some time. All you Manhattanites, afraid you'll explode if you leave.'

'Yeah, well maybe I'll trek there when I don't have to work so hard to manage my business.' She leaned in closer. 'Hey, Dakota's off in the shower. We don't have to pretend to like each other any more. Scram.'

'But I do like you.'

'One-way street. And you're driving the wrong way. Beep beep. Get off the road.'

She fell back against the cushions. From the easy chair she picked up a long tube of pink ribbon on bendy needles, knitted into the smallest of stitches. Georgia began knitting again, paying close attention to her stitches, not looking at him.

He was on the verge of overstaying his welcome but he didn't move to go.

'So what's that you've got there?'

'A gown for Cat Phillips.' She didn't look up. 'This is me, on a deadline, working hard. You can let yourself out – the door will lock behind you. I need to get this done for Cat.'

Cat. Yes, she was a piece of work. Had called him a few days after the party, asking to get together. He'd met her out of politeness, even though he no longer dallied with married ladies. She was pretty, in a much studied kind of way, her hair, make-up and clothes only the most fashionable shade and style. Georgia, though, she could have been the original Breck girl. If the Breck girl had had a wild mane of curls, of course, corkscrewing off her head in all directions. And a laugh that made you want to be in on the fun.

He'd assumed, of course, that Cat was going to make him an offer. *That* kind of offer. But it never happened; the only item on her agenda had been to talk about Georgia. How had they met? Why weren't they married? How long had Georgia had her shop? It had been strange, being asked so many questions, when he had very few answers himself. Uncomfortable, he'd made excuses and left, wondering, as he so often did these days, just why he wasn't with Georgia, anyway.

And tonight she'd just been there, pushing back at his attitude, unfazed.

Then she'd knocked over that box holding the shiny, silky pink yarn, all over the floor and they'd both bent down, scooping it up, Georgia exclaiming that it was worth an absolute fortune. That's when he'd kissed her. Good and properly.

*   *   *

She was practically hopping around the kitchen, anxious for Anita to call her back. Why did Nathan have to talk so long?

Georgia couldn't believe it. She had grabbed James and kissed him. God only knew what had got in to her. Maybe it was the decade of celibacy that made her lose all sense of reason.

This is the type of thing that happened when she let him return Dakota to the apartment, instead of meeting at the shop. It had all seemed so natural, so like the old days that she'd momentarily forgotten herself. She was even dressed in an old pair of shorts that pre-dated Dakota. He'd come in looking so fit, still perspiring a bit from racing bikes with Dakota, toned but a little softer than he used to be around the middle.

'Go have a shower,' she told Dakota, who bounced off to clean up. She could see that James was looking at her and it made her feel powerful.

Georgia said something that she hoped was sassy. That would make him realize she was off-limits.

Then James had sat on the sofa – the one he'd helped schlep over from the Salvation Army, by the way – and started yakking away about his latest work project. Still staring at her, though. She'd taken up her knitting, trying to look busy, avoiding his gaze. But it felt so surreal, sitting on furniture that had once been *theirs*.

She caught his eye as they both remembered, in the same instant, the nights they'd made love on this very couch. He leaned forward, as if to kiss her, and she'd jerked her leg, panicked, knocking over the box holding all of the luxurious, astronomically priced silk yarns she was using for Cat's powder-puff gown. James had leapt onto the floor, right away, helping collect everything. And she saw *him*, the old James, right there in front of her.

That's when she kissed him. Again and again. Until she

heard the bathroom door creak and she froze, telling him with a look that it was time to go.

Now, standing in the kitchen, Georgia Walker wrapped her arms around herself in a big hug, unable to stifle a giggle. She couldn't wait to tell Anita.

12

Puffing a bit as she reached the top of the stairs, Anita stopped to catch her breath. Maybe Nathan was right – she was getting a bit old. Since when had a flight of stairs been so daunting? For once, she wished she'd picked up one of those crazy neon sports drinks from Marty's instead of her usual coffee. Thinking of him, she tried to stifle a silly grin rolling across her face; trying to get her breath under control and stop smiling at the same time only led her to lapse into a terrible coughing fit.

She was so loud that she drew Peri to the doorway. 'Anita, are you okay?' said the tall young woman, reaching out to pull her inside. 'Gosh, you sound awful. Here, I'll take the drink; you go sit down in the office.' Georgia looked over from where she was stocking yarns, worry all over her face. She knew Anita well enough not to make a huge fuss; still, she was watching the older woman's every move.

'I'm' – breath – 'fine,' Anita insisted, a wave of her hand as if to swat them all away. 'Quit fussing.' She let Peri take her to the back office, though, if only to avoid the prying eyes of all the customers. That was something that had been lost with her generation, it was true – the fine art of minding one's own business. Okay, okay, a sip of water. Why did everyone seem to think water cured everything? All it did was wet the throat. Still, she took the glass, nodded a thank you to Peri, leaned back into her seat with relief when Peri left the office.

Goodness. So she wasn't in tip-top shape any more. Well, what of it? She'd kept her figure all these years; she deserved to take it easy. Good thing Marty wasn't taking her to the movies again – another tub of popcorn she didn't need. No, they were going to see the ballet. A surprising choice, really; she suspected Marty was trying to impress her. But if she wanted to be going out with a minister of cultural affairs, she would be. There was something so solid about Marty. He was just the guy to have on your side. And the way he always looked out for Georgia. It was something special to see.

There was no forgetting Stan, but you know what? There didn't need to be. Marty was his own man. Which was more than okay with her. Okay, just a few more minutes and she'd go back out to the shop, let Georgia have a turn to put her feet up.

'Anita?' She opened her eyes to see Peri's pretty brown eyes looking at her.

'I'm okay, dear.'

'I know – I just, well, wanted to ask you a question.'

Anita gave Peri her full attention.

'I've been wondering a lot about Dakota's father, James. He's got this whole European chic thing going on and I—' Anita cut her off before Peri got carried away in possibilities.

'Don't even go there, dear. It's a situation filled with emotional landmines and I don't think you're old enough to have developed the right armor.' She wagged a finger. 'Besides, I wouldn't date the boss's ex, no matter how many years have gone by. It's not smart politics.'

Peri sighed. 'It's impossible to meet anyone in the city. And I work with a bunch of women . . .' Her voice trailed off.

'Smart women, and don't you forget that.' Anita straightened her jacket, which had become twisted when she sat down. 'Don't worry, Peri, we'll get the blind date network in action when it's time. Until then, enjoy your youth.'

'But that's just it. I'm not enjoying myself. I go out with my friends for drinks, dinners, clubbing. It doesn't make me less lonely.'

'Well, that, my dear, isn't about finding a man. It's about getting to know yourself.' Anita patted Peri's cheek. 'You know, my generation had that all backwards – we married young, and then we were left on our own too soon. Nearly every girl in my class is a widow now. So either we ran to Florida to play mahjong with all the same people we already knew, or we toughed it out.' She continued. 'But I was lucky. I had a teacher to show me the way.'

'Who?'

'Georgia, my dear, Georgia. Now there is a woman who had to learn to know herself – and she embraces her life even when it's hard.'

'Yeah. Georgia's got it all together – she's one of the juggling-it-all supermoms.'

Anita let out a whoop of laughter. 'Oh, Peri, you've got it so wrong. Georgia is filled with exactly the same kinds of conflicting emotions and insecurities we all are. You. Me,' said Anita. 'The thing is, she loves herself in spite of that.'

Standing on the top of the ladder, Georgia could see the top yarn bin was filled to the back, far beyond what any customer under 7 feet tall could reach. She really had to come up with a better storage system because this one wasn't quite selling the merchandise.

A throat cleared.

'Hi.' Oh God. That voice. Then louder.

'Georgia. Hi. Umm, hi.' Georgia looked down the length of her body. There, just under the ladder, stood James. Staring up at her.

'Hi.' She felt her face grow hot, the thought of kissing him the Sunday before running on instant replay in her mind. Wanting to jump off the ladder and make out all over again.

'Just passing through the neighborhood on the way back from work and thought I'd stop by. To, you know, visit. Say hi.' James raised a hand in greeting. 'Hi.'

Dammit it all to hell, he thought to himself. He hadn't sucked this much at talking to a girl since asking Ellen Farris to the junior prom. Pull it together, James. Be casual. He put his hand out to one of the yarn bins, expecting to lean his weight onto the wooden shelf and awe Georgia with his masculine cool. The shelf, however, had other ideas, not accustomed to supporting more than a few pounds of wool, and rapidly collapsed on its brackets.

Georgia watched, as if in slow motion, James's body resting on the shelf for a nanosecond, then the piece of wood falling to the floor, as chunky heathered yarns in gray and camel rained all around.

'Oh, shit!' James was flustered, trying to catch the wool falling to his feet. It was good to see him a little frazzled. 'I'm sorry, Georgia, I didn't know, I . . . dammit.'

She took her own time climbing off the ladder, then reached out to take the skein he was holding in his hands, the occasional ball of yarn still sliding out of the bin.

'Hi, James,' she said, smiling. 'I was just thinking about reorganizing.'

'Yeah, well, I guess I helped you along with that. Sorry.'

Georgia stared at James for just a moment too long; she could see he was regaining his composure just as she was melting a little bit too much.

'Dakota's not here right now, she's out at a friend's.'

'I didn't come by to see Dakota – at least, not just Dakota.'

'Did you want to take up knitting?'

'No.'

'So . . .'

'I was just wondering if, maybe, you'd like to join Dakota and me on Sunday – you know, my previously scheduled appointment?'

'I know. I was the one who approved it.' Georgia noticed she was twisting the loose end of the skein, and promptly put the thick yarn in a bin to her right. With the sparkle ribbon. Ack, she had a tough policy on mixing up the materials – just ask Peri. She turned, abruptly, hiding the misfiled yarn with her back. As if James would notice.

He took her sudden movement as his cue to move a little closer.

'So what do you say? A visit up to Hyde Park?' His lips were getting nearer.

'Okey-dokey, Dakota will love it!' She took a step sideways, conscious of Anita and Peri and some pokey old customers debating about the merits of machine-washable toddler knits. Why couldn't she just pull out some kind of suave response, act as though men were flooding the store to ask her out every day?

Georgia checked her wristwatch.

'See you Sunday then – I've got to get this cleaned up before the club meeting. Bye!' And she turned around and began pretending to check inventory. 'Thanks for coming by, James. I'll just get back to work.' She could feel Anita's eyes watching her, so she purposely didn't turn round, preoccupied with replacing the shelf and putting the materials in their rightful place.

So Sunday it would be – a day together, just the three of them. It was only when the job was almost done that it hit her: a person didn't return home to the Upper East Side from a building site in Park Slope, Brooklyn, via the West Side.

James must have made a special trip.

Just to see her.

Women were streaming in for club – the soap actress was here for the first time, as were a couple of Barnard girls, part of the college brigade of knitters sweeping the nation – and Georgia was delighted to see them all. The regulars were all there, of course, K.C. and Lucie and Darwin. Georgia had expected Peri to dash out as soon as her work day was done; she didn't have class and it was a Friday; she rarely stayed for the meeting. But tonight she strolled over to the table, sat down next to Georgia.

'So how are things with James?'

She was taken aback, quite frankly, to have such a personal question from her employee. A dear employee, absolutely, but not someone with whom she'd swap confidences. She had listened to Peri many times; the sharing hadn't been reciprocal.

'Fine, thank you, Peri, everything is fine.' Georgia's tone made it clear: No more snooping. She changed topics. 'It's nice to see you staying here tonight.'

'Oh, I made a deal with K.C.: I'm going to tutor her for the LSAT in exchange for a lunch date with her cousin Jane, who's a buyer for Bloomie's.'

Georgia looked over at her old publishing friend, who was pulling a copy of *Ace Your Way into Law School* out of a worn leather briefcase. K.C. caught Georgia's eye, gave her the thumbs-up from across the room, then cupped her hands around her mouth as if she was yelling all the way down a football field.

'I've given up bad knitting for a more noble pursuit,' she hollered, as the drop-in knitters swiveled, surprised to hear such a noise coming out of a woman so short.

'Can people just come here and not knit?' asked one of

the college students, a tone of mild outrage in her voice. Oh, to be young and expect everything to be just so!

'Who woulda thunk it?' replied Georgia, with a wink. She caught the girl's look of consternation. 'No, everyone has to knit when they're here. I promise you. But not every person has to use yarn.'

13

The office at the back of the shop was transformed: tubes of lipstick, bottles of hairspray, and containers of powder and blush lay on the piles of paper covering Georgia's desk; the loveseat was even cleared off – miracle of miracles – save for the green and gold afghan tossed just so over the back, a video camera set on a tripod to one side. Anita perched precariously on the armrest, her back to Lucie.

'I have one word for you, Anita-pie,' said Lucie, standing behind the older woman, hairbrush in hand. 'Layers.'

Anita's hand rushed to pat her smooth silver bob, which fell to a sharp edge an inch below her chin.

'Oh, certainly not. I've worn my hair this way for years. It's who I am.'

'Well, it's smooth. It's shiny. It's exactly how I'd expect someone as polished as you are to look. But you know? I think it's time you went a little . . . more adventurous.'

Dakota, sitting cross-legged in Georgia's desk chair, perked up.

'A girl in my class dyed her hair with Kool-Aid. It's, like, totally orange.'

Anita shared a look with Lucie.

'I don't think Lucie has orange hair in mind for me, darling.'

'No,' agreed Dakota. 'But if you do it, then Mom might let me Kool-Aid my hair, too.'

Anita wagged a finger, but didn't say a word. She was busy concentrating on her lines. After much discussion, she, Georgia, and Lucie had finally come up with a game plan to go ahead with the knitting videos. They would simply run film at some of the club meetings, then later edit it and cut in separate, personal interviews with the knitters, followed by detailed images showing how to cast on, knit, purl and so on. In this way, the show would be so much more than a simple how-to video – it would capture the essence of the shop and of the pure fun of knitting together. A knitting club that anyone can join from the comfort of their own home, suggested Lucie; Georgia had been uncharacteristically enthusiastic – when she thought she was going to be mostly doing off-screen narration. When she learned just how much time on camera was required, she nearly put the kibosh on the whole thing. But Dakota, who had already been enlisted as the boom mic operator, let out the words that guaranteed all things were possible: 'This is way cooler than anything I've done with Dad!' And so the project was underway.

Right now Anita was getting ready for her close-up – she'd had a manicure that morning – and had taken care to wear a soft angora cardigan in a light sky blue that she'd knitted years ago, on tiny needles to keep the stitches delicate.

Lucie bent down so her mouth was very close to Anita's left ear. She spoke oh so quietly to keep Dakota from hearing. 'I guarantee a new "do" will take off five years.' Lucie clucked her tongue. 'Chop chop.'

'So when people see me on the street they'd say more than, "There goes a sixty-five-year-old senior?"' Anita didn't let on that she was really 72.

'No, they'll say "Who's that sassy lady? She looks awesome for *sixty*,"' Lucie whispered. 'Maybe even fifty-nine.'

Just then Georgia popped her head in. 'Dakota, your dad is here to take you for a bike ride,' she told her daughter, who had gone back to reading *Seventeen* at the desk. 'And how's the film crew?'

'We're taking a break,' answered Anita. 'I'm going out for a haircut.'

Lucie packed up the mess and put the camera aside for another day. Too bad; she was looking forward to having an excuse to keep herself busy. She hadn't told anyone about the baby, not even Will, who occasionally dropped her an email and wanted to get together. Wouldn't he get an eyeful? She let him down gently, explaining there was someone else in her life. She didn't say the 'someone else' was a baby. His baby. But she didn't think of it that way. Lucie thought of this baby as all hers.

And then there was Rosie, who was threatening to actually do what she hated most and make a trek into the city. No, she couldn't wait too much longer, not really. She was coming up to 18 weeks along; the baby was due in late October.

By Christmas, she'd be a mom of an infant.

The TV producer left the office door open and walked the few steps into the main part of the store, surprised to see Peri handing Darwin one of the shop's distinctive lavender-handled paper bags, the words 'Walker and Daughter' emblazoned on one side; you could certainly see Dakota's hand in that choice. More surprising, however, was seeing Darwin with such a bag, overflowing with chunky orange and fuchsia and lime-green yarns – a jarring combination, was she going to try and use them together? – and a new pair of size 15 needles, still in their plastic wrapper, poking out of the top.

Peri and Lucie exchanged a glance; Lucie winked at Darwin, who shrugged.

A wave to Georgia, who was off to one side helping a client assess her gauge and convincing her to go up a needle size, and then Darwin and Lucie fell in line with each other, down the steps and onto the street. They began to amble together in silence, heading uptown on Broadway, but without any announced destination.

'Well, we'll have to take a look at what you picked out there,' said Lucie. Darwin nodded, a little shy.

It was funny, thought Luice, how you could go from really not caring about a person to suddenly looking forward to seeing them. When you gave them a chance. She hated when such schoolyard wisdom had some basis. And she'd been surprised, the last few club meetings, to find herself scanning the room upon arrival for her new . . . what? . . . secret-keeper? What was Darwin to her, anyway? They didn't know each other all that well. Still. It felt good to walk uptown, the bright sun just hinting at the hot summer to come, passing all the Saturday shoppers poking in and out of the boutiques and restaurants, someone to talk to as she sauntered along.

'I have something for you, by the way. I picked it up earlier and was going to save it until the next club.' Darwin pulled a small packet out of her pocket and pressed it into Lucie's hand a little too roughly, commenting dryly: 'Ancient Chinese medicine.'

'What is it?' asked Lucie, finally accepting. Friend. She had really made a new, true friend in Darwin.

'Candied ginger. It settles the stomach and it's good for, you know.' Darwin made a rounding movement in front of her abdomen.

'We're out of the shop so I guess we can say it out loud,' Lucie giggled. 'I'm having a baby!' A feeling of elation came over her; she realized that was the first time she'd said the magical words out loud to anyone but her caregivers at Planned Parenthood. Even though she knew Darwin knew already, it felt fantastic just to say it. Before, when she turned 40 and no man in sight, knowing she couldn't afford the clinic donor thing, she had tucked away her hopes in that regard. And now that she'd found a way . . . she was blooming with excitement. A little shocked, sometimes, at what she'd done. But happy overall.

'Yes, you're having a baby!' Darwin repeated, grinning, looking genuinely thrilled for Lucie.

'All the tests have been really great so far, it's all good.' Lucie was overflowing now, caught in the joy of sharing her news. 'I just have to take it easy a bit, older pregnancy and all that, and things should be just fine.'

'Well, put your feet up when you get home and pop a ginger candy in your mouth. It's soothing,' said Darwin.

'Is this really a Chinese thing you learned from your mom or something?'

Darwin laughed. 'God, no, Lucie. I read about it in *Natural Health* magazine.' She shook her head. 'I think maybe the hormones are addling your brain. You may not have noticed, but I kind of skipped out on good-Chinese-girl classes? So no traditional remedies from me. I also avoided the all-American-sweetheart lessons, so don't ever expect me to toss the old pigskin or make you an apple pie.'

Lucie laughed. 'I'm kinda failing obedient daughter myself.'

'I'll drink to that! Here's a Starbucks – let's go get you a milk and me a venti caffeine infusion.'

'Hear hear!' agreed Lucie.

Darwin steered the pregnant woman through the doorway. 'I also need a favor – I still have to work on tying a damn slip knot onto a needle,' said Darwin. She paused for a moment to give their order to the barista. 'This knitting thing is all in the name of research. I want you to know that.'

'Of course it is! I don't think you'd knit unless you were under duress.'

'I just want to be clear. I'm not going to like it.'

'Right. Hey, can you get me one of those muffins, too.'

Darwin ordered two fat-free blueberry treats as Lucie,

hovering over two teenagers slowly making their way to leave, rushed in and sat down at the only free table in the place. A man who had also been fishing for a table gave her a scowl.

'Sorry,' she mouthed. 'Baby on board.' He raised his hands, palms open, as if to say, 'No problem.' Aha, thought Lucie, this baby thing might just change everything. It might not get her a seat on the subway – nothing got you a seat on the train in this town – but it might just let her get a chair in the coffee shop.

'I doubt these will be as good as those cookies of Dakota's but here you go.' Darwin handed over the goodie and the milk.

'Let me guess – that just cost you something around ten bucks. My treat next time.'

'I know! Living on the East Coast is astronomical. When I moved from Seattle I couldn't get over the price of food. Food!'

'It's crazy, I know. So, speaking of food . . . and other things that cause your waistline to swell, I need to get some new clothes.'

'Yes, you're kinda popping out of those ones.'

'Darwin, you're not supposed to agree. You should tell me I'm glowing.' In a way, Lucie enjoyed her new friend's candor even as she felt chagrined. She didn't look that bad, she thought, even though she'd taken to wearing an oversized old sweater that Will had left lying around before she'd ended their relationship. She wore it pretty much all the time: it was one of the few things that still fitted. 'It's just a little tight,' said Lucie.

Darwin nodded, making an elaborate show of keeping her mouth shut. 'Hmmmm hmmm hmmm,' she said, her lips pressed together. Lucie made as if to swat her head.

'Point taken, Professor.' Lucie smiled. 'So I need someone to give me a second opinion while shopping, since clearly the Annie Hall dressing in men's clothing didn't quite work the way it was supposed to.'

'I don't think Annie Hall was known for wearing gigantic sweaters with the too-long sleeves flipped back – but at least you were trying to make a statement,' said Darwin. 'I had no idea what you were going for.'

'So says Ms Fashion Police?'

'I'm about the mind, not the body,' insisted Darwin. 'Not ironing my clothes is my way of flipping off the patriarchy. I am not bound by rules.'

'And it's clearly working,' said Lucie, rolling her eyes. 'Are you coming with me or what? I have to go tomorrow before another week of work or I'm going to bust out of this skirt. As it is, it's pulled up to my boobs because my waist has expanded too much.'

'Well, I'm totally behind on my research and I have to master this damn slipknot thing.' Darwin saw a look of disappointment flicker on Lucie's face. 'In other words, count me in. Want to meet at Filene's Basement in Chelsea tomorrow morning?'

Lucie's face broke out into a wide smile. 'I'll be there.'

Welcome home to Jersey, thought Darwin, walking the two steps from the front door to her living room, tossing her keys onto the Formica counter in the galley kitchen, catching sight of the calendar and its pictures of tulips. April. She hadn't changed it since, well, that night. That night with Elon. She gave a shudder, fished her cell phone out of her backpack to call Dan.

'Hi, this is Dan, I'm either asleep or at the hospital, so leave me a message!' Typical. He was becoming impossible to reach. They talked every few days, but it was always rushed, Dan exhausted, Darwin insisting nothing was wrong in response to his exasperated concern. She felt as though, somehow, he suspected – even though there was simply no way he could know.

Flopping onto the faded mocha suede couch, the one they'd bought for $150 from the old lady moving out next door, she pushed aside a pile of laundry. At first, she had washed everything – all the sheets, all the towels, the ones that had been used, that Elon had touched, and then all the ones that had been resting in the linen cupboard. She washed and rewashed the offending jeans and panties and socks from that night, then did load after load from each dresser drawer until everything that could withstand water had been cleaned. The kitchen counters had been bleached, the floors scrubbed until the worn linoleum gleamed, the toilet turned blue with some tablet that promised months of disinfecting.

She douched.

The piles of clean clothes had lain, nicely folded, waiting to be put away or pressed. But Darwin had walked in the door of her compact apartment one day and, not really glancing at the work to be done, just sat down. In the dark. And cried. She hadn't done a speck of laundry since then, she hadn't ironed, hadn't put the clothes away, she hadn't cooked, she hadn't slept. Not in the bed, anyway. An elbow rested now on a pile of shirts that, if not exactly dirty, had probably been worn. Some of them. Maybe. She couldn't keep track. Most mornings now she just pulled out some sort of top from one of the many piles, gave it a shake, and left for class, her bottom half clad in jeans.

The only thing she could keep up with was the recycling – all the empty take-out boxes had to go. That much Darwin could keep straight. Because if she didn't do even that, then the formerly fastidious, iron-loving professor-to-be would be living with cockroaches.

And even she didn't deserve that, did she?

*   *   *

Her right index finger was already turning red and sore; she'd been casting on for hours and it was damn near impossible to get beyond that first row. How did Lucie and all those guys knit so quickly? She could barely pull the stitches off the left needle to get them onto the right.

'Aaaah!' Her size 15 needles went flying through the air, along with shirts and socks and dishtowels. And the ball of fuchsia yarn, tangling its way around the legs of the coffee table and the lamp.

'Fuck it all, fuck it, fuck fuck fucking stupid fucker,' she was crying now, her butt on the floor, laundry – clean, dirty, somewhere in between – blanketing the room as if someone had set off a bomb.

So this was it. You take a wrong step and you end up wearing yesterday's underwear, sitting on the carpet, trying to teach yourself how to knit. And even that doesn't work. She never expected it to be so hard. Life.

Her bags had been packed, her mind made up, and she floated across the country after college knowing that, finally, she was coming into her own. Going to celebrate women, elevate her peers, make a difference, kick all the old ideas in the ass. ('Be a feminist or whatever you call it, Darwin,' her mother had said the day she left for grad school. 'But just don't look like a dog's breakfast doing it.' Her mom was sad to part but also relieved: her parents thought she was Dan's problem now.)

He'd never been anything but supportive, though he didn't seem to think there was any pressing need for feminism any more. 'Everything's pretty equal now,' he said. 'Though I still wouldn't mind if you burned your bras.' Only equal, she pointed out, if all the men were just like him.

But now there was another thing, an idea just tickling the back of her mind. In all her planning and defiance, all her rejection of her parents' requests and values, all her talk of live and let live, she hadn't factored in one thing: she still believed in right and wrong.

Oh, yes, yes, she always had more than enough to say about how companies, societies, men and women should behave regarding each other. (If two people of the same caliber are up for a job, she would say, but one is male and the other female, the best choice for the society is to place the female in the job, thereby moving in the direction of correcting decades of inequality.)

But, at the same time, she'd also believed in this moral gray area, about sexuality and personal life choices and the importance of doing what felt instinctual.

And that belief, she realized with a clarity she had been missing for the past month, was naïve.

Right or wrong wasn't about being straight or gay or liking sex one way versus another. It was about disrespecting her integrity as a person. As an individual who had made a promise. A marriage vow. ('I still don't know if I believe in marriage,' she told Dan the night of their wedding, tangled in sheets on their air mattress, the only piece of furniture they owned at the time. 'I wouldn't expect anything else from you, wifey,' he'd said, teasing her. 'I know you'll always keep me on my toes.')

She'd spent so much time focused on the fear of contracting a disease from Elon – he'd said nothing to her to indicate such was possible – that she'd neglected to look at the situation from any other angle. It didn't matter whether she believed in it or not. Because she *was* in it. Being married wasn't just about who played Suzie Homemaker. It wasn't, really, in a good marriage, about that at all.

Running a relay race to cross the finish line healthy, happy, and whole. It was about being one half of a team.

And Darwin had basically placed a bet against hers.

Who knew what was going to happen now? It was impossible, really, to imagine a life without Dan. She'd spent so long fighting domestic expectations that she hadn't focused, very much, on the relationship itself. She'd gotten tangled up in the peripheral stuff. Focused more on being on the other side of the country than on being closer to Dan than anyone else on the planet. And now she might have to pay the price.

Hours later, she pulled herself off the floor, having cried herself to sleep, fumbled for the phone. If only she had Lucie's number! Instead, she looked at the lavender bag on the coffee table, the shop's info printed right there. It was only 7.30, it would still be open. She dialed. Heard the familiar voice announce 'Walker and Daughter.'

'Is Peri there?'

'Sorry, she's gone for the day, but is there something I can help you with?'

'Georgia? It's Darwin.' She waited for the sigh, the sound of exasperation when Georgia realized it was her. Instead, there was simply silence; she couldn't tell if the lack of sound indicated anger or disinterest. So she kept quiet, too, hesitating.

'Darwin?' Georgia's voice had just a hint of concern. 'Are you okay?'

'I'm, uh, Peri said I could call,' Darwin paused, her mind racing. She'd had some vague notion about trying to talk to Peri about the night with Elon. And now she wasn't even there. Georgia, though, was going to think she was nuts. She cleared her throat. 'I thought I'd try this casting-on thing and I'm having trouble.'

'Well, I can talk you through it. I bet you're pulling the yarn too tight, it's a common thing that beginners do. Are you having trouble getting the needle through the yarn? Uh-huh? Okay, let's start from the beginning, one needle in your left, one in your right . . .' Georgia began to walk her through the process, going all the way back to the slip knot. Darwin could do that part, of course; now she stopped working her hands as she listened to Georgia talk about the craft she loved. It was relaxing to hear her voice, a grown-up version of a bedtime story.

'There's lots of skill to knitting, certainly, but if you ask me, a lot of it is all about the muscle memory,' said Georgia. 'One day you'll just find your fingers making the moves and your brain will go to this deliciously soothing place, and all the knots in your brain will unwind just as your fingers make knot after knot after knot in the yarn.'

'Oh, I'm not trying to do that. This is all in the name of research, you know.'

'We know, Darwin, we know. Still, I'm surprised you're at home on a Saturday night trying to knit. You're young – why aren't you off trying to meet a special someone?'

'I'm married.' A rush of guilt over Elon.

'I had no idea! Darwin, you hardly ever say anything but how knitting is going to send us back to being barefoot and pregnant.' Laughter.

'Well, Dan's in LA now,' said Darwin. She kept her tone light. 'It's a temporary thing. He's doing his residency. And you know, the commuting marriage is very trendy right now. And I'm nothing if not trendy.'

More laughter from Georgia.

'You are just one surprise after another, Darwin,' she said. 'You should bring this fella of yours into the shop sometime.'

'I'd like that,' said Darwin. And she meant it. She'd really like to have Dan back in town. She'd enjoy introducing him to all the friends she'd made. He'd never believe it. Well, no, Dan *would* believe it. He'd always been his wife's biggest champion. It was Darwin who was surprised by being a part of the club.

And so the two women picked up the threads for a conversation, weaving a bit about Darwin's studies, Georgia's plans for the video with Lucie, some banter back and forth about Dakota's upcoming school project on the suffragettes.

And then goodbyes, a welcome but unfamiliar feeling of good will about each other lingering after the click of the dial tone, the store owner musing about the scholar's request for one of Dakota's recipes – it was an easy one, Rice Krispie treats; Georgia knew Dakota would roll her eyes at its simplicity. Her daughter was tiring of the women asking for nibbles that reminded them of their own childhoods. Don't they see I'm trying to expand my culinary horizons, Dakota had complained. If they're not careful, I'm going to make squid tartlets. With octopus sauce. Like on *Iron Chef*.

Georgia was wearing her good suit and nursing a cup of coffee from Marty's deli as she sat, reading the *Times* at the shop's table. The store was closed on Sundays but she was there anyway. Georgia tilted her legs just so, slightly uncomfortable because her skirt was digging into her waistline. Had she put on some weight recently? It must be all of Dakota's baking, sitting out there on the kitchen counter, begging for a taster.

Through the unlocked door, Darwin strolled in, big bags and a frozen yoghurt cone in hand; Lucie was right behind, crunching away at the cookie bits surrounding her frozen treat. She was dressed in a crisp white shirt and black cotton pants, the shirt large and loose but not ill fitting like the clothes she had on the day before. She looked like a new woman.

'Looking great, Luce,' said Georgia. 'But Ms Chiu, I thought you would know that buying clothes is just another way of supporting the patriarchy.'

Darwin put her hands on her hips. 'Ha, ha, ha,' she said, drawing out every sound. 'They're Lucie's clothes, not mine.

I only wear Fair Trade clothes anyway. Nice try, Georgia
Walker.'

Lucie and Anita exchanged glances, worried that another
day's filming would be derailed if an argument erupted
between those two. But the academic simply smiled. Georgia
returned the expression. Lucie and Anita, both perplexed,
raised eyebrows at each other.

'Indeed,' murmured Anita. 'Will wonders never cease? So,
shall we set up, Lucie?'

Anita had been adamant: if they didn't start filming the
video on one of Lucie's days off, they'd have to wait until
early June. Because Anita was going to see Nathan and his
family for the long weekend and it was only a week away.

The Memorial Day weekend – the official start of summer.
Which, frankly, Georgia was dreading. Easter dinner had
been one thing. James had seemed so sweet, complimenting
her lamb, and Dakota was delighted to have the entire family
together. And then they'd had that . . . moment. The kiss.
So it hadn't seemed like such a big deal when James
suggested, last week, that they spend a day, just the three
of them, doing something fun. She'd nixed the Hyde Park
idea, not wanting to be either trapped in a car or stuck on
a train ride next to James, making small talk but thinking
about kissing him. Instead, the three of them went to the
Central Park Zoo for a couple of hours, checking out the
polar bears and the monkeys. It had been surprisingly
pleasant, letting Dakota devour a hot dog from a street
vendor, sharing a bready pretzel with mustard with James.
The spring colors were out, the flowering trees in bloom,
and it had just been such a nice day that they rambled on
over to the model boat pond, renting a remote-control toy
for Dakota to sail. Holding hands when she wasn't looking.
A typical New York Sunday for a regular city family. Which
they weren't, of course. Not even close. But it was nice.

And she had let herself fall into it, the easy feeling of being with James, of feeling looked after, of fueling herself on Dakota's laughter.

Then came the price. Time to pay up, Walker. Because James Foster, as always, had something he wanted. No, not Georgia Walker. It was never Georgia, was it? No, indeed. The minute they had returned to the apartment, James began going on about his latest and greatest idea. He wanted to take his daughter (*his* daughter? Her daughter and he'd better get that straight in his mind, thought Georgia now) to Baltimore to meet his parents. And what more perfect time than the Memorial Day weekend? Georgia had been momentarily stunned. She'd expected this request at some point but not now, not after all the kissing and flirting and general stupidness.

James hadn't changed one bit: he had been trying to butter up Georgia just to get his way. Fake her out with a little pretend romance. Just to take Dakota away from her. It would start with a weekend, then who knew where it would go?

Everything was all about him. It always was. He didn't even think about asking Georgia first. He didn't even consider asking her to come along on the trip to Baltimore.

'Absolutely,' Dakota replied to his suggestion. So there was Georgia, left to play the bad guy.

She wasn't about to send her daughter out of town with the father that had just waltzed onto the scene less than a year ago. Even if this trip was the innocent little family meeting he claimed. Could she trust him to look after Dakota? After all, her little girl may have been a city kid but an annual trip to Pennsylvania does not make someone a seasoned traveler. What if they got separated and Dakota found herself lost in Baltimore?

And, God forbid, what if he just never brought her back?

'I don't think so, James,' said Georgia, her mouth a thin line. 'It's not going to happen.'

And Dakota had raced out of the room, slamming the door to her bedroom, her jagged sobs easy to hear through the thin walls. 'I hate you, Mommy, I hate you.'

14

Surely there comes a day when you're just resigned to it, thought Cat. When the negativity becomes so rote that you don't even notice it. But that moment kept eluding her, and she felt bruised by every cruel comment her husband doled out. By the lack of attention. By the overwhelming sensation of hate that left her imagining endless horrible deaths for him.

She should have left long ago, back when she'd still had a chance – at a career, another marriage, kids. Thirty-seven might not seem old if your life was your own, but Cat had signed hers away years ago. She was almost 30 when she clued in that her parents' admonitions that she couldn't just run home – their response to her crying phone calls in the early months of her marriage – was simply a long-married couple's reaction to the seemingly overwrought hysterics of a young girl, settled down before she'd fully grown up. If they'd truly known the verbal abuse and emotional rejection she received from Adam – from the entire Phillips family – she came to believe that they would have helped her, would have welcomed her back, encouraged her to pursue that Ph.D. in art history. But by that point she couldn't ask them, having buried them following a fatal collision with a drunk driver. And, well, Cat was well looked after, wasn't she? Didn't have any need of money. Or so they must have assumed, she having long since stopped complaining about Adam. Their will had given all their assets over to her siblings, left her some good pieces of furniture and her mother's engagement ring. Nothing she could use to steal away in the middle of the night and begin anew.

Instead, she absorbed a powerful lesson: she was all alone. Support was fleeting, at the convenience of the giver. There was no one to turn to and nowhere to go, unless she was willing to make a stand and find her own way in the world.

She'd tried to tell herself that she could suffer all the little indignities – his one-night stands, the emotional affairs, the relationships (Adam being a man who required a harem to service his ego and other, substantially smaller, parts of his anatomy) for the good silver and the unlimited charge card at Bergdorf's. Now she wasn't so sure. Home didn't exist any more, her siblings had their own lives, she had no skills, and a strong belief that Adam would wring her out in court if she tried to get her share of his money.

So who could believe it? That day at the dermatologist, the snappy article about some yarn shop and the quirky single mom who started it from nothing. The name jumping out at her, an echo she could barely hear, from a world she had long since given up as a dream. When she was herself.

Yet there it was. What had she expected? To find Georgia Walker waiting for her all this time, arms outstretched, remembering all the serious conversations and double dates and laughter? To find Georgia Walker still ready to fight her battles, to give her a hug, to back her up against all comers?

She knew that's what she had wanted. But to be confronted with Georgia's beautiful life, the darling little girl, the store filled with women (and a few men!) happy to be there, sharing a love of a craft. It had been agony. There had never been any doubt about Georgia. No, never any doubt about her. She was always the one who put her head down and got the job done. Cathy had been the dilettante, clever but never directed. She should have known she'd never get anywhere without Georgia.

*   *   *

Maybe if she'd been a famous knitwear designer *already*, Georgia thought, she'd have some sort of company that delivered her gowns for her. As it was, she offered six-for-the-price-of-one: designer, pattern-maker, knitter, seamstress, steamer, and messenger girl. Though at a very handsome price, indeed.

She sat in the front seat of the taxi, in between the driver's clipboard, water bottle, and newspaper to read during heavy traffic, glancing every other second at the two garment bags laid one atop the other in the back seat. The first, she knew, imagining the feel of the scrumptious golden material, a cashmere blend shot through with glittery threads to give it the shine and sensation of gold. The gown itself was a rather delicate affair, fitted repeatedly on Cat's slender frame, to hug every curve and shimmy over her body as she walked. The bodice was a low V, all the way down to the middle of Cat's abdomen (already toned but Georgia knew she'd been hitting the gym harder than usual), the two sections over the bust pulled together by only three skinny knitted bands. ('All the better to see your favorite assets,' Georgia told her, motioning to her bust line. Cat had loved it.) The sleeveless top was all garter, but the stitches were unbelievably fine – she was certain to need glasses after this job! – and the piece continued its tight descent down the body to the skirt, a separate section, all seed stitch to give it the texture of crushed taffeta, the glitter in the wool reminiscent of that ubiquitous party material. Only this version was more sophisticated and, thankfully, quieter. More slink than rustle. It blossomed just above the hip, making Cat's derrière look a bit more rounded, her waist even tinier, before falling softly to the floor, with just enough folding to maintain the feeling of fullness without verging into plumpness. It was an outfit to keep anyone guessing – eye-popping on the top, all softness below. Georgia named all of her unique creations, secretly talked to them as she worked the stitches. The golden dress she called Phoenix. It was her triumph.

And then her old friend had come up with a need for a second outfit! Georgia had outdone herself, completing it in just over four weeks versus the six weeks of intense labor it took to do the first one. The style and shape of the next dress – what she called Powder Puff in her mind – was Cat's homage to Audrey Hepburn. The material was made of raw silk fiber, which had certainly made it more of a challenge to knit, but it resulted in an exquisitely delicate creation. With a mandarin collar that revealed just the right hint of collarbone, and a cap sleeve that showed off Cat's toned arms, the dress nipped in at the waist before racing straight to the floor, the soft pink inter-rupted only by the flash of thigh, thanks to the slit in the skirt that was cut all the way up to the hip. The style hinted at demure but the wearer, who demanded the slit be ever higher, was anything but. It, too, was a showstopper, paired with dangling earrings that Cat had received from Adam the previous Christmas. ('Oh, these,' she had said. 'They're real diamonds – I had them appraised after he gave them to me. He must be in love with his latest paramour; usually, I just get a watch.')

Ten minutes late. Damn! Georgia hated to be delayed. The cab screeched off Broadway, began navigating the smaller streets – Mercer, then Prince, then Greene – before stopping at the entrance of Cat's building. Georgia rushed out, care-fully gathering Cat's dresses, and rode the elevator, the one that opened right up into the loft, for what she figured would be the last time. No more Wednesday afternoon meetings, no more fittings, redesigns, scrambling to get enough luxury yarn for the project. She felt a little ooky. A kind of twinge she couldn't quite put her finger on. A sprinkling of anxiety. She was always sad to say goodbye to her creations, to Phoenix and Powder Puff, just like all the baby blankets and sweaters that had gone before them. The doors opened up and there was Cat, dressed casually in overpriced jeans and a boat-necked cream shell, a fine-gauge cotton cardigan wrapped preppie-style around her shoulders, a pair of shiny new cowboy boots gleaming on her feet. Her hair, typically blown out smoothly, was instead moussed and teased to make whatever wave was naturally in there come alive. She looked like an upscale version of Georgia. Cat stood there, grinning, motioning the knitter to come in.

'Hey! Notice anything different?' said Cat, smiling wider. Two months ago, Georgia would have been so completely offended. Would have presumed parody, instead of flattery. But now she could see what had been obscured by the mascara and that attitude. The glimmer of a girl she once knew. Funny. Exuberant. Playful.

Georgia felt that little something boogying around her stomach. Yup, hard to believe, but that bad feeling probably wasn't about Powder Puff. Or Phoenix.

It was going to be sad to say goodbye to Cat.

Scanning the foyer of the museum in one quick glance, pleased she had chosen the golden gown after all, a sheer gossamer wrap in an almost translucent shade of nude dangling from her hands, Cat did a quick evaluation. She was definitively the best-looking woman in the room. One-two-three . . . contact. Every man's – and his wife's – eyes were drinking in their fill. And right on cue, Adam broke away from his little pack of buddies talking money in the corner, squared out his chest with pride and began swaggering his way over to claim her. Show the crowd she was his.

'Hi, sweetheart,' she purred.

'Well, don't you look like a million dollars, babe,' he replied, stepping to her side in preparation for putting his arm around her shoulders. The public display of ownership.

She moved away, just a bit. 'Don't muss the hair, Adam,' she cooed, giving his friend Chip a little wavy-wave as his eyes lingered. Cat didn't turn her head, continued speaking to her husband.

'I have a little something for you, Adam.'

'Will it wait 'til we get home or do I have to sneak you into the men's room?' He chuckled, that conservative white-male laugh of satisfaction.

'Oh, no, let's do it right here, darling dear.' Cat had stopped smiling. She shook her arms free of her wrap, a manila envelope underneath in her hands. 'Mr Phillips, you've just been served.'

15

Glancing at the clock, Georgia realized that she'd let Dakota stay up way too late. It was 9.30 on a Tuesday night!

'Hey, shoo,' she said to her daughter. 'I'm going to lock up here so go up to put on your jammies and I'll be home in two shakes.'

'Do you mean *pa*jamas? Jammies are for babies.'

'Put on a scuba suit for all I care, kiddo, just get up and into bed.'

She walked Dakota over to the door just as Cat – looking fantastic in the golden Phoenix dress – rustled in. Dakota, she noticed, walked right on by and up the stairs.

Cat, wild-eyed, shut the door behind her and rushed over to grab Georgia's hands.

'I did it!'

Georgia nodded, pleased to see her design in action. 'I'm glad the dress got the reaction you wanted.'

'Yeah, it was fantastic!' Cat was shouting. 'I socked it to him, right in front of his cronies and their wives, half of whom have probably slept with him anyway.'

'You what?'

'I ditched Adam. Sayonara, baby.'

'Cat?'

'Yes?'

'Why are you *here*? In my store?'

'Because I'm wiping my slate clean. I'm time traveling back to the eighties and I'm going to fix everything I did wrong.'

'Ah, Dartmouth again.'

'Yes. Dartmouth.' Cat walked over to the window. 'Georgia, when you didn't take up that place at school . . . eventually, I moved off the waitlist and was offered a real spot. And I accepted it.'

'Figured that out, Cat, but thanks for the update.' Georgia began emptying out the till. 'By the way, sweetie pie, I didn't accept the Dartmouth offer because *you* didn't get in. And we'd promised to stick together . . .' She left her voice trail off. Accusing.

'I didn't want to leave you behind!' Cat turned away from the view of the dark street, her upswept hair coming loose and falling around the top of her golden gown. Georgia's face offered no reaction.

'Okay,' Cat pleaded. 'I wanted to go to a school like that. But I didn't want to leave you behind. It's just, my parents – the guidance counselor – everyone said, "This is your big chance, Cathy," and I believed it. Then I didn't make anything of it and you, you've become this big success. I see it all so clearly now.'

'See what?'

'All that life-is-what-you-make-of-it crap! It's true.' Cat plopped down at the table, looking at Georgia across the room. 'It's true.'

Georgia pushed the register drawer closed and hesitated. Then she strode across the store and sat down across from Cat.

'I didn't have a choice. Sink or swim. I had a daughter to support.'

'That's not the whole story, Georgia Walker. You could have gone home to Bess and Tom anytime.'

'Never to leave again.'

'I used to call Bess, you know.' Cat sat back with her legs crossed, picked up the hem with her fingers and began to rub it lightly. Quit playing with Phoenix, thought Georgia; I spent a ton of hours making her fall straight. 'Georgia? Did you hear me? I used to call Bess, after I left for Dartmouth. "Hello, Mrs Walker, will you please let Georgia know I telephoned." "Mrs Walker, did Georgia get my Christmas card?" And you never replied.'

'Of course, the old "It's in the mail" excuse.' Georgia shrugged. 'I never knew; Mom didn't let on.'

'No?'

'No.'

So there it was. Cat had tried to apologize, she had tried to hold on to their friendship. All those years ago. And something more: Bess, the mother who always seemed so uninterested in Georgia, had tried to shield her from a girl she believed couldn't be trusted, who would hurt her only daughter even more. Knowing that was a gift, the closure Georgia hadn't actively been seeking but wanted nonetheless.

'Thank you, Cat, for telling me.'

'Georgia, I want us to be friends. Real friends. Like in the old days.'

The store owner regarded the glamorous blonde, careening toward a bitter divorce and an uncertain future, no doubt fearful and looking for something solid to cling to. But Georgia didn't have time to be anyone else's mommy but Dakota's. And she was all out of second chances, James having squandered what optimism she had left.

She shook her head.

'Okay, I get it,' said Cat, her voice cracking with emotion. 'I get it. You're done. You've been done for a while. Of course you are. Who would blame you? And so there's just me, right? On my own.' She began pacing around the shop as Georgia watched her with mounting concern.

'Oh my God, Georgia, I'm all alone,' whispered Cat, still

pacing. 'What's going to happen to me?' She pointed to the cover of a knitting magazine in a wall rack, started breathing fast as though she might begin hyperventilating. Georgia suspected she was having an anxiety attack.

'Okay, so, okay. It's done. What's done is done.' Cat took the magazine off the shelf, tossed it to Georgia. 'So tell me, how much would it cost to get a few things for my new Adam-free life? One of those blanket things, an Afghanistan? A tea cozy? Curtains?'

She was getting more frantic. Georgia had to admit, knitted curtains would be an intriguing choice. Granny-gone-wild decorating. She reached out a hand, gently touched an arm.

'Cat, Cat, what are you doing?'

'I don't know. I don't know!' Cat tilted her head and nibbled at her lip. Georgia saw again the willowy girl who had so often wanted her to take the lead.

'But while I'm figuring out this new life of mine, I think I might need a sweater or two or something.' Cat wasn't about to let the matter drop. 'I can still pay you – I'm selling off my jewelry.'

Cat folded her arms across her chest; her bare arms had goosebumps.

'Can I come over on Saturday before the store opens? Maybe help you come up with a pattern? I'm staying at the Lowell. It's not far. I'll just cab it.'

Georgia pursed her lips together, held them tightly closed; they made a popping sound as she eased the tension in her face. Cat stood stock still.

'Okay,' said Georgia, her voice cautious. 'Okay.'

'Mom! Mom! Are you ever going to get up?' Georgia cracked open one eyelid. She could barely believe she'd had a night's sleep since seeing Cat in the shop. Now she was surprised to find Dakota standing before her, dressed in a blue merino

V-neck that she had knitted for her the previous Christmas. Already it was just that little too tight, pulling at the bust line.

'Wow, look at you . . .' started Georgia, before catching herself. Best not to make some dumb comment about her daughter's breasts and make her self-conscious. Still. The signs were all there. Her baby was growing up; she'd be thirteen by the summer. Georgia felt a lump in her throat, sitting up in bed, sneaking a peek down the front of her pajamas at her own breasts, just that little bit less perky than they once were. She and her daughter were both getting older.

'It's almost eight o'clock! I'm completely going to be late for school – your radio has been playing for over an hour.' Dakota was not amused. 'I'd be on my way if you didn't insist on walking with me every day. I'm not a little girl. I can go on my own.'

'Hey, hey, what's with all the attitude, young lady?' Young lady. Did she just say that? Omigod, she was turning into her mother Bess, all bossy boots and dourness. She swiveled to look at the clock, disbelieving the time. 7.50 a.m. She hadn't slept through her alarm in ages, had always been a morning person, more often turning off the radio before it could flip on and padding out in her slippers to enjoy an early coffee and the paper at the kitchen table. Dakota, on the other hand, was always sleeping in, grumbling through breakfast and dawdling on the walk to school.

Should she just give in, let Dakota go to school on her own, and fall back into another hour of sweet slumber? She still had the heavy feeling of exhaustion, enticing her head back to her pillow, where she could just close her eyes and let herself drift slowly . . .

'Moooom! Are you getting up or what? I have a math test today.' Dakota's words were coming out in a rush. Georgia flipped out of bed, grabbed a pair of jeans and pulled a fleece

over her pajamas; it may be May but the morning air could
still be cool.

'I won't walk you the entire way – just to the school block
but not right to school,' explained Georgia, seeing Dakota's
look of horror at her outfit. She made a pit stop in the bathroom, a quick brush of the teeth, and a token attempt to pat
down her hair, all without looking in the mirror. Somehow,
it had happened: she'd turned into one of those crazy mothers
who took their kids to school in their pajamas. 'At least it's
just my pajama top,' she insisted to her little girl. 'When I
was growing up, there were moms who dropped their kids
off in robes, slippers and hair curlers!' She waited for Dakota's
laughter as she gave her a quick pinch.

'Yeah, like hair curlers are the last thing you'd need,' her
daughter replied, sullen. 'Let's just go. And we don't need to
talk, okay?'

Where did her sweet baby go? Had she slept for more than
a night?

It was as though a teenager had come in the night and
stolen her darling muffingirl. Even though there was no logic
to it, Georgia had just sort of assumed the hormones and
moodiness wouldn't really kick in until after Dakota's thir-
teenth birthday in July. Well, old momma, she told herself,
guess again.

The sun was barely up but Lucie sat in her dining room –
really just a corner of the living area, a folding chair and
two IKEA chairs set up – and slowly crunched her way
through a bowl of granola with milk. Then another. After
all, she *was* eating for two. Thanks to the hormones, she
still had nights when she couldn't sleep. Lucie flipped
through the calendar to October and the big red star she'd
made: Baby! God, if this little one didn't come out on time,
she'd turn 43 before it arrived. Rosie had been considered

an older mother when she gave birth to Lucie at 35. Oh, how things change.

Just a year ago she was settling into the idea of being a single woman, confident and capable all on her own. And now she was going to become a mother. She finished off her food and got down to the day's business, planning to watch some of the raw footage from last week's club meeting and then the explanations of slip knotting and casting on, filmed separately with Georgia and Anita. It had gone well last Sunday, once she'd convinced Georgia that she didn't need to dress up as though she was going to be an extra in *Harper Valley PTA*. So Georgia had ditched the suit, changed back into her usual attire, and brought down some knitted pillow covers her granny had made years ago, just to show Lucie. She'd been impressed by the mosaic pattern, to be sure; also amused that Georgia had misinterpreted her comment that she wanted to start focusing on smaller projects. As in tiny. Infant-sized. Why couldn't she just say it? Baby baby baby. Everyone had to be suspecting, but, God bless 'em, the members of the knitting club were a classy bunch. Not even K.C. had said boo, every person allowing her the space to just be. To share her news in her own good time.

She flipped on the camcorder, watching on the LCD screen. There was Georgia, opening the door and strolling into the shop – okay, a bit too Mister Rogers, she'd have to cut that – and introducing the viewer to her store.

'Welcome to my . . . world,' Georgia's voice on the tape was shaky. 'I'm Georgia Walker and this is my yarn store on New York City's Upper West Side . . .' – a quick pan of the bins with the colorful chenilles, cottons, bouclés, mohairs, then coming to rest on the table – '. . . and this is the spot where it all happens.' Her voice was becoming more assertive. 'This is the home of the Friday Night Knitting Club,' continued Georgia, walking into the shot now, pulling out a chair and sitting down, followed by Anita. 'And right here, at this very table, with my good friend and mentor Anita Lowenstein, is where we pass along all the techniques and secrets of knitting that makes it such fun' – here was the point when Lucie was going to splice in some of the club footage and then jump back to Georgia – 'and also the challenge that keeps it interesting.' Cue Lesson 1: Anita explaining a slipknot. Lucie switched off the camcorder. So far, so good. She still had to do more in-depth interviews with Georgia and Anita, to find out about the beginning of the store and the hows and whys of when the women learned to knit.

Lucie stood up, stretched, went into the bathroom, as she did several times every day, pulled off her shirt (one of the new ones Darwin had helped select), and turned sideways, evaluating her swelling abdomen in the mirror. 'Looking good, kid,' she told herself, cupping her belly with her hands. This baby was going to be so loved, cherished by a mommy who was eagerly anticipating its arrival. She still wished, though, that she could go home for the annual Brennan start-of-summer barbecue, ribs on the grill and red sauce simmering on the stove. Could see her mother, Rosie, wearing white sunblock on her nose as she coached the boys – now in their 50s – playing touch football on the grass; her dad, now elderly, would offer up play-by-play from his plastic lawn chair. But Lucie wasn't ready to risk her family's reaction to her new, expanding figure. She grabbed her top and ambled back to the couch, considered going back to work before she remembered the bag that Georgia had handed her earlier this week, which she'd just dumped into her messenger bag before schlepping on home. 'Hey, I know we're paying you – sort of – but it's not enough,' Georgia said. 'So take this, just a little something.'

Lucie had been so busy she hadn't bothered to look, knowing it was yarn, of course. Now, a bit idle, she zipped open her case and up-ended the Walker and Daughter bag onto her lap. Six skeins each of sunny yellow, white and celery green multi. Acrylic blend; machine washable. Soft. Lucie rubbed a corner against her cheek. Very soft. She turned over the skein to read the gauge, then smiled to herself, finally in on Georgia's little tease with the knitted pillow covers.

'Toddler Touch' proclaimed the label.

Yup. Georgia knew.

New York City was always quiet on holiday weekends – especially during the summer. How could you tell? Well, it wasn't completely impossible to book a table for brunch at Norma's on 57th and, unless it was raining, it was pretty easy to catch a cab, the yellow cars circling the streets in search of patrons who'd fled by Friday noon to the Hamptons or the Jersey Shore. And yet those were the Saturdays that Georgia loved, the opportunity to organize the shop and take stock while still remaining open for the handful of customers who just had to get some chunky yak wool. Hey, it happens.

She knew Cat was coming in to go over a sweater pattern, aka sort out her life with the only thing akin to a friend that she had, but right now, in this moment, Georgia was okay with it. After peeking in on Dakota and rearranging the covers she'd kicked off during the night, Georgia took a quick shower and hit the shop early, around 8 a.m. (Clearly Wednesday's little sleep-in adventure had just been a stress reaction, she reassured herself, and she was back to her usual morning-person self.)

Shortly after doing a quick tidy of the shop and pulling out her inventory log, Georgia heard the familiar sounds of music from her apartment upstairs. MTV, again. Oh, well, choose your battles, right? By 9 a.m., Cat was there, pretending to care about sweaters. (Earth to Cat – it's May. Summer is coming . . . Georgia just rolled her eyes and half listened. She knew Cat was mostly afraid of confronting a long weekend with no parties to attend, no home to go to, no overbearing husband to rail against.) At 10, she opened the shop for business – and was pleased to see a steady stream of customers roll in.

Finally, when Peri showed up for her shift at noon and Dakota had yet to make an appearance downstairs, Georgia left Cat sitting in the office, still pretending to look through pattern books, and marched to her apartment, ready to let her daughter know that it was high time she turned off the television and did something productive with her day.

But Dakota wasn't in the living room. The TV blared, skinny men in leather pants kicking up their legs on the screen and screaming, but her little girl wasn't there to see it.

She wasn't in the bathroom, the kitchen, sleeping in her bed. Georgia raced into her own bedroom, hoping to find her daughter snooping in the private boxes in her closet. She threw open the door.

'Dakota,' she yelled. Even though she could see her baby wasn't there. 'Dakota?' Running through the rooms again, in case a second look-round would produce her missing child. 'Dakota!'

Her feet crunched on a discarded Walker and Daughter bag that had fallen onto the kitchen floor. She picked it up and saw, in her daughter's handwriting, a message.

GONE TO BALTIMORE

That was all.

And in an instant, she knew. With every bit of blood and bone in her body. James had taken her child. Waltzed in with kisses and stolen her baby's heart right from under her.

She grabbed her cell phone, dialing his number.

Voicemail. 'Please leave a message for James Foster . . .' said the recorded voice. She slammed down the phone. Fucker! Picked up, hit redial. 'Please leave a message for

James Foster . . .' She threw the phone across the room, dashed over to retrieve it, and hit redial. 'Please leave . . .'

A beep. An incoming call. Dakota?

'Baby, is that you?' Breathless. Hoping.

'Georgia! This is James, I was on the line with my boss but your number keeps coming up—'

'You stupid bastard, you took her!' Crying now. 'Where is she? Just let me talk to her! Please!'

'Georgia, what's going on?'

'Where is Dakota?'

'Isn't she at home?' Concern creeping into his voice. 'Georgia, where is Dakota?'

'I don't know! She left a note, "Gone to Baltimore", that's all it says. You said you'd take her there. She's with you!'

'Georgia. Listen to me. I'm at the work site in Brooklyn. You kiboshed the Baltimore thing, it didn't happen.' Shivers down her spine, a realization that anything could happen to her little girl. Dakota was out there. Somewhere. On her way to Baltimore. All alone.

16

James's voice was still there. On the other end of the line. Go to Dakota's room. Do it now, Georgia. What's missing? Did she pack anything?

Opening the closet, her dresser, looking under the bed. A list of what's missing: a striped backpack. The felted purse she had just made with Peri. The tiny stuffed tiger she still took to bed at night. The sock where she kept her allowance. Everything else seemed just as it always did. Georgia wandered around the apartment, in a daze, looking for a clue. And then she saw it. Or, more precisely, didn't see it.

Dakota's bike, typically propped up near the doorway, was missing.

'A twelve-year-old kid wouldn't really believe she could ride her bike to Baltimore, Georgia.' Peri shook her head. 'There's no way.'

'Is James on his way?' asked Cat. The back office wall was right against the stairs; Cat had heard Georgia come peeling down the steps, yelling. Now they were all in a huddle, as the three of them tried to decide what to do next. Yes, James was on his way. No, she didn't want to call Anita in Atlanta and worry her.

They assessed the ways to get to Baltimore. Car. (Oh, please God, not hitchhiking.) Bus. (Was there any place more skeevy than Port Authority?) The train. Penn Station.

'You can take your bike on the train!' Words tumbled out of Peri. 'College kids do it all the time.'

'I had no idea—' began Cat, the least likely to have ever used public transportation.

'Let's go,' cried Georgia, all three ready to dash out of the shop and leave the customers behind. They ran down the stairs, paused.

'I'll watch the store – you go.' Peri raced back up, leaving Cat and Georgia on the street. Georgia's cell was ringing; James's number.

'We think she's riding her bike to Penn Station,' she yelled into the phone, standing in the street and frantically waving her arms to attract a cab. One pulled over. Cat opened the door and they clambered in, Georgia realizing too late that she'd forgotten her purse.

'I don't have any money on me. Shit!'

'Georgia, I've got it,' said Cat, then shouting at the cabbie, 'Penn Station and fast!'

'I'm on my way from Brooklyn – I called my parents and told them if someone named Dakota calls or shows up to welcome her and let me know right away,' said James. 'Needless to say, they were a little startled but I didn't go into the details of who she is.'

'Oh, James, what if something has happened to her? What am I going to do?'

'Nothing is going to happen to her, baby.' His voice was reassuring. 'We are going to find her and yell at her until she's good and scared and then we're going to just go home and sort out the whole mess.'

Georgia was sobbing now as Cat's arms grabbed her in a big hug.

There was no traffic. It was a holiday weekend. Light after light was green. And still, it was too slow. Lincoln Center. Columbus Circle. West 57th.

'Head over to ninth Avenue when you get to fiftieth! Skip Times Square!' Clearly Cat was used to getting around above ground in Manhattan; Georgia knew every subway route on the West Side but she'd be damned if she knew the quickest way to navigate the streets by car.

And then they were flying across 34th, stopping in front of the side entrance to Penn Station/Madison Square Garden, and Georgia was out the door, leaving Cat to settle up. Down, down the steps, and through the dark tunnels to Amtrak.

And there, at the front of the line, five-foot-five tall and beautiful, stood her in-so-much-trouble-now-but-thank-you-God-she's-alive daughter. Felted purse over her arm. Backpack at her feet. Sock in hand as she doled out dollar bills to the ticket taker.

Georgia race-walked the last few steps to stand behind Dakota.

'Thanks,' she told the man at the counter. Not wanting to draw attention. The last thing a single mom wants is to draw attention.

Steering Dakota to the side.

'What the hell were you thinking?' Her voice hard behind gritted teeth.

'I just wanted to see my family!' Dakota wailed.

Georgia knew, of course, that this was the moment where she was supposed to be all tough love and punish Dakota for her irresponsibility. But that wasn't what was in her heart. She was so grateful to see her only daughter, alive and shouting, holding her in a tight hug, that she decided to listen first, yell later.

'You wanted to trek all that way just to see some fusty old relatives you don't even know?'

'Yes, I do, Mom. I need to know where I come from.'

'You come from New York. Pennsylvania. You come from me.' Georgia shook her head at her naïve daughter, rushing off to meet the grandparents who might not even know about her. James had never even said if he'd told them yet.

'I know, Mommy, but it's not enough.' Dakota was crying now, frustrated at her inability to find the words.

'You want to know your history.' Georgia filled them in for her daughter. 'Well, it's not all Baltimore and Foster, little girl. If you want to know your roots, then I'll show you. I'll take you to them.' She stroked Dakota's hair, smoothed it out of her eyes, oblivious to Cat, who had joined her a moment ago, and the thousands of anonymous strangers walking by, rushing to trains late and on time.

James had found them now, panting; he'd clearly been running through the rabbit warren that was Penn Station.

'Dakota, what has gotten in to you?' He was frowning, angry. Georgia held up her hand.

'Situation under control, James, thank you very much,' she said, the teamwork of the past hour lost in a renewed resentment of the complications he brought into her life.

'Dakota and I have made a decision: I'm taking her on a trip to meet her granny in Scotland.'

Mastering a Complicated Stitch

It becomes exciting as you begin to see the pattern take shape, when you can go row after row without even looking at your hands, when you move on from knit and purl to cable and slip stitch and intarsia. (There's nothing like your first argyle!) It's the reward for perserverance. Don't let it go to your head or stick to the same moves; learn new stitches and see how far you can go.

17

The three adults swayed on their feet for a bit, all of them
– even Georgia – surprised by her sudden plan. For one
thing, Georgia didn't make spontaneous decisions. For
another, it wasn't as though she could just leave the store to
baby-sit itself. There were lots of complications. Not to
mention that the morning's excursion had left them more
than a little exhausted. 'Maybe let's find some water,' she
suggested.

Dakota sensed none of the adults' stress, her fists pumping
the air, whoops and hollers coming out of her mouth. At least
she wasn't so close to being a teenager that she wouldn't act
like a goof in public, thought her mother. Her daughter, mean-
while, was already soaring, in her mind, on a 747 – her first
plane ride and over an ocean, too! – and busy deciding which
of her friends she would call first.

'Hey, Mom – are we leaving tomorrow? There's a lot I
have to do before we go.'

'Soon, sweetheart, soon.' Georgia was savoring the look of
consternation on James's face. She wasn't, actually, paying
much attention to Cat at all.

But Cat was listening to her every word, watching Georgia's
every move. Seeing her hold Dakota in her arms as if everything she ever needed or wanted was right there. The spirit
of Cathy Anderson left in her soul always nudged at Cat
Phillips. Telling her she wasn't doing enough with her great

education, her natural flair for style, her God-given intelligence. Would it have been different if she'd been a mom?
Maybe. Probably. But the situation, as it stood, left her with
no marriage, no career (Career? There'd never even been a
job!), and barely anyone on the planet who cared about her
or who she cared for. Her life wasn't anything like she imagined it would be.

Cat had nothing and Georgia had everything – and Cat
knew, just absolutely felt in her gut, that her old friend was
the only one who gave enough of a damn that she could
teach her how to have it all, too.

After a certain age – following college, perhaps, or upon turning
30 – there's so much stuff in the brain that other things get
shoved out. To the back of the line. Sometimes a woman just
doesn't remember everything that's taken place in her life. And
who could blame her? Georgia didn't have that experience all
that often. Her life centered on such a small core group of
people, but, on occasion, K.C. would regale her with some
amusing anecdote from their time at Churchill Publishing and
how Georgia had made some comment or other that really
put so-and-so in her place. And Georgia would have no memory
of the event, but smile anyway and go along, not sure if K.C.
was misremembering or if she was losing her own mind.

So when Cat, standing in the background at Penn Station,
responded to Georgia's declaration about Scotland with
enthusiasm, Georgia was pleased. In a mild way. She wasn't
really considering Cat's take on the matter but support was
always welcome. She'd been expecting a more insecure reaction when Cat absorbed the fact that she would suddenly
find herself without any support system for a few weeks. Yet
she was totally blindsided to hear what Cat had to say.

'Omigod, that's the trip we always said we'd take together
after college!' she squealed. Had they made such a pact?

Georgia was caught off-guard, any such utterings made while she was still a high-school student long erased from her memory and also considered, by the logic of adulthood, null and void by now. Right?

'It's a great idea,' continued Cat. 'I'll use my air miles.'

'I, uh, was thinking of a mother-daughter trip, Cat.'

The blond woman – dressed today, Georgia noticed for the first time, not in a power suit, but in a pair of casual slacks and a pressed, but plain, sage-colored blouse – made a pained face.

'You know my mom is gone, Georgia,' she said. 'So it'll just have to be me.'

Back at the store, Georgia gave Anita a quick ring to let her know they'd found Dakota, lest she hear it all from Marty and get upset. Not that Georgia knew if Anita and Marty were talking while she was down in Atlanta with Nathan's family. Still. She suspected the seeds of a real relationship were blossoming between those two.

Georgia waited, sitting at her office desk, doodling until Anita came to the phone.

'Darling! I'm so glad you've called,' said Anita cheerily. Then her voice dropped. 'Can you hear me?'

'I can hear you, Anita.'

'It's been forty-eight hours and they're driving me bonkers. Taken me to see two retirement communities on the golf course – who takes up golf at sixty-five, I ask you – because I said the guest house was too small.'

'You're not sixty-five.'

'Georgia, you're missing the point. They're trying to lock me away!' Then Anita giggled. 'And they hate my new hairdo! Nathan said he thought it looked too mussy.' Georgia thought about Anita's shorter, flirtier 'do', the face-framing blunt cut softened with layers and wisps of bangs that drew attention to her gorgeous eyes. Lucie had been right; Anita did look younger. And no one, especially a middle-aged man, suddenly wants to see his mother start looking less like mommy, more like a sexy woman. Who might be dating someone other than his father. But that was a topic for another time.

She filled her friend in on the details of the upcoming trip – no, the flights and all those particulars hadn't been finalized but yes, yes, she was committed to doing it.

'I know school isn't over but it's only seventh grade,' Georgia insisted. 'And I just want to reconnect with her, spend some time with her before Mr Let-me-buy-you-a-fancy-bike-so-you-can-ride-to-Baltimore comes up with any more bright ideas.' She paused to listen. 'I know it's not his fault, exactly, Anita. But it sort of is.'

And then she rehashed the story she'd gone over with Anita already, the kiss, the store visit, the trip to the zoo, and then, once she'd taken the bait, the hook. James had wanted to take *his* girl to Baltimore.

Anita was quiet for a moment. 'Are you sure that's what he said?' she asked. Did Anita know something about James that she wasn't letting on, Georgia wondered? 'Are you absolutely certain he said he only wanted to take Dakota?' Anita repeated.

'Yes! His girl! His girl! His girl!' Saying it so fast made Georgia slur the words ever so slightly, a little bit of a *zzzz* sound at the end.

His girl*zzz*.

His girl*s*.

Plural.

There was no time to talk to James. Besides, what was she about to say anyway?

'That ship has sailed,' Georgia said aloud. 'And it was the Titanic.'

'Huh?' Peri stood in the doorway of the office. 'If you want to sail to Scotland, the Queen Mary might be a better choice.'

Georgia shook her head. 'No, no, we're going to fly. If – and it's a big if – you feel ready to step up and manage the store in my absence.' She motioned for Peri to come inside and shut the door. 'We'll let Cat stay out on the floor for a moment and pretend she has a job or something. It will put a little zing in her pants. You and I, let's talk.'

Peri pulled up a chair and sat across the desk from Georgia.

'I wanted to talk to you as well,' she began. Oh, no. Was Peri going to quit on her now? 'K.C.'s cousin has bought fifty bags for Bloomingdale's and I have until the end of July to deliver them. I was going to ask for some time off, what with tutoring K.C. for the LSAT and school and . . .' Her voice trailed off.

Georgia leaned back. If this conversation had come up yesterday, she would have panicked. But after this morning's brouhaha, she'd acquired a new perspective on life's little hiccups.

'Peri,' she began. 'Let me be the first to say "Congratulations". You had a dream and you're out there, making it happen.' Georgia reflected on her early days, on Anita – then Mrs Lowenstein – challenging her, encouraging her, believing in her. 'But I still need you – and want you – to be here. Is there a way we can make it all come together? Maybe if we tried to adjust things so that . . .'

And then she began to sketch out a plan, shortening the shop hours over the course of the time she would be away in Scotland, Peri assisted by a part-time clerk who could ring up sales while she set up her sewing machine and her knitting at the table.

'You'll make those bags on time and have room to spare,' concluded Georgia. 'Anita is scheduled to be back in two weeks – you can count on the fact she'll be here sooner than that – and you can tell K.C. that all tutoring takes place in the shop.'

And then she offered the bonuses that clinched the deal.

'Plus I just got in a box of new worsted multi that should felt up very nicely, in all sorts of shades of eggplant and celadon and sunshine. It's yours – at cost.' Georgia had always been generous with discounts; this offer was above and beyond. 'And when I'm back from Scotland, I promise you I will take on purse duty, and help you get those suckers knitted and felted and all your PeriPocketbook labels sewn on straight and tight. You'll be a success, Peri, and I will help you make it happen.'

They both stood up, shook hands over the desk, grinning, a new partnership of sorts forged from their old manager-employee relationship.

'I better get one of those bags for free!' Georgia joked.

'At Christmas, at Christmas,' Peri responded, laughing. She sat down again, feeling more comfortable just hanging out, for a moment, with Georgia.

'So when do you leave for the big trip? Dakota's been telling all of the customers.'

'I'm thinking about the overnight flight, later this week.' She was finally going to dig deeply into that bank account from James. His little Baltimore plan had started the wheels in motion, after all.

'Just you and Dakota?'

'Well, we're going to stay with my granny,' answered Georgia, smiling, giddy with anticipation of placing the call to her beloved grandmother, the curt 'Very good' unable to mask Gran's pleasure. She leaned back in her chair. 'And, of course, every trip needs a third wheel. Ours is Cat. I'd tell you she's coming along to carry our luggage but, knowing her, she's going to try to make it go the other way round.'

Georgia got up and motioned to the door, followed Peri out to the shop.

'All right, let's get out here and sell some seriously expensive cashmere so I can pay for that assistant!'

Peri pivoted to look at her boss.

'Thank you, Georgia,' she said with a sincerity that made the storeowner, residual waterworks still close to the surface after the morning's shenanigans, feel teary. It was nice to be appreciated.

'You're welcome, Peri,' said Georgia, giving her waist a quick squeeze. 'All I want is to see everyone happy.'

18

The rain drizzled down the windows of the car rental office at the Edinburgh airport, really just a small trailer in a large parking lot of cars. It had been a tremendously long flight. Not so much the time, mind you. Just the company.

'I'm not too pleased about this situation – I could have arranged a driver for us, Georgia.' Cat's arms were crossed over her body as she stood next to her tired old friend at the counter; Dakota was looking through the glass at the selection of cars.

'Can we just pick any car?' she asked Georgia. 'I like red.'

'You're in luck – the Vauxhall has your name on it,' declared the tall, reedy fellow behind the counter. 'Can I give directions?'

Georgia leaned closer to peer at the map, trying to hide her justifiable fear about driving a car (she did so once a year, during Christmas in Pennsylvania) and her apprehension about ending up on the right, er, the left side of the road.

'Just remember: the passenger is always on the curb side of the street,' the car rental rep told her cheerily. 'We haven't had a client in a bang-up in quite a while. I'm sure you'll be fine.'

Cat was right – she should have made some sort of arrangement for a driver. But the expense! The way to become rich is to not spend your money on frivolous things, Gran had said, and Georgia had followed that advice in building the business and squirreling away funds for college, rainy days, and important trips to rediscover her roots. Well, to be honest, she hadn't exactly planned on the last one, except in the most vague someday-ish notion. Now, though, she was committed to driving this car to Gran's house near Dumfries, her mind set even firmer because of Cat's snarky tone.

Sure, Cat had been kind enough to use air miles to buy all three tickets – their seats in coach had taken roughly the same number of points that Cat had planned to use for a first-class spot. And it prevented Georgia from having to plunder the bank account. But really, if she had to hear Cat refer to their economy class location as 'steerage' one more time!

'You know, I think we can try something a little nicer,' Cat was saying to the car rental clerk. 'Let's upgrade to a Mercedes – like that big black number out there. We can put it on my card.'

Georgia put her hand over the credit card.

'No.'

'Yes.'

'No.'

The clerk reached across the counter and slid the card out from both of their hands; probably on commission, thought Georgia. He looked up at her briefly, waiting for her to give in. She wasn't about to deny the man his extra funds; she'd settle up with Cat later.

'Just zip it through and let's be on with it,' demanded Cat. Georgia inclined her head ever so slightly to give her assent and the clerk was down to it, punching in numbers on a keypad and sliding the credit card through the reader, whistling. No doubt calculating what portion of the upgrade would go in his pocket. Well, good for him, thought Georgia. We worker bees have to stick together. A moment, then another. The credit card was swiped a second time. Then the man – who'd stopped whistling by this point – picked up the phone.

'Just need to make a call here, the card company, you know,' he said by way of explanation.

'It must be because we're in a foreign country,' Cat said to Georgia.

'My card didn't have a problem.'

'Well, yours probably has a much smaller limit,' responded Cat, primly.

'I see, I see, right then, okay.' The employee had angled his body ever so slightly so he was no longer looking directly at the women but at the wall behind them, the phone cord pulled around his body. He turned back, a blush rising on his cheeks, as he returned the receiver to its cradle on the counter.

'Ah, well, then,' he began. 'There's been a slight problem, Miss . . .' – he glanced at the card now – 'Phillips. Seems you were only an authorized user on this card and that the account holder has withdrawn authorization. I'm very sorry but there's nothing we can do. Shall we go back to the Vauxhall then? It handles well, what my wife and I drive ourselves.'

Cat put out her hand for the card. 'I'll call myself,' she insisted.

'Ah, that's fine, Miss. But I'm afraid I've received instructions from the company to cut up this little bit here,' he said, pulling out the scissors. His face was now in full flush. He lowered his voice. 'I'm desperately sorry but it'll be my job if the company complains. You know,' he looked past Cat, who was making a rather alarming squeak as though wavering between crying or yelling, and appealed to Georgia.

'Snip it up and let's get ourselves on the road,' she responded.

'No!' screamed Cat, her face ashen as the scissors sliced through the plastic rectangle, finally realizing that the bank of Adam had absolutely and truly closed.

A nub of plastic with a holographic image landed face up on the counter.

'I'll just take this bit,' said Cat, clutching the remnant of the card and following Georgia meekly out to the vehicle.

'Shotgun!' Dakota was quick on the draw, all right.

'What?' Cat was in a daze.

'My little girl has beaten you for the front seat, old friend,' said Georgia, putting on a broad and fake accent, vaguely English-Scottish. 'Now let's get our stuff in the boot. Pip, pip!'

Dakota held a giant golf umbrella overhead as Georgia began loading the bags into the trunk. Cat stood there watching, arms at her side, little girl lost at 37.

'It's a good day, Cat.'

'How can you say that?'

'You've just reinforced for Dakota two of the most valuable lessons any girl can know.'

'Don't serve your jackass of a husband with divorce papers?'

'Hmmm, nope, not what I was thinking of. I figure that goes on a case-by-case basis,' said Georgia, puffing a bit as she wrestled with lifting Cat's overpacked pieces of luggage. 'But you've just demonstrated Rule of Life Number One. Dakota?'

'Be your own safety and security!' Dakota shouted out to the sky, jostling the umbrella so that a little rainwater plopped right into Cat's eye. The blonde made a little squeal.

'And addendum to Rule Number One – listen up, Dakota,' said Georgia, slamming the trunk shut and tapping on the closed lid for emphasis. 'Every woman should have credit in her own name. Wouldn't you say so, Cat? Ladies, our carriage awaits.'

Dakota charged up to the front seat lest Cat get there first, saw the wheel was on the side she was accustomed to being the passenger's spot, and bolted around the front bumper. 'I almost lost it there!' she laughed as she clambered into the passenger seat, pulling down the umbrella and shutting the door. Georgia held her hand over her head to stave off the water drops but Cat remained motionless, still standing, shoulders slumped, by the back end of the car.

'I really *have* lost it, Georgia.'

Georgia Walker took a few steps towards the woman who felt at once an interloper and a bosom companion. She couldn't deny that she'd felt a little thrill watching Cat's card get turned down, seeing the disappearance of the wealth and privilege previously flaunted. But she felt sad for her, too, knowing very well what it was like to find yourself without an idea of how to get from A to B. Landing in a situation of one's own making doesn't mean it was the circumstance that was truly wanted.

'Well, CathyCat, let's see if we can help you find it again.'

'Like what?'

'Like I don't know but it's up to you to figure it out.'

The rain had progressed to a shower and both women were soaked; Georgia gave up on trying to keep the rain off her curly hair. She knew there was no way to avoid the frizz now.

Motioning to the car, she took the few steps to the driver's door and reached out for the handle.

'But I'll tell you Rule Number Two – and this one came from my gran, good old Glenda Walker herself: "Your life is what you make it."' She reached out for the door handle.

'Georgia?'

'Yeah?'

'Do you have these rules written down somewhere? Because I think it's time I got myself a copy.'

And without making eye contact, Cat climbed over the driver's seat that Georgia had pushed forward, dripping water off her coat and hair as she settled into the back seat of the red 2-door hatchback. She buckled in, and then leaned forward, resting her chin on her knees as Georgia put her fingers to her lips and gave the universal sign of 'be quiet' to her daughter. Dakota nodded as Georgia fired up the engine and offered a silent prayer that she didn't kill them all trying to get through the roundabout to exit the airport.

One hour and several wrong turns later, the women were long past any moment of shared understanding.

'That's the twenty-third car to pass us,' moaned Cat from the back. 'I think my legs are going to be permanently cramped in this tiny backseat. When are we going to be there?'

'I think that's my line,' said Dakota, peering around with a grin. Georgia stared straight ahead, ignoring both of them, white-knuckling the wheel. Goddamn it was hard to drive on these tiny little roads! Hadn't the public works heard of shoulders on a highway? Though you could barely call these compact lanes a highway, could you? Just winding, swerving lanes flowing through the countryside, the farms on either side overflowing with a billion sheep, some with their fluffy butts painted a mysterious red or blue in some secret Scottish sheep code.

In a rare moment of solidarity, Georgia felt a new appreciation for her mother Bess and how she had dreaded all those trips to visit Gran. The journey was a heckuva lot easier when none of the responsibility rested on you, she thought, as Dakota kicked off her shoes and put her feet up on the dashboard.

Vroom! Another car passed them as she slowed prematurely, wary of driving through yet another country village with its compact houses and stern churches built right up to the side of the road. Most of the time she thought of all of New York's rules and regulations for renovations to be just an excuse to keep more paper pushers in their jobs; now she had the evidence right in front of her for the need for building codes. Some of these homes must be unbelievably old, she realized, feeling a sense of *déjà vu* and pride as she thought of her people, her ancestors, toiling it out and getting on with things.

'I wonder if these people can sleep at night, worried that someone might drive right into their bedroom?' she commented lightly.

'I'd think the car would probably be pretty banged up before it got too far into these stone walls. And you'd need to be going a great deal faster than you're going right now . . .' Cat let her sentence trail off.

Georgia glanced over the dashboard. 'Slow 30 mph' was painted in large letters on the asphalt. She looked quickly at the speedmeter. Fifteen. Ack! Cat was right; it would be nighttime before she made it to Gran's. She accelerated slightly, caught sight of a young couple coming out of a doorway and hit the brakes – though the man and woman were in no danger and well enough off the road.

'I didn't know they had such stop and go traffic in the Scottish countryside,' said Cat dryly. 'We'd have done better to travel by sheep.'

Georgia didn't reply directly.

'Dakota, did you know that Cat failed her driver's test four times when she was in high school,' said Georgia, her eyes still glued to the road, feeling slightly guilty for calling her out in front of her daughter but mostly wanting to let Cat know she hadn't forgotten.

Dakota's eyes grew wide as she swiveled around to view the crunched-up figure of Cat, rumpled and fuming, in the back.

'You failed?'

'I passed it on the fourth try,' Cat responded curtly. 'Which means I only failed three times. And failure, if you want to know, Dakota, is just another opportunity to try again.'

'Touché,' said Georgia.

'So like what did my mom do in high school? Did she ever get in trouble?'

'You mean like the time she climbed out her window and down the big oak tree in front of the house to go to the biggest party of the year at Rich Holloway's house?'

'Mom! You snuck out?'

'Should I really be copping to this? Thanks for bringing it up, Cat.' Georgia focused on the road for a second before she replied.

'I guess I thought my mother was being too strict – it was summer, after all, and I'd done all my work around the farm.' Georgia waited a beat. 'But now I realize I should have listened to my mother because she probably knew best. Because someone who shall remain nameless tripped over a tree root and screamed to high heaven because she sprained her ankle. Just as we were almost home free. Literally.' She leaned over and stage-whispered to her daughter: 'The culprit is in the back seat.'

'Did you get grounded?'

'No, she did not, Dakota – and you want to know why?' Cat leaned up from the back, not that she had too far to go.

'Man, I'd forgotten all about that part of it,' said Georgia quietly as Cat continued, Dakota hanging on her every syllable.

'Because I told her to sneak on up to her room and I told Mr and Mrs Walker that I was just arriving to convince Georgia to come with me to the party. And she got into her nightie and by the time they came up to her room, she was totally acting like she was asleep.'

'Wow. So did you get in trouble, Cat?'

'Trouble schmouble. There was a consequence, though. That's when Mom and Dad insisted I get the job at Dairy Queen to keep myself busy.'

'Didn't you live on a farm?'

'No, we lived in town. Dad worked at the bank and Mom worked at throwing dinner parties for his boss.' Cat gave a little snort. 'I guess the apple doesn't fall far from the tree.'

Dakota, though, was more intrigued by the idea of an ice-cream shop.

'So could you just eat whatever you wanted? Did they let you invent your own sundae flavors?'

'Not anything so grand, I'm afraid. A lot of ringing up soft-serve ice cream and cleaning out the Blizzard machine.'

'And you couldn't run the cash register! Oh man, do I remember this now!' Georgia was laughing so hard she was very near relaxed; her foot was easing into the gas pedal so that the Vauxhall was almost – not quite – going at the speed limit.

'You couldn't run the till?' Dakota, who had grown up above the yarn shop her entire life, was absolutely incredulous. 'I could run one when I was, like, seven.'

'They were harder to run in those days. Lots of buttons.'

'They still have lots of buttons.'

'Okay, okay, it's true. I couldn't operate the cash machine and I was put on probation.'

'On her first day,' added Georgia.

'On my first hour,' corrected Cat. 'So I spent the entire time flipping burgers in the back. And then I called Georgia, who scammed out on the hay baling to drive into town . . .'

'And showed up right at closing to ask the boss for permission to help her figure out how to run the register.'

'Did you work at the Dairy Queen, too, Mom?'

'No, sweetie, I was either at the farm or at school working on the paper – with Cat as my star columnist, no less.'

'So how did you know what to do?'

'I just jumped in there and kept at it until I'd figured it out. And you never know when a skill is going to come in handy – I was awfully glad I didn't have one more thing to learn when I started the shop. I had enough on my hands raising a genius baby!' Georgia reached over to give Dakota's cheek a light pinch.

'Someone read the signs – I think we're coming up to the M74.'

'Righty ho,' announced Dakota with glee, then looked at her mother with concern. 'It's a big roundabout.'

'Well, then, we'll just go around and around until I can get us out of it.'

'Hmmm, where have I heard that before? Oh, yes, about fifteen minutes ago—' Cat's sniping was cut short by an insistent buzzing sound.

'What is that?'

'Is that your cell phone?'

'Your cell phone works here?'

'It's GSM – very pricey.' Cat looked at the display. 'Oh, shit, it's Adam.'

'Hey, watch your language!' said Dakota. A little surprised to hear Cat swear, a little thrilled by it too.

'Yeah, not in front of my wee lassie,' said Georgia, more keenly focused on the coming lane switch.

The buzzing continued.

'Should I answer it?'

'Up to you, Cat,' said Georgia.

'I don't know. I didn't tell him I was going. Do you think he's calling to yell or woo me back?'

'Didn't receive a memo on that one while I've been driving around all these Scottish roads, Cat, so I don't know,' Georgia replied. 'Maybe the credit card company called him.'

'Oh, shit!'

'Hey! Not in front of me!' Dakota wagged her finger at her mother's flustered friend.

The buzzing stopped.

'It's gone to voicemail. Okay, what a relief,' said Cat. 'He could be mad. Should I pick up the message now, you think? Or maybe later?'

She felt a rush of excitement at the idea that Adam was trying to reach her. Maybe he realized that she was pretty damn great, after all. Then again, he hadn't cared enough to keep her on his credit cards. The phone began to vibrate again, startling Cat into dropping it on the floor of the car and having to paw around her feet to find it again.

'Shit! Shit! It's him again! Georgia! Should I pick up?'

The roundabout was directly ahead and a steady stream of traffic was hurtling into the triple lanes, all the other drivers knowing exactly how to navigate the circle to get to where they needed to be. Shit.

'Here, give it to me,' said Georgia, reaching her hand back without removing her eyes from the cars ahead. Cat passed forward the noisy, pulsing handset, still shrieking and muttering. Georgia took a quick glance, saw 'Adam' clearly displayed, and leaned on the window button to roll down the glass and drop the mobile phone onto the roadway.

'Oops,' she said, without even an attempt at sincerity. 'Charge!' Georgia accelerated a bit into the roundabout. There were angry honks as she crossed all three lanes at once. 'Oops,' she said, really meaning it this time, ignoring Cat's swearing and Dakota's eye-rolling as she successfully made her way out of the circle and onto the roadway.

With any luck, they would be at Granny's by teatime.

After passing by, oh, another million sheep – Dakota was counting 'One lamb, two lamb' all the way – Georgia was relieved to pull up to her granny's house, a compact brick cottage with a trim around the windows that was painted a sunny canary yellow. The same paint decorated the rounded front door, which looked to be taking up a full third of the front of the house. Funny, she'd always remembered the house being bigger, thought Georgia as she parked the car and released the newly cell-free Cat from her backseat bondage. They'd walked barely a step when the massive door opened and onto the front concrete landing came a petite elderly lady in a collared white blouse and a red buttoned cardigan over black slacks, laced-up oxfords on her feet and her back as straight as a rule. An orange tabby beside her on the step meowed a greeting. Funny, Gran was tinier than Georgia remembered, too.

'The Walker family together at last!' called out this five-foot-five dynamo with the tight white curls, holding out her arms to greet her five-foot-five counterpart with tight dark braids. Dakota was grinning from ear to ear even as Granny used all of her 90-year-old strength to hug the stuffing out of her.

It felt good, truly awesome, to be back in the place she loved so much. Why had she stayed away so long?

Slowly she walked up to the front walkway, staring down at the ground as though not to seem undignified in front of Cat and run into her grandmother's arms as she had done when she was Dakota's age.

'Hello, Gran,' she said to the wee old lady with the bright blue eyes, arm in arm with Dakota already.

'Ach, Georgia,' replied the woman, her face positively glowing. 'The heart of my heart.'

And then the older woman reached out to give her adult granddaughter a tight squeeze and in that moment all of Georgia's fears and responsibilities faded away, back to that other time and place across the ocean. For now, all that mattered was Gran and all the days and nights ahead, drinking tea and knitting or walking around the fields and showing Dakota all the history that was theirs together.

And Cat Phillips? She was seeming more like Cathy Anderson every minute.

*   *   *

Not too much later, the guests were settled into their rooms – Georgia and Dakota to share the big bed in the guest room, Cat (who'd realized her plans of a country house hotel might not work out once her credit had been nixed) set up in the daybed in the corner of Gran's sewing/knitting room. They'd had the grand tour, a peek into the lounge with its matching navy loveseats and coal-burning stove, the wallpaper of roses and vines in the dining room and the tidy, efficient kitchen with its gleaming white appliances and painted cupboards, a wall-mounted plate rack displaying Gran's wedding china. (Intertwined leaves and a gold border on a cream back-ground.) The rooms were cozy but somehow they didn't feel small, mainly because the furniture was just the right size. Gran's house was the anti-McMansion.

'It's like a doll house for people,' said Dakota, admiring the colorful striped afghan on the wide iron bed, the knitted cozy on the teapot, the cotton dishrags that her gran had stitched together and actually used. (A good texture gives better scrubbing action, she told Dakota conspiratorially. A pattern should be, at its core, a practical plan for achieving a goal.) Georgia was comforted, somehow, to see the advice-giving had started already. Gran was not one for idle chitchat about what was on television or the last book she'd read. No, her grandmother had always been one to say what needed to be said to get a job done, or to pass along important wisdom. Which could, of course, be anything from how to get an extra meal out of leftovers to choosing a husband. Advice, thought Georgia, thy name is Gran.

She sat down at the old wooden table in the kitchen – the breakfast nook – in the same spot she'd sat at every visit, with a view out the back window to the yard and garden and the farm fields beyond. The tea things had already been laid out, the cups and saucers, spoons, a generous pitcher of milk, the sugar bowl, and a plate of still-warm shortbread and another of homemade bread and jam. Gran was swirling around just enough hot water to warm up the teapot, then dumped it into the sink. She dropped in three spoonfuls of loose-leaf tea and filled the teapot near to the brim with just-boiled water from the kettle, then brought it all over to the table to steep.

'Hands washed?' she asked.

'Yes, Gran! I'm thirty-seven years old.'

'Never too old to be looked after, I say.'

They sat down to wait for Cat, hearing instead the sounds of the bath being run.

'Most unusual.' Gran had the gift for few words that said much.

'Gran, about Cat coming here. It's just that . . .'

'Happy to have her, dear. Any friend of yours is more than welcome. Even if they do take a bath at teatime.'

'Well, it's just that she's not really, well, I don't know if I ever told you.'

'I may be old, Georgia, but my mind is clear. I've kept every letter you ever sent and enjoyed rereading them on occasion, to be honest. Keeps me company. So I know very well who Cathy Anderson is, whether or not she's calling herself by the name of a domesticated animal.'

'I don't think she's very domesticated,' Dakota chimed in. Georgia shot her a look.

'I think you're right about that, my dear. This one is growing up quickly, Georgia, she's seeing the world as it is,' said Gran, catching Georgia's look of exasperation quite well. She reached out to tap her grown granddaughter's hand. 'I know, dear, I know. It's always hardest on the mothers.'

19

Georgia woke up to a burst of light on her face.

'What the . . . !'

'Half the day is done, love, it's gone ten,' said Gran, standing next to the curtains she'd just pulled open.

'C'mon, Mom, it's time for breakfast – I made muffins. And shortbread for tea later.'

'Oh, she's a delightful one in the kitchen, Georgia – she's got the knack. Just like my own mother, who could take a practically empty larder and turn out a brilliant feast.'

Dakota soaked up the compliments. And the connections. She'd spent a fascinating morning with her old granny, as she creamed the butter the old woman had left out the night before, mixing in flour and sugar and vanilla. They'd rolled the dough into a long tube, slicing it off into thick rounds, giggling all the while. Baking in pajamas! Then they'd sat down to a quiet breakfast, just the two of them. Boiled eggs with salt and toast soldiers, watching the sun come up as they stood on the step at the back door, Dakota still in pajamas but bundled up in an old emerald green cardigan of Gran's. It had been early, but Gran hadn't ever lost the habit of rising with the sun – an old farmer's wife's habit – and Dakota was jet-lagged, her body clock all crazy. She'd fallen asleep the previous night shortly after tea and her mother had decided to let her sleep. Which resulted in Dakota waking up early and raring to go. Good thing her great-grandmother was prepared.

'I don't think I've ever seen a sunrise,' she told Gran.

'It's something your eyes never tire of,' said her white-haired counterpart.

They gazed at the streaks of pink and gold for a while; then Gran broke the silence.

'Your mother tells me you're looking for your roots.'

'Yeah.' Dakota stared down at her hands. 'I need to know where I come from.'

'Indeed. That's a big thing in America. Where you've come from.' Gran nodded sagely. 'Well, you've come to the right place, Dakota my dear. We're your people here.'

'I don't really look like you, though, Gran.'

'Ach, that's only on the outside, little one.'

The pair walked off the step to inspect the garden, the manicured bit of lawn and the very large flower patch to the right – the irises, clematises, and rare blue poppies in bloom – and the even more substantial vegetable garden to the left, Dakota salivating over early strawberries and tender carrots she could use to make muffins. The fields surrounding the house stretched back over a mile, bordered on all sides by fences made of hard stone, all shapes and sizes packed in place with skill and worn together by age. The stones, Gran said, were plucked out of the ground by the ancestors of her husband Tom Walker, Sr, all those Walkers working their way up from a past as tenant farmers to finally having a spot of land to call their own. When she was a girl, the Walker name had been well known in these parts, and young Tom was considered quite a catch, she told her great-granddaughter. And they had been very happy together.

'But then he went off to fight in the war and he just never returned home,' said Gran simply, a fact she'd long ago accepted. 'My father-in-law ran the farm for years and years until my oldest son stepped up to the work, and my youngest boy – that's your grandpa in Pennsylvania – helped him at it until he caught the bug for America and sailed away.'

'So my mom never knew her grandfather?'

'No, she knew him, Dakota. She knew him through me. But she never *met* him, which is a different thing altogether.'

Dakota tilted her head for a moment, considering. 'So all these old Walkers I've never met . . .' she spoke slowly, thinking it through, '. . . are still people I *know.*'

'In the very essence of your soul. Quite right you are. Because they *are* you.'

'Gran?'

'Yes?'

'I think you probably know pretty much everything.'

'You may be on to something there, little one.'

Hours later, the two of them were dressed, still in cardigans knitted long ago by Gran, she in her favorite red and Dakota in green, making the two of them look distinctly Christmassy when they stood side by side. As they were doing a lot, quite taken with their matching height.

Georgia raised herself on one elbow.

'The two of you have been making muffins?'

'And watching a sunrise and picking the poppies and sneaking in to Cat's room to get the knitting bag –'

'Being very careful not to disturb your guest who seems to have a penchant for snoring,' interjected Gran. 'But I think we'd do best not to tell her she's such a noisy sort.'

'And now we're here to wake you up, Mom. Hurry and get dressed – Gran's going to teach me how to knit a Fair Isle pattern.'

'What's the chance I can get breakfast in bed?'

'The same chance there's always been, Georgia dear,' said Gran. 'None at all.'

Georgia laughed and made as if to get up, which appeased her daughter and grandmother enough for them to leave the room. But she lowered herself back down into the bed once the door was closed, her back sore – from the plane ride, no doubt – and her stomach nauseated. It was only 5 a.m. back in New York and she was desperate for a few more minutes of rest. But she couldn't seem to drift back as she lay there, her mind swirling over the events of the past few months, the reappearance of James and Cat, the fighting with Dakota, and the sheer fun of hosting the knitting club in the store. A bright spot in a crazy spring. It had been a crazy night, over a month ago, when Cat had lurched into the shop and demanded they all do something that scared them. And what did Georgia do? Spend a few hours with James, kissing him, being stupid. Pretending to the club that she was meeting Cat's dare.

But that was a bit of a con, wasn't it? Because she wasn't really scared of James now – she was angry with him, sure, but it wasn't the same as when she was younger. When he trashed her heart and wandered off without a care.

No, Georgia was afraid of James from back then. Afraid of what she didn't know about his affairs. The lying. All the nasty things he probably really thought about her.

She was afraid of those unopened letters. The ones she'd kept in the box in the closet all these years, careful never to give in to the urge to read them. She'd just check on them, every year or so, reassuring herself they were still there. She thought of them as the answers, James's reasoning for his actions, and the idea of them had always felt, in the back of her mind, as a sort of closure she could go get when she was ready.

Someday, she would tell herself, someday she would read them.

It hadn't been strange, really, when she was pulling out her suitcase from the closet in New York and fretting about taking a trip with Cat, to take down the box and reread that old year-book passage. To see the two letters. What had been unusual had been the impulse to bring the letters.

She had given in, tossed the envelopes into the bottom of the case. Maybe. Maybe not.

Did she really need all the details? The great last gasp of blame and retribution?

Yes, she did. She did. Now.

Georgia padded in bare feet across the carpeted room and went to her suitcase, began rooting around calmly through the piles of clean panties and tees. She knew she'd packed those damn letters. Where were they? With increasing stress, she began to dump clothes and shoes out of the case onto the bed, searching through zippered pockets, flipping through books, sorting through her toiletries case. Where were they? She went over to her carry-on bag and rummaged through, came up with nothing. What if she had lost them? After all this time?

She was barely able to breathe as she sorted through the pile of clothes on the bed a second time, frantically folding and refolding shirts, pants, pajamas. And then, from the leg of her favorite jeans, the letters shook out. With a fit of frustration and relief, she slid her thumb under the flap of the first envelope and ripped away at the edges.

Standing in her sleep shirt, legs bare, she braved herself to read the letters James had sent from Paris.

> *Georgia*
>
> *It's hard to find a place to start. I was wrong. I made a mistake. I know I hurt you and that's just not right. I don't know why I did it – it just happened. But I want you to know that I quit my job and I won't see my former boss again. I took a great job in Paris that should have lots of room for growth. And I think we should try again, make a fresh start.*

Maybe we could all live together here? I really do love you. I feel so good when I'm around you. Happier than I've ever been.

Maybe I was just testing you? Anyway, it was stupid. I know that now I really want – need – to hear from you.

Love,

James

P.S. And I was stupid not to bring you to Baltimore. I'm ready to take you anytime you want to go.

I, I, I. God, it was all about him, wasn't it? Georgia bit her lip, feeling uncertain, and then tore into the final note, anticipating – hoping, even – that this would be the nasty letter she'd always assumed he'd sent.

G—

I'm truly sorry. I love you. And I love our baby.

Please get in touch.

J.

What? Where was the blame, the demands, the lies? She'd spent years nursing her resentment of James. Not just the cheating – that was beyond wrong – but the lack of concern for her and the baby, for the way he just walked out of their lives without a second thought. Off to Paris. With great glee, she'd assumed.

And now, to learn he'd cared! Her stomach was in a twist; panting for air, Georgia dashed out into the hall to go to the bathroom, splashed cold water from the sink on her face and held on to the counter for support.

Wishing, just wishing, she could purge all her regret away.

After enduring a breakfast that had morphed into brunch – and suffering an annoyingly perky Cat refreshed from her sleeping-pill-induced evening of rest – the women pulled on their shoes and light jackets and headed out to the rental car.

It was time, said Gran, to take her guests to town and show them off to the locals. No one noticed that Georgia was quiet, assuming she was merely jet-lagged. She made a mental note not to ruin her grandmother's big trip to town with long-ago problems that were too old to be resolved.

'I've been bragging about the two of you for years,' Gran explained to Dakota as they buckled into their seats. 'Just for fun, we can say Cat is a celebrity – she's so thin and pretty they're sure to believe it.'

Cat beamed at Gran from the back seat.

'Hurry up now, Georgia, I want to make sure we've done the rounds by teatime.'

The drive to town – all one street of it – took a good three minutes, four with the need to slow down for the tourists jaywalking across the street.

'Where to, Gran?' Georgia marveled at the main street of Thornhill, a collection of artisan boutiques, pubs, a separate fishmonger and butcher, and one very fancy dress shop. And, of course, a store for knitted woolens.

'Start at the top of the street and we'll walk our way down.'

'So this is it?' Dakota hadn't quite realized, when they drove through the afternoon before on the way to Gran's house, that these few blocks of main street were simply part of the road they called a highway. Georgia found all sorts of images coming back to her, could recall walking the trip to town when she was a young girl, ever hopeful of getting an ice cream for the return stroll.

'I can't believe the designer dresses in that window,' Cat was saying, crunched in the back with Dakota. 'Gran, I am totally impressed. I thought this was going to be hicks in the sticks.'

'Thank you, dear, I think,' said Gran.

Georgia parked the car and let out her passengers, offering her arm to her grandmother.

'Don't need that,' scoffed Gran, who was moving briskly into the first store facing them. 'Now, Muriel always works on Mondays and I know she'd love to see you.'

Georgia followed behind, a vague memory of a girl she'd played with long ago, a feeling of homecoming enveloping her. They walked into the boutique, past the display of Camilla-style headgear, and found themselves warmly greeted by women who knew all their pertinent details and seemed overjoyed to see them. It was fantastic.

Dakota looked back at Georgia, a bit thrown to be immediately surrounded by strangers clucking with approval and complimenting Gran on everything from her great-grand-daughter's posture to her height.

'Aren't you two the vision of twins,' the shopkeepers said, as Dakota and Gran stood just as they had been doing since they met, arm-in-arm and permanently joined at the hip, dressed in their co-ordinating knitted cardigans.

'Not quite identical . . .' began Gran.

'But that's only on the outside,' finished Dakota, laughing. The two of them were a veritable comedy team, thought Georgia. And it was a delight to see her little muffingirl so happy, the Penn Station adventure long forgotten.

They made their way along the street until Gran declared it was time for a spot of refreshment. The tea house – really just a little room attached to a shop selling a hodge-podge of soups and scones and toasted sandwiches – was kitted out with standard-issue frilly curtains and doilies under the sugar bowls on the tables. But a display shelf at the back of the store held handmade wooden carvings – all available from the Web, of course – in a variety of distinctly non-Scottish themes, from fat-bellied Buddhas to a replica of the Twin

Towers. The corners of the room were filled with iron sculp-
tures of a sort, confusing twists of metal with tags attached
offering, by way of explanation, names such as 'Conundrum'
and 'Hullabaloo'. Gran followed Dakota's eye.

'Local artists,' she said simply. 'It's not all porridge and
tartan around here, you know.'

'I'm really surprised by how sophisticated it all is,' said Cat.
'I've been thinking about what I should do with my career
and I just feel so inspired.'

'Good to see that twenty-four hours is all you need to
figure out your life.' Georgia was feeling a little tired of Cat's
exclamations of every store and person as 'darling' and 'so
authentic!' Gran gave Georgia's knee a little press, inclined
her head for Cat to continue. Always the good manners,
thought Georgia. Maybe she'd been in New York too long.

'I'm going to move to Scotland,' declared Cat. 'After I saw
that dress shop, I realized there's really an upscale clientele here.'

The old woman looked alarmed. 'We're rather downscale
on the upscale ladder, I assure you.'

'I bet you could stay with Gran,' Georgia offered, trying
hard to keep her face straight, pressing her knee back into
her grandmother's under the table. 'You might even be able
to move out of the sewing room.'

'Georgia, really, I'm serious,' said Cat. 'I think I should
bring an organic foods store to the area. Introduce healthy
eating to the Scottish people.'

Dakota looked up from her menu, which she had been
studying intently, trying to decide between cakes or scones.
She tapped her finger on the card. 'You might want to check
this out, Cat,' she said, her voice not giving anything away but
her eyes laughing. She was becoming a wit, Georgia realized.

The women glanced down. 'We use locally grown, organic
ingredients whenever possible' was displayed at the bottom
of the menu.

'Oh.' Cat looked crestfallen. 'I really thought I was on to something. I even wrote down a few ideas,' she said, pulling out of her purse a piece of paper on which she'd written the following: Tomatoes, Cucumbers, Cheese, Milk, Vitamins.

'I think, Cat, that's what most people know as a grocery list,' said Georgia, not unkindly. 'Maybe not so much of a business plan there. Besides, I imagine it may be difficult for an American to introduce being green to a country of people who drive tiny gas-efficient cars.'

'Georgia, I'm just trying to figure out what I'm meant to do in this life.' Cat shoved her list into her handbag.

'A commendable goal, Cat,' said Gran, with a tone that meant the time for Georgia's teasing has passed. 'Let's get ourselves some sustenance because we've still to make our way to see Maudie at the woolen shop. She'll want to know all about your yarn shop in New York City, Georgia. Well, I've already told her, of course, but she'll want to hear you tell it again.'

The ladies sipped PG Tips and nibbled baked goods and tried jams and cream as Dakota thought up treat ideas for the club back home and Cat threw out more ideas for her new career. (Yoga instructor? Nope, too spiritual. Personal stylist? No, too frustrating having to do all that shopping and hand it over to someone else. Antique dealer? Hmmm, maybe there was an idea . . .) She could do anything she set her mind on, Gran told her confidently, as long as it wasn't in Scotland. Or in New York, added Georgia, laughing. Cat looked hurt, then relaxed a bit as her old friend assured her she was only joking. Sort of.

It was nice, thought Georgia, just wasting away a Monday afternoon with these women she really cared about. Yes, even Cat, she had to admit it. She bit into a crumbly, buttery scone, savoring the burst of sweet raspberry jam and the cooling silkiness of the clotted cream, when she heard Gran give a little cough of annoyance.

'So who's this now?' Georgia looked up to see two dour-faced biddies at the table.

'Hello, Marjorie, Alice,' said Gran. 'This is my grand-daughter Georgia Walker, her friend Cat Phillips, and my great-granddaughter, Dakota.'

'Your great-granddaughter? My my, that's quite something,' said one to the other.

'Most unusual,' replied the second woman.

'Oh?' said Gran, her voice like ice. 'Whatever do you mean?'

'Just that we've never met the little one before.'

'Gran, those women are staring at me.' Dakota looked devastated, having heard her mother's stories and imagined Scotland to be some kind of Utopia.

'I wouldn't want you to get a swollen head but you are incredibly beautiful,' Gran said matter of factly, as the two women continued to hover over the table. 'Absolutely gorgeous.

'And if anybody is staring for some other reason –' she raised her voice, 'then they can kiss my arse.'

Georgia nearly choked on her drink. If she was ever going to need an enforcer, she'd be sure to call Gran.

'Now make room for some cake, girls, because we're not moving a muscle until we're good and ready to go.'

And they settled into their chairs, feeling strong together, encouraged by the other tea-takers' murmurings of 'Quite right!' and 'Good on you, Glenda,' and staying put until Marjorie and Alice were tsk tsked right out of the tearoom.

Gran pulled open the coat cupboard, a place for everything and everything in its place, she had said more than once over the past day to Cat and Dakota, who continued to fling their belongings onto the short wooden bench by the front door.

Georgia, long ago trained, hung hers up promptly and left her two charges to face the scorn of Gran, feeling tired and in need of a short rest. This time, Cat circled back from the hallway and took out a hanger, then followed Georgia, still talking about career ideas even as her friend declared she was no longer listening.

Dakota leaned against the wall next to the bench, kicking off her sneakers; Gran insisted she untie the laces properly.

'Dakota,' she said, lowering herself onto the bench.

'I know. I forgot to hang up my coat and you had to do it for me. And now the sneakers.'

'Well, yes, that's true. You'll do right next time. But there's something else I want to tell you.' Granny, still sitting, gently steered Dakota by her shoulders until they were looking level at each other.

'After the tea room, it's just . . . I want to finish our talk from this morning.'

'Okay,' said Dakota, looking down at her socks, pulling at them with her feet, trying to make a hole. Gran, uncharacteristically, didn't comment about her squirming.

'I know there's some who were not sure about your arrival, your mother being on her own and all. And she struggled to make a good life for the two of you but she's done it. The proof is in the pudding. The proof is in *you*,' said Gran, pulling Dakota's hair free of her collar and patting it down. 'Such a good girl. And every day you've been on this Earth has been a joy and a blessing.' She then took both of Dakota's hands in hers.

'You know, I raised two sons and olden days be damned, it was still hard to be a teenager. Even back then. Your Grandpa Tom was a scallywag. Always talking back. "What do you know?" he always used to ask me.' Dakota half giggled, amused by the idea of her gray-haired grandfather in Pennsylvania being anything other than an old man and a little sheepish knowing she had asked Georgia the very same question not too long ago.

Granny smiled as Dakota laughed but she didn't stop talking, glancing quickly in the direction of the rest of the house as if to keep an eye out for interruption.

'You'll have lots of questions to answer as you get older. Who you are. Who you want to be. What you think about things. Like politics. And romances. And whether you'll speak out or keep your mouth shut. It's always a challenge to work out the best way to live your life and as much as everyone tells you what to do, ultimately how you do things is up to you,' said Gran. Dakota nodded earnestly. It felt so good to talk to Granny.

'Was it like this when you were young, Gran?'

'Oh, yes, quite so. My mother was always keeping me from the dances to stay home and read to my ailing grandfather. I was quite outraged at the time. But you know? I've had a lifetime of dances and now I treasure that time with older relatives, and I know that my mother had a little bit of fore-sight that I hadn't yet developed. You try to remember that, Dakota.'

'Yes, Gran.' Was she going to fall into the 'listen to your mother' speech? Like she hadn't heard that one a million times, thought Dakota.

'But the main question is trying to work out who you are – and the way to find the answer is to look at where you've come from and to think of where you'd like to go. Only you know the secrets of your heart.'

Dakota frowned a bit as she stared, quizzically, at her granny, her wrinkly face surrounded by that curly fluff of blue-white hair.

'There's a lot of life in this old face, little one,' said Granny. 'You must feel so grown up – almost thirteen – and I see so much ahead of you. Lots of good times. I hope never bad days like I've known.' Gran's eyes were shiny wet but she didn't cry. She wasn't the type. But her voice had a slight waver. 'And I don't know how many times I'll see you again, what with my old bones and that great big ocean in between us. But all the lessons I learned and shared with my son and then with Georgia and now with you, those will keep you going long after I'm gone. Whether a person is physically in front of you or not, the love remains. Do you understand, dear child?'

Dakota brought her hand to her granny's cheek, caressing the lines and marveling at how soft and powdery it felt underneath her fingertips.

'The love remains,' she said simply.

'I'm not daft, Dakota,' said Gran. 'I know there are some who see you and wonder about your background, asking "Is she black?" And so you do have a whole other history to be proud of that I couldn't begin to understand. I'm just an old Scottish lady, here with my cats and my memories.'

Dakota's face was very close to Gran's; the older woman smelled of peppermint and hair spray. It was weird and nice at the same time.

'But just so you know that we are, each one of us – even poor Cat – held together by the invisible threads of our histories. And so yours is Scottish and American and African in some long ago time and place. But these strings are all the good and all the bad that our families ever experienced. And when the world tries to pull you loose – and it will – there may be some stretch. But someone like you, with so much love holding her together, will never fall apart.'

A draft was coming underneath the front door and they shared a shiver; Gran tugged at the young girl's sweater to pull it tighter.

'Do you understand what I'm telling you, dear child?'

Deep brown eyes looked directly into old blue ones, a shared communication. The twelve year old didn't fidget or sigh or make a joke; instead, she nodded slowly. Silently. In that instant, Glenda Walker could see the strong, proud, intelligent woman the child would become, and she was filled with relief and pride and hope. She patted the young girl's shoulders.

'Well, then,' she said, 'let's go and see what to do about dinner.' Even though they'd just come back from tea.

And, smiling, Dakota skipped off into the lounge to shoo the cats out from the knitting bag.

20

It was humans-only this morning: the cats had been unceremoniously kicked out into the garden. The table was set with Gran's good china, the leaf pattern with gold trim, and flowers from the garden in her prized lead crystal vase. Certainly, Gran had made a show of it every morning, going out of her way to lay the table with platter after platter of food, readying them for their day trips to Edinburgh to explore the castle and Dumfries to retrace the steps of Robbie Burns, or fortifying them for an afternoon pulling weeds in the garden, enjoying the sunshine and the invigorating hard work. Just the other day she surprised them with good Scottish smoked salmon on bagels – grocery-store kind, of course, but still! – and yesterday she had made a frittata from a cookbook that Dakota brought along. (Georgia couldn't remember a time when her grandmother would have gone in for anything quite like that.) And, additionally, there was always porridge and bacon and black pudding (and Dakota was the only guest who dared to taste that!) and eggs any style. An old-fashioned kick-off to the morning. Though Georgia, truth be told, was finding all that heavy food wasn't sitting so well. Not so her daughter.

'One thing I love about being here is the big breakfast,' Dakota was announcing, in one hand a fork overflowing with eggs and sausages, a slice of buttered toast in the other. 'At home it's just cereal and that's okay, but I always felt like something was missing. Now I know it's my Scottish side that needs porridge and bacon and eggs. Every day.' She leaned over to get her mother's attention. 'Every day,' she mouthed.

'Have you ever heard of cholesterol?' Cat was eating some cut-up fruit and a half-slice of bread with a very thin layer of Gran's homemade jam, trying to decide if she ought to add a cup of yoghurt to her simple breakfast.

'I know what cholesterol is,' said Dakota, talking with her mouth full. Gran cleared her throat until she closed her lips and swallowed. Dakota made a big show of blotting at her lips with her napkin and then continued: 'It doesn't affect nearly thirteen year olds. Or Scottish people.'

Gran chuckled. 'I wish that were so. But I daresay you're right, your Scottish side is needing a good breakfast in the mornings. Georgia, I hope you're not feeding rubbish food to this growing girl.'

She knew, of course, that Georgia was conscientious when it came to Dakota's diet. And Georgia was accustomed to her grandmother's sparing use of words and the way she often spoke in the negative. 'I hope you're not doing such-and-such' was a common way for Gran to make her feelings known, as if by taking that approach she wasn't outright telling someone what they *should* do. But Georgia still felt hurt. First that Dakota seemed to imply she wasn't doing enough. Kids complain; it's what they do. But this time, Dakota's comment hit home. After all, Georgia had been slower in the mornings, sleeping later, and sometimes leaving her daughter to get breakfast for herself. And then Gran had to jump in. Always with the advice-giving! Georgia felt so tired and her back hurt and she just couldn't seem to stop herself from snapping.

'I am not feeding her junk food for breakfast, Granny, and you know that very well!' She noticed with ire that Gran didn't look the least bit ruffled.

'Of course you don't, dear,' she said, telling Dakota to run out and pick some fresh berries. 'Dawdle for a bit, Dakota. It's time for a big girls' chat.'

Cat stood up and pushed back her chair, ready to leave the table.

'You. Sit right back down.'

The blonde took her seat.

Georgia was sputtering.

'Out with it then,' commanded Gran. 'What's the bee in your bonnet?'

It was all the opening that the New Yorker needed.

'I have done absolutely everything for my daughter her entire life, fed her all the right foods and splurged on special clothes and day camps during the summer and organized sleepovers and movie nights,' she said, her voice sharp. There was no blubbering. No, Georgia was angry. Really and truly angry. And not at Gran. She knew that. Sort of.

'I never had a date in all these years and I doled out discipline when all I wanted to do was give in to her demands and go take a hot bath. Do you know what I never have? Time to myself. Time to just relax. There's always something, the shop, or Dakota's father, or my back-stabbing best friend who can't seem to make a fucking decision and followed me all the way to your house.'

She was in full rant mode, punctuating her speech with jabs of her spoon into the air, and, at key moments, in Cat's direction, who was staring at Georgia with chagrin. 'And you know as well as I do, Gran, that my own mother never fed me a damn piece of sugared anything in my entire life and that didn't make me a better person,' said Georgia. 'Quite the contrary. Bess hardly said one nice thing to me in all my life and frankly, a bowl of Fruit Loops might have cheered things up a bit now and then.'

'I suppose it might have.' Gran's voice was even, her face calm. 'What else?'

'My mom never makes an effort, never comes into the city to see Dakota, she just stays out in Pennsylvania and is the once-a-year relative at Christmas. It's no wonder Dakota is obsessed with biking to Penn Station and finding her family! She barely knows them.'

'How do you know Bess doesn't make an effort?' Gran was contemplative.

'Because she never bothers—'

'—to do what you think she ought to.' The white-haired woman may have been old. But her mind was clear. And she didn't mince words. It was her turn now.

'Your mother has her own story, Georgia. I can guess that if my son is anything like his father, he's a demanding soul. Charming. Kind. But particular. Difficult. And what do you know about her secret sorrows? When have you ever approached her without wanting something from her?'

'You've never liked Bess, Gran, so how can you stand there and defend her?'

'Because I just listened to you complain about having a daughter who needed so much from you that you didn't feel as though you had anything left over.' Gran gave Georgia the most gentle smile. 'And then I listened to you complain about having a mother who never gave you enough.'

The old woman got up from the table and went to put the milk back into the fridge. 'I suppose when it comes to human nature I know more than my fair share. Widowed young. Raising children on my own. Feeling as though I was doing it all alone even though now I see I wouldn't have made it without the friends and family all around me.'

'I see where you're going with this, Gran, and you just don't know what it's like to be on your own in New York City. It's not like rural Scotland.'

'No, but I do know what it's like to be on my own with two hungry babies and a world war on my doorstep, Georgia, so don't you fall into the trap of thinking you've got the hardest lot.' Gran was curt. 'Stress is not about the situation, my dear, it's about the person. There's some who can handle it and there's some who can't.'

'I can't handle it,' added Cat, sympathetically. 'Never could.'

'And that's a load of rubbish right there. You' – she wagged a finger in Cat's direction – 'just haven't tried.'

She returned her attention to Georgia. 'And you, my dear, have spent a bit too much time ruminating on the past. Dare I say feeling a bit sorry for yourself. I can tell you – both you girls – that there's one thing about people that is constant. All people. You. Me. Bess. Everybody.'

'What?' asked Cat, breathlessly. Georgia turned her face away, frustrated.

'Sometimes people just don't get things right.' Gran began picking up the plates from the table and carrying them over to do the washing up. 'Did you hear me? People sometimes don't do the right thing.'

'So then what?' Georgia's tone made it clear that she wasn't satisfied. Cat, on the other hand, was hanging on Gran's every word.

'So then you're left deciding how you are going to react to what they offer. Because you can't make them change.'

'That's it?'

'That's it, then.'

Georgia flopped back into her chair. Sighed. Frowned. And then smiled. A little half-smile on one side of her face. If her folks weren't going to change then she could stop spending so much of her precious energy trying to make them do so. There was just something about getting a tongue-lashing from her grandmother to put things in perspective. To give her the get-out-of-jail-free card she'd been searching for.

Her eyes turned to Cat. The little smile grew into a grin, spread from ear to ear.

'Your turn,' she said, her voice challenging.

Cat shrugged. 'What are you looking at me for? I'm okay. I just don't know what to do is all. But I'm going to make it on my own.' She folded her hands in her lap and looked out the window, looking the picture of perfect calm, not meeting anyone's eyes.

Georgia let out a snort.

'Enough with the Mary Tyler Moore routine,' she said. 'Let's go back to the beginning: brilliant high-school student steals best friend's place at Dartmouth and grows up to become a vacuous socialite. Cue life crisis.'

'Vacuous? You think I'm vacuous?'

'I think you appear that way, yes.'

'Well, I'm not stupid, Georgia, and you know it.'

Gran swiveled at the sink and held up her hand, covered with soap bubbles.

'I think that, if I may say so, is precisely her point, my dear,' she said. 'You're not stupid. But you flit about as though you were a child.'

Cat's face turned beet; even she wasn't about to take on an elderly granny. So she focused her energies on Georgia and gave her a blast.

'I came to you, I looked you up, I paid you to make me a dress so I could boost your business!'

'Are you saying you did that to help me out? I didn't need your charity. That gown is a work of art. Or do you think that buying a gown from me makes up for college?'

'Yes! No! I don't know!'

'Good, get angry, dears,' soothed Gran, back at it and using a brush on the saucepan to pick up the bits of egg. 'That always gets to the root of things.'

'I saw the article in the magazine and I thought, "There it is. My chance to make things right."' Cat had pushed back her chair, was walking around the room and making wide gestures with her hands. 'And you looked so confident and capable and just like I remembered. All those curls. I thought I'd show you how I could afford something really expensive. Or maybe I'd soak up this great talent you have for being successful.'

'Don't confuse success with money,' said Georgia, dryly. 'They are quite different. And not a month goes by that I don't worry about the bottom line.'

'But that's just it, too, don't you see? You have all these things that matter: a business. A daughter. A man who's totally into you.'

'A man?' Gran now, her curiosity piqued.

'Don't go there,' Georgia growled.

The old woman continued to wash the breakfast dishes at the sink, her back to the table and her eyes scanning through the window to see Dakota, still picking strawberries, eating two or three for every one she put into her basket. She listened to the girls go at each other without commenting.

'And I saw all that you'd done and I thought you'd save me.' Cat crossed her arms in front of her body. 'I thought you'd save me from myself.'

There was a generous amount of head-shaking going on in the kitchen.

'It's like Gran says: I just didn't do things right,' Cat was saying. 'So there. I'm sorry and I've apologized and now I want us to be done with it.'

'Well, I have a few things to say to you first.' Georgia spoke slowly, began to idly play with the salt and pepper shakers. Gran continued tidying with gusto as though a gleaming countertop was her highest priority, though of course she was listening keenly.

'I won't deny you hurt my feelings. But there's a mistake I think you made. I think you gave up on life: you decided that your husband's accomplishments meant you didn't need any of your own.'

Cat tilted her head back as though in deep concentration.

'And now you're just doing a version of the same thing, tagging along with me to Scotland to see if I can be the person you'll attach yourself to,' said Georgia. 'And it's time for you to stand on your own. It's not about being the best or the most or the richest, Cat. You just have to be good enough. Good enough to get by, good enough to sleep at night knowing you made an effort.'

She'd seen her friend get upset with her – annoyed, mostly – but even then Georgia seemed to be in control. Now, she was just so . . . emotional. And honest. And right. There was no sarcasm, no teasing. Just plain talk. Laid bare.

So what now? Cat knew she'd been moping around, figured Georgia would fix her. Somehow. But the problem wasn't merely about too much Botox or filling her days with pricey shopping sprees to make up for the lack of something worthwhile to do. Cat had given up responsibility for herself. The only problem was that no one else had ever wanted to take it on. Then again, there was no reason they should have.

'It's up to me,' Cat whispered. 'It's really up to me.'

Her voice grew louder, almost triumphant, as she stretched out her arms. 'I can do it! I just have to harness my power and let myself fly.'

'Oh, my, I think we've gone all New Age on ourselves.' Gran interrupted Cat's speech with a bit of a face. She was a good one for drama, that girl. Though the old woman was pleased, having learned through the years that a true friendship never really ended. It could always come round again.

'Well, I wish I could get back that fifty grand I spent on therapy – I should have just come here for wisdom instead,' laughed Cat.

'You call it that because I'm old,' said Gran, reaching into her cupboard. 'But I'm not wise. All I'm preaching is common sense.'

The back door creaked as Dakota barreled in, berry stains around her lips and a full container of fruit in hand. And so the intensity was broken, lightened, enriched. Gran returned to the table – Georgia and Cat and Dakota back in their chairs – and brought over a fresh pot of tea and a bar of good dark chocolate. A bit of breakfast dessert, she said.

'Gran, you've gone soft,' teased Georgia.

'Maybe so,' she conceded, biting into a hard square. 'But it's better to loosen up as you go or you risk turning brittle.'

21

Dinner was finished and cleared away and Georgia and Gran were whispering in the kitchen, drying the last of the dishes. The two of them had spent many hours alone together since the Big Talk at breakfast over a week ago, and Georgia seemed noticeably different. She laughed more often. Listened for fifteen, even twenty minutes at a time, as Cat laid out her latest ambitions, stifling any unkind comments even as her old friend insisted she would make a great life coach: 'You know, I could really help women get their lives on track!'

'And so you could,' Georgia replied with gravity, doing her best Granny imitation.

The trip had been the perfect vacation, she realized. Sure, she checked in almost daily with Peri, knew that Anita had – as predicted – taken an early train and gone right back to work at the store. The club, they'd told her, was still going strong on their project, though the summer weather had resulted in uneven attendance. It was a fantastic June in the city, they said. And it was a glorious month in the Scottish countryside as well.

With Georgia and Gran talking at every turn, Cat found herself spending several evenings alone with Dakota, chatting about fashion and looking at magazines that she had purchased at the airport. At Dakota's urging, Cat helped her experiment with the tubes and tubs in her cosmetics bag, sweeping on a light blush and dusting on a little shadow underneath her brows, trying on reds and pinks on her lips.

'That can't be Dakota?' Gran said every time Cat called for their attention as Georgia's daughter strode in, looking so much like a young woman and so little like a girl playing dress-up that Georgia felt shocked each night. But she didn't criticize, could see how much Dakota enjoyed having Cat all to herself, touching her expensive clothes and hearing about glamorous parties and dinners. To Dakota, Cat was like a movie star. For Cat, Dakota's admiration kept her inspired when she felt overwhelmed by all the changes ahead. The coming divorce still didn't feel quite real, she'd admitted to Georgia one night after Dakota's bedtime. There was nothing like a separation to realize that maybe you did still have feelings for the guy, after all.

'I wouldn't know about that,' Georgia replied frostily, still putting up defenses even after her armistice with Cat.

'That's okay,' said her friend, so relaxed she was letting the orange tabby lie on her lap, pressed cream trousers and all. 'I know you're lying, Walker girl.'

And the women simply sat together, in comfortable silence, petting the cat and relearning how to enjoy each other's company.

The phone startled the women out of their quiet repose; it was their second to last evening and they were spending it as they had so many others, with Gran at her knitting, Cat at her planning, and Georgia reading and dozing, all curled up in the armchair in the corner. Dakota, exhausted from a day of weeding with her great-grandmother, had taken herself off to sleep even though it was not yet 9 p.m.

'I wonder who's ringing at this hour?' muttered Gran as she made her way to the telephone – an older black model, mounted on the kitchen wall, receiver attached to the base by a cord. (Dakota had marveled at the sight of it, suggested it ought to be donated to a technology museum.)

'Yes?' Gran had that peculiar habit, so common to the elderly, of shouting into the phone. 'Yes, she's here. Who is this? I see. And you're where? Um-huh. Indeed. Well, continue on the M60 until you see the monument in the middle of town, and then keep straight on for another two miles down the road. It's the farm with the whitewashed brick and the yellow trim. You'll recognize the house because the rhubarb flowers in the front garden are looking quite spry. Yes, yes, all right.'

Cat felt shivers go up and down her spine, a mix of fear and excitement. He'd found her. Adam had called the credit-card company to find out exactly where she'd used her plastic and had come to get her. With time and distance, he'd finally come to see clearly just how much he needed Cat. And she'd make him do his penance, of course, but maybe with the help of her therapist they could find a way to come together, maybe he could even help her with her new career.

She walked over as if to take the phone and was surprised when Gran placed the receiver back in its cradle on the wall.

'Was it Adam?'

'Adam? Oh, no, dear.' Gran settled back into her chair. 'No, that was Dakota's father. James. He'll be along shortly.'

Georgia was bolt awake, looking quickly to Cat for confirmation that she hadn't misunderstood.

'Gran, I wasn't expecting, I don't know, James and I aren't . . . together,' Georgia said with emphasis. 'Where is he? And why did you tell him how to get here?'

'Because he's already nearby, at the petrol station. And I thought you said he was seeing Dakota again? I thought you said you'd kissed him?'

'Yes, but it was stupid. I told you that part, too.'

'Oh, but I thought . . .' Gran was becoming upset. 'Now

I've gone and done the wrong thing. Well, I'll just send him packing. I won't let him in. I'll tell him you're busy.'

'So we're just going to pretend we're washing our hair?' Cat was amused. 'How very Harrisburg High.'

She went to get herself a cold drink even as blinds were being pulled down in the kitchen and the lounge around her; Gran was also turning down the lights and whispering.

Cat sipped her Coke, watching the two Walker women dash through the compact house.

'Hey, Georgia, didn't you just tell me James was no big deal?' She shouted just to make a point. 'Sure seems like you're going to a lot of trouble to avoid the man. And by the way, your rental car is still outside. Shall we hide it in the barn?'

Georgia stopped moving, paused, and then lunged towards the keys on the kitchen counter. Cat put out an arm to stop her.

'I have a better idea.' Her voice was quiet now. 'Let's just put on a little lipstick and quit acting like maniacs. So James is here. You can deal with it. Besides, you're turning Granny into a hysteric.'

The older woman was puffing now, having collected up all of her guests' coats and boots from the front cupboard and dumped them onto her own bed, seeming to think she needed to sweep the house clean of any trace of Georgia.

'Gran? Let's just forget it. We'll let him in, it's okay.'

The 90 year old dabbed at her face with a tissue, nodded. Relieved. The two younger women went off to the sewing room, emerging minutes later with Georgia outfitted in dark indigo jeans and a body-hugging V-neck silk sweater in celadon, her curls tamed back with a multi-colored scarf tied as a headband. A touch of mascara and a bit of shine on the lips gave her that perfectly 'natural' look.

'You're a picture,' said Gran, restored to her seat in the

lounge but too keyed up to knit. Cat offered to put on the kettle as Georgia hovered around, not wanting to wait by the front door but reluctant to be too far away, too. They saw the headlights come up the drive, shining through the farmhouse window. And then he was there.

'I was in London on business,' said James, then shifted his weight in his chair. They were sitting in the kitchen, the place where all big talks took place in Gran's world. He cleared his throat.

'Actually, I went to London a few days after you left the city, trying to work up the courage to come here. I stopped into the local V hotel on made-up business just so I wouldn't end up unemployed.' He laughed self-consciously.

'I wanted to see you, Georgia. I had a great plan. I was going to come up here and whisk you off to Sweetheart Abbey—'

'The medieval ruins. I know it; we did the Solway Coast with Dakota last week.'

'Well then you know the story: Lady Devorgilla builds a monument to her beloved husband in twelve hundred and something, creating a final resting place for her and his embalmed heart she carried around after his death.'

'Rather gruesome. Dakota couldn't decide if it was cool or gross. And a little, uh, over the top maybe? I mean, come on, James . . . Sweetheart Abbey?'

'Well, some plan it was. I flew up to the airport and rented a car and promptly drove off in the wrong direction. I was halfway to North Berwick before I realized I was heading east instead of south.'

Georgia laughed. 'I had some trouble driving around here too.'

The tall man stretched out his legs; the compact kitchen chairs made him seem more substantial than ever.

'Just so you know it wasn't my plan to show up here late at night. But I knew if I went to a hotel, I'd lose my nerve by morning.'

'Your nerve to what? Harangue me at my grandmother's house?'

'Is that what I do? I bug you?' James sounded tired. Defeated. 'Well, maybe I do. I'm trying to, I don't know, do something. Reconnect. I guess.' He twisted a napkin to a point. It was unbelievable. How he could walk into a room armed with blueprints and ideas and convince a team of skeptical corporate types to spend multi-millions on glass and steel. How he felt so vulnerable in this spotless little kitchen, surrounded by knitted dishtowels and pictures of Dakota stuck to the fridge with magnets.

'Georgia,' he said. 'Georgia, Georgia, Georgia. Could we take a walk?'

Why not? Her daughter was safe in bed, and Gran and Cat were conspicuously eavesdropping in the other room. They could head down the lane to the road and back; she'd tuck a flashlight into her pocket though she suspected there was enough moonlight to see their way. Nodding, she went to get her jacket from the cupboard, then remembered it was on Gran's bed. She rushed to grab it so James wouldn't wait too long at the front hall, wouldn't find himself questioned by the other women.

'Don't worry, we'll definitely wait up,' called out Cat as they exited.

Zipping up against the cool night air, Georgia remarked that she was surprised James hadn't commented on her old friend's presence.

'Nah, it's not shocking,' he said. 'You used to talk about her a lot in the old days.'

Georgia threw him a quizzical look.

'It's true. You talked about how she hurt you but mostly

you talked about how you had a hard time getting to know people in New York. And how you missed your friend Cathy.'

'I did miss her. I do. But Cat is growing on me. Slowly.'

James stopped walking and angled his body to face hers. 'Do you think you have room in your life for another old friend?'

'James, we've been through this. More than once. Why do you show up here and go through it all again?' Georgia was blunt. 'Is it an ego thing? Am I the girl you want to keep around in case nothing else works out?'

'That's fair, but it's not the truth.' James shook his head. 'I did everything back then out of fear we would work out.'

'Huh?'

'It was so good with us back then. I was really happy. But I thought, oh, different cultures, different colors, it will never last, so why even bother? Eventually we'll split up so just get it over with now.'

'So you dumped me?'

'Nooo,' said James, speaking carefully. 'I cheated on you so that you would get mad and dump me.'

Georgia felt like throwing up. 'Guess it worked then,' she said, walking away from him and back to the house.

'It's about being honest. For once. Look, I didn't know that's what I was doing at the time,' he called after her. 'It took me a long time to figure it out. But that's all I've been doing for years. Thinking about you.'

She slowed her steps, listening to his voice.

'I'm sorry. Really and truly sorry. To hurt you. To not be around with our daughter.' He strode after her, catching up quickly. 'I made excuse after excuse, about me being black and you being white and then about how you never answered my letters and how I'd made too many mistakes to go back.'

He glanced back towards the road, watching a car drive along, trying to keep composed.

'But then, a few years ago, I was sitting in a sidewalk café in Paris and there was this family walking down the street, a black woman and white man, and these gorgeous kids, and they were all laughing and holding hands, and I began to cry. Right then and there. In public.'

James wasn't about to stop now. He had to let her know.

'I began stockpiling presents for Dakota in a closet, planning for some day when I'd see her again. I had Barbies, pink ponies, paint-by-number books, Pokémon cards, Monopoly, soccer balls. Storybooks in French, in English. I'd go into a children's boutique and buy clothes in every size because I didn't know what would fit.' James was practically choking out his words. 'My lifestyle, all that partying, it was kaput. And thank God for that, if you know what I mean. I had this idea that I would become a better man, a good man, the best dad, and then I'd come back to New York and it would all be okay.'

'James, that is so . . .' Georgia hesitated. 'Naïve.'

'I'll do you better. It was presumptuous,' said James. The two of them were on the move again, away from the lane and into the flowered side of the garden, over to a bench near the rhododendron.

'Arrogant and foolish and pretty darn rude,' he concluded. 'And then I show up and realize she's almost a teenager, she doesn't want that collection of Barbies, and all the clothes I bought weren't her taste anyway. Because I don't know her at all. And it's not about spending money, anyway.'

'You did send us checks, though, and that helped.'

'That's what I told myself for years! "I'm not a deadbeat because I pay child support."' said James. 'But that was just another rationalization. It still didn't make up for me not being there.'

'No,' Georgia admitted, motioning for James to sit down. He shook his head.

'Go ahead.' She settled in, willing to listen. She'd had good practice with Cat over the last while.

'I made a mistake. A big one. But I've gone from thinking I should just walk away from Dakota to mourning that I could never go back to hoping there's another chance out there for me and my daughter,' he said. 'And for me and you.'

'We're not a two-for-one deal, James.'

'Then that's okay. It's up to you.'

'Yeah,' said Georgia. 'So answer me a question: who was that woman who called on the way to Cat's party? Lisette, I think.' Georgia knew darn well what the woman's name had been.

James gave her a funny look.

'Lisette?' He paused. 'She was my secretary in Paris. We logged a lot of time together.'

'Your secretary?'

'I'll have you know, Georgia, that she's very attractive,' James said, cracking a smile for the first time that evening. 'But she's somewhere upwards of sixty years old. She was more like my mom, as likely to criticize my choice of tie as to type up a report.'

'Oh.' Georgia was embarrassed. But James felt a surge of hope, encouraged that Georgia felt a little jealousy.

'I need to know that I told you how I really feel.' He was imploring her now, his voice soft and gentle. 'I love you. It never went away. You just amaze me. You're so smart and funny and sexy and tough. Dakota adores you. Anita adores you. Cat's afraid to let you out of her sight. And I chase you around the globe like an idiot. Georgia Walker, you are the kind of person who sears into the soul. I have never been able to get you out of my mind.'

'I doubt that.'

'Don't. You, all of you, you're so beautiful.' He reached out to her but she held up her hand and turned away. There wasn't much more to say. He felt in his pockets, nervously rubbed a quarter between his thumb and forefinger. A distraction.

'I've got to go.' His voice was almost inaudible. 'Don't want to take up any more of your time.'

'James,' she said. A statement. James. Standing in front of her. In Gran's garden.

It couldn't really happen back at home, back in New York, surrounded by all the memories and lingering grief. Here she could see him, finally, not as the enthusiastic up-and-comer he was once and not as the selfish guy who had left her, but really and truly as the man he was today. Older. At once more sophisticated and less sure of himself. With a maturity to match his graying exterior, the flecks of salt and pepper at the temples. There was no boyishness left around his edges; Georgia could see his entire life story in the tiny wrinkles around his eyes, see the memories of good times and the crush of regret when she looked into his eyes. How can you forgive the unforgivable? She didn't know. Yet, somehow, she already had. (Thank you, Gran!)

Georgia rose, walked slowly round to the back of the bench, and began to gently touch the polished wood. Without looking at him.

She thought about his letters. She thought about late nights sitting up with Cat talking about the men they would marry. All the ramblings of a teenager. The certainty. The insistence that she'd never take back a man who'd cheated on her. Cat had agreed. And then spent fifteen hellish years with a philandering jackass. Now, in front of Georgia, stood her own heartbreaker. The great love of her life. One and the same.

And Georgia knew. She would take him back. Not because he was Dakota's father, though that counted for something. A lot. And not because she'd been single all these years. She'd had herself for company and that had turned out to be enough. Just enough. Nor was it because he'd been trying so hard to make amends, or because she'd read those long-ago letters, or because he'd grown up and she knew that, truly, this was a person she could trust. Though, yes, surely, all those things had an impact. Offered her closure, promised a beginning.

But there was a greater reason, one that Georgia could openly and honestly admit, now that the posturing and the defenses and all the misunderstandings were out of the way.

She loved him. Simply and completely, with an intensity and purity that startled her awake. She loved him, too.

And she knew then that she would take him into her arms and reveal that he'd always been in her heart.

Ripping it Out

All you have to do is forgive.

22

It was Georgia's first time being met at the airport. There was something so special, so civilized, about not having to schlep out to the cabs or the shuttles or meet a stranger holding a placard with her name. No, James had been there, having returned to London to tidy up a bit of business and subsequently flown home before the trio even left Granny's cottage. They'd been apart just long enough for Georgia to begin to feel nervous that somehow, some way, this relation-ship – if you could call it that – would fall apart. Again. That it had all been a dream: the hours of conversation in Gran's garden, the coming inside, the caressing and kissing and the slow walk to the bedroom, where they sat on either side of the bed, holding hands and watching their daughter sleep. Whispering. Until exhaustion took its toll and James went to crunch up his tall frame on Gran's compact flowered sofa, legs dangling over the ends, Georgia to tuck in beside Dakota.

It had been one of the best nights of her life.

Still, she'd fretted throughout the flight, flying all day Friday, readying herself for the disappointment. But he had been there. Just like he told her he would be. Standing in arrivals. With a sign that read 'Walker and Daughter'.

They were back just in time for club, the second last meeting of June, then a weekend's worth of sleep to get on to their regular time clocks and one last week of school for Dakota. James double-parked on the side street, then began the time-consuming process of carrying their bags up to the apartment.

'Head on up to the shop – I'll throw these into the living room,' he told her. And Georgia didn't even protest, eager to be back home. In the store. It was very much the same, she saw – the shelves of yarn in all the colors of the rainbow (and good to see the new box of merino had finally come in), the bright sun coming in the large window, a last gasp of summer day before twilight, the wooden floor swept shiny clean, a handful of customers milling about. It felt so good just to smell it again, the wool and the warmth and the coffee always on in the back. And yet it was different: Peri had set up an extra table by the register where she'd placed an assembly line for her purses, getting a much-needed assist from Anita (who ran over to give a big hug), Lucie (who gave a thumbs-up, making a motion with her hand over her belly) and Darwin (struggling to put the pocketbooks into plastic bags; she offered a shy wave, tape on her thumb). K.C. had turned the back office into an LSAT study center, a pile of books all over the papers Georgia had left covering the desk, and a ready supply of Raisinets, chips and soda (diet, she clarified, as though it would bother Georgia less) on top of the file cabinet.

'Comfortable?'

'Actually, Georgia, I was going to suggest you get a new chair,' said K.C. 'This one hurts my butt. Chip?'

'No, thanks. When do I get my office back, pray tell?'

'What? You're not going to just order me out, kiddo?' K.C. came up to Georgia and did a mock-check for fever, her hand on Georgia's brow. 'Nope, you're not delirious. You must be . . . relaxed? What put you in such a good mood over there in Scottish sheepville?'

She walked out to the register, speaking in a stage whisper. 'I think Georgia had a good vacation, if you know what I mean, ladies.' K.C. gave a dramatic wink to Peri and Lucie. Anita made a sound of disapproval; K.C. gave her a double wink-wink.

'Why are you being so weird, K.C.? You look like you're having a spasm.' Dakota. Sky-blue backpack over her shoulders, a pin of the Scottish flag on her denim jacket. Already getting a big squeeze from Anita.

'Hey, little sparky, good to see ya.' K.C. gave the girl a tug on her hair. 'Why don't you run upstairs for a sec while we talk to your mommy?'

'Okay. My dad said we could order Indian tonight anyway and I want to make sure we get extra samosas.'

'Your dad? He's in the apartment upstairs?'

'Yup. He came to see us in Scotland and then met us at the airport and now he's staying for dinner with me.'

'Oh really?' K.C. put on a very serious expression. 'I think your mother needs to give a debriefing of this little trip to see your . . . what did you call her again? Oh, right. Grandmother. Was that code for something? Cough it up, honey. 'Cause I'm not moving out of that office until I get full details.'

Georgia hemmed and hawed, and then caught Cat's eye, not able to stop herself from breaking into a wide smile.

'Ah, I don't know,' she said, trying to stall. 'I thought I'd save it for the club meeting.'

'Gang's all here, buddy,' insisted K.C. 'And we ain't budging without the details.'

It was hours later. James had ordered enough food for everyone, though he conspicuously stayed upstairs with Dakota, watching TV as her jet lag took over and she tumbled off to bed. Georgia was eager to be upstairs with him and yet completely excited to be the center of attention, filled with a giddiness she hadn't expected to ever feel again. It was great to be the girl with the story everyone was dying to hear. Even Cat looked happy, she noticed, though in a flash her mind was back on James upstairs. Was he planning on staying over? It's not like they were going to go from zero to sixty in three days, was it? Or was it? Good thing she'd put on a nice pair of panties and done her legs. Just in case. It had been a long time coming for her to have a 'just in case' reason. And it made her feel fantastic. She was so happy to see her friends, sure. But she could barely keep her mind on them!

'Georgia? What do you think?' It was Darwin, shoving a mangled piece of fuchsia and lime-green chunky yarn into her face.

'Isn't it a good start?' prompted Lucie. Georgia regarded the piece in her hands. It was the sloppiest, messiest rectangle of mixed-up stitches she'd ever seen, the short end picked up and knitted halfway through the piece and sections in which the purl had obviously not been brought forward, the tell-tale scrunch of stitching. It was, in short, awful. And really cute, when you considered the source.

'. . . I kept forgetting which way to bring the string but I said to myself "Just go, Darwin," – and I really did talk out loud, you know – because I just wanted to show you that I'm ready.' Darwin's face was glowing.

'Ready for what?'

'I'm going to make the sweater, too. Look,' Darwin began to pull brand-new yarn out of a lavender bag. 'I've picked out some very nice wool.'

It was one of the most expensive cashmeres they had. Exactly the pricey kind of wool that would make a newbie like Darwin feel nervous about wasting – and thereby increasing her chance at mistakes. Plus she suspected that a grad student couldn't really afford to be spending so much money on knitting supplies. She gave a quick frown to her employee.

'She insisted on that wool,' said Peri.

'Of course she did,' replied Georgia smoothly. 'But, you know, Darwin, this isn't the type of wool you need.'

'It isn't? But Lucie used that.' Darwin seemed crestfallen; who knew how many hours had gone into that practice piece. Or was it meant to be a scarf? Hard to tell, but it was clear Darwin had spent hours trying different stitches – there might even have been a pattern in there if one wanted to look past the slipped stitches and holes to find it.

'Yes, yes.' Georgia was thinking quickly. 'But remember how Lucie was making a winter sweater? It's June now. That's why you should be using a cotton yarn. I'll exchange this and refund the difference.'

Darwin shrugged.

'Okay, if you say so,' she said. 'I'd rather use wool, though. Something like that gray heather over there. If you think I'm ready?'

Georgia went over and pulled out some super bulky wool-acrylic blend and tossed it over to Darwin. 'You, my dear, are more than prepared to take on the sweater! Especially with women like K.C. forging the way.'

'Oh, I see your grandmother didn't chastise your talent for mockery.' K.C. pretended to be put out. 'I'll have you know I've found a welcome recipient for my much-maligned baby sweater.' She pointed to Lucie.

'What can I say? It literally just popped out one day. One minute a little bulge. The next? A basketball.' Lucie pulled at her tan cardigan. 'See? I can't even do up the last sweater I made!'

'But you're going to dress the little creature in this spicy number – you tell her.' K.C. waved a needle holding the rows that would make up the back of the sweater, the multicolored acrylic masking potential flaws.

'You were already on the back of the sweater when I left!' Georgia was laughing now.

'And like you can just knit and study at the same time?' K.C. was making a 'stop' gesture with her hand. 'So, okay, you probably could. Well, I can't. I just added a few new rows last night. Because I didn't have a man to kiss my lips and distract me.'

A collective 'whoo-hoo' went through the group as Georgia blushed. She'd filled them all in on the basic details of James's trip to Scotland. And she'd provided the play-by-play to Anita, who had shared the details of her early return from Nathan's and that she and Marty were a going concern. The two had made a pact to find some time to talk – without Cat and the other women from the club hovering around.

Did they have handbooks on getting divorced? Because that's what Cat could do. She could write the book on it. K.C. could hook her up and get it published. The challenge, though, was surviving this latest ordeal.

Cat waited anxiously for her lawyer's assistant to come for her. She'd been smart, of course, to prepay at the hotel for three months, one fewer thing she'd had to worry about after the credit cards were pulled. (Though, now that she thought about it, the huge charge was probably what got him to cut her access in the first place.) Still, three months had seemed like the right amount of time – most of the summer season without Cat as his perfect hostess – and a vague assumption she and Adam would drift back together as the year gave way to fall. Because he couldn't live without her, of course. Her stunt was designed to recapture his attention. Make him see her as a real person. With ambitions and ability.

Oh, she'd been more than ready to leave him. That was true enough. But deep down she still believed that Adam could change. Look at James, right? And being on her own wasn't nearly as easy as it was in her imagination. For all her big talk, Cat had been having doubts.

Now she sat, waiting, summoned to hear what Adam was offering.

'You should come down so we can go over the details in person,' her lawyer had said. And it wasn't as though she had somewhere better to be on this hot summery day. (The world was so much hotter when you didn't have an air-conditioned car waiting everywhere you went, she was learning.) She'd done her morning with Georgia – 'bugging' her, as she'd been told – and then spent the lunch hour at the gym followed by nails at a little corner shop. (Part of her new cost-cutting measures: no more spa manicures.) And then she'd sauntered on over to . . . the knitting shop. To meet up with Dakota and chitchat about the mornings she spent at some sort of day camp, filled with games and sports and making little knickknacks.

That's what they need for jobless divorcees, she realized. Day camp.

Georgia had pointed out to her, of course, that she couldn't actually spend all of her time hanging out with an almost-13-year-old girl. And Cat knew in her heart that there was something, well, lame about a grown woman who had, as the high point of her day, an hour or two looking at *Teen Beat* and watching Beyoncé on MTV. It's just that it made her feel as though she was doing something important. Something that wasn't, entirely, all about herself.

Still, even Dakota asked her the question. And she hadn't even been mean about it.

'Don't you have any other friends?' she said, raising her eyebrows, as Cat talked about all the fun they could have through the summer. 'I mean, I'm going to work in the store like always, and I have drama club on Tuesdays and Thursdays in August. You know: getting ready for the day when I'm going to be on Food TV. Sorry, Cat, I guess I don't have as much free time as you do.'

Thirteen years old. And already she had direction.

'I think I've just been dumped,' she told Georgia.

'Or maybe you've just been pushing a little too hard,' pointed out her friend. 'She's a lucky kid: you and Peri for fashion advice and boy talk, Anita to be her fairy grandmother. And her tired old mommy to pay the bills and tuck her in at night.'

There was no one tucking in Cat these days. Though it was not as if Adam had ever been the pampering, considerate type. So she shouldn't actually be missing him. It was the same thing she told herself, every night as she went to bed, crying. She'd hated him for years. So why should she be longing for him now?

'Mr Elkins is ready, Mrs Phillips.'

Cat followed the young girl – maybe she should become a lawyer like K.C. was going to do? – and sat down across from the good-looking man who represented her.

'How are you, Howard?'

'Fine, Mrs Phillips, just fine.' He typically called her Cat, flirted a little. Now he was straight down to business. 'Mr Phillips doesn't want to contest the divorce action. In fact, he has offered a settlement. No hashing it out in court. Just cut and dried, you get this, he gets that.'

'Well, I thought you said this type of thing could take years.' She was surprised, had expected Adam to make a play to win her back. That he wasn't doing so . . . that he just wanted to talk through lawyers . . . stung. Wasn't she more valuable to him?

'It could have, except that he's willing to deal: a considerable lump sum and he's offered to buy you an apartment, up to five million, on the agreement that you waive alimony rights.'

'An apartment?'

'Could get you a classic six with a park view in a good

building. He's willing to pull some strings to get you into a
building you'd enjoy.'

'And in exchange?'

'No alimony, and you agree never to talk to the media –
or anyone else – about the marriage or the settlement.'

'Why is he doing this?'

'These things can be very messy – it's best not to create
a fuss.'

'No! That's not what I mean!' Cat was becoming emotional.
If it was over, so be it. She had wanted the chance to be on
her own. But she wasn't prepared for the feeling of rejection
that was welling up inside her. Her voice came out in a
whisper.

'No,' she said again. 'Why is he just letting me walk away
without a fight?'

23

One month of bliss. No arguments. No misunderstandings. Just lots of dinners in, mostly with Dakota, sometimes without. Bike rides in the park – yes, Georgia had even tried out that damned bike and ended up exhausted from a short trek, thank you very much – and evening walks to get a soft serve from the nearby candy shop or even just braving the tourist horde to hang out at the Temple of Dendur at the Met. James had treated them to a boat cruise to see the Macy's fireworks on the Fourth and tickets to Cirque du Soleil on Randall's Island. In the middle of July, all of them – Cat and Anita and Marty included – had taken the subway up to Yankee Stadium and watched the Bronx Bombers blast their opponents with home run after home run. It was, in a word, awesome.

She'd asked Anita to take Dakota out to the movies this Sunday night, had shaved her legs again, made a trip to Victoria's Secret for something special. A little purple cami set over which she donned a black V-neck tank and a not-too-skimpy-but-short-enough denim skirt.

'It's like I'm getting to know the most amazing guy,' she told Anita when they made the arrangements. 'And guess what? We already have a daughter together. It's very post-modern.'

Georgia had used that logic on herself when she whipped together a quick pasta supper: nothing to be nervous about because they've already been together. Obviously. Just look at Dakota. But her stomach fell through to the floor when the buzzer rang. She ran her sweaty palms over her hair, intending to smooth her curls, instead creating instant static electricity. Out of breath even though it took three steps to cross the living room and pull open the door.

James leaned against the doorway, in a bright white polo and crisp khakis.

'You look hot! And yes, I'm leering.' He nodded appreciatively.

She thought about the fusilli on the stove, just tossed with garden vegetables and a light olive oil and garlic. And she thought about the recently opened bottle of wine, the half-glass she'd gulped just a moment ago. Then she thought about Gran and the great charade she had been going to pull, telling James they weren't home when he turned up. Things worked out better when you were straight up.

Georgia decided to be direct.

'James,' she said, reaching out a hand to tug on his shirt collar. 'I think it's time you stayed the night.'

She didn't have to ask him twice; he was inside the apartment and pulling her into his arms instantly, his mouth on hers. Smiling as he kissed her, tasting so good, familiar but different. His technique was better. More experienced. She pushed the thought of all those other girls out of her mind; he was hers now. Hers and hers alone. Memories of long-ago sex with James flashed in her mind, triggered by the way he ran his fingers up and down her spine – she had forgotten that! – to how he loved to bite at the hollows of her collarbone, not so bony as they used to be. He wasn't as impatient as when he was young, either. Taking his time to look at her body as she undressed, reminding himself with his fingers and tongue of all of his favorite places. (And when she jumped off the bed in a panic to pick up any stray items of clothing, lest Dakota come home early, he helped her do a quick apartment check.)

He spoke to her, not in the shady sex lines of a Master of the Universe talking about how she made him hot, baby, so hot . . . but the soothing, laughing tones of a man as excited in his mind as his body. Loving every moment. Georgia had expected to feel embarrassed by her appearance, by the faint tiger stripes on the side of her abdomen that marked her long-ago pregnancy; she had been sneaking in crunches over the past month and tried using some miracle stretch-mark remover cream. (Ha!) But, instead, James had kissed every line. Being with him was just like returning home after a long journey. To a really mind-blowing location, to be sure, but a safe, familiar, beautiful place nonetheless.

James was truly hers. And she was his.

Being invited into a person's living quarters in New York City is a huge gesture of trust. Certainly their choice of artwork, furniture, paint color, reveals much about their taste and style. But that's the case anywhere, isn't it? New York is different, it remains a city of neighborhoods built up along the lines of class and race: the Upper East Side for Old Money, the West Side for New. Downtown for the Trendies. And all sorts of strivers and dreamers and regular middle- and working-class folks sprinkled everywhere in between, snapping up any apartment that is bug-free (please!) and not too overpriced (pretty please!). But it's not necessarily the location or address that defines a person: you can lease a tiny rent-controlled studio just off the East Side's Madison Avenue – or, one building over, own a massive multi-bedroom flat inherited from a wily old grandfather. In midtown offices, co-workers wonder if their peers are pulling themselves up by their boot-straps or are really just trust-fund babies. When impressions are everything, would you want anyone to know the truth either way?

That's why regular, work-a-day New Yorkers 'entertain' in

restaurants. Cocktail bars. Meeting up at the museum. Oh, sure, you'll hear people say it's because of the size of their apartment. That the kitchen is too small to make a reasonable meal. But that's just part of the equation. Because unless you go out of your way to live hugely above or below your means, letting a friend, a colleague, a significant other into your home reveals everything: your attitudes, your sense of style . . . and the state of your pocketbook. It's one thing if your home is so grand as to intimidate, though in New York, there is always someone who has more, bigger, seemingly better. Opening your apartment door invites envy or condescension. It changes the playing field.

The truth comes down to this: in a city obsessed with wealth and status, there are few gestures more intimate than being invited into someone's home.

So when Marty suggested to Anita that it would be fun to just stay in for a night, cook a meal together and enjoy some wine, she panicked. Not because she worried that he was expecting something for dessert beyond a slice of cake – he'd always been a complete gentleman and let her know that her company was more than enough. She panicked because they'd never discussed where they lived. In ten years of casual acquaintance, it had never come up. Which was, in New York, extremely typical. Ask someone where they live and they'll give out a cross street – 95th and Third, for example – rather than an actual address. And she'd always told him that she lived 'on the way to the park'. Marty, on the other hand, had never mentioned where he called home, either. And he was such a wonderful man, so proud of his deli and its success, that the last thing she wanted was for him to see her apartment. In the San Remo. One of the most beautiful and exclusive buildings in the entire city.

Anita was proud of her means, it signified Stan's hard work and his love for his family. But, for the first time, she was also embarrassed by it, aware of her wealth's potential to create discomfort. To make Marty – possibly, she couldn't be sure – feel inadequate.

'That's a great idea,' she said to Marty's suggestion, barreling right through before he could reply. 'Let's do it at your place. I can come over and cook.'

'No, you can be my sous-chef,' Marty said with a grin. 'I'll be in charge.'

A few days later, she found herself on a tree-lined West 81st Street. He lived in Apt. 1A in the building, he'd said, so Anita was surprised to come to his address and find a tall 1890s-style brownstone, wide steps going up to the double front door and a street level door below. Once single-story homes for the well-to-do, many brownstones had been converted into multi-family dwellings over the previous century, then, in the 1990s, began going back the other way.

The double front door opened and a toddler wobbled uneasily over to the railing, followed by an attractive young woman, visibly pregnant and pushing an empty stroller.

'Oh, let me help you with that,' said Anita, moving up the stairs to take an end and help the young mother carry the equipment down the steps.

'It's okay, my husband is coming right down,' said the woman. 'It's a nice night for a summer walk.'

'Yes, it is a nice night,' answered Anita, standing at the top of the stairs. 'But I think I've got the wrong address. I'm looking for Marty Popper.'

'Oh, Marty? He lives in the basement apartment. You can ring his buzzer here or just knock on the door downstairs,' she said. 'He's so sweet, he built us a big deck with stairs down to the garden.'

Just then a tall man came out the front door, an overstuffed diaper bag over his body and a toy donkey in his hand; the family set out for their adventure while Anita walked down to ring the doorbell for the basement apartment, feeling ever more certain that not going to her place had been the right decision.

Marty came to the door, hair still damp from a recent shower, in a long-sleeved collared shirt and a pair of navy dress pants.

'Come in, come in,' he said.

She walked in, let Marty take her purse, heard him taking a deep breath.

'You smell very pretty,' he told her. Anita smiled. She noticed the gleaming wooden floors, saw the staircase going up to the parlor floor but closed off at the top for the family above, admired the pocket doors leading to the rooms. Original? Off to her right was a large living area with two upholstered couches, an exposed brick wall, a large television, a desk with a computer. A round table and four chairs stood in the center of the room, and then there was a massive kitchen, outfitted with the latest stainless-steel appliances. Beyond the kitchen area was a glassed-in sunroom with French doors to the garden beyond, and to the left of the kitchen was a door that most likely led to his bedroom.

The apartment was gorgeous. Positively, absolutely gorgeous. Marty had surprised her once again.

'My niece, Laura, helped me choose the furniture,' he offered by way of explanation. 'She gave me two choices on everything – this one or that one, that one or this one. Couldn't go wrong.'

'It's fantastic,' said Anita.

'Come on over to the counter, I've been putting out toppings.'

'Toppings?'

'Yeah,' he said with a chuckle. 'I thought we could make our own pizzas.'

It was more fun than she would have guessed, chopping

up vegetables and grating cheeses, sneaking tastes, bumping into each other as they made trips to the fridge or fumbled in the drawer for Saran Wrap to cover the ingredients until they were ready to place the items on the dough.

'Ooh!' yelped Marty.

'What is it?' She was concerned.

'I nearly chopped my thumb off there – and I've been slicing pepperoni for nearly fifty years!' he said, before dropping his voice. 'Guess I just can't keep my mind on things when you're around.'

Anita felt that little dance of nerves in her belly, caught sight of her reflection in the gleaming stainless-steel stove. Even the distorted angles couldn't hide it. Her face was beaming.

She was in love.

It's something every person needs to learn, Georgia was telling Cat a few days later as she packed Dakota's backpack with extra socks and underwear and the new training bra she'd purchased at Bloomie's. (She figured she'd just tuck that in there, let Dakota find it on her own.) Don't – no, really, don't – agree to things when you're lying together in bed after making love. It's what leads to adventures like a family trip to meet the couple who should have been your in-laws, if everything hadn't been such a disaster for all these years.

But she'd agreed, somewhere between kisses and tickles, that of course Dakota could meet her Foster grandparents. And of course Georgia would come and meet them too.

'What are you? Nuts?' Cat was lying on top of Dakota's bed, pretending to flip through a copy of *Teen People* but actually closely reading the stories on the rivalries among a gaggle of pop queens. She sat up, conscious that Georgia had noticed her interest.

'I like to keep up with Dakota,' she said, tossing the magazine onto the floor. 'But, seriously, Georgia – you do remember that these are the people who didn't want James to date a white woman in the first place? And you're still, well, white.'

True enough. The only white person in the room, in fact, when she stepped into the foyer of the Foster family home, as country in style as James's apartment was modern gleaming steel and black leather. Here, the soft blue couches were over-stuffed and welcoming, wooden shelves groaning with books and endless framed photos of children: Georgia recognized a young James and three girls, youngsters in short dresses with empire waistlines to teenagers in bell bottoms and then young women in corduroy blazers and ruffled blouses. There were the requisite graduation photos on the walls, and over the mantel hung a large photo of the entire family – those young girls now women entering middle-age, their children and husbands gathered round, James in the center of the grouping with his arms around his parents, towering over everyone.

He had called ahead, he told her, to let his parents – Lillian and Joe – know they would be arriving. He had just forgotten to say exactly *when* he'd called.

'When James telephoned last night to say you'd be taking the train up today, I must say we were . . .' His mother's voice faltered as she searched for the right word. 'Unprepared. But I want you to know that we are very glad to meet you, Dakota, and to meet your mother, of course.' She extended her hand.

About five foot four and curvy, Lillian was a dynamic-looking woman, dressed in a red silk blouse and a flowing shirred skirt, large hoop earrings framing her face, her hair short and natural. She, like Joe, was a teacher, had made a career out of teaching kids to love the classics; Joe had taught chemistry for 40 years before retiring a few years earlier.

Nearly six feet tall, Joe was a strong-looking man whose

hair had hardly grayed over the years; wearing a polo and dark pants, he looked more like James's older brother than his father.

Dakota was entranced, shaking her grandparents' hands solemnly as befitted a serious occasion, before launching into a mile-a-minute monologue followed by a series of seemingly endless questions. Lillian ushered her in to the front room, took down an old photo album and began poring over the snapshots of the family, while Georgia perched alongside her daughter. She wished she hadn't come.

They had sat down to a lunch of sandwiches and green salad, Georgia grateful that the food gave her something to do with her hands, as Dakota filled them all in on her trip to Scotland. And her upcoming birthday.

'So I'm going to be thirteen soon and that's huge – starting eighth grade in September and I'm pretty smart. I got mostly As last year,' she said, catching a look from her mom. 'Not to brag,' she finished quietly.

'That's not bragging if it's true,' said Lillian. 'Your father was a smart one, and so were his sisters. Your aunts.'

'Will I meet them today?'

'I think we'll introduce you to the whole family just as soon as can be,' the woman smiled gently. 'All your cousins and aunts and uncles. They'll love you. But today it's just time for us to get to know you. And I thought you and your dad could play a little card game with your old Grandpa Joe there while your mom and I do the dishes.'

Georgia threw James a mental SOS with her eyes.

'I'll help, Mom,' he started, but Lillian held up her hand.

'No, I'd like to have Georgia give me a hand right now. Please and thank you. Georgia, is that all right with you?'

The two women brought in plates and condiments in silence, Georgia lining things up on the counter in the way of someone unfamiliar with that particular kitchen, Lillian moving with brisk efficiency as she loaded the leftovers back into the fridge.

'Mrs Foster, I am so sorry this is so out-of-the-blue, it's just that . . .' Georgia stood by the sink, making a row of glasses, nervous.

'I love my son, Georgia, make no mistake,' said Lillian, stepping out from behind the fridge door. 'But we've got a royal mess of a situation here.' She washed her hands in the sink.

'But I'd like to have you tell me a bit about yourself. What do you do in that big city up there?' Lillian had a certain kind of presence – honed from years in a classroom – that commanded acquiescence. Georgia felt as though she was back in high school, called up to the blackboard.

'I run a yarn shop.'

'Your own business?'

'Yes, I started it when Dakota was a baby. First I'd take on knitting commissions. And then the business grew and I got a bit of a loan, from my friend, Anita, and I branched out to selling yarn. I've had the store for years and it's been a solid living.'

'So you're a businesswoman. Good for you. And have you ever been married?'

'No, I never, it's just, well, I . . .' Georgia decided to be frank. 'I think I've been waiting for James to come back all this time.'

The older woman nodded, rubbing down the counter with vigor, then tackling the stainless-steel sink with a spray of Windex. It shone.

'So you're patient,' she said, still polishing the faucet. 'You're a shock to the system, Georgia Walker, that's for sure, but sometimes it's the little jolts that keeps things lively. Don't you think so? Now let's finish up here.'

And the women loaded the dishwasher as Georgia told

James's mother about Dakota's hobbies and friends, Lillian occasionally sharing a story or two about James as a child. In fact, it wasn't as bad as she had expected. Well, at least not for Georgia.

'She's got spirit, that's for sure. Spunk.' Lillian Foster looked out at her grassy backyard, surveying the plantings, the sun starting to go down. She'd convinced them all to stay for another meal but they'd soon be catching the train – and she wasn't going to miss her chance to talk to her son. Alone.

She'd asked James to help her outside, leaving the rest of the company in the house.

'How old are you now, James?'

'You know how old I am, Mom.'

'I *know* I know! But I want to hear you say it. Out loud.'

'I'm going to be forty in September.'

'So you are, son.' Lillian reached out to stroke James's hand. 'I remember when you were a tiny baby, those little hands and feet. James, I would have liked to have known Dakota as a baby.'

'Yeah.'

'No, it's not all "Yeah" and "Sorry". Is that what a forty-year-old man says to explain why he's kept his family apart for over a decade? James Aaron Foster, there's a twelve-year-old girl in my living room who is my own flesh and blood and I just met her this morning. This morning!'

Lillian gave James a hard look; her voice was rising. 'Your father is so upset he doesn't know what to do with himself. He hasn't slept a wink since you called last night.'

'Mom, I'm sorry, it's just that you always told me, "Don't bring a white woman to this house!"'

'So now it's my fault? Because it isn't, son.' Lillian stepped off the deck stairs, motioned to James that he should follow. 'Let's go check out my roses,' she said. A few seconds later they came to the prized red blooms, growing up the back fence on a white trellis. She started pulling off the flowers past their bloom.

'I'd like to dead-head you, if you really want to know,' she spat out, not glancing in James's direction. 'You're damn right we told you not to marry a white woman. We also told you to marry a Baptist and as far as I can tell, you've never even dated a true Christian.'

A large sigh came from James. He wasn't in the mood for a lecture.

'Oh, you'll listen to me now. Being married is hard. Period. And it can be even harder when you come from different worlds – race, religion, nationality. It wouldn't have been so easy if you'd married a black woman over there in France. Our advice wasn't just about color, James, though there's a lot of history there. Especially in this country. But this isn't a school lesson. I'm trying to teach you a life lesson and please let it not be too late.'

'I know what you're going to say, Mom.'

'Oh, you do, do you? Then good, you'll catch on the first time. Do you see how I've got to tend these roses? Always something to do. Prune, feed, water, get them started on this trellis so they grow up straight and true, reaching for the sky.' Lillian cut off one bloom that was just opening, not yet in full flower, and handed it to James. 'That's what parenting is – you throw out a lot of rules and good advice and you hope something good blooms. Even when your baby is almost forty years old. Your father and I have always been proud of you. Worried, too, that you never married or seemed to settle down. Now we know why.'

'I love Georgia.' James was glum. Feeling guilty.

'Well, now we're getting somewhere.'

'I just didn't want to disappoint you.'

'No, James, you cherry picked what you wanted from everything we ever told you and then left the rest. What you found was a convenient excuse to run when you were scared.'

James looked at the flower in his hand.

'I've been over all of this with Georgia and she's okay with it, Mom.'

'Well, I'm not so sure I am, mister,' said Lillian, her clippers in one hand, wagging her finger with the other. 'Because the minute the two of you conceived a child, it stopped being about what your father and I always told you. That's when it became about your family – that beautiful child and that long-suffering woman who somehow found it in her heart to forgive you. Black or white, that is some remarkable woman you have in that Georgia Walker.'

'She's pretty special,' admitted James. 'Georgia is smart and funny and she just rolls with it, takes life in stride. She makes me want to be a better man.'

Lillian was shaking her head.

'I'm glad of that, but I want you to understand. It's not what I would have chosen for you. But your father and I would never shut our door to you. Or to that little girl. In this family, we don't turn our backs on each other, no matter what.'

James held the bud to his nose and inhaled the light scent. He could hear laughter coming from inside the house and he smiled in the direction of the living-room window.

'I know that now, Mom, more than I ever did,' he said, taking her by the arm and guiding her back inside. 'And I'm not running anywhere ever again.'

24

After that last trip to see Nathan nearly two months ago, she was more than ready to just stay put, Anita told Georgia, inspecting the latest shipment of cotton rag.

'My age is catching up with me,' she said. 'I am just drained all the time. The kids are telling me I'm working too hard. But you and I know I've hardly done anything the last few months but knit or take naps in the office.'

'You have seemed really tired – have you thought of seeing a doctor? Or maybe it's just too much going out with Marty?'

Anita snorted. 'Now you sound like my mother, God rest her soul. That woman never wanted me to have a boyfriend. Just wait until you're married, she would say – though I had no idea how that was going to happen since I wasn't allowed to go out with anybody until I was over eighteen!'

'So, adjusting for inflation, that's a modern age of what? Thirty-five?'

'Very funny,' said the silver-haired woman, using her hand to brush her layered bob behind her ears so she could reach into the box and pull out an armful of yarns. 'Though, when I'm with Marty, I do feel almost eighteen again. I'm enjoying it much more this time around.'

'Anita? Are you – you and he – you know . . . ?' Georgia let her voice trail off with suggestion.

A flush came up on Anita's face.

'Goodness!' she said. 'There are days I'm glad you're not really my daughter and this is one of them.'

'Am I supposed to feel good about that?' Laughing, Georgia grabbed her clipboard and marked down some inventory details.

'And it's not really any of your business, but no, not yet.' Anita dumped her group of cottons onto the table, relieved that the store was free of customers and that Peri had gone off for a class at FIT. Thank God no one was around to hear a discussion about her sex life! Then again, it was pretty exciting to have something worth talking about in that regard, wasn't it?

'But we have been talking about going away for a romantic weekend,' she offered. 'With two rooms, I'd like to point out.'

'I wouldn't assume otherwise.'

'It's not like your situation, Georgia – I've just met Marty, really.' Anita was exasperated. Young people today did a lot of hopping in the sack, in her opinion.

'Anita, you've known him for years.'

'But we've only just started dating officially.'

'So is this about propriety? Or restraint?' Georgia decided to press her mentor. 'Or fear?'

'I'm not the type of woman who just jumps into bed with the first man she talks to!' The older woman's voice squeaked.

'I know you're not, Anita, and I'm not really suggesting you have sex with Marty.' Georgia began loading up the merchandise for display. 'To be honest, this whole conversation is kinda freaky.'

'So now it's crazy, the idea of me and Marty?'

'Not crazy as in insane. Just kind of weird. Like thinking about my parents.' Georgia shuddered.

'Well, it's not weird. It's normal. And I have no one else to talk to.' Anita bristled at the idea that she was too old to have sex, and launched promptly into a speech about how she was a single woman – a grown woman – and what she did on her own time was no one's business.

'Righto,' said Georgia, focusing on the task at hand. Then

she sighed. 'Though it sounds like you're giving *yourself* a pep talk.'

'Georgia, this is very difficult for me and now that you've brought up the topic, I'm going to be direct.' Anita opened up her purse and took out a small notebook and a pen. 'Marty and I might, or we might not, take our relationship to the next level. But I'm out of my element here. I think I need the name of a good gynecologist. Or a psychiatrist to have my head examined.'

'You're out of luck on the psychiatrist front but I do know the name of a great gyno,' said Georgia, going to her office and returning with a tattered red address book. 'I haven't gone in for a long time but I used to see Carrie Spelling over on Park Avenue.'

Her hand shaking just a little, Anita wrote down the phone number.

'Hey, it's nothing to be nervous about,' said Georgia. 'I mean, I'd rather go to the movies, but it's not totally awful.'

'No, I know, dear,' replied Anita, capping her pen. 'It's just that after Stan died, I figured I'd gone through the menopause, so why bother? Now I wonder if it's too late for me to, well, you know.'

'Aaaah,' cried Georgia, putting her hands over her ears. 'Okay, okay, I have a great idea: I'll go to your appointment with you and sit in the waiting room – a little moral support. In return, we'll never talk about our sex lives ever again.'

'It's a deal,' said Anita, snapping the clasp on her purse. 'I think I'd prefer it that way too.'

It's funny how a friendship can grow with very little encouragement. Just kind of springs up, a little weed of an acquaintance, and then it just doesn't go away. Becomes hard to imagine a day without the other person around. And, slowly, you begin to like it.

That's how Lucie felt about Darwin. Sure, she had all her old friends, off married in the 'burbs and filled with all sorts of boisterous encouragement about how she could pull off the single mom thing. And she had no doubt they'd all call after the birth and send a ton of gifts. But would they show up beyond the initial 'Let me see the baby!' visit? No, they'd all be too busy with their own lives, no doubt. And who could blame them, right?

But Darwin was different. She had her own life, too, had school and the thesis that never ended, had a husband far away. Still, she never seemed to find Lucie's calls an intrusion. No request was too demanding. Would you come with me to look at a daycare? Had she ever heard of baby sign language? Did she think the more expensive baby gear was really that much better? As she was getting bigger and more tired, Lucie found that she really wanted that support, the kind of back-up she guessed other women got from their baby's father.

Maybe it hadn't been such a well-thought-out plan, anyway, the idea of becoming a single mom at 42. But it would have been harder if she hadn't made a new friend in Darwin, who, underneath all her sharp-tongued edges was really just about the most generous, thoughtful pal she'd ever had. First the ginger, then a baby book, then an address for a single moms' group. Not Lucie's style, but still. Thoughtful.

And now she wanted to ask her the biggest favor of all.

They were meeting at their usual spot – the Starbucks near the shop – and Darwin was early, as usual, downing her second cup before Lucie arrived.

'I'm glad you called this morning,' said Darwin, a little wired on caffeine.

'Yeah,' agreed Lucie. 'Me, too. I was wondering . . .'

Darwin took a gulp of coffee, waiting.

'Would you be my labor coach? I mean, maybe that's too much to ask, but I don't really have anyone else and—'

'Ah, the old "I don't have anyone else so Darwin will have to do" routine,' said Darwin, no trace of emotion on her face.

Lucie made a gasp of horror. 'Oh, no, I didn't mean it to come out that way.'

Darwin's face broke into a goofy grin. 'No worries, Luce. I'm just working on my deadpan,' she said, picking up muffin crumbs with her fingers. 'I'd be happy to do it. But first, I have to tell you something. And this is really important. No joke.'

She took a deep breath, reflexively pulled at her long dark hair. 'I'm really glad I've gotten to know you and I just want to be honest. I think I wanted to be your friend because you're pregnant.'

'What?'

'I am really . . . enthused . . . about your baby. It makes me feel good.' She could see the way Lucie's face had scrunched up, perplexed. Darwin crumpled up her muffin wrapper and napkin, continued speaking.

'I had a miscarriage, about a year ago. And I couldn't do anything afterward. Couldn't talk about it with Dan, couldn't complete my research for school, nothing. Every time I saw a pregnant woman I'd end up crying in the bathroom.'

'Oh, Darwin, I didn't know.' Lucie felt close to tears herself; it was the hormones.

'No, hardly anybody did. And then my cousin told me to get a hobby, suggested knitting. Me! Knitting!'

Lucie laughed as they both recalled Darwin's early days at Georgia's shop, and her recent attempts at making stitches. Both disasters, really.

'Well, you know how that worked out.'

'I think it's worked out pretty well.' Lucie wagged a finger.

'I just, I'm telling you about the miscarriage because I don't want to overstep with you,' Darwin said. 'I don't know how or why, but being around you and this baby is making me feel so much better about mine. I miss her – I don't even know if it was a her! – but I miss her all the same.'

'Of course you do.'

'I really want to make sure your baby is okay and I'm really glad you asked me to be your coach,' said Darwin. 'I'd like to do it.'

Lucie reached out to give Darwin a gentle punch in the arm.

'Good enough, then,' she said. 'So how would you feel about coming for a sonogram appointment in the next hour?'

Darwin looked startled, but then her face relaxed and she let out a long breath.

'You know, Luce, I'd really like that,' she said, before standing up and coming around to pull Lucie's chair back. 'Coming through, folks, make way, pregnant lady on the way to the doctor.'

Yup, thought Lucie, feeling stupid and special all at the same time; she'd picked a good one in Darwin. A really good one.

The doctor's receptionist answered after only two rings: 'Dr Spelling's office. Can I help you?'

'Hi, uh, I'm a patient – my name is Georgia Walker – but I'd like to make an appointment for someone else. She's in her seventies.'

'That's fine, older women should still come in for an exam. Is this your mother?'

'Oh, no, just a friend – but I said I'd come with her for support. You know, sit in the waiting room and all that.'

'You've recently had a pelvic yourself?'

'What? Uh, no. But I'm fine.'

'How old are you?'

'Thirty-seven.'

'Then if you haven't had an exam in the last year, you

really should come in. And since you're going to be here anyway . . .'

Georgia didn't really want to do the whole feet in stirrups with the little look-see between the legs. But she didn't think she was going to be able to get the receptionist off the phone otherwise. 'Okay,' she said.

'We'll see the two of you next Wednesday at nine, Ms Walker. Have a nice day.'

Well, that didn't exactly go as planned, thought Georgia. But then what ever does?

25

Pancakes on a Monday. Well, why not? The shop was closed as usual, she'd muddled her way through the dreaded visit to Dr Spelling the previous week, and she and James and Dakota had come off an absolutely stellar summer weekend, including a Saturday night birthday party in which they'd taken their daughter and ten of her closest friends to see the latest teen flick. It was awesome, just being all together. As a family. Their own kind of family. And as for their elaborate machinations to keep the intimate side of things under wraps – the way James would ring the doorbell in the morning, as though he hadn't just spent the night – well, Dakota didn't seem to be buying it. Georgia suspected as much but somehow it had just seemed too strange to discuss James's sleepovers.

'Hey, honey, Dad is staying the night tonight!' Nah. It had been easier to make James throw on a pair of sweats and run down to Marty's for coffee, pretend he'd gone for a morning jog in the park. Never mind that his apartment was across town on the East Side. It was feasible. Technically.

But last night, James sprung his theory that he thought they should be open. Really open. As in moving-in-together open.

Georgia offered several reasons why they shouldn't, of course, past history at the top of the list.

James's rebuttal: if it's real, why wait?

'On that logic, we should just get married, silly,' she'd said, expecting a smart-ass response. She didn't get one.

'Okay.'

Georgia lay there, stunned, watching the ceiling tiles. Counting them. There were a lot. Eighty-two, in fact.

'Um, that wasn't a proposal.'

'Oh,' he said, unfazed. 'Too bad. So how's that moving-in thing looking to ya?'

'Maybe a little better than a few minutes ago.'

'I would marry you, Walker.'

'Yeah.' Georgia propped herself up on one elbow. 'I think that's what I'm afraid of.'

It had taken a long time to fall asleep, which meant they almost missed waking up early to toss James out on the street for him to 'arrive' while she and Dakota were eating breakfast. Or, as was the case today, making pancakes.

James rang the buzzer, having bought a bottle of water at Marty's to slap some 'sweat' on his face. It was his little nudge to Georgia.

'Hey, honey, Dad's here!'

'I was just jogging again and for some reason, ran across Central Park instead of in it.' James's voice boomed theatrically.

'Hi, Dad.' Dakota didn't look up from the griddle. 'Pancakes are almost ready and today I put in blueberries.'

Georgia walked over to the table and, for the first time, noticed that her daughter had set it for three.

'Smart kid,' muttered James so only his lover could hear. They sat down to eat, this new Walker and Foster unit, passing the orange juice and the milk for coffee, glancing at sections of the *Times*. Just like any other family.

'Where's the syrup?' James.

'I eat 'em straight up, with just butter.' Dakota.

'Well, I have both butter and syrup!' Georgia said, rummaging in the cupboard for a container of maple. The clinking of knives and forks on plates was interrupted by the beeping of Georgia's cell phone. A message.

'I'll just get that and see who it is – Dakota, make sure you eat some fruit, too.' She flicked open her phone and dialed in to her voicemail, then turned off the cell.

'Who was that, baby?'

'Nothing much, just someone following up, uh, on an order for the store.'

And then she watched as her daughter and her . . . boyfriend – yes, her boyfriend! – as they washed and dried the dishes, not even leaving the griddle to be scrubbed later but putting it away clean as new. She read the paper on the bed as James took a quick shower and got dressed and gave a thumbs-up to Dakota's shorts and tee ensemble for day camp, then stood at the door in her pajamas waving them off for the day.

They'd forgotten to talk to Dakota about moving in together. She had, in fact, neglected to tell them anything.

'Anita?' It was barely three hours later; Georgia was talking into her cell phone on the street, wearing a hooded sweatshirt even though it was a warm July day. Not New York sizzling, to be sure, but sunny and bright. With a breeze that was picking up in intensity.

'Georgia, I'm so glad you called!' Anita was chatting away. 'So you won't believe: I snore in my sleep. The doctor said so. Can you imagine?'

'You snore,' Georgia repeated, straining to hear over the noise on multi-laned Park Avenue as the taxis honked and screeched their way uptown and downtown.

'Yes, and what a shock. I have a condition called sleep apnea – I saw it on one of those newsmagazines years ago but I thought you had to be a fat man to get it,' Anita was laughing. 'Good thing I didn't you-know-what with Marty or I might have snored him right out the door!'

'So it's not serious?'

'Well, not if you treat it – but that's why I've been so tired. I'm not getting enough oxygen,' she explained. 'So I'll go to a sleep disorders clinic and get some sort of mask I can wear at night. It's very Darth Vader.'

'And you don't think that'll freak out Marty?'

'Oh, no, dear. Men love contraptions.' Anita spoke with confidence. 'In fact, you can always—'

Georgia cut her off. 'Did you hear from Dr Spelling?'

'The gynecologist? Oh, yes, last week, I'm all good. Didn't think to mention it. A bit of advice on getting back into the swing of things, though. So we'll see,' said Anita. 'So did you tell Dakota about James?'

'What? Uh, no, I didn't.'

'I thought that was your plan?'

'It was. But I got a phone call, Anita, a phone call from Dr Spelling.' Georgia's voice cracked. 'And I saw her again today.'

'Oh my goodness, you're pregnant. I knew it!' The older woman was making cheering noises in the background. 'Another baby! Oh, it's so wonderful. A little quick, maybe, but who am I to judge?'

Georgia stopped moving on the sidewalk, bothered by the wind blowing in her face and the tightness in her chest. She turned around so the gusts were hitting her back and put a finger in her right ear to block out the street noise, pulling the cell phone close to her mouth.

'No, Anita, just stop. It's bad. Really, really bad.' Georgia lowered her voice to a whisper, though no one was paying any attention to the curly-haired woman talking on her cell phone in the middle of the sidewalk. They just maneuvered around her, on their way to job interviews and lunch dates and shopping sprees with the girls. All the oh-so-important details of a regular life. Was this really happening?

'Dr Spelling says I have a tumor on my ovary. A big one. And it looks malignant.'

There was a gasp on the other end of the line.

'What did you say? I don't think I heard you properly.'

'I have cancer,' said Georgia, snapping her phone shut and swaying slightly in the sea of people walking around her, listening as the phone began to ring and ring. Knowing Anita was calling her back.

'I have cancer,' she said to no one in particular. 'Cancer.'

Starting Again

Every knitter has a sweater left unfinished; the bags of bits and pieces stashed away and never picked up again. And why? A change in fashion? A change in season? If that was so, you'd just pull out the stitches and use the yarn for something new. No, there's a secret hope that makes you hold on, to dream that you'll get it right someday, that you'll go back and take it up again and it will finally come out right. That this time all the pieces will fit. The mistake is waiting until you feel renewed enough to give it another try. You simply have to pick up the needles and keep at it anyway.

26

She'd gone several blocks before hailing a cab, ignoring the phone all the while; it had become silent by the time she was riding across the park to the West Side. Georgia got out at the curb, could see Marty through the glass of his store window, looked up at the big window one floor above and the Walker and Daughter sign hanging there. Thank God it was Monday, and she didn't have to focus on customers and the shop; James was at work, Dakota at camp, Peri enjoying a day off, and Anita . . .

She knew where to find her. Climbing the stairs, Georgia wasn't surprised to see the door to the yarn store unlocked, to see her dear mentor sitting at the table in the center of the shop, hands in her lap, waiting. Like a child caught being naughty, Georgia skulked her way into the room, for once not glancing around and taking in all the colorful merchandise that lined the walls. She sat down and faced Anita. Not sure of what to say or do next. The older woman brought her hands out of her lap and reached across the table; Georgia did the same. They held hands for a long time across the table, silently.

'Okay,' said Anita, finally breaking the quiet. 'We'll just figure out how to get through it.'

'Okay.' It felt better to just agree. Her mind was spinning.

'So tell me everything the doctor said.'

'I have a tumor on my ovary. And it's big.'

'And?'

'The fatigue, the upset stomach, the bloating – all the little stupid things I've been complaining about for the past little while,' sighed Georgia. 'It's all been symptoms, probably.'

'But that's like having a flu,' said Anita. 'Isn't there supposed to be some big thing, a can't-miss clue?'

'I guess not – she said the signs can be vague.'

'But you're so young! I'm twice your age and I've never had a tumor.'

'I don't know any more!' Georgia groaned. 'I can barely remember what she said.'

Anita nodded; she'd had enough friends experience breast cancer scares to know how the brain just turned to mush when you heard a doctor say that word. Cancer.

'So we'll call the doctor and I'll be on the phone this time and we'll take notes.'

'Okay.' Georgia was staring at Anita, holding her hands so tightly, willing her old friend to know how to save her.

'Let's start at the beginning, though, and you can just tell me as much as you can.'

Georgia took a breath and then shared the details of her appointment with Dr Spelling the day she'd gone with Anita, how the MD had felt something that she thought was most likely a benign cyst. Something common. They'd done some blood work and she had her receptionist make an appointment for an ultrasound, which Georgia had gone back to do the previous Thursday morning, before the shop opened.

'Why didn't you say anything when we left Dr Spelling's?' Anita frowned.

'She said it was just routine, and I decided I wouldn't worry anyone unless there was anything to worry about.' Georgia pulled her hands back and ran them through her curls. 'I wanted to keep things under control.'

'So why didn't you tell me on Thursday?'

'Because the ultrasound technician told me before she even

started that she wasn't able to comment – her job was just to perform the procedure,' said Georgia. 'I didn't want to be a pain in the ass, so I didn't press her. I tried to sneak a look at the screen but it was hazy and hard to figure out what was what.'

'And then?'

'And then Dr Spelling's office called today and said I needed to come in and boom! "Here are the findings and look, now we need to get you to a specialist."'

Tapping her fingers on the table, Anita seemed lost in thought for a moment. She made a clicking sound with her tongue. 'So, okay, I'm going to start making some calls.'

'I thought you didn't know any doctors in the city?'

'That's different: I didn't know any doctors that I wanted peering down there and I wasn't about to ask my son David to recommend someone.' Anita was dry-eyed and reflective; rummaging through her handbag for that pen and paper again, ready to make a list. Georgia had expected her to be all emotional and blubbery. But the silver-haired dynamo was all business. 'Some of my friends have sons and daughters who became doctors, and I'll call David to see if he has a connection with the kind of specialist you need.'

If it had been something else, something not so dire, Georgia would have pooh-poohed Anita's help, saying it was too much trouble. Don't spend so much effort on me, she would have said, it's not important. Or she would have insisted that she could figure it out all by herself.

But not this time. She needed the help and she knew it.

'Thank you, Anita.'

'Thank me when you're fifty-five and playing with your grandchildren,' responded Anita in a clipped tone. 'Until then, let's save all our energy for dealing with the problem at hand.'

* * *

Thirteen is a magic age. Old enough to know too much; still too young to know everything. Georgia had watched Dakota so closely at dinner the previous night that she had made her daughter self-conscious.

'What? Do I have food on my face or something?'

'No, I just enjoy looking at you,' she'd said. 'You're my favorite person in the whole wide world.'

Dakota had grinned, turned to her dad. 'You know what that makes you, Dad? Chopped liver!'

And they had all laughed, James and Dakota with gusto, Georgia with restraint. Why tell them now? She'd wait until she had more details. And when James had brought up the moving-in-together thing again, she'd put him off, suggested that he go to his own apartment to sleep.

'I'm just tired,' she said.

'Me too. Let's just go to sleep,' he replied. 'I don't know how long I can keep up this daily sex thing anyway! We might have to cut back, you know, or run the risk of a heart attack.'

Georgia barely responded.

'I'm just joking,' James said. 'I'll go home if you want but I'd rather stay here. And just sleep. I promise I'll run out in the morning and pretend I've just come from a yoga class or something.'

'I just kind of want a night to myself.'

James considered for a moment, wavering between hurt and anger, and then moved on to reasonableness.

'You know what? You're right. I might be a little smothering,' he admitted. 'I just wanted to make up for lost time. But absolutely, take a night for yourself. Can I still see you tomorrow?'

'Yeah.'

'Can we make fajitas?' Dakota had just walked into the room.

'Sure, baby,' said Georgia, who was relieved to know she'd have some hours to think.

Now it was Tuesday morning and she lay in bed listening to the sounds of Dakota thumping around, changing her outfit several times before being ready for her first day of Drama camp. Anita had made some decisions, about having Peri come in early to watch the store today while the two of them made calls and did Internet research in the apartment upstairs. (Having delivered her huge order of PeriPocketbook felted purses to Bloomingdale's on time and in a variety of shapes and colors – with cute labels sewn in by Lucie and Anita and Peri herself, of course – the fledgling handbag designer was more than happy to accommodate Georgia's change in schedule. No problem, she told Anita, I'll let myself in and stay the entire day if you need me.)

Georgia hauled herself out of bed to sit in the kitchen while Dakota chowed on cereal and juice.

'Where's Dad?' asked her daughter. 'I thought he'd come by after yoga class or something.'

Two hours later, Georgia was still in a T-shirt and sweatpants when Anita came to the door, armed with phone numbers and lists and books, everything from upbeat little life affirmation quote books to serious medical tomes.

'We can't leave those around for Dakota to see.'

'Why not?'

'I'm not going to tell her.'

Anita screwed up her lips in a pucker, then released them and made a big popping sound. 'I see,' she said, with a wave of her hand as if dismissing the comment. 'Well, I'll just make a list about that too. How to talk to people about this. *If* there's anything you need to tell her. First we need to get you a second opinion.' She consulted her pad of paper.

'Dr Spelling already called this morning with the names of two specialists. Onco-gynecologists,' said Georgia.

'See? There you go,' Anita replied. 'Let's see if we can find out what's really going on inside your body, and then come up with a plan to fix it. Have you told James?'

'No.'

'Cat?'

'No.'

'I see. So you're pretty much going to suffer in silence and let everyone else carry on in their blissful way?'

'Yup.'

'Of course you are – what was I thinking? Well let me tell you something: this is out of your control.' Anita was exasperated, frightened, upset. 'If it's confirmed, you're going to have to tell James and Dakota. There'll be no way around it.'

She made another call but was told the doctor was booked up for at least three weeks; Anita tried another name from her list but got a similar reply: ten days unless there was a cancellation.

'But this is important,' she said.

'It's important for everybody,' came the reply.

Georgia began to pace as Anita kept dialing. It was one thing to lean on the woman who had, essentially, saved her more times than she could count. It was easy just to lean in for a quick hug, or a pep talk. But how could she ever let James or Dakota see her as anything but strong and in charge? Wasn't that part of why people liked her? That she was so capable, so confident, so certain? Some people are the partyers, the fun-time Charlies – like K.C. – and others are glamorpusses, like Cat. But Georgia? She was the Tortoise: slow and steady wins the race.

When you've been rock solid, it just seems unfair, somehow, to fall apart. Doesn't it?

'Georgia? Earth to Georgia?' Anita was waving across the room. 'We need to get you in to see a specialist. And we need the best doctors in the city. So, whether you like it or not, I'm going to bring Cat in on this.'

'Why?'

'Because she's got as many connections – more – than I have and she's way more tapped in to the health field,' said Anita. 'I'm sure her Botox man knows some great doctors. Who can pull strings. Besides, Cat is downstairs already, unpacking a new espresso machine.'

Of course she was. Cat was still coming in to the shop every morning, and frankly, Georgia had found herself comfortably falling into a rhythm of enjoying a good hot cup of joe with her friend. It was, in a way, just like school, when you'd talked to a friend the night before but you couldn't wait to see them at the first bell to rehash everything you'd already discussed hours earlier.

'Okay,' she said. 'Get her up here and see if she's got anything to add.'

In a flash, Anita was downstairs, trying to act casual but effectively rushing into the store with great commotion and scurrying into the office, where Cat sat amidst Styrofoam packaging, pieces of the contraption in either hand. Peri poked her head in, curious, but Anita made up a story about how they were redecorating Georgia's apartment and needed Cat's advice. Redecorating? Georgia? If Peri had stopped to think about it, she wouldn't have believed for even a nanosecond that Georgia would essentially skip work to toss around a few throw pillows and slap on a can of paint. But there was already a line of customers at the register – there was always a mini-rush on Tuesday mornings of the diehard knitters, who'd run out of this or that when the shop was closed on Sundays and Mondays – and so Peri went back to work immediately.

Cat, on the other hand, was positively over the moon to be brought into a décor consultation for Georgia. It made perfect sense to her that her friend would stay home to spiff up her apartment. But one step inside, with Georgia still in pajamas and books and papers lying all around, and Cat was wise to something else going on.

Filling her in on the details, Anita asked her straight out: who did she know and what could they do?

Staring at the Hudson and New Jersey beyond, Cat passed cruise ships and tug boats as her cab sped down the West Side Highway. It had been a long time since she'd been down in the financial district; she had rarely bothered to see Adam during the work day. Or, more precisely, he had never asked her to make the trip. Now she was meeting him at his office – she told him she wanted to discuss the settlement; he refused; she insisted it would be worth his while; he was intrigued. You can have ten minutes, he told her. Hope it's enough.

If there had been more time, she would have gone back to the hotel and put on something fabulous, would have spent an hour on make-up. Instead, she pulled a tube of lipstick and another of mascara out of her purse, and decided her white cap-sleeve tee, khaki skirt, and nubuck mules would have to do. I'm not out to impress, she told herself, I'm here to make a deal.

Adam's office was oversized, with a wall of windows and a view of the Statue of Liberty and Ellis Island beyond. The orange-colored ferries between Staten Island and Manhattan chugged in the waters below. Cat watched them motor along, standing at the window, waiting for her husband – her soon-to-be-ex-husband – to return from a meeting. There was a brief moment where she thought, deliciously, of jumping onto his computer and finding secret information about his finances (an idea rejected because it most likely was not there, instead kept with his personal accountant) or sabotaging his work (rejected again because she doubted she could access any documents). Then, with a squeeze of anxiety, Cat realized she had never known Adam's computer passwords at all.

What sort of marriage was that?

'Hey, Cat, what a delightful surprise.' Adam's voice was gracious. Cat turned around, excited and pleased. Her heart sank. Behind Adam stood his mentor, an older gentleman long retired from the firm.

'Adam,' she said coolly. 'Hello, Stephen.' She offered her cheek as the older man came forward and said his hellos, then went on his way.

Adam closed the door.

'So now then,' he said, 'it's just us. Is this room okay or would you like something a little more private?'

'Private?'

'Well, I hear so much about exes falling in bed together, I figured you needed a little . . . tending to.'

'You thought I came down here to sleep with you?'

'Sleep? Not so much. Sex? Maybe.'

'You're loathsome.'

Adam laughed and took a seat behind his desk, leaving Cat still standing.

'All right, now that the niceties are out of the way, what do you really want?'

'I need a favor.'

He leaned back in his chair and stroked his chin theatrically.

'Favor? I don't know that I do favors.'

'I need you to call Chip, and get an immediate appointment with the top onco-gynecologist in the city.'

'Are you sick?'

'Hoping to delay the divorce until I keel over?' Cat spat out.

'It's a genuine question.'

'No, I'm not sick,' she replied. 'It's Georgia.'

'I see.' Adam watched his wife silently. It was an old habit of his; she always broke down and spoke first.

'I'll accept the settlement as is if you call Chip.' She sat down in a club chair in front of his desk.

'You could call him yourself.'

'I really doubt he'd take my call now that we're getting divorced, Adam.'

'True.' Adam smiled. 'True enough. That little stunt at the museum kind of sealed your fate. No one trusts a girl who airs her dirty laundry in public.'

'You call him, I'll accept the settlement.'

'Cat, Cat, Cat.' Adam got up and rested part of his weight on the front of his desk, leaning his body into his soon-to-be-ex-wife's personal space. 'You'll take the settlement as is anyway. I know it. You know it. So why should I call Chip?'

'Because we'll cross out the bit about you buying an apartment.' Cat felt desperate: she thought of Georgia's pretense of being calm, the fear that was so obvious in her face; she thought of Anita's look of relief and confidence when she'd said she could find her friend a doctor this week.

'Repeat that?'

'I'll take the money you offered but you won't have to buy me an apartment,' she spat out. 'I'll sign the divorce papers without a fight. But only – and I mean only – if you get Georgia in to see the top guy this week.'

'Why, Cat,' whispered Adam, bringing his face close to hers. 'I never knew how exciting it would be to negotiate with you. We should have done it more often. Want to find that private room now?'

As if by instinct, she brought up her hands and pushed him away.

'Get away from me,' she hissed. 'You just make those calls and get back to me with an appointment time ASAP.' Heading for the door, she turned around, willing her brain to come up with something harsh and brilliant that would make him see she wasn't his victim. That she was willing to pay any price to save Georgia. To repay her. Not out of guilt. But for her faith in Cat all along. She opened her mouth but Adam interrupted. His eyes were downcast; he looked sad.

'I would have done this for you anyway, Cat,' he said softly. 'Even without you giving up the apartment.'

Her stomach lurched. Was he here now? Her true Adam? 'You would?'

The man at the desk began to chuckle, then brought his hands together as if to clap.

'No!' he said, looking at her with a mix of pity and leering. 'Jesus, Cat, you never wise up, do ya?'

Yanking open the office door, she bolted into the hallway and counted the steps to the elevator.

It's worth it, kid, she told herself. Anything is worth it to save Georgia.

The rest of the week had dragged along, a waiting game, until the appointment on Friday afternoon that Cat had managed to secure. You had to hand it to her, thought Georgia as she pretended to work in her office on Thursday morning, her old-new best friend had really come through for her. She must really be connected, to be able to just pick up a phone and make it happen. It must be lucky to have power like that. It must make you feel good.

All through the week, Georgia had consistently put off the one thing that made *her* feel good: James. She avoided his calls, canceled the fajita dinner by claiming she had to go over the books with Anita in the evenings just as they always did around the beginning of a month. Of course, they'd checked them over the week before. Business wasn't quite as booming as in the earlier part of the year, but then that was typical. People tend not to think about wool when the weather is warm.

This morning, James phoned to say that he wanted to take them all back to Baltimore on the weekend, go to the aquarium with Dakota and his parents; Georgia agreed readily though she suggested that father and daughter do the weekend trip alone. That, more than anything else, made James suspect something was going on.

'What? You always want to be in on the action when it comes to Dakota – and you've only met my parents once.'

'They certainly seemed nice.'

'Okay, let me rephrase. We nearly came to blows over going to Baltimore the first time, then we went as a group and I practically got my head chopped off by my mom while you suffered the third degree. Now I say we should go back . . . and you're just completely fine with it?'

'Yup.'

'Just go have a nice time?'

'Yup.'

'What's with all this "yup" business? It's like you never want to talk to me any more.'

'What do you mean? I spent all of last weekend yakking your head off.'

'But since then you've been one-word answers all week. Even Dakota said you were grumpy.'

'She did? When did you talk to her?'

'When I came by the shop last night and she was manning the register. Peri was throwing K.C. test questions because she's cramming for the big test on Friday.'

'Oh.'

'They told me you'd gone to dinner with Anita – but I had just seen Anita talking to Marty in the deli downstairs.'

'Oh.' In fact, Georgia had made excuses to Peri, gone up to sit in the bathtub and cry. She'd stayed until the water turned cold, the only place that felt safe enough – private enough – to let out her emotions without fear of being seen.

'What's going on, Walker? Is it me?' James was hurt.

'No, it's just, I . . . can't tell you.'

'Georgia, if I'm doing something wrong again, just tell me. I'm smarter this time around. I'm sorry I've been pushing the moving-in thing.'

'No, James, it's not that. Trust me. I just need some space right now. And it would be great if you'd take Dakota for the weekend – she'd love to meet all those cousins.'

'Okay, but can I see you on Friday night, then? It's been days.'

'Oh, uh, I've got club on Friday. In fact, why don't you guys go up early that day? Could you get out of work and take her around noon?'

'Sure, but I really want to see you.'

'Then I'll see you when you come to pick her up.' And Georgia hung up before he could say another word. Call back, call back, she thought to herself. Demand that I tell you everything that's going on. Force it out of me.

But of course he wouldn't. No, James would be respectful of her request. And as smart as he may be, he wasn't a mind reader.

So she had done what any stressed-out working mom facing a health crisis would do: she went to work. Came up with plans to reorganize the store, ordered in some more cotton skeins – it was really selling quickly as folks dreamed of finishing summery sweaters before Labor Day – and spent far too long reading medical stories on her computer. Dodging Anita at every turn, who was bringing her orange juice and fruit salad and kept suggesting she take a rest.

What she needed was a break – a real break – something to focus on that had nothing to do with what might or might not be lurking inside her body. And the unexpected arrival of Lucie towards the end of the day on Thursday – moving far slower these days now that she was lugging a 25-week-old in utero – was just the ticket. (She still didn't look her age, thought Georgia. The red bandana around her growing sandy hair could stay – no doubt Lucie's response to the sweltering August heat and the fact that she couldn't dye her hair while pregnant – but that darn messenger bag simply had to go. Sure, it weighed less when the strap was across the body, but the way it fell on her front made Lucie's swollen breasts look positively massive. It was almost impossible not to stare!)

'Georgia,' panted Lucie, holding herself up in the doorway to the back office. 'I so absolutely have to talk to you. I need advice on having a baby solo.' As she closed the door and wriggled her way out of the messenger bag, flopping onto the loveseat and looking plaintively at her comrade-in-arms, the only other single mother she knew, Georgia felt a surprising sense of elation.

See? she comforted herself. Things weren't that different after all.

I'm still the go-to girl in a crisis.

I'm still the one voted Most Likely to Succeed at Harrisburg High.

I'm still me.

For over an hour, the two women talked, first about Lucie's raw footage for the knitting video, and then about the cost of everything from child care to strollers. Finally, they got down to the nitty-gritty: how hard is it, really, to run a single-parent household?

'Well, it's true you never have to compromise with someone else – and that has its advantages,' Georgia said. 'But then you can never hand off the kid and go take a nap. It's all you – twenty-four-seven.' She shrugged. 'But I was lucky. I had a great kid and a lot of help from unexpected places – like Anita.'

'That's what I need – an Anita.'

'Well, she's one of a kind. But you can reach out to support groups and to your friends and to your family.' Georgia smiled. 'I didn't think that was really an option for me – the family thing – but I may have been a bit too hasty at twenty-four on that score.'

'Yeah, I, um, haven't actually told my parents that I'm having a baby.'

Georgia nodded with understanding. 'I hear you. So what is your hesitation?'

'Big Catholics. My brothers and I used to refer to my parents as the Pope . . . and her husband.'

'And you're not, um, religious?'

'If by that do you mean do I feel guilty about how I conceived this child, then no. And let's just say I didn't go to a sperm bank.' Lucie laughed, then turned serious. 'But if you're asking do I believe in God, then the answer is yes.'

'I can't say I've spent too much time thinking about God.' Georgia was thoughtful.

'Me neither – at least until I found out I was really pregnant,' said Lucie. 'Now I think about that stuff way more.'

She looked at her watch, rooted around for a hairbrush in her messenger bag, and pulled off her bandana. 'And, speaking of the Big Girl Upstairs, I have an appointment to meet a priest and talk about returning to church. Also known as getting my child baptized.'

'So you're not a true believer?' Georgia was keen on the topic.

Lucie busied herself with heaving up her body from the loveseat. 'Whew, that gets harder every day,' she said. 'And I don't know if I'm a believer – I guess I'm a questioner. But I figure they need people like me too.'

'I bet they do,' said Georgia, with warmth. 'But I'm surprised Darwin isn't with you – the two of you seemed joined at the hip.'

'Ah, Darwin,' nodded Lucie. 'She says organized religion is a tool of the patriarchy – and I don't think she's going to back down the way she did with knitting. I'm on my own with this one. Unless you want to come along?'

'Oh, no, I'm a Presbyterian,' said Georgia. 'Not that I've darkened the door of a church since I moved to New York fifteen years ago.' She whistled. 'I can't believe it's been that long.'

Lucie began to close the snaps of her messenger bag.

'You know what? In my later months, I used to carry a backpack around instead of a bag,' said Georgia. 'It balanced out my belly.'

'Really?'

'Yeah, I'll trade you, if you want.' She upended her knapsack, letting loose a pile of newspapers, a sweatshirt, and a paperback from her trip to the park with James and Dakota the weekend before.

'My bag here is a piece of crap,' said Lucie, indicating the fraying at the edges.

'Dakota say that's the new style,' answered Georgia.

'I haven't made a trade since third grade.'

'Then I say it's high time for one.' With a Why-not? shrug, the two women exchanged bags. Lucie repacked her hairbrush, a baby-name book, a make-up case, a pair of size 6 rosewood needles – on one she had a half-foot of a yellow striped baby blanket – and one ball each of yellow and white machine washable acrylic. Plus a bottle of water, a pack of Saltines, an apple, and a meal replacement bar.

'Okay, I'm off – last chance to come to my big meeting with Father Smith and talk to God.' She made a face and, with a wave, headed out the door.

'Wait up.' On impulse, Georgia decided to go. Even though she knew Lucie didn't really expect her to come along.

But then, she didn't know that Georgia had a few things she wanted to say to God, too.

27

'I haven't got a prayer against all those young Turks.' K.C. was drinking a beer in the back office, even though it was only noon on a Friday – and Georgia would positively kill her if she knew. But Georgia had left the office a half-hour earlier and said she'd be out the rest of the afternoon with Anita, and K.C. had taken the opportunity – after a particularly dismal score on her practice test for the week – to rush down to Marty's and bring back lunch for herself and her tutor.

'Along with a cold bottle of brewski,' she told Peri, taking a swig and leaning back in Georgia's chair. Peri was used to her moods by now, the way she'd burn out at the end of a long week of study. Still, K.C. was clever, and Peri had no doubt in her abilities. K.C., on the other hand, was starting to get cold feet. She'd even sent in a few résumés to publishing houses, half hoping a job would materialize and she could declare her plan to become a lawyer officially kaput.

'What law school is going to want to take on someone who'll be fifty when they graduate?' she asked between mouthfuls.

'Lots of them, I bet,' said Peri. 'Just think of it this way: your application will definitely stand out. They'll sit around talking about the impressive old broad.'

K.C. held up her hand in the 'stop' gesture at the word 'old'.

'If you keep up the abuse, I won't tell you about the

PeriPocketbook I saw this morning.' Oh, she was a sly one, that K.C.

'You saw one of my purses?' Peri was getting excited. 'This isn't one of those trick things, is it, where you say "Oh, I saw it on the shelf of this shop."'

'No, my dear tutor, it's not.' K.C. spoke in low purr. 'I'll give you a guess: it was around fifty-ninth and Lex.'

'Bloomingdale's. Um, yeah, I know, I delivered them.' Peri gave a shy smile. 'I spent most of last Sunday hovering around Bloomie's, watching to see if anyone bought any. But no one did while I was there.'

'Maybe that's because they weren't getting the right exposure.'

'What do you mean?'

'Well, honey, I ran over to check out the shoe sale before all the good ones were snapped up and guess what I saw in three windows? Mannequins with PeriPocketbooks as part of their ensemble. You could totally see the labels – and, as chief plastic bagger, I completely remembered them. One mannequin had a pink and white purse slung over its shoulder, another had that red multi hobo bag that Anita finished and the last window was all evening wear, with the black silk clutch.'

'In the windows? The windows!' Peri was jumping up and down. 'K.C., this is fantastic! Oh my God, I wish I could go over there now. With a camera!'

Coming from around the desk to offer a solid punch in the arm to her friend, K.C. relented and gave Peri a quick squeeze.

'You don't tell Georgia about my beverage indiscretion and I won't tell her you ran out to get a cab and do a quick drive-by across town,' she said. 'Don't worry – I'll stop drinking away my LSAT blues long enough to ring up any customers.'

* * *

These are the times when people say they need a good, stiff drink. To blunt the edge. But Georgia didn't want to take off the edge. In fact, it was just the opposite. She wanted the numb feeling to simply go away.

They'd made it; got through the week to the Friday afternoon appointment with Dr Paul Ramirez. The preeminent onco-gynecologist in the entire city, he of the 'Best Doctors' profile in *New York* magazine and the wall of degrees from Harvard and Yale, was a short man with exquisitely long, manicured fingers that he laced and unlaced as he talked; Georgia couldn't take her eyes off him.

The doctor yakked on and on about how he'd looked at the ultrasound and agreed that surgery was needed, about how they'd know what to remove after they opened her up but that it was likely she would lose both ovaries, possibly also her uterus, a chance they might remove some of her bowel. What's going to be left? she asked, and the doctor tilted his head and offered a half-smile. As though she had made a joke.

Anita was in the room, taking notes, asking questions from a checklist she'd found on the web. They covered the likelihood of chemo, about survival rates and long-term prognosis and the possibility of losing her hair; she watched Anita scribble away. But everything that was up for discussion were all things being done *to* her body; they weren't things Georgia could see any way to affect or control. And throughout the meeting she had the strangest sensation of floating, as if she wasn't actually there.

Dr Ramirez had gone on about positive attitude and blah blah blah, but she'd really tuned out at that point, wondering instead how many times he'd had to deliver this same speech. Watching his lips and those long fingers. Did he use the same words, settle on a phrase that worked best to illustrate the complexities to his non-medically minded patients, select some pat words of comfort?

Did he ever go home and sit in his bathtub and cry?

'Do you have any questions, Georgia?' This was what he asked. Any questions. Any questions? Um, yes, she had a question. A big question.

Was she going to live?

His answer was filled with numbers and details and 'if this, then that' scenarios.

Useless.

'We'll need to touch base as soon as possible. Take the weekend to think things over and then I'd like to schedule a surgery.'

The weekend. Of course. Not like she needed any longer to decide whether she'd like to be sliced and diced.

'I think that went very well,' Anita had said as they left, biting her lip as Georgia threw her a dark look.

She hadn't much wanted to go to the club meeting after that, had walked all the way up to her apartment without stopping to see how things were at the shop. Anita followed her but they didn't speak, Georgia simply kicking off her shoes and climbing into her bed, clothes still on, lights out. Anita sat on the edge of the bed, rubbing her back, as Georgia struggled between wanting to cry and scream. A few gurgled sounds came out, but mainly she lay there, silent. Staring at nothing.

'I think this is good,' said Anita, stroking her hair. 'You stay here and hide out. I'll bring you a little something to eat after club.'

She closed the door softly behind her and went down to the shop; fifteen minutes later, Georgia was there – eyes red and puffy – but there. Cat and Anita were in the corner by the window, heads together. Her trusty employee saw her first.

'Hey, are you okay?' Peri pushed aside her digital camera, having waited anxiously all day to show her Bloomingdale's windows to Georgia. Even K.C. took her nose out of the study guide on the counter, and Lucie paused from her second hour of trying to teach Darwin how to do a basic increase so that she could tackle the sweater project. Georgia had forgotten to tame her hair after her lie-down and it was sticking up more than usual; her shoulders sloped forward. She looked exhausted and dazed.

'Heya,' said Georgia, as she was surrounded at once by the women of the Friday Night Knitting Club. There wasn't anyone else in the shop: just the die-hards. All the other drop-ins were probably on the Jitney to the Hamptons or simply not in the mood to knit on such a warm summer night.

She paused for a moment, weighing what to say. She could obscure the situation, be secretive, be stoic. But a week of doing just that hadn't done much other than leave her feeling adrift and also with an unexpected sense of shame. There seemed to be only one way to make it all real. And that was to be open about what was really going on. To practice, just like she guessed the doctor did, the right way to break the news to the people she loved. To her sweet girl. To James.

But first to her friends, her fellow knitters, experts and beginners alike. Georgia looked at the waiting faces around her and took a deep breath.

There wasn't much to say as they descended the stairs to the street, Peri leading the way and Darwin a step behind Lucie, who was hanging on tightly to the railing to steady her top-heavy body.

'I have an idea, guys,' said the academic, whose knitting skills remained marginal. 'What if we all start working on an afghan that Georgia can have with her in the hospital or in the recovery? We could all make a section and then sew it together. A sort of surprise.'

'It's a great idea but I don't know if we'd get it done –

Lucie's the only one of you who's finished her sweater!' Peri had been blown away by Georgia's revelation, thinking, of course, about how to help her dear employer, but also worried about what battling cancer could mean for the shop. Would she need to find another job?

'It's a good impulse, Darwin – I'll help you figure out an afghan. Something simple – no increasing.' At the bottom of the stairs, Lucie gave both her labor coach and Peri a big hug. To reassure them. To reassure herself. It's a scary thing, when a person you admire is suddenly revealed to be absolutely, truly human.

K.C. was still upstairs, not wanting to leave Georgia. Of course, Cat and Anita were loitering around as well, doing their best to convince her to stay overnight with one or the other.

'Come to the Lowell or just let me sleep in Dakota's room until she gets back,' Cat had been saying as the rest of the group packed up the knitting they'd barely touched over cooling cups of tea and coffee and fervent discussion of people they'd known who had beaten the disease. They talked about the shop and how they could operate a version of the schedule they'd run while she was away in Scotland – *if* Georgia opted for surgery – and they talked about vitamins and exercise and the need for rest.

There had been something wonderful about it, for Georgia, to suddenly be the center of attention. Not that she was enjoying being ill – she certainly wasn't – but it was such a welcome reversal of how things typically were. From as long as she could remember, when she was a child, a teen, a young mother, she had been the organizer, the worker bee, the behind-the-scenes manager of life. Keeping her head down, doing the right thing, using her energy to make things easier for everyone else. It had been like that at home with her parents, loud Donny distracting Bess and Tom's attention. At school she'd edited the newspaper and kept everyone on deadline, but Cat had been the columnist, the showstopper, the one who wore mini-skirts to her jeans. She'd always been comfortable to be in the background, to move at her own rhythm, confident in her own thing.

Georgia's sense of satisfaction came from the collective happiness of those around her. It had been that way at the store, too, when she taught beginners how to cast on and saw the pride in their eyes. Or when she found a small supplier of a high-quality yarn and knew that she was giving a boost to the supplier and delighting the customer all at the same time. She loved the win-win. She loved to make it happen.

Still, she'd hung back, all those months ago, when the women started meeting on Fridays; now she was pleased that she'd risked letting her guard down. That she could sit at the table in her pretty little yarn boutique with this unlikely collection of women and call them her friends, that she could share with them how her body was betraying her and that they would truly, genuinely care.

It felt good. It felt right.

Like anyone does from time to time, Georgia had tried to be her own seer and figure out how her future was going to be. In college, she obsessed about careers. In the days of James, she fantasized about white picket fences and suburban backyards. In the first year of the shop, she imagined a franchise across the nation. Or a descent into bankruptcy. And of course she was still predicting now, was making special deals with God to save her (I'll go to church! I'll give to charity! I'll help old ladies across the street!), and had imagined all week the moment when she would tell the people in her life that she had cancer. Would she just blurt it out? Scream it in frustration when Peri asked for time off, when K.C. messed up her desk once again, when Cat used up all the paper in the printer trying out fancy font styles for her résumé? Or would she whisper it softly, play the role of the always capable Georgia, not wanting any special treatment, so brave, so amazing.

The truth was that, increasingly, she did feel a bit set apart by the news, as though she'd finally been given a hall pass to get out of the work-a-day drudgery and responsibility and her overwhelming need to make sure everything – everyone – was quite all right. Finally, she could use the I-have-cancer revelation to excuse away any decision, any behavior, any desire. And no one would question her. No, it didn't mitigate all the possible consequences or reduce her fears, but it seemed that being diagnosed with cancer had a surprising effect: Georgia finally felt that it was okay – more than okay – to put herself first.

And what she'd needed that Friday night was not to struggle by herself or spare everyone's feelings or simply assume that their problems were larger than her own; no, she needed – she wanted – to reach out. To open her heart. To share her pain.

Her friends were shocked. By the news. But they didn't recoil at Georgia's vulnerability.

Instead, they listened, they brainstormed, they joked when the tears pricked at their eyes, and they were there. Just there.

For her.

28

The sun was blazing hot by 8 a.m. on Saturday morning; Georgia wanted not to have to think, to just sleep the day away since Dakota was off in Baltimore. But the little window-unit air-conditioner was no match for the sticky, humid weather. The air was stifling.

And so were the decisions weighing on Georgia, about surgery and side effects and statistics. That's what she didn't want: to become just another number. Another anonymous patient battling a devastating diagnosis.

How do you fight cancer anyway? You can't reason it away. Georgia had always tried to think things out, not react hysterically, but simply weigh the pros and cons and make informed decisions. It's how she approached the business, how she looked at the idea of romantic relationships (after the first go-round with James back in the day), how she dealt with her complicated exchanges with Bess and Tom.

Telling the club had been good. The choices were still hers, but now she had the ideas and input from the entire group. It made her feel stronger somehow. Braver.

After a quick shower, curls still wet and ringlet-like, Georgia decided to take a walk around the block, maybe grab a bagel before opening the store. She didn't have to; Peri had offered to take another full day, but now that the cancer wasn't a secret, she didn't feel so much as though she had to hide.

A summer Saturday means corner fruit stalls all around

the city, as street vendors push grapes and tomatoes and peaches for super-cheap prices, far less than in the grocery stores. Trucked in from farms upstate, the produce was fresh and delicious – a bargain sweet treat for every New Yorker trying to stretch her food budget. Buying fruit on the sidewalk was a city ritual, something that Dakota and Georgia loved to do, deciding beforehand to spend only $5 and then seeing what they could get for the money, rushing home to make a giant fruit salad. Rounding the corner of Broadway, Georgia saw the regular corner vendor and waved.

He held up a basket of Rainier cherries.

'Fresh, fresh,' he said, gesturing to her.

She swerved around a few pedestrians on the sidewalk and came over to inspect the fruit, standing alongside some other customers surveying the table.

'Okay,' she said, pointing to a few plums as well. 'I'll take them.'

It was a busy morning at the fruit stand. The woman next to her was buying corn, carrots, lettuces; a dark-haired man in a black polo shirt selected fourteen apples.

'An apple a day,' he joked. 'Or two, for extra insurance.'

That voice. Seemed vaguely familiar. Which was, by definition, unusual. She didn't interact with a lot of men: most of her customers were women, and she had basically four men in her life – James, Marty, her dad, and Donny. So why did this one sound like someone she knew?

Georgia looked over.

It was Father Smith. From the church. The priest Lucie had introduced her to when she went to discuss baptizing the baby. Georgia'd said, what, three words to the guy? He wouldn't even remember her. To be safe, though, she avoided his eye, waited for the vendor to hand her the plastic bag of cherries and plums so she could scram out of there.

'Oh, hello,' boomed the priest.

She looked up from staring down the celery.

'Oh, Father,' said Georgia, feigning surprise. 'I didn't see you there. You look different without the collar.' She brought her hand up to her throat, pantomimed a collar. Idiot!

The priest nodded. 'I love the fruits of the season,' he said, hoisting up his bag of apples.

'Me, too,' she said. 'Gotta go.'

She turned to leave and then hesitated. Why not? Why not just ask him? She pivoted on her heel.

'Father Smith,' she began. 'I'm not Catholic. But I was wondering if I could ask you something.'

'About your friend Lucie?'

'Nooo,' she paused, thought about abandoning the conversation. 'About me.'

'Shoot,' he said amiably, standing on the street corner, bag of apples in hand, in a black shirt and khaki knee-length shorts.

'You don't dress like I expected you would.'

'Is that your question? I always get that one. I don't know why people are so keen on what priests wear.' He chuckled. 'Don't always wear the collar on my free time.'

'Oh. Do you want a coffee? My friend runs the deli around the corner.'

Father Smith looked carefully at Georgia for a moment.

'I'd love one,' he said. Even though he'd had his personal limit of two cups a day already. 'I like that deli – they have great pastrami.'

'My knitting shop is right above it,' said Georgia. 'Walker and Daughter.'

'Are you the daughter?'

'No, I'm the mother – Georgia Walker,' she said. 'And I guess the mother thing is kind of why I want to talk to you.'

They went inside, got two cups of hot coffee from one of

Marty's employees, and sat down at one of the tiny tables inside.

'Father, I want you to know that I'm not into all sorts of churchy mumbo-jumbo,' she began.

'Okay, I'll try to keep the mumbo-jumbo to a minimum.' To her surprise, he didn't seem the least bit offended.

'I didn't mean to be rude,' said Georgia. 'It's just that I, well, I'll get straight to the point. I've been diagnosed with ovarian cancer.'

'Yes, yes, I see. That's a trying thing.'

'I haven't told my daughter yet. She's thirteen. And it just seems so unfair. Unreal. I just want to know why this happened to me.'

She waited, expectantly. The priest looked back at her, pensive, nodding.

'Well,' he said, after a time. 'I don't know. But I do know it's not because you did something bad, if that's what you're thinking. It's not something you deserve.'

'It's not, right?'

'No, Georgia Walker, it isn't.' Father Smith shook his head. 'I'll tell you right now that I don't have all the answers you may be looking for. I'm not God. But I can tell you some things that I believe.'

'Please.'

'I believe sometimes medical issues just happen – they're not cosmic tests, they're not retribution for all the naughty things you've done over a lifetime,' he said. 'It's not some moral righting of the unvierse. It's just something going wonky with the wiring.'

'Okay, and . . .'

'And I think God cries when we're in pain, he cries with us and he supports us. But I also believe he stands back and lets us sort things out. Lets the doctors do their work. Lets your body heal itself.'

'And if it doesn't?'

'Then he welcomes you with open arms. God isn't really about the body, you know, he's about the soul.'

'So if I pray hard enough then I'll get better?'

'No, no, that's not what I mean at all. Praying isn't a form of divine insurance. It's just a way of communicating, just a way of opening your heart.'

'By that definition, an honest conversation with anyone is a form of praying.'

The priest tapped his nose. 'You're right on there, Georgia Walker.'

The chat had lasted for a long time and left her feeling, if not exactly certain, then at least reassured that everything could work out all right; in the end, the Father had told her his door was always open and offered a blessing, which Georgia felt good about receiving but assured him she had no intention of ever coming to Mass. They parted with smiles and a warm handshake, and she'd met up with Peri at the shop and given her a big hug, had asked about the purse sales at Bloomie's and looked at the pics of the mannequins holding PeriPocketbooks. Anita, K.C., Darwin, Lucie, Cat – they'd all pretended to have a reason for stopping by, streaming in and out of the store. But it was good to have them around, to know she had their support. To talk with them and offer it up to God.

It was late afternoon on Sunday when Dakota and James finally hustled their way in the apartment door, dragging behind them a giant stuffed whale and a bulging shopping bag.

'Mom! It was fantastic!' Dakota ran to give her a big hug. 'I met everybody. And they all seem to really like me.' She was aglow.

'My parents pulled out all the stops,' explained James. 'Impromptu visit number two turned into a massive family barbecue and birthday party for Dakota, complete with gifts and a giant ice-cream cake.'

'So that means I got two parties this year.'

'Pretty lucky, I'll say.'

It was nice to see James and Dakota so animated, so relaxed with each other. But that just made what she had to do next that much harder.

'Guys? Let's sit down for a sec. There's something I have to tell you.'

29

Fuzzy. Faces. Looming above. 'You're fine.' 'You're fine.' 'You're fine.'

Voices nattered at her: Anita. And James. She'd had a vague fear, after she told him about the cancer, that he'd cut and run. But instead he'd been at her side like glue until she went to the hospital, had even tried to get Peri and Anita organized to keep the shop running. (Georgia had told him not to get over involved. A phrase that, to be honest, she'd never imagined tossing out at the guy who had hardly been around for most of Dakota's life. Crazy how things work out sometimes, she thought.) And now there he was, peering at her, his lips moving.

'I love you,' said James. 'Do you hear me, Georgia, I love you.'

She mumbled in reply, felt Anita's cool hand stroking her cheek.

'There, there, dear. It's okay to cry.'

It had been her idea for Dakota to stay back at the apartment with Cat, to not see her so drugged up. And she was glad for that. God, she felt as though someone had parked a truck on her chest. And tired. Very, very tired. Georgia closed her eyes, just for a moment, just to try to make sense of everything.

Hours later, she woke up, the same faces hovering around the room.

'Hey,' she said, weakly.

'Oh, you're doing great.' That was Cat. There she was. Looking perky in a navy and white striped dress. And there was something different about her.

'You cut your hair,' said Georgia, her voice raspy.

'Like that's important,' said Cat. 'It's my break-up hairdo. You know, clean slate and all that.' She smiled at Dakota over the bed: the two of them had spent the previous day getting their hair and nails done. She'd told the teen that it was to make themselves look extra-special for Georgia, but really it had been the best distraction she could find. For Dakota and for herself. There was so little she could really do, thought Cat, glancing about the room. It was private, another thing she'd quietly arranged for Georgia. If there was one thing money could buy in America, it was good health care. And pride? That could get you in to see the top doctor; she'd signed all the documents agreeing to the settlement the same time Georgia got in to see Ramirez. Adam was always true to his word when it came to money deals.

'Mommy?'

'Hi, baby,' said Georgia. 'How long have I been asleep?'

'You woke up a few times in the night – do you remember?' interjected Anita.

'No.'

'Well, it's morning. Tomorrow. You got out of surgery yesterday afternoon.'

'Are you in pain, Mom?'

Everyone was talking all at once. It was overwhelming. Georgia held up her hand.

'Okay, okay, everybody, I think that's the signal that we've come on a little strong,' said James. 'Besides, if the doctors catch all of us in the room at the same time, we'll be in trouble.'

The group filed out, leaving only Dakota with Georgia.

She reached out for Georgia's good hand; the other one was hooked up to the morphine drip and a push button clipped to her finger, in case she wanted more medication.

'Are you okay, Mom?'

'I am now, sweetheart,' said Georgia. 'Now that you're here.'

The week was a blur of sharp pains and a constant throb of soreness that permeated every movement, of indignities large and small, of trouble going to the bathroom and seeping out in other spots as the incision healed. Georgia felt exhausted, yucky, relieved to be through it; her excessive sleeping and soap-opera viewing interrupted daily by visits from the usual suspects. She tried hard to be attentive and listen to Dr Ramirez explain the surgery: her ovaries and uterus had been removed, and she'd needed a small amount of bowel resection as well. She nodded sagely when he explained that they'd taken all the cancer they could see, but that it appeared she was in Stage III, which was serious but certainly not hopeless. They would have to stay the course with chemotherapy and possibly, down the road, a second-look surgery.

'Bring it on,' she told him, her face pale beneath the bravado.

It was difficult to tell one day from the next, though Cat's daily morning flowers helped her keep track. On the fifth bouquet, she was surprised to get a knock on the door. Typically, when it was Anita, James, or Dakota, they all barreled inside, filled with chatter and carrying magazines and candy bars. This time, the visitor waited, then knocked again.

'Come in?' No one entered. Georgia assumed it was the morphine; maybe she was finally hallucinating and dreaming up phantom visitors?

The knock came again.

'Come in!' yelled Georgia, causing a sharp jab in her abdomen as she automatically stretched her body towards the noise.

The door opened. And there, in a beige belted trench coat that was too hot for a New York August and holding an over-sized brown leather handbag, stood her mother Bess. Shadowed closely by Tom, all white hair and big hands that he kept pulling in and out of his pants pockets.

'Hello, Georgia,' said her mother. Primly. 'Your father and I have come to see you.'

A moment went by as Georgia thought about what to say. But no words came out. Just a mangled cry and searing, hot tears that made her insides feel as though they were going to rip apart. Bess's arms were around her instantly as mother and daughter rocked together.

Turned out she didn't have to say anything at all.

It was a funny reunion, in a way: Georgia in a nightdress, her curls sweated to her head, Bess and Tom dressed in suits as though they were going to an important dinner. They made a motley crew. 'I brought you something,' said Tom, and then proceeded to pull out, from a plastic bag, an old stuffed toy she'd had as a child.

'Thanks, Dad,' she said, touched by the gesture but not having thought about that toy in years.

'I hear you had a good time back at the farm,' he said.

'Yes,' said Georgia. 'And I just sent Gran a letter, told her about what's been going on.'

'So how's things at the store then?'

'Good enough.'

'Good, good, that's real good.'

It was awkward, straining for conversation, dancing around The Big Topic.

'You're so young,' said Bess.

'These things happen, Mom,' explained Georgia. 'It can be genetic if there's a cancer history, but in my case it's just a fluke.'

Bess paused, then reddened. 'Well, my mother went away for a while when I was young,' she said slowly. 'A woman's illness, that's all I was told then. People didn't talk about breast cancer in those days.'

Bess began to get teary. 'I didn't realize it mattered,' she said.

There was a time – before the talks with Gran in Scotland, certainly – when Georgia would have railed at her mother for not sharing these types of details. For always holding back. For always holding Georgia at arm's length. But would it have made her go to the doctor more often if she'd known? Would it have made the cancer not happen? Probably not.

And now she was having the best, most honest conversation of her life with her parents. It was surreal. It was great. And she could thank Cat for their arrival, as Bess admitted she had been the one to call them in Pennsylvania.

'I didn't realize you were still friends with Cathy Anderson.' Her mom had dried her eyes now, seemed even a bit hurt.

'We got over our differences,' said Georgia. 'I don't see why it should bother you.'

'I just thought you might have told me, that's all.'

Georgia cocked her head sideways. Could Bess really think she was the one who was closed off? It was an intriguing idea.

'Well, if you're into hearing things, I might as well tell you that I'm back together with James,' she said.

'Dakota's father?' Tom's voice boomed around the room. 'Yes.'

'I see, I see,' he said, stalling, waiting for his wife to react.

'That's nice, Georgia,' said Bess, settling into the chair by the bed. 'It's been a long time coming.'

* * *

Darwin knew she'd been putting off the talk for far too long. If there was one thing she'd learned from watching Georgia, it was that it was hard to see what's coming round the corner.

She hadn't seen her husband in almost seven months, had cancelled multiple prearranged plans to trek out to Los Angeles and told Dan she was too busy with her research to spend any time with him when he suggested he make the trip himself. Her apartment was still a shambles and her original research was all but abandoned. The plan to look at the resurgence of knitting as a throwback had also stalled; to her chagrin and then delight, Darwin found herself quite liking the handcraft. Even if she was, well, less than good at it.

But there just comes a time, doesn't there? When it's time to face up to things. She'd done a lot of thinking, and she realized, finally, that she'd checked out of her marriage a long time ago. Back when she lost the baby. And, if there was any hope of salvaging her relationship with Dan, it was to start at the beginning. She opened up her instant message window and hoped to find him online, too.

Dansgirl: You there?

Medguy: Yeah.

Dansgirl: I have to tell you something.

Medguy: Miss you.

Dansgirl: No, big stuff. I have to tell you big stuff. About the baby.

Medguy: It's been almost a year.

Dansgirl: I know. But I didn't want it.

Medguy: What?

Dansgirl: I really didn't want to have a baby. I thought I did. But then I found out I was really pregnant and I did things to make it go away.

Medguy: ? I'm calling now. Pick up NOW!

The phone rang, and she considered letting it ring. But she couldn't do that to Dan.

'Hello?'

'I'm not going to get mad, Darwin, but I want you to answer me right now: did you have an abortion?'

'No.'

'Then what are you talking about?'

'I'm a bad person, Dan. A bad mother. A bad wife.'

'It's been months of this, Darwin – you crying into the phone, you not answering the phone when I know full well you ought to be at home. I want to help you. I really do. But I don't understand what's wrong.'

'Remember how you said I should see a therapist after the baby?'

'Yes.'

'I didn't go. I took the money out of our bank account and I, well, I've used most of it to buy wool. Really expensive wools.'

'Okay, well, maybe that will help. Can you even knit?'

'No. Not really. But Lucie's teaching me; she asked me to be her labor coach.'

'Are you sure you can handle it?'

'I don't know. I think so. Yes. Well, I don't know. What I think I need to do first is to wipe my slate clean.'

'Where are you going with this? Are you breaking up with me?'

'I never wanted that baby,' said Darwin. 'I found out I was pregnant and then I freaked. I went online and read all about old wives' methods of getting rid of pregnancies, herbs and hot baths and falling down stairs.'

'And did you do something?'

'Yes.' Darwin's voice was barely audible. 'I wished it away.'

Dan moaned with frustration. He'd been up for thirty hours straight and had spent the better part of a year trying to get his wife to tell him how she felt; still, he felt stymied.

'Oh, Darwin, thoughts don't cause miscarriages.'

'Yes they can,' she said. 'I told the baby I didn't want it, that it was interfering with my plans for graduation. But then I missed it when it went away. I dream about it.'

'First off, it didn't just go away. There was something wrong with the fetus; it's normal.' Dan was using his doctor voice. Authoritative. 'Second, I love you and I want you to know that it's also typical for some pregnant women to feel ambivalent.'

'But it doesn't make any sense! I didn't want it and so it left and now I think about that baby all the time,' she yelled. 'Don't you understand? It was my body! I was the mommy! And I fucked up, Dan.'

She wheezed over the phone line, out of breath, anxious. Pacing around the apartment, dodging the crazy piles of laundry. The newspapers.

'Why didn't you leave me?' She was making herself frantic.

'What? Over a miscarriage? Darwin, honey, you've made this thing bigger than it is . . .'

'It's big to me! It's big to me! I couldn't look at the research on midwives any more, I couldn't see a pregnant woman without wanting to puke.'

'Then why are you doing this labor thing with Lucie?'

'Because don't you see? She's including me. She's letting me be part of it. I can get it right this time.'

'Babe, it's Lucie's kid. She gets to take it home from the hospital, not you.'

'I know that. You said all year that you wanted me to talk,' Darwin was screeching. 'Well, I'm talking now. You went off to Los Angeles and got all doctored up and I've been sitting here, alone.'

'I didn't abandon you, Darwin; we talked about this. We had a plan.'

'No, Dan, we talked *around* this. And I don't care if I agreed to you taking this residency. I've changed my mind. It still feels as though you walked out on me.' She went to the bathroom to turn on the faucet, get a glass of water.

'Okay, I'll figure out something. I'll quit, I'll I-don't-know-what, but I'll do something.' Dan was alarmed: Darwin could be demanding, she could be scathing, but she was almost always calm.

'No!'

'What do you mean?'

'Then the past year would be a waste. All the time apart. It can't be a waste.'

'Darwin, you are making no sense.'

'I know, I know.' She sat down on the bathroom floor. 'Dan?'

'What's going on, baby?'

'There's something else.'

'What?'

'I cheated. I slept with another man.'

She was about to continue with her confession when she realized.

Dan wasn't on the line any more.

Binding Off

You can't keep your garment on needles forever; eventually it's going to have to exist on its own, supporting itself. The trick is looping the stitches across each other so they can be pulled away from the needle without coming all apart.

30

Darwin knew she should be working on her thesis. The days were ticking by, one by one, and she was no farther in her writing than before August started. But she just couldn't concentrate.

She'd tried Dan's cell about, oh, 800 times since telling him. Why did she admit what she'd done? Surely she could have lived with a guilty conscience for the rest of her life, surely the pain would have blunted after a while.

No, she admitted to herself, it probably wouldn't have. Better to live your life in the open rather than exist on borrowed time, waiting for the great unmasking.

Lucie picked up on her change in mood immediately; it didn't take much cross-examination for Darwin to spill it.

'I told my husband I cheated on him,' she said dully, as they carried bags bursting with onesies and impossibly small socks and footie pajamas from Macy's. Soon, they were going to set up the crib and the nursery. (Just a cleared-out corner of Lucie's bedroom.)

'Did you?' asked Lucie, as they waited at the traffic light. No more jaywalking for the pregnant woman, a hard habit to break for any longtime New Yorker.

'Yes, with some guy who is friends with Peri, if you can believe it,' said Darwin. 'I always knew to be suspicious of knitting. It ended my marriage.'

Lucie got a kick out of that one.

'Darwin,' she said. 'If knitting led to sex, I'd have seen a lot more action. But I'll admit it: you are filled with surprises.' And that was all. No recriminations. No signs of shock. Or horror. Or declarations that she'd just lost the post of labor coach. Just a gentle smile and an inquiry, as Lucie pulled open the door to the corner pizzeria, if she'd prefer pepperoni or plain cheese.

Actually, she wanted Supreme: everything on it.

After lunch, she and Lucie took the train up the West Side, wanting to go by Walker and Daughter.

The shop was still a place of business, of course, but it had also, unofficially, become the Georgia update center, with everyone gathering there in the afternoon to hear the latest news on the store owner's condition. Though there was still the chemo to contend with later, the doctors were cheered by how quickly she was recovering.

'She's feisty,' Anita told them. 'It's looking good. She should be out soon.'

'We've played a few hands of Go Fish, and Mom says she's all caught up if anyone needs an update on every single soap opera,' added Dakota. It was a tough time for the newly minted teen. She'd kept up with her Tuesday and Thursday Drama club – 'I paid for the entire session, so you're going!' Georgia had insisted, even as she packed for the trip to the hospital – and then spent every afternoon visiting, reenacting relaxation exercises she'd learned from the drama teacher ('Don't pretend to faint unless someone is going to catch you,' pointed out Georgia) or offering a reading from scenes in the 5-minute play she was writing. ('It's not mandatory,' she told her mother. 'I figured I'd just explore my creativity.') The story, Georgia could see quite easily, was a simple one: a family meets up after years of being apart and, in the words of the character who was the daughter, 'No one has to go to the hospital so we're all okay.'

Georgia had applauded with gusto, doing her best to seem

relaxed so that Dakota never worried but still experiencing post-op pain. She sent her daughter off to get her a large can of soda and to find Cat, who was probably off in the gift shop buying her too many magazines again.

'Don't forget ice,' she said to her daughter, before turning to Anita.

'Dr Ramirez says it's normal, and that you're healing really well,' said Anita.

'I know, I know, but it still hurts.' Georgia was pouty. 'Did you bring the stuff I asked you to?'

'Every day, it's something new. First you think you'll knit, then it makes you too tired. Then you want make-up. Then a sweater. I'm just a pack mule here. Schlep schlep schlep.' Anita sounded annoyed.

Georgia didn't buy it. Her mentor was trying to distract her and she knew it.

'The bottom drawer in my office desk – did you bring it?'

'What's your rush? We can't do a little bit of visiting here? Let me start on a list of what else you need.' She began to rummage through her purse.

'Anita, c'mon. Let's have this talk.'

'You're doing fine.'

'Exactly. And that's the perfect time to make sure all my wishes are in order.'

The older woman pulled out the tickler file, the one she'd grabbed from the bottom drawer, from a large handled bag.

'Fine then. Here is all of it: Will, insurance, everything.' Anita's mouth was a hard line. She wasn't happy.

'Oh, Mrs Lowenstein, I do believe you're cranky.' Georgia looked through the papers, things she hadn't looked at in years. Everything was in order, but it didn't reflect what she really wanted. 'My life has changed a lot in a short time – let's make sure to see a lawyer so I can update some of this stuff.'

Anita made a sound of disapproval.

'You don't need to worry about this now.'

'If not now, then when?' And Georgia had stuck out her tongue and laughed, welcoming Dakota back as she carried in the Sprite and handing off the papers to Anita.

'It is what it is, Anita,' she said cryptically so Dakota couldn't follow the conversation. 'Now let's talk about what we're going to do when I'm out of here.'

'We could have a party in the shop,' suggested Dakota. 'With confetti and a disco ball. I could make Shirley Temples and brownies.'

'Excellent,' said Georgia, pretending to be impressed.

'We could just have rest and relaxation at my apartment,' piped up Anita. 'A lot of peace and quiet.'

'Or we could do what Georgia wants and take me home.'

Anita sat on the edge of the bed and squeezed Georgia's hand.

'We'll be in a car the minute Dr Ramirez signs the paperwork, sweetheart,' she said. 'Don't you worry.'

Back at the shop after that visit, Anita had filled in Darwin and Lucie on the specifics: she'd wanted Georgia to stay at the San Remo but, to no one's surprise, Georgia was insisting on coming home to her apartment. A home care nurse would take care of the dressings and Cat would still be there, having moved in to be Dakota's 'roommate', taking up residence on an Aerobed on the floor. (The floor!) And James would be around a lot of the time, too. But all their help was still needed to keep the shop going even with Georgia out of the hospital.

'I know I've hardly been around and so much has fallen on Peri,' Anita said.

'And me,' piped up K.C.

'And me,' said Lucie, who'd taken to doing evening shifts.

'And me,' said Darwin, who sat in the back office many nights, pretending to write, but was really just afraid to go home. To see the answering machine that had no messages and smell the regret that scented the air.

'Yes, you've all helped, and it's just been wonderful. Thank you.' Anita looked pleased, but tired.

James had been in and out of the shop to pick up Dakota and such, but he had been spending most of his available time at the hospital. Then he'd stop by late to his East Side apartment to get a change of clothes and return to sleep on the couch in Georgia's apartment, just to feel close to his family. He got up early so Cat wouldn't notice he wasn't sleeping in the bedroom; it was too lonely without his Georgia next to him.

He had taken several days off work when she'd first had the surgery, then gone back, saving up his vacation days for the chemo to come. Still, he showed up at 12.15 daily, using his lunch hour to sit at her bedside and tell her jokes; he came back later for the evening visit, annoying the nursing staff by staying too late.

'I figured you'd cut and run,' Georgia said to him after a few visits, a teasing tone but real sentiment underneath.

'Oh, cutting and running,' he said. 'Been there, done that.'

He tried little ways to make her feel better, buying her an iPod and downloading her favorite songs, bringing framed photos of Dakota to put at her bedside, finally buying a knitting book and reading aloud the patterns.

'You do one kay, then one pee, asterisk, repeat five,' he read. 'Then yo, kay two tee, and yo again. This is wild stuff, isn't it?'

'It's awesome,' she said. 'You're doing great. Keep going.'

He sat up late with his daughter in the apartment, trying to be reassuring but really just faking his way through answering all her questions – 'I don't know' does not bring a restful night's sleep to a worried 13 year old – and he brought in sandwiches and coffee from Marty's, just to do something to thank the women from Georgia's club who were covering the shop. He and Anita kept up with their lunches, in a manner of speaking, now meeting for quick bites in the hospital cafeteria between sitting with Georgia and talking to doctors and trying to get in as much work as possible.

His mother Lillian even took the train from Baltimore and brought a selection of homemade casseroles, making sure that he and Dakota could have a home-cooked meal. And she brought a card and a plant for Georgia.

'She doesn't need a woman she just met barging into her hospital room and getting up into her business,' Lillian explained. 'But she does deserve to know we're thinking of her and wishing her a speedy recovery.'

Sometimes it made him feel worse, everyone being so understanding and thoughtful, especially given the fact that he hadn't been around for very long.

'I don't deserve everyone being so kind,' he confided in Anita, who was heading into Georgia's room with her latest request: her red leather journal and some pens.

'We don't always get what we deserve,' she replied, patting James over his heart. 'Sometimes we get more, sometimes we get less. At least we get something.'

He'd insisted on carrying her up the stairs in a wheelchair, turning it around and pulling her up backwards. Which was good, because she didn't fancy two steep flights, thank you very much. It was good to be home, thought Georgia, sinking into the soft spots on her faded old couch, noticing the large new window air-conditioning unit that James must have purchased.

The apartment was cool, unbelievably clean, and desperately quiet. Even though there were five of them in the room.

'How do you feel?' asked Cat, breaking the silence. 'Too cold? Need a blanket?'

'I made you some cookies, and fudge,' interrupted Dakota. 'Are you hungry? Do you want both? Let me get it.'

'Don't fuss so much, you'll excite her,' warned James.

'I think she needs some sleep,' insisted Anita. 'I'll stay here and you can all go get some dinner.'

'Whoa, hold on there, folks.' God, Georgia really loved all of them so much. But they didn't know when to back off. 'I am actually right in front of you, so don't talk about me as if I'm not here. Next, I know what I need, and it's a hug. Four of them, in fact. So line up, one after the other, and let's go.'

Ah, Georgia was back. Even if she was lying down on a sofa. The lady was in control.

'Now bring on this fudge and let's call this a homecoming party,' said Georgia, as everyone began to relax. 'Psst, Cat – you won't believe how much weight I've lost. I think I'll be borrowing your clothes from now on.'

Being at home wasn't easy, though, especially as the new school year drew closer. Dakota went shopping with Cat and came home with far too many new outfits, but Georgia just gave her a thumbs-up as Dakota modeled each one, the glittery jeans and fluttery-sleeved tops and the bright Lilly Pulitzer dresses. (She passed on the matching frock Cat bought for her.) They'd been through so much, why not splurge on a little retail therapy?

She'd been home a few days, mostly on the couch, often in bed, when Cat gave her a heads-up.

'The club wants to come up and have a meeting – a little one,' she said. 'Are you up to it?'

She was. And so the Friday Night Knitting Club became, for one day, the Friday-it's-still-afternoon Knitting Club, hanging a note on the shop door and thundering up the stairs like a herd of little elephants. A round of hellos and get well cards later, and Darwin brought forward a large box wrapped in comics as Georgia rested on the couch, her living room filled to bursting with women.

'Ta-da!' she said, as everyone clapped.

'Who knew getting sick would mean constant presents?' said Georgia, tearing off the paper. With Anita's help, she lifted out the afghan. 'Whose idea was this?'

Another day, another Darwin would have jumped to the front of the line. But not any more. She hung back for a moment, then spoke up.

'It was the club's idea,' she said. 'A group effort.'

Soon after Georgia let them in on her illness, Darwin had presented Lucie with several afghan patterns she'd found on the Internet, trying to select the prettiest blanket for Georgia.

'You do realize this would take me a long time to do – and I am, let's be honest, pretty good with a pair of needles,' Lucie had pointed out matter of factly looking at the lacy extravaganzas. 'Why don't we come up with something simpler? I mean, where are you with things right now?'

'I can do a pretty mean garter stitch,' said Darwin. 'I've been working on the hem of the sweater back and it's looking fine. Check it out.' She brought forth fifteen rows of heather-gray garter hanging off her needle.

'Isn't it a little, uh, substantial for the hem?'

'Oh, I'm getting creative, mixing it up.'

'But it won't match the front. That has a much shorter hem,' said Lucie. 'And I thought you got tired with doing the front – did you even get to the neck?'

'Nope. I bought a second set of needles and just started the back before I finished the front. I just like hems.'

'Darwin, most people don't invent a pattern for their very first project, you know that, right?'

'I know. But I'm not like most people.' Darwin was confident, beaming with pride over her little piece. 'I'm generally advanced.'

'How long did this hem take you?'

'Four hours.'

Lucie let out a breath.

'So here's what we're going to do,' she said. 'We can make this afghan thing happen, but we're going to have to get the whole club involved. And I mean everybody.'

She was Johnny-on-the-spot by the next meeting; Georgia had barely been in the hospital by that point. But Darwin had handed out photocopies of the basic pattern with zeal (thanks in no small part to Lucie): a basket-weave pattern in which everyone would do one long – but thin – row. On big needles – size 15 – with the softest, chunkiest machine washable acrylic in the store.

'So, okay, cast on 34 and do 16 rows of garter stitch – my favorite,' explained Darwin, to the room of K.C., Peri, Anita, Lucie, and Dakota, who had just come back with Anita from the evening visit at the hospital. A few of the more frequent drop-ins were also in the shop, and they took photocopies as well. 'That's the border. Then we'll do 8 rows as follows: knit 4, purl 5, knit 5, purl 5, knit 5, purl 5, knit 5, knit 4. Then do 8 rows this way: knit 4, knit 5, purl 5, knit 5, purl 5, knit 5, purl 5, knit 4. Repeat 30 times. Then finish up with 16 rows of garter stitch. It's still my favorite.'

She had grinned with excitement, imaging the moment when she would show Georgia the blanket she had organized. A little bit of a thank-you, you know? For everything.

Now the finished product was in Georgia's hand, a rainbow of sorts. Darwin had let everyone pick out their own colors and that may have not been the wisest choice, she realized. But still, the afghan had that particular kind of beauty that appears when something is made with love.

Lucie had sewn all the pieces together, making them fit

quite well, even though the tensions had all been so different. Darwin's stitches were tight, her frustrations and anxieties over Dan squeezed into every row of forest green. K.C.'s section was a Silverman Special, the yellow littered with mistakes and lines in which she'd mixed up the knit and purl. Anita hadn't slept in weeks, even with her sleep mask to fight the apnea, kept awake by her constant fretting over Georgia, and had found the time to do a long white section that formed the middle of the afghan, the stitches even more stunningly perfect when flanked by the segments done by Darwin and K.C.

Lucie had made certain to do both end sections, one in a bold pink and another in red, so that the edges were smooth. Peri had quickly knitted up a sky-blue segment – Georgia's favorite color, she knew. Then she had worked on another in dark blue, making a point to ask Dakota to knit some rows and then, with great care, giving the needles to Cat for the final garter stitch border, placing her own fingers over Cat's hands to work the stitches for her.

'It's amazing.' Georgia was genuinely moved. 'But I guess this means you're all behind on your sleeves!'

31

Zero zero zero zero zero zero. She counted the numbers once, then twice. A tidy sum, indeed. Cat had figured that receiving a big fat check from Adam – it was actually a wire transfer – would make her feel secure. Finished. Complete. Instead, she once again found herself with the sense that she was lost, while everyone else knew where they were going. Georgia had been home for weeks and was recovering with ease, building up her strength for the chemo that would start by the middle of September. But she was already spending part of every day in the shop, and made a point to get up with Dakota in the mornings. Cat was still sleeping on the Aerobed, but lately she'd sensed that it wasn't so much that she was needed to help out as that mother and daughter were reluctant to upset their rich little transient.

'I need a career,' she told Georgia for the umpteenth time, eating her Cheerios dry. 'No, really, I do.'

'Have you heard back from anyone about your résumé?'

'Got a few calls when you were in a hospital but it just wasn't a good time for me.'

'You're never going to get hired with that attitude, Cat.'

'I just want to be like you, Georgia,' she said. 'Inspired by something I love.'

'Oh, please,' said Georgia. 'I was single and pregnant and couldn't afford child care. I liked to knit! So poof I started a business? Um, no.'

'What?'

'I worked shifts at Marty's, knitting on commission, and then I got a big fat loan from a major supporter.'

'Anita.'

'Right you are,' said Georgia. 'Cat, I'll let you in on a little secret. We don't all love our jobs every day. And doing something you have a passion for doesn't make the work part of it any easier.'

'It doesn't?'

'No, it just makes you less likely to quit.'

The first session – on a Friday – had been fine. Really. Cat had gone with her as they hooked her up to the chemo drugs and waited; the nurses were chatty and upbeat and frankly, it didn't seem so bad. There was even a little gift at the end of the treatment, courtesy of Cat: a pair of gorgeous diamond earrings set in platinum.

'I figured they're putting platinum into your body with those drugs, we might as well put a little on it, too,' said Cat, pretending to be casual. 'It's a little motivational technique: you show up, you get a present for every session.'

'Part of your life coach thing?'

'Part of my support Georgia's life thing.'

But she didn't need any extra motivators that first time. In fact, Georgia felt good enough after that initial round of chemo to go back to work, had even stayed up a little late to hang out at club, admiring Darwin's mismatched (and unfinished) front and back of the sweater, had even given her a new pair of needles to start on the sleeves.

'She's all yours,' she said to Lucie, who had finished her own sleeves up quite nicely and bound off, all her pieces ready to go. (Not to mention the entire layette she'd worked up on her own time, while waiting for all the slowpokes to get on with it.)

'Now I see why we started on a wintry sweater,' added

K.C., suffering through the increase on the sleeves of her baby sweater. 'Because it takes a fucking year to make one of these things.'

'I thought all that practice on the afghan would have made your needles move a little faster, K.C.?'

'Oh, please, honey,' she said. 'I knitted that afghanistan out of sheer fear.' K.C. winked at Georgia. 'I'm glad to see you back around here, kid.'

And they spent the rest of the session focusing on K.C., who was going to write her LSAT the next day; they took turns shouting out questions and Cat offered words of inspiration she'd gleaned from one of her many self-help books.

'If it's meant to be,' Cat told K.C., 'it will be.'

'Oh, blow it out your ear,' K.C. answered. 'If I don't kick ass on this thing I'm going to spend the rest of my life packaging purses for one Miss Peri Gayle, handbag designer.'

'Gee, not like I even pay you,' said Peri, who was using almost all of her free time and a good chunk of her working hours on her bag line.

'Yeah, that's the worst part about it,' said K.C., then asked if she could borrow Georgia's iPod to play Queen's 'We are the Champions' before writing her test.

'But of course,' said Georgia, reclining in the leather desk chair that Anita had rolled out of her office. 'If the seventies inspire, who am I to stand in your way?'

It was standard club. Lots of chatting, too much eating, a teeny amount of knitting getting done.

After the next session of chemo about two weeks later, Georgia didn't pause to check on the shop, just went home to sleep and fight the nausea.

'It's killing me,' she wheezed to James, as she lay on the couch and he unpacked some takeout cashew chicken, prompting a run to the bathroom.

'That's the idea, babe,' he said. 'We'll knock any stray cancer cells right out of there.'

'Yeah, but the rest of me is hurting too,' she said, crying as he wiped away her tears. 'Let me get it all out before Dakota comes upstairs from club. I don't want to freak her out.'

'I'm here, baby. Just you and me. It'll be okay.' He rocked her in his arms.

'At least my hair isn't coming out,' she said. 'I've hated it for years and now I'm just happy to have it around.'

She patted her head then burst into another round of tears and hyperventilated.

'And my fingers are all thumbs, I can't even knit any more, or do up my buttons very well.'

'I know, Georgia, but it's temporary. Just a chemo side effect.' Dr Ramirez had gone over all the possible changes that chemo could bring, but it's one thing to see a list on a piece of paper, quite another to suddenly find yourself with a peripheral neuropathy that leaves you numb. James sat there, holding her, wishing he could make it all go away.

'I know, James, this is hard on you,' she said. 'But I'm going to get better.'

He'd always known, in the back of his mind, how strong Georgia was, raising Dakota, running her business. But he'd never really known the core of her strength until now, as she sat, tears streaming down her face, her body battered, but her spirit intact. Her faith in herself was undiminished.

She was still crying when there was a knock on the apartment door. James went to open it, came back.

'It's Lucie,' he said. 'I told her you probably didn't want to see anybody.'

'No, let her in.'

'Georgia?' Lucie was huge, that compact little figure overshadowed by a big round belly.

'Have you suddenly had a major expansion?'

'It's the last month and I am desperate – absolutely begging – to have them rip this baby out of there,' Lucie said. 'I hardly got up the stairs to here, and that's after sitting around in the shop for an hour after climbing the first steps from the street.'

James excused himself to the bedroom so Georgia would have some time to hang with Lucie.

'Did you tell your mom about the impending arrival yet?' asked Georgia.

'I sent her an email.'

'Have you heard back from her then?'

'Um, no. She only checks her computer if you call and say you sent a message,' admitted Lucie. 'She'll get it the next time one of my brothers is there – they always clear out the spam.'

'I think this is what Cat's psychology books call "avoidance". She's been reading non-stop lately,' Georgia laughed, then grimaced. 'It's a bad night for me. The chemo didn't sit well today.'

'Want me to go?'

'Nah. I've been waiting to hear about the how-to videos – Darwin told Peri who told Dakota that you were almost done.'

'That's why I came up – I edited all the footage we had, and came up with some basic skills videos, and then one based on making the sweater.'

'Tell me you didn't include anything by Darwin or K.C.?'

'I made sure that all shots of them were above the hands!' Lucie giggled. 'I feel bad. Just a little.'

She attached some cables and did some plugging in, and the videos were on the screen.

'They're great, really informative,' said Georgia, after watching a segment of the first few how-to lessons. It was true, they were good. Lucie was skilled with a camera; in some shots, Georgia's hair looked almost as if it had been styled.

'I wanted to show you something else, though,' said Lucie, switching a tape. 'I had hours and hours of extra footage and I just put together a bit of a short film about the club. I figured I could show it at a meeting or something.'

Georgia watched as everyday scenes from the shop appeared in front of her, the stand-ups from May, then shots of Peri's purse assembly line from June when Georgia was away, to the newer appearances on-camera of Cat (spouting what she likely imagined were homespun wisdoms), and then seeing the birthday cake that K.C. had brought in for Dakota, the entire club singing off-key, and on and on, right up until last week, when Darwin and Anita had engaged in a mock duel, using their knitting needles as swords and giggling like maniacs.

'Omigod,' said Georgia. 'We're all completely nuts.'

'Pretty much.'

'It's fantastic, Luce. Real slice-of-life stuff. Should make everyone want to start a knitting club with a bunch of complete strangers.'

'I guess it's just a little fun something.'

'You know what you could do? Kind of polish it up, put in a little narration or something. Call it "The Secret Lives of New Yorkers".'

'What do you mean?'

'No, on second thoughts you need to have "Sex" in the title. That's what sells these days.' Georgia was starting to wheeze again, this time from too much amusement.

'Do those drugs make you high or something?'

'I wish,' said Georgia. 'No, they just make you able to see things very clearly. Luce, you've got a little something there. I daresay a bit of an eye.'

'Aw, you're just like my college professor from film school.'

'You went to film school? No wonder,' Georgia said. 'Well, that clinches it. Lucie Brennan, you go home and turn this little production into a documentary. A real one. The how-to videos are great, but I say take the extra footage and use it. On one condition: cut out any scene in which my hair is more than this' – she held up her hands – 'high off my head.'

The suggestion was preposterous. Really, Anita knew she'd been out of her mind to say she'd consider it. Moving in with Marty? How would they figure out expenses, split things 50/50 or do that modern thing and each portion out according to a percentage of their income? (That could be a real disaster, thought Anita.) Would he expect her to do all the cooking? And how much baseball would she really have to watch?

Oh, there was no shortage of reasons against it. But there was still something enticing about the idea of waking up beside Marty morning after morning, hearing him sing Bobby Darin hits in the shower. She had to admit, there was something darn nice about spending time with someone from the same generation. It saved a lot of time typically spent on translation.

She decided to float the idea by Georgia. They'd settled into a new rhythm, with Anita covering the shop in the mornings, then going upstairs to have a cup of tea and help Georgia get ready, as needed, before the two of them returned downstairs for a few hours in the shop. Peri had taken over the noon-to-8 p.m. shift with ease, and had even found a morning class at FIT that she could fit into her schedule.

'So it's stupid, of course, for people our age to move in together,' finished Anita. 'My mother would have been aghast.'

'When was she born? 1900? And it's not like she's here to really know about it,' said Georgia. 'I think it's a great idea. But then I'm partial to this love thing these days.'

'But what about my apartment at the San Remo? We can't

live there – it's my home with Stan,' said Anita. 'And I don't even know if the board allows subletting.'

She helped Georgia ease into a shirt, did up the buttons.

'And the San Remo apartment has so many memories, the kids would all be upset,' continued Anita. 'Well, really just Nathan, I don't think the other boys would care so much.'

'You could get a house sitter.'

'How would you find someone you could trust?'

Georgia paused for a moment, then grinned fiendishly.

'Oh, I know how,' she said. 'Let's go talk to the blonde beauty sleeping late on the Aerobed in Dakota's room.'

Sewing It all Together

It's always easier to knit a sweater in sections: the front, the back, the sleeves. The benefit is that if one section is frustrating you, it can be put aside and you can move on to something else until you're ready to finish. That's not the same as giving up: that's being smart. Just work at it little by little until each and every part is ready and then you'll be able to match it up. Stitch together with a large-eyed needle and thin thread of yarn of matching color, sewing through every second stitch. (Remember: if one side appears longer than the other, then stitch just every other stitch and fudge it. Wool is very pliable and you can make all the pieces sew together quite easily. Trust me.) And it's never a mistake to block your piece, to lay it on a board and let the wrinkles steam out so that it has a smooth, finished look. Sometimes you just want to gaze on things a while, to keep them fresh and perfect as long as you can.

32

The warm days were all but gone; it was definitely jacket weather. There were changes in the apartment above Walker and Daughter, too: the big new air-conditioner was removed from the window (to keep the heat in), James had splurged on a new blue microfiber sofa to replace the faded old peach and yellow one, and Cat had finally deflated her Aerobed. 'It's a happy October,' she said, a set of matching luggage at her feet in the living room. 'Cat Phillips is out of the building.'

'I'm not pushing you out,' replied Georgia. 'It's more of a pinch to get you going.'

Cat's full wardrobe – a rather substantial collection – had been shipped from storage, along with a few framed photographs of her parents, to the San Remo. Anita had assured Cat that she was, of course, much more than a simple house sitter.

'I want you to take care of all my treasures,' Anita told her as she opened the door to her exquisitely bright living room, filled with antiques, the sunlight streaming in. Large picture windows overlooked the park, framing the leafy trees that were changing to orange and gold.

Still, Cat felt awkward as she moved into the roomy bedroom that had once been home to Anita's son David, even though it had been remodeled into a second master suite in the 20-or-so odd years since he left for college. Even though Anita had emptied the closet of the boxes of vests she had made since Stan passed on, had sent a selection of her favorite creations to her boys and donated the remainder to a men's shelter. Even though Cat was grateful to have a home.

It felt a little bit more comfortable after she threw a bit of a dinner party – just the Walkers and the Foster – and made the meal herself, a plain risotto (the bottom of the pan was a mess!) and grilled salmon (a tad overcooked but still edible). It had taken her all day, of course, but then that just changed things up from her usual dallying around the shop. Dakota brought dessert, a selection of squares from several recent rounds in the kitchen. Georgia, still feeling nauseated, ate a little bit of soup that Cat had warmed, took a few bites of risotto.

After dinner, they all went into the kitchen, a group clean-up effort. Dakota cleared, while James volunteered to scrub the bottom of the saucepan; Georgia watched, perched on a chair by the counter and holding a dish towel, but not really doing much.

'Finally, I've found the excuse to get out of all the world's drudgery,' she joked. She was tolerating the chemo well and Dr Ramirez was encouraging, but she was still tired and had been extra nauseated lately. But lots of sleep and some new medication and she was doing a-okay. Of course, she'd skipped the wine, leaving Cat and James to split a bottle, which they were still polishing off as they tidied up.

Cat was doing her part, trying to clean the spillover on the stove from her cooking extravaganza; she spritzed delicately with a bottle of blue cleaner. ('Hey,' said Georgia in a stage whisper. 'That's for windows. Try the other bottle in the cupboard.') Turning too quickly, the blonde knocked over her glass of cabernet, the red wine rapidly soaking into her pale green blouse. She began rummaging through drawers for napkins or towels, not remembering what was where. She came upon drawers of cooking utensils, flatware, oven mitts, spices, and, to her surprise, the ubiquitous junk drawer, stuffed with takeout menus and manuals for running the microwave and the coffeemaker.

'Anita has a junk drawer!' exclaimed Cat, as though she'd just uncovered the older woman's most shameful secret. 'I never would have pegged her for a junk-drawer person.'

Georgia eased off her chair to come take a gander as Dakota rushed in carrying the last dirty glass from the dining room.

'Let me see,' said her daughter.

'You guys are spying,' admonished James, loading up the dishwasher a few feet away.

'I know,' said Cat, pulling out papers and twist ties and an old orange-handled screwdriver, absentmindedly dabbing at her blouse with Georgia's dishtowel.

'Not much to see,' added Georgia, looking over her shoulder.

'Except this,' mused Cat, showing Dakota a stack of old, faded postcards held together with a rubber band. Cat pulled them loose and began flipping through, a collection of mountains and monuments. Turning over the first one, she began to read out loud.

'You can't do that!' said Georgia.

'It's simply addressed to Anita,' said Cat. 'There's no message. A total blank.'

'I think Stan did some traveling with the boys,' ventured Georgia.

'I know Anita is afraid to get on a plane.'

Curious, they sorted through postcards of Big Ben, the Eiffel Tower, the Great Sphinx, the Coliseum.

At that one, Cat frowned.

'What is it?' asked Georgia.

'Just made me think of Rome,' she said. 'I spent my junior year in Italy for my art history degree. I had this fantasy that I would become a curator dealing with antiquities. And now look at me! I'm a divorcee who house-sits.'

'Well, maybe you could . . .' Georgia trailed off, thinking. Could what?

'Oh, please, Georgia,' said Cat, sighing. 'I don't think I can bust into the business of ancient artifacts after being out of school for years and never working in between. The best I could do is take a chunk of that money from Adam and become an antiques dealer, surround myself with things I love and pass them on to others who will do them right.'

'For the right price,' added James.

Cat laughed. 'Exactly. Hang up my shingle and away I go.'

'Exactly,' echoed Georgia. Cat bunched up the postcards again and put them away in the drawer, shaking her head.

'I'm serious,' insisted Georgia. 'You can do this.'

'Like Manhattan needs a new antiques dealer on the scene? Come on.'

'Okay, where else?'

'I just got settled into Anita's place and I promised I'd stay put so she doesn't get cold feet at Marty's.'

'Okay, okay, I get it. Quit looking for problems,' said Georgia. 'So where could you open up shop but not have to move?'

'I don't know. Westchester? The Hudson Valley?'

Georgia threw Cat a look of challenge. 'I think you could do it,' she said.

'I think you're insane,' answered Cat.

'I think the two of you,' said James, 'make a frighteningly brilliant little team. I only wish I could read some of those old issues of the Harrisburg High *Gazette*.'

'Oh, I have every copy,' said Georgia and Cat in unison, beaming at each other.

By Sunday, Georgia was tired from her evening out but spent most of the morning on the couch, talking to Cat on the phone about how to start a business. It was an exciting time, throwing out all sorts of zany ideas, dreaming. After a nap that seemed far too short, James sat on the couch and kissed her cheeks until she woke up.

'We're going to be late for Anita and Marty's cocktail hour,' he said. 'It's the big housewarming event.'

'This has really been a party weekend.' Georgia grinned. 'I'm exhausted, but it's been really fun.'

'Especially the getting out of doing the dishes part,' said James.

'Oh, darling, you know me too well,' she replied.

With Dakota leading the charge, they arrived only ten minutes late or so at the brownstone. Cat was already inside, running off her mouth at Anita about all her plans for an antiques business.

'Georgia thinks it a great idea,' she announced as the family followed Marty into the living area.

'So do I,' said Anita, patting Cat on the knee and then getting up to give Georgia a big hug. 'Welcome to our little home.'

The apartment was just as beautifully decorated as it had been the first time Anita saw it, but now it had a throw pillow here, an original painting there, and vase after vase of fragrant fresh bouquets.

'It smells like you,' said Dakota. 'Good.'

They received the grand tour, ending up on the patio in the back garden for a few minutes, even though the air was cool.

'All right, I'm going to ask something that I know we all want to know,' declared Cat. Anita froze, expecting a comment about there being only one bedroom. 'Marty, do you own this brownstone?'

A chorus of 'Cat!' echoed through the group.

Marty seemed nonplussed.

'Nope,' he said, taking a sip of his beer. 'I'm afraid I just rent this apartment.'

He took another sip.

'From my brother Sam, who retired down to Delray. It's his brownstone and my niece lives upstairs with her family,' he continued. 'I just own the building on Broadway.'

'Say what?' It was Georgia. '*You* own the building?'

Marty looked down at his hands, a bit chuffed. 'Yeah,' he admitted.

'So you're . . . Masam Management,' said Georgia. 'Of course you are. That explains the barely-there rent increases over the past few years. I thought it was just some landlord out of touch with the spiraling costs of the city. But no, it's you.'

'It's me.'

'Very savvy, Marty,' commended Cat. 'You're a regular Donald Trump.'

'Just a guy that worked hard, saved his pennies, and had a goal.'

'What goal was that, Marty?' asked James.

'To make a good home and then find the prettiest girl in the world,' he said. 'And that's just what I'm doing.' He put his arm around Anita and raised a glass.

'To us,' he said, then winked at Georgia. 'To all of us.'

It was just a rough cut, Lucie was saying to Georgia as she arrived as the workday ended. But still, it was almost there. They'd snuck out of the shop – a quick wave to Anita to let her know they were going – and headed upstairs for the preview of the film.

'I remember when I used to run up and down these steps a million times a day,' she told Lucie. 'Now I move from sitting on my butt in the apartment to sitting on my butt in the office.'

She unlocked the door; Dakota was banging around in the kitchen, frosting chocolate cupcakes.

'Are we disturbing you, sweetie?' Georgia called out.

'Nah, just finishing,' said Dakota, who joined her mom on the sofa.

Lucie started the film, reading a narration from a piece of paper. 'I'm going to do the voiceover at the TV station this weekend,' she told Georgia. 'My boss is really cool. The job still doesn't pay enough but the health insurance and the easy access to an editing suite has more than made up for it. Plus they're going to top up my maternity leave with some extra time.'

'It's awesome, Lucie, just great.'

'I love it,' said Dakota. 'I think I've grown taller since I made that felted purse.'

Georgia kissed the top of her head. 'You're really growing into quite a young woman,' she said, ignoring Dakota's eye roll. 'And you, Lucie, are growing into quite a filmmaker.'

'I had so many hours in the can and then I shot a ton more since you gave me the go-ahead,' she said. 'You've really been kind to me. To Peri. All of us. I kind of wanted to make a film about that, about women pursuing their dreams and being independent. Show this baby how it's done.'

'Don't give me all the credit,' said Georgia. 'Save some for yourself.'

'I'd like to show the club when it's finished.'

'I have a better idea – let's make it a real premiere,' said Georgia. 'I'll rent out some equipment and we can set up the shop as a little bit of a screening room. Put up some posters in the shop and at Marty's with time and place. Think you can get it done for next week?'

'Absolutely – I'm almost there.'

'Well, we can move the table against the wall, and there'd be enough room. I bet we'd get quite a few people to show up.'

'Maybe,' said Lucie, considering. 'Do you think perhaps that news anchor from Channel 4 or something, the one who comes by sometimes?'

'Sure, or maybe someone we don't even know yet,' said Georgia, getting excited. 'It's New York. Everybody always has a connection to someone who can make it happen.'

'Thanks,' said Lucie, genuinely touched.

'You bet.' Georgia hoisted herself off the sofa and slid into a pair of mules. 'Now let's get back downstairs – we've all been so distracted with everything that we've fallen behind in our project. But I'm finally going to show Darwin and K.C. how to do the sewing-off on their sweaters if I have to tie them to their chairs!'

A half-hour later and K.C. was planning a mutiny. 'I failed sewing in high school,' she sulked. 'Georgia, I thought you were going to finish it off for me like you always do.'

'It's just a bit of zigzagging with a needle and yarn,' replied Georgia. 'Make sure it's the same tension as the stitches and you're good to go.'

'It's not sitting right,' said K.C.

'Well, it would have worked better if you'd blocked and pressed it,' pointed out Anita. 'I went over that last week.' Her tone scolded, but gently.

'I thought that was optional.'

'It looks better if you do it.'

Then Georgia noticed that Darwin was sewing her sleeves together to make a tube – but not attaching them to the front and back pieces, which were still folded up in her bag.

'Darwin, you've got to do the shoulders first,' said Georgia, as Lucie returned from her third trip to the bathroom to take her seat beside her labor coach. She was a good egg, thought Georgia, doing her finishing along with the group even though she'd knitted a zillion other things all along the way.

'I didn't finish them.'

'What?'

'I didn't finish the front and the back.'

'Oh,' said Georgia. 'Okay.' And she walked over to help some other customers sew everything together.

'Why not?' Lucie asked Darwin.

'Because I was knitting this sweater for Dan,' she said dully.

'Well then, I think you'd definitely want to finish it,' said Lucie, her eyes on her stitches. 'Don't you know what knitters call it when they put all the pieces together?'

'No.'

Lucie leaned out across her big tummy and took Darwin's sleeve, began to take out the seaming. Then she reached into Darwin's bag and gently handed her the front section.

'I think it's time you got yourself to the point where you can try it,' she said. 'Because it's called "making up".'

33

The following Tuesday, Darwin pushed her way into the knitting shop with a large box in her arms and a big backpack over her shoulders. 'Got any tape?' she called to Peri, who had started working an extra day on Tuesdays to help out while Georgia recuperated.

'What have you got there?'

'Posters for Lucie's movie,' Darwin said, dumping the box on the table just as the filmmaker in question walked through the door. 'It's totally done and we're going to paper every surface we can find in this town with posters about the premiere at Friday night's club meeting.'

Georgia, sitting at the table looking at some figures, pulled a poster out of the box. 'Great job, Lucie, on the design,' she said. 'Dakota already made a handmade sign on the wall over there but these look much better.'

Darwin pulled out the chair next to Georgia and put her head down, her long dark hair falling all around.

'Hey, what's with this, Professor?'

Darwin didn't move. 'I'm tired,' came the muffled reply. 'I've been pulling all-nighters.'

'Did you finally get going on that thesis?' Georgia said with enthusiasm.

'No,' said Darwin. 'I finally took Lucie's advice.'

The pregnant woman turned round at the mention of her name. 'You finished the sweater?'

'You finished the sweater!' repeated Georgia.

'Darwin finished her sweater?' said Anita, coming out of the back office with Cat.

'What happened?' asked Cat.

'It appears Ms Chiu has finished her sweater,' said Peri with mock drama, as though reading a news bulletin.

Darwin raised her head to make a face when K.C. threw open the door.

'I got my results back and I kicked ass!' she screamed. A genteel elderly customer looking at the cashmeres dropped her skein on the floor and scurried out the door. But Georgia couldn't be mad at her old friend. Not now.

K.C. was crushing Peri in a hug. 'My hero, my LSAT genius,' she screamed. 'I'm going all the way. Columbia Law or bust!'

She pointed a finger at Georgia, still sitting at the table next to Darwin. 'I knew it was a good idea to take that smart young assistant to lunch at Churchill Publishing,' K.C. said. 'She's good people.'

All of a sudden Lucie bent over and moaned. Cat, standing next to her, jumped back with alarm.

'Oh my God,' she yelled. 'I think she's having the baby.'

'It was bound to happen,' said Georgia, feeling a real tightness of emotion in her chest over the success of her friends.

'Darwin, I think this is your cue,' added Anita.

But even as she spoke, Darwin was already flying across the room, dragging over a chair for Lucie to sit in.

'Aaaah, this really hurts,' cried Lucie, a look of shock on her face. 'No, really, really.'

'Breathe through it, okay now,' said Darwin soothingly, to the bemused admiration of Anita and Georgia.

'You'll be great, Luce,' said Georgia, catching her eye. Lucie gave her the thumbs-up.

Darwin began to whirl around in all directions.

'K.C., get down to the street and flag a cab,' she instructed. 'Peri, call the hospital. And can someone do me a favor and hang up these posters today? We've got a hospital to get to.'

'Don't you need Lucie's things, dear?' prodded Anita.

'All here in my backpack, thanks,' she said with confidence, guiding Lucie out the door.

They paused for a moment, Cat and Anita by the door, Georgia still at the table. Then Peri ambled over to the office to get the tape and took a handful of posters down to Marty's.

'Looks like we'll have a new member of the club very soon,' she said on her way out.

'Wow,' said Cat. 'I've never been that close to a woman in labor.'

'It's a painful, crazy, beautiful thing,' said Georgia, who was starting to feel exhausted and lightheaded, really quite nauseated. Her stomach hurt. Sympathy cramps for Lucie, perhaps.

'Indeed,' seconded Anita.

'Okay, so are we going to finish up that business plan?' asked Cat, walking back towards the office. 'I'm ready for you to read it now, Georgia.'

Putting both hands on the table and breathing hard, Georgia tried to push herself up. But the shop skeetered around in front of her eyes and her legs began to wobble. She doubled over as pain seared her abdomen. In seconds, Anita and Cat were on either side, easing her down.

'Hey,' Georgia panted as Anita held her head. She took several shallow breaths before speaking again. 'I think we need a cab to the hospital, too.'

34

The cab snaked its way down a busy Broadway; it was barely
1 p.m. and traffic was bad. 'Step on it, buddy! And run all
the yellow lights.'

'Wow, Darwin,' puffed Lucie. 'You really mean business.'

'Yes I do,' she said. 'I'm a full-service labor coach, instructions to cabbies included.'

Lucie moaned as another contraction began to build.
'Distract me,' she begged.

'Um, okay, well.' Darwin hadn't expected regular chitchat;
she'd prepped for discussing epidurals and demanding extra
ice chips. 'I really finished the sweater. I sent it UPS to Los
Angeles last night.'

'A wool sweater to California.'

'Yup,' she said. 'And not just any old wool: it's itchier than
I expected and I screwed up in a few places. Just what he
wants: an ugly sweater riddled with mistakes from a soon-
to-be-ex-wife.'

'You don't know that's what he's planning,' insisted Lucie,
blowing out small breaths.

Darwin shrugged. 'There's always a chance,' she admitted.
'Now let's breathe it out, Luce. I'm not letting you have this
baby in a cab.'

'Don't stop for yellow lights – and there's a hundred bucks
for you if you get us there pronto.' Cat scrambled into the
backseat of the cab as Marty placed Georgia next to her.

Anita had raced downstairs to get help; K.C. had joined in to help Peri with the posters and they'd already plastered the deli window. Now they stood by as Anita took her place alongside Georgia. Peri opened the passenger door and reached over the front seat to put her hand in Georgia's for a moment, then leaned sideways for K.C. to do the same.

'You're tough, kid,' said K.C. 'We'll see you soon.'

Marty shut the back door as K.C. and Peri joined him on the street, watching the taxi pull a U-turn and head downtown.

James rushed down the hall, Dakota in tow. He could barely remember getting Anita's call and leaving the hotel building site in Brooklyn, making his way to Dakota's school and arriving at the hospital. Georgia was resting comfortably, Anita said, as he peered through the window in the door and saw her sleeping, an IV in place and an oxygen tube under her nose.

'What's going on?' he asked.

Anita looked at Dakota. 'Should we step away for a moment?'

James shook his head. 'It's happening to Dakota, too. You can tell us both.'

By nine o'clock that night, Darwin was sweaty and exhausted. And she wasn't even the one having the baby. Lucie had been in labor eight hours and it looked as though they had several more to go.

'First babies can take a while,' the obstetrician explained when she came to check in on her patient.

'But she's so tired,' fretted Darwin, taking the doctor aside. 'Why don't you just call it a day and do a C-section?'

The doctor smiled kindly. 'She's doing great. This is how the system works.'

Lucie motioned Darwin to come back. 'Get my cell phone,' she said. 'I want to call my mother.'

Darwin fished around in the backpack, taking the phone out of a little knitted cell-phone sock (Lucie was always sneaking in little projects, she thought with a bit of envy), and handed it to her friend.

'I'll step outside so you can have some privacy,' she said.

'Okay,' smiled Lucie. 'Go call the shop and tell everyone how it's going. We kinda left in a flash.'

An obstructed bowel was causing the problems, the doctor had explained to Anita and Cat after the first round of tests. They'd put Georgia on fluids and massive doses of antibiotics, but it was going to be touch-and-go as they waited it out, hoping to prevent a perforation and stem any infection from moving into her bloodstream.

'I think we'll find a way,' said Cat. Her voice was quiet and assured.

'Yes, there's always a chance,' added Anita.

Georgia's breathing was becoming labored, but her right hand was still grasping tightly onto Dakota's fingers, while Anita held the left tenderly.

'I'm open to second chances,' rasped Georgia. 'But I may have had more than my fair share already.'

She slept for most of the afternoon and into the evening, not even stirring as medical staff poked and prodded. Georgia woke up briefly around 10 p.m. for a while, then dozed until well after midnight. Shortly thereafter, Anita noticed a figure at the door, looking into the window.

'It's Darwin,' she said aloud, surprised. She'd forgotten all about that other drama.

'Did Lucie have the baby?' mumbled Georgia, barely awake.

Anita took the few steps to the door and ushered Darwin inside.

'It's a girl,' said Darwin quietly. 'Ginger.'

'Good,' Georgia breathed. 'Good job.'

Darwin stayed for a few moments, then gently touched Anita's shoulder to let her know she'd make her way out. In the doorway she passed James, returning from talking to Dr Ramirez again. The latest test results were in.

His bottom lip was trembling but he held his voice steady: 'Hey, Walker, how are you doing?'

Georgia nodded, weak from the complications and not getting any better from the medication. Her face was pale but her green eyes shone brightly; she seemed completely aware. He came over to stand by Dakota, one arm around his daughter and the other hand stroking Georgia's curls.

Cat stood by the bedside, her arms dangling at her side, her face blank. 'Come on over here, CathyCat,' whispered Georgia. 'I may have only two hands but surely you can grab on to a finger.'

Cat inched closer to the bed; Anita reached out and pulled her hand forward.

'Oh, Georgia,' blurted Cat. 'What's going to happen now?'

Lying on her hospital bed, Georgia attempted a smile.

'I'm not about to stop talking, you know,' she said. 'Guess we'll just have to carry on our conversation in a different way.'

'I just wish . . .' interjected James, stepping over his words. 'That it had been different.'

'Maybe,' said Georgia. 'But then it wouldn't be the same, would it?'

They kept up a banter for several minutes, talking, just talking. About nothing. About everything.

Then, with great effort, Georgia turned her head and stared lovingly at Dakota, and though Cat and James and Anita surrounded the two of them, she focused every ounce of her energy on her beautiful little girl.

'You,' she said to Dakota, pressing her daughter's fingers to her lips. 'It'll always be you.'

'I'll be good,' answered her daughter, her voice rising in fear.

'No,' said Georgia, in her strongest voice of the entire night. 'Just be yourself.'

Her eyes began to flutter as though she was struggling to stay awake.

'I'm sleepy,' she said, triggering Anita to rush in and begin wiping her forehead with a cloth.

'It's okay, it's okay, it's okay, it's okay,' her dear old mentor repeated, as if unable to stop the words.

'It is,' said Georgia, bringing up her left hand to quell Anita from her fevered motions and motioning for everyone to come in closer.

'It really is,' she repeated, drifting off to sleep in the arms of the ones she loved the most.

There was a moment, a hiccup of time, as they all held their breath and waited for her to wake up. But then the machines stopped their monitoring beat and it was clear.

Georgia Walker was gone.

Wearing What You've Made

This can be the most fun: to show off some funky scarf that reveals your inner cool. And other times it's just so hard to wear something that seems less than perfect or didn't turn out the way you wanted it to. But just put it on anyway; celebrate your hard work and your talent. And your love. Every knitter stitches with love, even when they're just starting, all red-faced and frustrated. Why else would we create? Especially in a world that doesn't need homemade anything. That's when we need homemade everything. It never matters if things don't end up just the way you planned. Every moment is a work in progress, every stitch is one stitch closer. There may be worse, but there is always better. When you wear something you've made with your own hands, you surround yourself with love, and all the love that came before you. The real achievement, you see, is being proud of what you've made. I know that I am.

35

Walker and Daughter stayed closed, of course, in the long, empty October Wednesday that followed. James and Dakota bunked in the other guest rooms at the San Remo apartment, but couldn't sleep. Instead they wandered around its big rooms, like Cat, shocked and bleary-eyed. Marty stayed up all the next night as Anita sat in the living room, stunned, unable to rest either.

By Friday, she and James were busy with all the to-dos that come afterwards, all the stray ends that need to be tucked in. And she talked to Peri, who felt strong enough to open the shop.

'Georgia wouldn't want Walker and Daughter to sit empty,' said Anita. 'Let's just figure out some shifts and keep things going until we can figure out what's what.'

'I think K.C. wants to come by,' said Peri. 'And Lucie's out of the hospital.'

'Yes, call everyone and tell them we'll be open this evening,' agreed Anita. 'If they want to stop in.'

No one had given a second thought, since Tuesday afternoon, to the posters advertising Lucie's film. Nor had anyone taken them down.

And so Peri waited in the shop, not able to say anything as she rang up purchases for customers who were casually browsing, buying wools and needles and patterns. She held it all in until K.C. arrived and then the two sobbed and held on to each other for a time.

'I didn't know it would be the last time in the cab,' cried
K.C. 'I don't want her to not be here.'

It didn't seem real, especially when the rental equipment
arrived; no one had remembered to cancel Georgia's order.
Then the tears burst again as Darwin came into the shop,
with Lucie, a newborn Ginger in her arms, and Lucie's mother
Rosie at her side. Anita showed up too, leaning heavily on
Marty, and so did Cat, holding one of Dakota's hands as
James grasped the other.

It was a somber group, some sitting, some standing,
repeating the same phrases over and over again, recounting
everything that had happened, trying to make some sense of
it all. But they held on to Ginger, too, and K.C. helped Lucie
dress her in the little baby sweater it had taken her months
to make, and that felt a little bit better, even as everyone's
hearts squeezed tightly with grief.

And then it happened. A few of the more frequent customers
– and then some complete strangers, including a certain
mega-watt movie star in town to do a play – began to walk
through the doorway of Walker and Daughter. At first Anita
thought they had heard about Georgia's passing. But then it
became clear they wanted to see Lucie's film. She turned to
the new mom.

'Uh, I think there's a copy still in the box we brought in on
Tuesday,' said Lucie, her eyes red. 'I guess we could play it.'

'We'll play it,' said Dakota. 'My mom liked that movie. She
said her hair looked good.'

Lucie's taped voiceover boomed through the shop.

'This is the story of the Friday Night Knitting Club . . .'
she was narrating, over images of the outside of Marty's
building and the shop sign on the landing, before the camera
settled on an image of Georgia sitting at the center table with
the entire club, covering her mouth to stifle a giggle and then

giving in to a great burst of laughter, her chestnut curls shaking all around. 'And this is the story of a gutsy New Yorker named Georgia Walker who led the way.'

It had been a tough night, thought Darwin, as she entered her dark apartment. Lucie had offered her a spot on the couch, but her friend wanted to give her some time with Rosie.

Instead, she opened up her laptop, knowing very well that she wasn't about to get any sleep. She tapped the keys, surfed the Internet, tracked her sweater package on UPS – it had been delivered – and checked her email. Nothing.

Then she opened up a Word document and sat there.

One word. That's how Darwin finally started her thesis. With one word.

Knitting.

Does this skill have validity for the modern woman?
Yes.

There is tremendous power when women hold on to – or reclaim, in the case of many young women today – the traditional skills of women who went before us. In the developed world, knitting is at once a reminder and a connection to the struggles of our collective past, when warm clothing was a necessity that could only be made by hand, and a joyous celebration of the ingenuity and creativity of our mothers and grandmothers.

Darwin looked up from the screen. And, she thought, it's just plain fun.

A noise in the hallway startled her awake. Darwin was splayed out on her couch, the laptop – with several pages of text – resting on her stomach. It was 8 a.m. and light outside the window.

'Ugh,' she said, her neck sore from her awkward nap, her mouth dry.

She heard the sound again. A jingling at the door.

With a dash she was looking out the peephole, then unlocking the two deadbolts and the chain.

Standing there – wearing the ill-fitting gray sweater with one sleeve three inches too short, the other two inches too long – was her husband. Dan.

And he was smiling.

36

It had been a difficult winter. For everyone. But they'd made it through. And somehow, improbably, spring had come. Just as it did every year.

Walker and Daughter had remained open, with Peri keeping up her schedule, making room for a larger display of purses and hiring a part-timer to help out. It was decided that she should take over the upstairs apartment. She'd cleaned and repainted all of it after Dakota agreed it was time to see it change. K.C. had rented a car and taken a road trip – she'd always been so focused on New York that she realized she'd never really visited her own country; it was her last gasp of freedom before starting law school in the fall. Darwin had worked day and night to complete the first draft of her dissertation, just in time to find a new apartment in the city near the hospital. Dan was coming back, had found a way to transfer his residency, had been able to forgive. And Lucie, at home with Ginger and getting too little sleep, used the middle-of-the night hours to plan a new cut of her documentary and submit it to the Tribeca Film Festival.

Dakota's grades had slipped, for a bit, but James took immediate action, asking for a leave of absence to be with his heartbroken little girl. There had been no confusion over rights and wishes; Georgia Walker had made sure she was always ready for whatever might come her way. It was a challenging transition, to become a full-time parent as he mourned his loss. But he was making it work: James had taken Dakota to Baltimore for Thanksgiving, then to Pennsylvania for the annual Christmas dinner, braving the Walkers over eggnog and shortbread. They were somber holidays, to be sure, but he was at his daughter's side through it all, had pledged to take her to Gran in Scotland when school ended.

His East Side apartment was empty now; James located a new home for the two of them, around the corner from the shop and close to both Anita and Cat. Dakota helped in the store on Saturdays. Marty rewrote the lease: for as long as he owned the building, Walker and Daughter would never pay rent again.

It had, in its own way, all worked out. Except that Georgia wasn't there.

And so, one spring day, Anita took her dear Dakota out for a walk, a Walker and Daughter bag in her hand. They had been taking a lot of strolls together; it was easier for the teen to speak when she didn't have to look anyone in the eye and let them see her pain. 'Let's go to the Park,' suggested Anita. 'I'd like to show you something.' They sat together, quietly, until Anita reached into the lavender paper bag, and pulled out a sweater, wrapped in tissue.

'My mom made this?' asked Dakota.

'She did,' confirmed Anita. 'I met her right around here, and you were just a bump. This is where I commissioned her to make this very first creation from Walker and Daughter.' She gazed on the red and white tulips, the yellow daffodils, the grass bright green, remembering the young woman with the dark curly hair, crying on the park bench.

'And your mother trusted me to give something else to you,' said Anita, handing over a red leather journal to Dakota.

'It's where she put her ideas for patterns. And where she wrote the secret to making the perfect sweater.'

'The secret?'

'It's in there. Trust me.'

Dakota thumbed through the pages of drawings and came to a long section of writing. She began to read out loud.

'The Gathering,' she began. 'Choosing your wool is dizzying with potential: the waves of colors and textures tempt with visions of a sweater or cap (and all the accompanying compliments you hope to receive) but don't reveal the hard work required to get there. Patience and attention to detail make all the difference . . .'

She rested there a long time after she'd finished, crying but not wanting to be watched, as Anita waited patiently beside her, an arm over the back of the bench but politely looking the other way.

'C'mon now,' she said after a time. 'We promised her we wouldn't be too late.'

They met up with James on Central Park West; he was double-parked in a rental car.

'Hi, Dad,' said Dakota, climbing into the back seat so Anita could take the front. 'Let's go.'

It was a nice day for a drive, sunny and breezy; the 45-minute ride in the car passed by quickly, easily. And then, suddenly, they were there, pulling into a leafy little town within commuting distance of Manhattan.

It would have been hard if Cat had opened her antiques shop in the city, hard to see her doing what Georgia had done. But out here, away from the city, it was different somehow. It felt right.

James let them out at the entrance and went to park the car. Dakota heard the faint sound of chimes as she opened the clear glass door to the ground-floor store, with its artistically arranged display of mahogany tables and cherry wood bureaux, landscape paintings, individual pieces of china and crystal from rare patterns, fireplace mantels leaning against the wall, and a stately old grandfather clock that still kept time. For inspiration there were two mannequins in either corner, each draped in one of the gowns Georgia had knitted and with a small label marked 'Not for Sale'. Anita made her way carefully through the shop, glancing at the antiques and the pink mandarin-collared dress, touching, looking, admiring.

'I'm proud of you, Cat,' said Dakota as she rejoined Anita at the front of the store. They were gazing intently at the stunning golden gown. Phoenix, Georgia had called it.

'You are finally your own woman,' added Anita.

Cat smiled, touching Anita's arm and gently taking Dakota's left hand, as the young girl caressed the golden gown. They made a circle, the four of them there. Anita, Dakota, Cat. And Georgia's dress. A stunning achievement of design and planning and skill. Rivaled only by her greater creation standing before it, all round cheeks and smooth skin and endless potential. Georgia's darling Dakota.

'Please,' said Cat, breathing deeply, finally ready to take everything she'd ever learned from her dearest friend – the ambitious teenager, the tenacious businesswoman, the lion of a mother – and become the woman she'd always wanted to be. That Georgia had always believed she could be.

'Please,' she said again, holding on tightly. 'Call me Catherine.'

Darwin's first scarf!
Every knitter has to get started somewhere. Here's what you need to get going:

1) **A pair of needles.**
You can use metal or wood.
   Your project will knit up faster if you use big needles: Try size 15 or so.
   Want a less chunky look? Opt for size 8.

2) **Yarn.**
Color and texture is up to you! Use what catches your eye and fits your (Peri)pocketbook! You'll need at least 200 yards for a thin scarf; 300 yards will allow you to make it wider and longer. (And be sure to add extra if you want to make a fringe – though that step is optional.)
   Go with a super chunky yarn for the size 15 needles.
   Try a worsted weight wool if you're using size 8 needles.

3) **A yarn needle and crochet hook.**
You'll use this for fringe and for finishing your work.

4) **Basic skills.**
Go to WalkerandDaughter.com for tips, tricks, and more.

5) **The Pattern:**
Cast on at least 20 stitches, up to 30 stitches for a wider scarf. Knit straight across, then turn your work, and knit across again. Simplicity is key: using the knit stitch over and over will produce what is known as garter stitch, and your finished scarf will look the same on both sides. (No worrying about which is the front or the back!)
   The other great thing about doing a scarf is that you can keep on knitting as long as you'd like. Every now and then

try out the length – simply wrap the scarf around your neck while it's still on the needles and check it out in the mirror. Need it longer? Keep knitting!

If you're running out of yarn . . . don't worry! Wait until you get to the end of a row, turn your work, and then tie a new ball onto the yarn that you've been using. (The end from your original ball of yarn will be coming down from the front of the needle.) Push up the knot you tied with the new ball of yarn until it hits the first stitch on your needle. Then simply start knitting with the new yarn. When you're all done, you'll use your yarn needle or hook to sew in those pesky ends. For now, just ignore them!

Keep counting . . . every so often, count your stitches to make sure you are still doing the same number per row as when you cast on. Sometimes you may forget, or you may add an extra. If you've made a mistake, you can rip it out and do it again – or embrace the beauty of your one-of-a-kind handicraft and just try to keep doing the same number per row. Your scarf is as unique as you are – and as beautiful!

You'll cast off when the scarf is as long as you want it to be. Again, see WalkerandDaughter.com for techniques – and then use your yarn needle to weave in the ends. (Simply sew the ends into the scarf so they don't show.)

Want to add a fringe? Cut a long piece of yarn – about 5 inches or so – and fold it in half. Then place the yarn on the crochet hook. Slip the crochet hook through a stitch in the last row of the scarf (near the edge) and pull up, making a loop. Remove the crochet hook. Using your fingers, pull the two ends of yarn through the loop and tighten. *Voila!* And repeat. You'll add between 15 to 25 loops, depending on the width of your scarf and how dense you want the firnge to be. Just be sure to space them evenly across the scarf. (You can also use different colors of yarn for a unique look.)

Your beautiful scarf is done.

Dakota's Oatmeal, Blueberry & Orange Muffins
Bursting with fruit flavor – and pretty good for you, too!
Makes 12 muffins

Ingredients:
1 cup plain rolled oats (90 gm / 5¼ oz)
1 cup whole wheat flour (120 gm / 5 oz)
1 tsp each baking powder, baking soda & salt (5 ml each)
Grated rind of one large orange
1½ cups flaked sweet coconut (180 gm / 7½ oz)
½ cup liquid pasteurized honey (120 ml / 4 oz)
1 egg
3 tbsp corn oil or *extra-light* olive oil (45 ml / 1½ oz)
1 tbsp vinegar (15 ml / ½ oz)
Juice 1 orange & add water to make one cup of liquid (237 ml / 8 oz)
1 to 1½ cup fresh or frozen blueberries (237 to 315 gm / 8 to 11¼ oz)

Directions:
Preheat oven to 350F (176C).
Line a muffin tin with paper cups.
Combine the dry ingredients in a large mixing bowl: oats, flour, baking powder, baking soda and salt.
Next, add the coconut flakes and orange rind to the dry ingredients.
Get a separate bowl and beat the egg. Then incorporate the wet ingredients: honey, oil, vinegar, juice and water.
Add the wet ingredients to the dry mix and stir until just moist.
Then fold in the blueberries.
Pour batter into muffin cups, careful not to let any batter spill onto the tin.
Bake in a preheated oven for 20–25 minutes. (Check to see

if the muffins are fully baked by inserting a skewer before removing from the oven; it should come out clean.) Remove muffins from the pan and cool on wire rack. Enjoy!

Acknowledgements

There's a long way to go from writing at home to, seeing a book in a store, and I am very fortunate to work with the talented team that I do: my agent, the always enthusiastic Barbara J. Zitwer, my thoughtful editors Rachel Kahan in New York and Sue Fletcher in London, their assistants Eve Adler and Swati Gamble, and all of the hardworking folks in sales, marketing, publicity, editorial, production, and design. Their commitment has helped make this book a reality and I am so appreciative.

An enormous debt of gratitude is owed to the delightful Jane Langridge, CEO of the Ovarian Cancer Coalition, and to Dr Kris Ghosh, who offered valuable input regarding the medical aspects of the story. Ovarian cancer is often called a 'silent killer' because the symptoms can be non-specific, demanding of all of us women to know our bodies and our family medical history, to keep up with regular exams and all that good stuff. If there are any flaws in the medical details, I know they are mine alone.

When it comes right down to it, I am beyond lucky to have as many smart, talented people in my personal life as I do. A dear group of friends – some knitters, some not – took on the role of early readers and were extraordinarily generous with their time: Rhonda Hilario-Caguiat, Shawneen Jacobs, Tina Kaiser, Rachel King, Alissa MacMillan, Sara-Lynne Levine and Megan Worman. Christine Tyson was particularly supportive and helped to develop the yummy muffin recipe. And I remain tremendously grateful to Mike Gerber for making the call, to Dani McVeigh for her website design, and to Jennifer Fields, Kate Powers, Sasha Zikic and so many others for their consistent encouragement.

Finally, to my husband, Jonathan Bieley, who listened to me yak on about the club, read every version multiple times, and loved me through the writing of this book anyway. Thank you.